T0112887

"Holton's trademark wit and prose are present throughout *The Secret Service of Tea and Treason*, and there is no shortage of sparks between Alice and Bixby. You'll find yourself laughing out loud and swooning at numerous parts of the story."

—Paste

## *The League of Gentlewomen Witches*

"A brilliant mix of adventure, romance, and Oscar Wildesque absurdity—one of the wittiest, most original rom-coms I have read all year."

—Evie Dunmore, *USA Today* bestselling author of
*Bringing Down the Duke*

"There's no literary experience quite like reading an India Holton book. *The League of Gentlewomen Witches* is a wild, rollicking, delicious carnival ride of a story, filled with rakish pirates, chaotic witches, flying houses (and bicycles, and pumpkins), delightful banter, and some serious steam. You've never read Victorian romance like this before . . . and it'll ruin you for everything else."

—Lana Harper, *New York Times* bestselling author of
*Payback's a Witch*

"Fantastical, romantic fun! Sparkling with witty allusions to Shakespeare and Austen, whimsical adventure, and tenderhearted romance, *The League of Gentlewomen Witches* is a book lover's dream come true."

—Chloe Liese, author of the Bergman Brothers series

"Sexy, funny, and utterly charming, *The League of Gentlewomen Witches* is like a deliciously over-caffeinated historical-romance novel. Not only does Holton treat us to a fiery feminist witch as our heroine and a dashing pirate as our leading man, but she also gives us lyrical prose and crackling banter to enjoy on the side. Buckle up, readers, because this is a ride you won't want to miss."

—Lynn Painter, author of *Mr. Wrong Number*

## The Wisteria Society of Lady Scoundrels

"Holton is having as much fun as the English language will permit—the prose shifts constantly from silly to sublime and back, sometimes in the course of a single sentence. And somehow in all the melodrama and jokes and hilariously mangled literary references, there are moments of emotion that cut to the quick—the way a profound traumatic experience can overcome you years later."

—*New York Times Book Review*

"This melds the Victorian wit of Sherlock Holmes with the brash adventuring of Indiana Jones. . . . A sprightly feminist tale that offers everything from an atmospheric Gothic abbey to secret societies."

—*Entertainment Weekly*

"*The Wisteria Society of Lady Scoundrels* is easily the most delightfully bonkers historical-fantasy romance of 2021! Featuring lady pirates in flying houses and gentleman assassins with far too many names, I enjoyed every absorbing moment."

—Jen DeLuca, author of *Well Played*

"The most charming, clever, and laugh-out-loud funny book I've read all year—it is impossible to read *The Wisteria Society of Lady Scoundrels* and not fall in love with its lady pirates, flying houses, and swoon-worthy romance. India Holton's utterly delightful debut is pure joy from start to finish."

—Martha Waters, author of *To Have and to Hoax*

"India's debut is charming, clever, action-packed, with masterful bantering-while-dueling choreography: it reminds me of *The Princess Bride*, except swoonier and more fantastical. It's an instant beloved favorite." —Sarah Hogle, author of *You Deserve Each Other*

"With a piratical heroine who would rather be reading and a hero whose many disguises hide a (slightly tarnished) heart of gold, *The Wisteria Society of Lady Scoundrels* is the perfect diversion for a rainy afternoon with a cup of tea. What fun!"

—Manda Collins, author of
*A Lady's Guide to Mischief and Mayhem*

"Holton's writing is gorgeous and lyrical, her dialogue clever and witty, and her characters lovable and unforgettable. The story contains so many enthralling elements—lady scoundrels and spells, pirates and explosions, romance and flying-house thievery!"

—Raquel Vasquez Gilliland, author of
*Sia Martinez and the Moonlit Beginning of Everything*

"With secret identities, secret doors, and secret histories to spare, this high-octane layer cake of escapism hits the spot."

—*Publishers Weekly*

"In this joyride of a debut, Holton draws us into a madcap world of courtly corsairs, murderous matrons, and pity-inspiring henchmen. . . . As if the Parasol Protectorate series met *The Princess Bride* and a corseted *Lara Croft: Tomb Raider*." —*Kirkus Reviews*

"A tongue-in-cheek swashbuckling adventure." —*Library Journal*

## TITLES BY INDIA HOLTON

# THE ORNITHOLOGIST'S FIELD GUIDE TO LOVE

## INDIA HOLTON

BERKLEY ROMANCE

New York

BERKLEY ROMANCE
Published by Berkley
An imprint of Penguin Random House LLC
penguinrandomhouse.com

Copyright © 2024 by India Holton
Excerpt from *The Geographer's Map to Romance*
copyright © 2024 by India Holton
Penguin Random House supports copyright. Copyright fuels creativity,
encourages diverse voices, promotes free speech, and creates a vibrant
culture. Thank you for buying an authorized edition of this book and
for complying with copyright laws by not reproducing, scanning, or
distributing any part of it in any form without permission. You are
supporting writers and allowing Penguin Random House
to continue to publish books for every reader.

BERKLEY is a registered trademark and Berkley Romance with
B colophon is a trademark of Penguin Random House LLC.

Library of Congress Cataloging-in-Publication Data

Names: Holton, India, author.
Title: The ornithologist's field guide to love / India Holton.
Description: First edition. | New York: Berkley Romance, 2024.
Identifiers: LCCN 2023045886 (print) | LCCN 2023045887 (ebook) |
ISBN 9780593547281 (trade paperback) | ISBN 9780593547298 (ebook)
Subjects: LCGFT: Romance fiction. | Fantasy fiction. | Novels.
Classification: LCC PR9639.4.H66 O76 2024 (print) |
LCC PR9639.4.H66 (ebook) | DDC 823/.92—dc23/eng/20231128
LC record available at https://lccn.loc.gov/2023045886
LC ebook record available at https://lccn.loc.gov/2023045887

First Edition: July 2024

Printed in the United States of America
1st Printing

Book design by Katy Riegel

*For Amaya,*
*with northeasterlies,*
*wild oceans,*
*and love*

## TABLE OF
## SIGNIFICANT CHARACTERS

### IN ORDER OF APPEARANCE

BETH PICKERING . . . an intrepid professor of ornithology

HIPPOLYTA SPIFFINGTON-QUIRM . . . a high flier

DEVON LOCKLEY . . . a young man who has not yet seen
the error of his ways

KLAUS OBERHUFTER . . . a stain on the noble name
of beak bagger

LADY TRIMBLE . . . a bearer of exciting news!

MISS FOTHERINGHAM (À DEUX) . . . binate birders

MONSIEUR TARROU . . . verminous

MR. CHOLMBAUMGH . . . pronounced *chum-bum*, alas

ASSORTED ORNITHOLOGISTS

VARIOUS REPORTERS

MESSRS. FETTICK AND FLOGG . . . on pressing business

MONSIEUR BADEAU . . . but please note, he is not really here

MR. SCHREIB . . . not who he seems to be

ELIZA WOLFE . . . an adversary

A BOATLOAD OF FRENCH FISHERMEN . . . f(r)iends

MISCELLANEOUS LOCALS

MR. AND MRS. PODDER . . . an entirely chance encounter

ROSE MARIN . . . a model of professional ornithological
    behavior

MRS. HASSAN . . . coincidental

GABRIEL TARRANT . . . a grumpy cousin

LAZ BRADY . . . beholds the swelling scene

PROFESSOR GLADSTONE . . . the big birder of Oxford

# THE
# ORNITHOLOGIST'S
# FIELD GUIDE
# TO LOVE

♥

# CHAPTER ONE

For the master ornithologist, trouble is like water off a duck's back.

*Birds Through a Sherry Glass*, H.A. Quirm

*Spain, 1890*

IT WAS A fine day for birding. Almost too fine. Sunlight glazed the sky of northern Spain, unrelieved by cloud or breeze. Heat pressed down on the forest path.

Mrs. Quirm and Miss Pickering strolled beneath the shade of hats and lace parasols, employing their white-gloved hands in the manner of fans to cool themselves. Every now and again they lifted delicate silver binoculars to search the surrounding trees. Several birds flitted between branches, singing, courting, and generally participating in occupations typical to the avian species. But the ladies' quarry was one bird in particular, far shyer than the common breeds. They had seen glimpses of it throughout the morning and were intent on pursuit, despite the overbearing weather.

"By Jove, I could use a glass of lemonade right now!" Mrs. Quirm declared.

"Indeed, it is atrociously warm," Miss Pickering agreed.

"Rupert!" Mrs. Quirm snapped her gloved fingers. "Lemonade, if you please."

Rupert, walking behind her, turned to the contingent of porters, guides, and servants walking behind him. He gestured, and a man hurried forth with bottle and glass. Lemonade was poured, the glass was set on a silver tray, and Rupert presented it.

Mrs. Quirm took the drink, but before she could bring it to her robust lips, she sighted something that caused her to gasp.

"A bastard, here in the forest!"

Miss Pickering stared at her with astonishment. One simply did not speak of people born out of wedlock if one was a lady, and in all her twenty-four years, Miss Pickering had met none more ladylike than Hippolyta Quirm, despite the vigorous galumphing of her vocal cords.

"You do well to be surprised, Elizabeth!" the woman said in what would have been termed a shout had it come from a less reputable person. "The great bustard has no business being in a forest! It is a bird of the fields."

"Oh, a *bustard*," Beth said with relief. No doubt the heat had suffocated her ear canal as it was attempting to do with her lungs.

She blew restively at a chestnut brown strand of hair that had slipped over her damp brow. If only it was decent behavior to remove one's hat in company, or loosen one's collar, or leap naked into a nearby river! Ornithology tended to be a mucky venture—scuffed shoes, snagged stockings, guano-splattered parasols—but the worst of it was the perspiration.

When Hippolyta had announced they were going to Spain in search of the elusive pileated deathwhistler, Beth had considered feigning illness so as to remain behind. She was British right through to her tea-flavored, rain-colored core, and the thought of a summer without fog and storms horrified her. But in the end she had been unable to resist the opportunity such an expedition offered. To capture the deathwhistler would result in universal accolades. And if anyone could pull it off, it was Hippolyta Quirm, field ornithologist, wildly famous authoress of *Birds Through a Sherry Glass*, and at only thirty-one, a five-time recipient of England's prestigious Best Birder award.

Beth was pleased to be the woman's associate. The moment they met in Epping Forest, accidentally smacking each other over the head with their nets while their mutual quarry, a fine specimen of rain-singing robin, flew away in a teeny-tiny storm, they knew they'd work well together. For one thing, Beth was prepared to take all the blame for the mishap, and Hippolyta was glad to give it.

"You can extend your postdoctoral research into the psychic habitats of thaumaturgic birds," the woman had suggested as they walked back to town together afterward, "and I can get your help in the field."

"Yes," Beth had said without pausing for thought. Then again, even had she taken time to consider it, she'd have answered the same way. Hippolyta might at times be more discombobulating than a whole flock of thunder-winged loons, and certainly traveling with her left much to be desired in terms of quiet reading time, but that was a small price to pay for the literal broadening of one's horizons. Over the past two years, in between teaching classes as an Oxford University professor, Beth had visited places of whose existence she'd never before known, thanks to Hippolyta's resources. Certainly it was more than she'd have been able to afford herself on a professor's salary. Now she was even beginning to think that one day she might reach New Zealand, land of the giant carnivorous moa.

First, however, she had to not drown in her own sweat.

*Buck up*, she chastised herself. At least it was not as bad as chasing the fire-breathing sand curlew in Cairo. Granted, she'd been dressed in black at the time, to honor the anniversary of her parents' death, but heatstroke almost saw her following them into the grave. More than once, the only thing that saved her from feverishly tumbling off a camel's back had been the ballast of her petticoats. If Hippolyta hadn't discovered that the curlew liked arrowroot biscuits, and was thus able to lure it into a cage for the voyage back to London, Beth's career would have burned out before it properly began. Again, literally as well as metaphorically—which seemed to be the usual state of affairs when one was involved in chasing magical birds.

"The great bustard can be taken as a good sign," Hippolyta was saying, and Beth pulled herself out of the Egyptian frying pan back into the Spanish fire. "No doubt it was attracted to our deathwhistler's thaumaturgic vibrations. We're getting close, mark my words. Oberhufter tried to convince me to search farther south, but I knew he was talking nonsense. He always does. I am a far superior ornithologist to him."

"Absolutely," Beth murmured loyally.

"I still cannot believe that man was voted High Flier of the Year. What rot! He is an idiot, and I know for a fact he bribed the awards committee with spotted nightspinner feathers."

"Mm-hm," Beth said, in lieu of pointing out that Hippolyta had bribed them with strix claws, despite having no hope of succeeding since, in addition to the spotted nightspinner,

Herr Oberhufter had bagged a scarlet thrush, a fire tit, and even a breeding pair of horned frogeaters that he donated to the London Zoological Gardens (and then had to come take away again, as they made such a noise they drove several nearby residents to the brink of madness)—all in the second half of 1889.

Granted, in the course of getting these birds, he had also broken the leg of one rival ornithologist and tricked another into catching a train to Siberia, from whence they sent an excited telegram reporting they'd found the mythical yeti owl, and thereafter were never seen again. The awards committee, however, cast a blind eye to such nefarious behavior. A bird in the hand was worth more than two birders in the bush, any day.

"Oberhufter will go down in history as a knave and cheat," Hippolyta persisted. "And once we return to London with the pileated deathwhistler, I shall campaign to have his International Ornithological Society membership revoked."

"Good idea," Beth said, blowing at the wayward strand of hair again.

"A little blackmail should do the trick. But if that fails, you can always seduce the membership committee chairman."

"Um," Beth said.

"He won't be able to escape your feminine wiles, not in those ridiculous sandals he wears over his socks."

Beth, having been unaware until this moment that she possessed feminine wiles, and not entirely sure what they involved, could make no sensible reply. It did not matter however, for Hippolyta's attention had returned to the trees.

"The deathwhistler is near, I can feel it in my water! And my water is never wrong! Keep your eyes peeled, Elizabeth. We're looking in particular for charred leaves or swarms of insects." She turned her head to shout at the servants. "Insects, gentlemen!"

The servants looked back with expressions suggesting they would like to take her advisement and shove it somewhere with significantly less sun than the Spanish forest.

Suddenly, the trees rustled. Hippolyta and Beth paused, their faces lifted and their senses straining for a sight, sound, or magical vibration of the pileated deathwhistler. Behind them, the servants took this opportunity to lay down their burdens (literal: tool bags, birdcage, heavy boxes, picnic hamper, picnic table and chairs; and metaphorical: weariness for the drudgery of their job). They wiped their brows and pushed up their sleeves in a manner Beth would have envied had she not been so intent upon the trees.

"There!" Hippolyta tossed aside her glass of lemonade without looking (braining a red-tufted mousetwitter that happened to be pecking about in the undergrowth, thereby bringing an end to its species on the Continent and losing herself, had she but known it, several thousand pounds). Her attention focused instead on a flutter of gold among the leaves. "Quick, the net!"

But even before Rupert could order a servant to obtain the net from a porter and bring it to him, whereupon he could present it to Hippolyta, the deathwhistler was off. With a swoop of wings, it lifted its coin-colored, peacock-size body from a branch and began to fly away along the forest path.

"After it!" Hippolyta shouted.

Beth lifted the hem of her long white skirt and hastened after the deathwhistler, Hippolyta hot on her heels with a rustle of yellow taffeta. They ran along the path, parasols bobbing, dust billowing as their boots struck the dry earth. The servants watched them blankly.

"Faster!" Hippolyta urged.

But suddenly, Beth staggered to a halt. The bird glided on a short distance, then descended to the path, its wings folding, its bronze crest glinting in the sunlight.

"Why do you stop?" Hippolyta demanded—and, at Beth's urgent reply, staggered to a halt herself before she ran headlong into a chasm. Dropping her binoculars in surprise, she watched them plummet several hundred feet to break against jagged rocks below.

"By Jove!" she shouted.

"The deathwhistler seems aware of our predicament," Beth said wryly as the bird flickered its long-feathered tail at them.

"The chase is not over yet!" Hippolyta averred. "I am determined to protect that bird from unscrupulous hunters [i.e., her rivals] and see it safe in the Duke of Wimbledon's aviary. No deathly chasm shall stop me! Propellers!"

Beth tugged on a cord attached to her parasol handle. Hippolyta did the same with hers. Long metal shafts arose from atop the parasols' caps and, with a whirring buzz, began to spin. The two ladies proceeded to rise from the path.

Behind them, the servants sagged down onto boxes, hamper, and chairs. Before them, the pileated deathwhistler pecked the ground as if entirely undisturbed by the introduction of this boisterous new avian species. A glint in its small dark eyes suggested, however, that it was amused and intended to wait for the most aggravating moment possible before taking off again.

Hippolyta and Beth angled their parasols in such a manner as to traverse the deep but narrow cleft in the earth, then alighted on the other side. As they drew the parasols shut, Hippolyta held out a hand toward Beth, palm up, without removing her steely gaze from the bird.

"Net," she commanded.

"Er . . ." Beth said.

Hippolyta snapped her fingers impatiently, but to no avail. They had forgotten to bring the net with them.

"Bother!" Hippolyta said. "Well, never mind." After all, she had not become the preeminent field ornithologist of the British Empire, and the slightly-less-eminent but still famous field ornithologist of the Continent, without being able to bounce back from such calamities. She began divesting herself of her puff-sleeved jacket. "We shall sneak up on it and toss my jacket over its head."

"Good plan," Beth said. She was about to wish Hippolyta luck for such a risky venture when the older woman handed her the jacket.

"Now, remember, Elizabeth! When frightened, the death-whistler makes a dreadful, fatal noise, like—"

*"Oi! Look out below!"*

At this holler, Hippolyta and Beth did exactly the opposite of what it commanded: they looked up, into the canopy of the forest. A man came leaping down from a tree, his long brown coat soaring behind him winglike.

Birds startled and took to the air. For one awful moment, Beth heard the first perilous notes of the deathwhistler's cry. But even as her heart began to shudder, the man snatched the bird and tucked its beak beneath his arm, rendering it silent. Tawny feathers ruffled wildly, briefly, then settled into calm.

The interloper bowed as much as was possible with a sizable bird in his arms. He was slightly unshaven, and a lock of black hair fell over one dark eye roguishly. "Good afternoon, ladies," he said, grinning.

"Mr. Lockley!" Beth's exclamation shook her vocal cords, which were used to only gentle employment. "What do you think you are doing?"

His grin deepened. "I think I'm stealing your bird, Miss Pickering."

"Who is this rogue?" Hippolyta demanded.

"Devon Lockley," Beth explained as the man brushed back his hair. "He's a professor in Cambridge's ornithology department." She had been introduced to him during the annual Berkshire Birders meeting last month. He'd not made much of an impression—shabby coat, nice smile, more interested in the sausage rolls on offer than in talking to her. A typical male professor. He certainly impacted more today, jumping down before them in a style that evoked derring-do, bravado, and no cumbersome petticoats. It was provocative behavior, to say the least, and his unstarched trousers, clinging to strong thighs, only made matters worse. Beth absolutely would not blush, for she was an Englishwoman—but inside, her heart was fanning itself urgently with a handkerchief.

"Cambridge," Hippolyta said in the same manner with which one might open their steak pie and say *maggot*. "And what sort of name is Devon Lockley?" she added, never mind that her own name, Hippolyta Albertina Spiffington-Quirm, ought to have disqualified her from asking.

"The sort that unimaginative parents living in Devonshire give their child," the man said. "It's an honor to meet you, Mrs. Quirm, especially as you so kindly shepherded the pileated deathwhistler into my trap. Both myself and my associate, Herr Oberhufter, thank you."

"Oberhufter!" Hippolyta immediately withdrew a dainty

silver pistol from a pocket of her dress and aimed it at him. But Devon's smile only quirked.

"I sympathize, madam, but there is no need to do that."

"There certainly is! Hand over my bird at once, you rapscallion, or I will shoot you!"

"Perhaps I misspoke," he replied calmly. "What I meant was there is *no point* in doing that. We took the liberty earlier of removing your bullets."

Hippolyta gasped and shook the gun, as if this would inform her of its contents.

"We?" Beth asked.

In response, Devon glanced over her shoulder. The ladies turned to see half their servants tied and gagged and the other half absconding back along the path with tools and food hamper. Seated at the wrought-iron picnic table was a large gentleman in a tan suit; he lifted his derby hat to the ladies in cheerful greeting.

"Oberhufter!" Hippolyta exclaimed again. "By Jove, this is outrageous!"

"No, madam," Devon said. "It is ornithology."

DEVON KNEW HE ought to have immediately hotfooted it out of there. Hippolyta was the wiliest, most ambitious birder on the circuit, and she'd just proven the lengths to which she'd go in order to obtain possession of the deathwhistler. But he couldn't resist sparing a moment to smile at Miss Pickering. He remembered her from a recent meeting in Berkshire, where he'd been utterly bored and had asked for an introduction to the pretty Oxford professor, intending to flirt a little to pass the time. She'd proved so courteously agreeable, however, that his boredom veered toward stupefaction, and he'd been forced to risk the digestive perils of the buffet just to make himself feel alive.

But dang it, she really was pretty, with eyes as blue as the Alaskan cat-catching warbler, a mouth as soft as a morning kiss, and a sweet, heart-shaped face—although it was also a rather sweaty face, and currently scowling at him as if she'd like to stab him with her furled parasol. He wished she would. Pretty was nice; naughty was ever so much better.

He had a job to do, however, and Hippolyta was reaching for her hatpin in a manner that suggested a mastery of naughtiness even he could not handle. So he took an abrupt step forward and snatched Miss Pickering's parasol.

She gasped. "Good heavens! There is no need to be so zealous! I'm sure we can negotiate—"

"*Negotiate?!*" Hippolyta cried out with horror.

"I'm happy to negotiate," Devon said. "Here is my offer: I take the bird, and you wave goodbye nicely."

With that, he flicked open the parasol and engaged its propeller. Miss Pickering's eyes widened, and Devon feared she might cry. Poor girl, so downtrodden by Hippolyta, so timid, she was no doubt—

Er, actually, she was beating him with Hippolyta's parasol. Having grabbed it from the older lady, she spared no effort in whacking Devon about the legs as he began to rise from the path. Delighted, he grinned at her. Then, with one kick, he knocked the parasol from her hand, causing it to fling away into the chasm.

"Sorry!" he said without the slightest remorse.

"I do not accept your apology!" she called out in reply. This defiance cast a lively flush upon her face, and Devon considered some flirtatious provocation, perhaps a blown kiss, just to see if he could tip her into truly bad manners. But the mechanized parasol was already carrying him away.

*Until next time*, he promised silently, and his body throbbed at the thought of it (or possibly due to the beating she'd given him).

BETH SEETHED IN a most unladylike way as she watched Devon fly across the chasm and land easily on the far side. Beside her, Hippolyta had forsaken 'ladylike' and moved directly on to unseemliness, with several muttered profanities escaping from between her clenched teeth. (Beth could not fully hear them but nevertheless was rendered shocked indeed.)

On the other side of the chasm, Herr Oberhufter rose languidly, fanning himself with his derby hat. He performed an extravagant bow to the ladies.

"Thank you for your assistance in tracking the bird!" he called over.

"Blighter!" Hippolyta shouted, firing her gun several times at him, thus proving its chambers were indeed empty.

Herr Oberhufter did not even do her the courtesy of laughing nefariously. He turned to help Devon place the pileated deathwhistler into the large iron birdcage Hippolyta had brought for this very purpose. Devon covered the cage with Hippolyta's picnic tablecloth, thereby creating a calm darkness to appease the bird before it could utter its deadly cries. Then, without further ado, the men walked away, carrying the stolen deathwhistler (which is to say, attended by one of the ladies' servants carrying the stolen deathwhistler), leaving Hippolyta and Beth in the middle of the forest, miles from civilization, several thousand pounds poorer, and almost certainly not in the running for an award at the International Ornithology Conference in September.

"I'll pluck your feathers yet, Oberhufter," Hippolyta shouted after them.

"Too right," Beth agreed. And, as Devon Lockley turned his head to throw one last crooked smile at her, she wiped the back of her hand across her heated face in the most scandalous manner indeed.

# CHAPTER TWO

The greatest tool in an ornithologist's equipage is the
fellowship of her peers.
    *Birds Through a Sherry Glass*, H.A. Quirm

A WEEK LATER, BETH and Hippolyta finally changed the
topic of conversation. Herr Oberhufter had been con-
signed to as many degrees of misery as Hippolyta's imagination could contrive, and Devon Lockley dismembered,
figuratively speaking—and forcefully speaking, since tempers
remained high all the way through Spain and across the border
into France. But at last, something new touched upon the
ladies' offense.

"Do they call this tea?" Hippolyta scowled into the dainty
cup she held before her. "It tastes like dishwater!" She set it
down on its saucer with a loud *clink* that resounded throughout
the elegant gilded tearoom of Hôtel Chauvesouris. Diners at
neighboring tables glared in response, but Hippolyta was far
too genteel to notice other people staring.

"Trust the French to make a revolting pot of tea," she
grouched. Selecting a macaron from the tiered plate at the
center of the table, she sliced vigorously through it, nearly putting someone's eye out with the resultant explosion of crumbs.

"So true," Beth said, although her own drink tasted entirely tea-ish. She had long ago learned that the safest passage through conversation with Hippolyta Quirm was simply to agree.

"We should have stayed at the Hôtel Meurice instead."

"We should have."

Hippolyta frowned. "Don't talk nonsense, Elizabeth. You know that would be impossible under the circumstances."

"Of course," Beth said, executing a one-hundred-and-eighty-degree change of opinion with well-practiced ease. "You are right."

"Hôtel Meurice is at least *five miles* from the university hosting Chevrolet's lecture. One might tramp all one likes about the countryside, but walking across town is entirely déclassé."

"Yes, indeed," Beth said. This explained why Hôtel Chauve-souris was crammed with twitchy birders. Monsieur Chevrolet was reputed to have the mustache of an Adonis and the thighs of a Zeus—and a highly informative manner of lecturing, of course. His seminars about thaumaturgic birds were always sold out. And while Paris offered several good hotels, ornithologists liked to keep a close eye on each other, in case of fowl play. Governments paid handsomely for the delivery of dangerous or endangered thaumaturgic birds to sanctuaries—and smugglers paid equally handsomely for their delivery to fashion houses and the secret laboratories of mad scientists—and one never quite knew where one's colleagues stood on that ethical divide (partly because so many of them straddled it, depending on price). Or what they were willing to do to bag a bird. Beth had counted seven of her and Hippolyta's rivals in the tearoom alone, and she knew others were taking a more bohemian approach to dining at the coffee shop across the road.

It was seven people more than she wished were present. Indeed, the entire scene threatened to overwhelm her brain. There were simply too many things to observe, analyze, and theorize about. She would have much rather had a tray delivered to her hotel room, so that she might continue adding the pileated deathwhistler's details to her field journal in a peaceful environment. But Hippolyta had started tossing out words like "antisocial" and "hopeless" and "you will wither on the vine, Elizabeth!" until she'd relented. As a result, here she sat, not so much as thinking about the unusual length of the deathwhistler's fibula, or the unusual angle the bird took when ascending in flight. She even wore the white lace dress Hippolyta so admired, despite its waistband being prejudiced against breathing. And now the selection of minuscule sandwiches for her plate having been achieved, the tea slandered, and her cutlery straightened to exactitude, nothing remained but for her to await death by boredom while Hippolyta made such small talk its point was practically invisible.

"I think mmffmm iff a mmff ffpiff," the woman declared while chewing on the macaron. She gestured with her fork. "If mmf, fen mffpf!"

"I agree," Beth answered.

Hippolyta swallowed. "By Jove! Are you even listening to me?"

"Of course," Beth replied automatically. In sad fact, however, she'd become distracted by a new arrival to the tearoom. It was the bird thief Devon Lockley, consulting with the maître d' as to an available table. Gone were his dusty coat and (alas) tight trousers; he had got himself up as a very fine gentleman indeed, clean and shaven in a dark suit and tie, his jet-black hair smoothed back. Looking at him, Beth's boredom vanished as a strange fluttering overtook her nerves.

*It must be guilt*, she decided, in defiance of an intellect that had always placed her so far at the top of her classes they had to keep inventing new ceilings for her. She owed the man an apology. He might have stolen her bird (and her parasol) (and at least some of her good sense), but that presented no case for violence. Not only had her behavior been dreadful, but the loss of her and Hippolyta's parasols had left both ladies exposed to the hazard of suntanning—as Hippolyta had pointed out a few times during their walk back to town (seventy-nine, to be precise). And no doubt Mr. Lockley had told Herr Oberhufter about their skirmish, which meant the entire circuit knew by now.

Instinctively, she reached for the cup before her. *Tea is the reservoir of peace*, her mother used to say, and Beth had lived by that motto ever since. Granted, she did not actually like the taste, but that was of no consequence. When one was an owl in a world of seagulls, one took any balm available.

The cup trembled slightly as she raised it to drink, but as milky warmth eased through her, she felt restored to, if not peace, then at least the safety of self-control. Plainly, the right thing to do was ~~sue Devon Lockley for the cost of the parasols~~ send a note of contrition to his hotel room, along with some chocolates wittily shaped as roosters. That would clear the path for a better relationship between them going forward: friendly nods across the field and assassinating each other's character via the polite channel of academic papers.

She had just settled upon this when Mr. Lockley removed his gloves—*despite not yet being seated to dine!*

Beth's nerves began to flutter anew. This time, however, the only possible diagnosis was . . . um . . . disapproval. Yes, so much disapproval! Why, just look at the outrageous way he exposed his naked hands, leather sliding over skin, long fingers taking the gloves in a strong grip that might lift a woman from the ground if he—

"Elizabeth!" Hippolyta's bark pulled Beth from her reverie and caused their neighboring diners to jolt. "You have dripped tea into your saucer!"

Flushing, Beth hastened to repair this catastrophe.

"*Tsk!*" Hippolyta's tongue flicked against her teeth. "So appalling."

"Sorry," Beth said, but then realized Hippolyta was in fact not looking at her. Following the woman's glare, she saw that Herr Oberhufter had joined Devon Lockley at the tearoom entrance. A deathwhistler feather protruded jauntily from his bowler hat, and smoke from his cigar made a little cloud for it.

Beth did not hate anyone, since that would take mental energy away from thinking about important things, such as birds, and quality paper, and how to keep that paper dry while hiking over foggy moorlands to sketch birds. She made an exception for Klaus Oberhufter, however. The man might rescue dangerous thaumaturgic species from communities who would like to kill them (granted, to stop the birds from killing the community first), but he also readily sold them to aviaries that were little more than tourist ventures and that cared nothing for the birds' quality of life. Hippolyta was more scrupled—she only sold to people who could provide the birds with a deluxe haven, since they were the only ones who could afford her exorbitant fee.

"Villains," Beth muttered as the two men began to cross the tearoom to a thankfully distant table.

"Bamboozlers," Hippolyta agreed. "I hear he's some kind of academic wunderkind."

"Really?" Beth asked without much interest, stirring her tea with a dainty silver teaspoon. "I'd have supposed Herr Oberhufter too narrow in his thinking to allow for genius."

Hippolyta snorted. "I meant the other one. The bird thief."

Immediately, every overeducated instinct in Beth's body perked up. She studied Devon Lockley anew, as if she might assess his intelligence from the unhurried way he followed Herr Oberhufter.

"Really?" she asked again, her tone still nonchalant but her interest becoming so rich she could have bought a small nation with it.

Just then, Devon Lockley glanced over. His dark gaze met Beth's with a small, crooked smile that implied he'd known exactly how long she had been eyeing him up—and therefore that he'd been eyeing her up too. Villain, indeed!

And academic wunderkind? Ha! A strident little voice inside Beth's mind, hidden behind stacks of apologies and reminders to open doors for other people, urged her to march across and inform the man of her academic honors, including that time Oxford's chancellor had called her "worryingly clever" (which almost certainly had been intended as a compliment). British women had enjoyed tertiary education ever since Queen Charlotte had developed such an admiration for the astronomer Caroline Herschel that she'd convinced universities to enroll women (her ~~bribes~~ donations had helped), but Beth was the country's youngest professor regardless of gender. Whereas

Devon Lockley must have been at least a whole two, if not three, years older than her—and merely a professor of Cambridge, to boot. She pinned him with a stare to rival that of the basilisk owl, which could turn a person to stone.

He winked in return.

"Why don't you give up," Hippolyta suggested wryly, "and drink out of your saucer?"

Beth looked down at her teacup and discovered she'd bashed the teaspoon around its interior so much, she'd made another flood. While she mopped and apologized, Hippolyta entertained herself by pressing macaron crumbs to a finger and sucking this finger noisily until clean. But both ladies were diverted from their culinary concerns when suddenly a cloud of floral perfume engulfed them.

"Why, if it isn't Hippolyta Spiffington-Quirm, as I live and breathe! I heard you were lost in the Spanish jungle!"

The ladies stared up at what appeared to be a perambulating wedding cake. White froth, lace, and flounces were topped with a flower bouquet in service as a hat. Amid all this was a round dark face beaming in happy assurance of its humanity. Beth smiled at her, but Hippolyta was less welcoming.

"Lady Trimble," she said, managing to pack at least two insults and an innuendo into the name. "I daresay a few beech trees do not a jungle make. But of course you would not know that, since you specialize in *urban* birds."

Beth winced. Hippolyta had just outright called Lady Trimble a quack.

Lady Trimble's smile tightened. As the wife of a baronet with an unplumbed castle and several lifetimes' worth of debt, she outranked Hippolyta, a mere millionaire's widow, but could not mention this without lowering herself. Beth found such social intricacies ridiculous (although if the women were birds, she'd already have her notepad out so as to record their every move). Bored even before Lady Trimble said another word, she began thinking back to the deathwhistler's flight pattern—

*"Egad!"*

Beth jolted. At the neighboring table, Misses Fotheringham, elderly twin birders, were chattering excitedly over a newspaper.

"Good gracious!" Hippolyta complained. "Such uncivilized behavior!"

Suddenly, the Fotheringhams leaped up, causing their table to clatter and a spoon to fall on the parquet floor. The entire population of the room gasped. Miss Fotheringham and Miss Fotheringham paid no heed, rushing out as fast as their elaborate dresses would allow.

Hippolyta shook her head in disgust. "Some people have no dignity," she said, dunking half a macaron into her tea. Lady Trimble moved back hastily to avoid the consequent splashes. "In my day, ladies took dainty steps when in public."

Beth kindly refrained from mentioning that, at thirty-one, Hippolyta was not only still enjoying her day, but indeed spent most of it striding hither and yon in search of birds, tea, and lucrative publishing deals. Lady Trimble, however, had no qualms about saying so, judging from the gleam in her eye. "I suspect—" she began.

*"Mon Dieu!"*

As the shout rang out, teacups everywhere went down in saucers with a concertedly outraged *clink*. Monsieur Tarrou, president of the Parisian Ornithological Union, was staring openmouthed at a newspaper that he held open with one hand while, in his other hand, marmalade dripped from a slice of toast. Suddenly, he flung the toast to the table, grasped hat, gloves, and newspaper to his heart, and dashed from the tearoom.

"Something's afoot," Hippolyta said with remarkable perspicacity.

"Maybe it's about the latest news from the International Ornithological Society," Lady Trimble suggested. Smirking, she produced a folded newspaper clipping from within her purse. But before she could name a price for handing it over, Hippolyta snatched it from between her delicate fingers. Snapping it open with one brisk shake, she rapidly scanned the news.

"Upon my word! IOS is announcing a special contest!" She held up the clipping long enough for Beth to glimpse the words CALLING ALL BIRDERS before lowering it to read again. "A caladrius has been sighted in England! Whoever finds it will be named International Birder of the Year!! Regardless of their work thus far!!!"

She and Beth stared at each other wide-eyed.

Lady Trimble, however, wrinkled her nose. "Why would the International Ornithological Society waste everyone's time with such tomfoolery? The bird could be anywhere! No sensible person would hike all around the country looking for it." She stepped aside as an ornithologist elbowed her on his way to the exit. Around the room, others were quaffing tea and shoving expensive cakes into their mouths with unseemly haste. "I say," she added, "have you heard the rumor about Monsieur Chevrolet's sideburns?"

But Hippolyta and Beth were lost in a feathered dream and had quite forgotten Lady Trimble's existence. Neither needed to explain to the other how they felt. The caladrius was the ornithological holy grail. (Indeed, some said the bird had been at the Last Supper, eating crumbs Jesus tossed to it.) Sightings of its pure white wings and sorrowful eyes were as rare as hen's teeth. If one truly was in Britain—not just an albino plover but an actual *Caladria albo sacrorum*, capable of removing illness from a person's body and flying it high into a cleansing sunlight—hundreds of ornithologists from around the world would flock there, even without the impetus of a competition.

Hippolyta gave a longing sigh, then peered closer at the newspaper clipping. "Wait, there's more! Universities in several countries are offering whoever bags the caladrius—"

"Five thousand pounds!" Lady Trimble burst out, trying to regain her grasp on the conversation.

"Is that all?" Hippolyta said, but her eyes lit up. Beth, on the other hand, sipped tea to prevent herself from rudely scoffing. While she could appreciate why a field ornithologist, motivated by fame and fortune, would be aflutter at such money, as an academic she believed the only reward that ever *truly* mattered was coming to understand a bird, seeing all its—

"And if they're professors, they'll win tenure," Lady Trimble added.

Beth set her cup down so distractedly, tea spilled across the tablecloth. Hippolyta gasped, but Beth did not hear it over the zinging of her thoughts.

**Tenure!**

It was the ultimate dream, offering a chance to really delve into her theory about the connection between psychic territory and phylogenetic relationships! She was years away from attaining it by the usual process, and in the meanwhile, Oxford's head of ornithology, Professor Gladstone, refused to countenance "any wanton mixing of systematics and naturalism." The fact that he was also chairman of the International Ornithological Society meant Beth risked not only her job but her future prospects if she tried defying him. But if she could win tenure now, she'd be able to safely bypass Gladstone and his antiquated notions about ornithology, female scholars, and exactly who should be washing the dishes in the faculty lounge.

Realistically, though, she understood her chances to be poor. For one thing, her idea of "flair" was using color on the segments of a pie chart. And more to the point, she lacked the ruthlessness of other ornithologists, most of whom would have recognized Ivan the Terrible as a kindred spirit. Even now, from the corner of her eye, she noticed Herr Oberhufter trying to wrestle a newspaper from Mr. Cholmbaumgh of the British Birders Coalition, heedless of how the man was in turn bashing him with teaspoon. Nearby, a pair of Irish birders had torn the front page of their own paper in two and were each threatening to set their piece alight if the other did not surrender.

But the worst behavior came from Devon Lockley, who sat quietly with an elbow on the table and chin in hand, licking crumbs from a cake fork as he stared across the room at her. His dark eyes gleamed with wicked humor. His smirk might as well have said out loud, *Why, Miss Pickering, that is an awful lot of detail you are noticing from the corner of your eye.*

At once, Beth snapped her attention back to Hippolyta.

"We must procure train tickets to Calais immediately," the woman was saying. She smacked her hand against the newspaper clipping, and Lady Trimble, who had just been reaching for it, squeaked like a fluffpuffin. "Indeed, we will buy up as many tickets as we can, to prevent others from traveling!"

Hearing this, two gentlemen at a neighboring table promptly abandoned their sandwiches and hurried from the room.

"We'll also need a cage from Delacroice's. I would trust none other. Once we have the caladrius in our possession, we cannot risk losing it."

"But what if you don't find the bird?" Lady Trimble asked.

The question was so ridiculous, it couldn't possibly have been spoken; therefore the ladies ignored it. "Rupert should go ahead to organize a team. He can take the first train north to Calais, and then a ferry onward to Dover."

"I'll tell him," Beth said, rising at once. But she got no farther than that, for a glance around the room revealed it to be unoccupied by all but a few gobsmacked tourists. Cups lay askew in their saucers. Napkins littered the ground. On one table, a plate was still rattling.

"By Jove!" Hippolyta ejaculated.

"I dare say in five minutes there will be not one train ticket left in all of Paris," Lady Trimble remarked cheerfully. "You should probably run."

"Nonsense!" Hippolyta's initial shock vaporized; she took another macaron from the plate and hacked at it with her knife. "Ladies don't behave in such a vulgar fashion. We shall employ smarter tactics. Seduction, for one."

"Um . . ." Beth said, for despite being recently informed of her feminine wiles, she had not yet found a satisfactory description of them in her field guides and remained dubious about the whole concept.

Hippolyta chuckled. "Don't worry. Although you know plenty about the birds, you know nowhere near enough about the bees, and we're in too great a hurry for you to catch up. Why don't you take a more innocent role? Steal something for us."

"Steal?" Beth exhaled with relief.

"Yes. The Musée des Oiseaux Magiques on rue de Rivoli has a traditional caladrius call in its archives. It's just the advantage we need! While I set about locating train tickets, it should prove no difficulty for you to visit the museum unnoticed by our competitors, obtain entry to the locked archives room, locate the call among hundreds of other objects, steal it, and exit the museum without being caught. I'll see you back here in an hour, shall I?"

"Yes," Beth said automatically. Then she paused to consider the scope of the task. "Perhaps an hour and a half."

"Are you certain, Hippolyta?" Lady Trimble murmured, frowning anxiously at Beth. "It seems inappropriate for a young lady to be robbing a museum unchaperoned. The world is a dangerous place these days, you know."

"Nonsense!" Macaron crumbs sprayed from Hippolyta's lips like tiny pink exclamation marks. "Elizabeth is both capable and sensible."

"Thank you for your concern, Lady Trimble," Beth added with a smile, "but I shall be quite safe. After all, what possible trouble could I encounter in a museum?"

# CHAPTER THREE

An ornithologist must be proficient in the three
fundamentals of fieldwork: finding a bird, identifying
a bird, and getting the hell away from that bird before
it eats you.

*Birds Through a Sherry Glass*, H.A. Quirm

ALL ALONG THE streets to the museum, Beth met no trouble. Her plain brown coat, accompanied by a small hat, gloves, and air of cultivated intelligence, triggered fear in any man who glanced her way: one catcall, and she might *educate* them.

Slipping past museum staff to enter the archives with the speed and stealthiness of a well-trained ornithologist, she also met no trouble.

Wending a narrow path through shelves and cabinets to the back of the chamber, she met no—

"Hello."

Beth stopped so abruptly her hat shuddered, and only because of her stiffened posture did it retain its place upon her head. "You!"

Devon Lockley gave her a lithe smile. "You," he replied, his tone more friendly and thus far more dangerous than hers. Worse, he'd removed his dinner jacket and unknotted his tie. The bare, olive-toned skin visible where he'd unfastened his shirt collar took "trouble" and dunked it in a glass of hot, rum-infused devilry. Light from the small, dusty windows slid across his mouth languorously, stroking the smile.

Beth looked away, clearing her throat.

Shelves of boxes stood to the right of them, and to the left a row of specimen cabinets. A wide, shallow drawer lay open in the cabinet directly beside Devon, revealing assorted bird-calls, bird lures, and bird thingamajigs whose purpose had long since been forgotten.

"I haven't found it yet," Devon said.

"I'm sorry?" Beth replied innocently. "Found what?"

His expression tilted with sardonic humor. "I suspect you're not in the basement of the Museum of Magical Birds for the purpose of an afternoon stroll, Miss Pickering. You've come for the caladrius call."

Beth applied to her sense of decorum for a suitable response, but it took one look at the man and turned away, busying itself with dusting its precious antique collection of curtsies. Left to her own devices, she gave him a second, considering look.

He was implausibly handsome for a university professor, who in Beth's experience were a pallid lot, rather musty, with a constant yearning in their eyes for dinner, wine, and their latest lecture to magically write itself. But if there was any yearning done in regard to Devon Lockley, it was almost certainly not by him but *toward* him. Not that Beth felt any such yearning. Heavens no! She was far too sensible for that. The riotous sensations in her stomach were merely due to French tea.

She also suspected him of possessing masculine wiles. He probably kept them up his sleeve or in a trouser pocket—upon which thought, Beth glanced at said pocket, and managed to prevent herself from blushing only by dint of general aggravation. She hauled her vision up by the scruff of its neck and discovered Devon watching her smugly, as if he could guess her thoughts and was considering whether to reach his naked hand into that pocket and bring out something truly scandalous indeed. Her aggravation increased by several notches.

"I am here to do some research," she said, silently reassuring herself that it was the whitest of lies; beige at most. "However, this seems a convenient opportunity to apologize to you for our fracas in Spain."

"No need," Devon answered easily. In response, Beth's aggravation forgot about climbing notches and took flight instead.

"Absolutely there is a need! I was an ill-mannered scoundrel of the worst kind to assault you with a parasol!"

He leaned back slightly. "Er . . ."

"You ought to be stern and judgmental." She thrust out a gloved hand. "I insist upon apologizing. Kindly frown at me and then shake hands, so we may reestablish a civil rivalry between us."

"All right," he agreed—then ruined it by adding, "My pleasure." He gave her a frown that was clearly wearing nothing more than a wicked grin beneath its coat. But before Beth could summon offense, he took her hand.

Immediately, she knew she'd made a tactical error. His bare fingers were warm even through the kid leather of her glove. His grip was firm in a way that made the description "firm" seem altogether salacious. An electric sensation rushed through her body, setting off alarms hither and yon. All that saved her was remembering the job she'd come to do.

"How do you know about the caladrius call?" she asked.

Devon shrugged. "You told me."

"I beg your pardon—?—!"

"Well, to be precise, you told my spy, Lady Trimble, who then told me."

"Egad!" Beth gasped. "That's *cheating*!"

"Come now, Miss Pickering," he said, laughing. "All may be fair in love and war, but this is ornithology. Cheating is practically one of our scientific principles. Or did they not teach you that at—let me guess, Liverpool University?"

He *wanted* to aggravate her. "Oxford," she answered in her politest tone. After all, she could climb trees without showing her petticoats and wrangle birds into cages without swearing. No man was going to disturb her equanimity.

He smiled.

"Villain!" she remonstrated at once, before she even knew what she was doing. And once she'd got going, alas, there seemed no stopping her. "Don't try that charm on me, if you please. I will not succumb like some—some—*liberal arts undergraduate*."

"If you say so, Miss Pickering," he answered, still smiling. "I do beg your pardon. And while I can't apologize for using Lady Trimble to spy on you, I will point out that at least I chose to run here and find the call before you might, rather than steal it from you outright. Not that such virtue did me any good." He frowned askance at the open drawer. "This collection looks like a pack of first-year students have held a keg party among it."

The apology, such as it was, mollified her. "Perhaps we aren't the first to come searching," she suggested in a calmer tone. "Hippolyta cannot be the only one to know about the call."

"Which also means others might appear at any moment." Devon glanced over her shoulder as if expecting a sudden influx of ornithologists bearing lockpicks, pistols, and emergency marriage certificates for use upon discovering a bachelor and spinster alone together. Beth's nerves ruffled all over again. Really, this encounter was going to drive her to drink, and she did not think there was enough tea in all of Paris for the purpose.

"I suggest a compromise," she said. "I will search for the call, and you will stand guard, and once I've found it we will leave quietly so as to not draw attention to ourselves. What say you?"

"I say you need a better dictionary," Devon replied, grinning. He looked over her shoulder again; glancing back, Beth thought she saw a darkness move between shelves, but she blinked and it was gone. "I'm being paranoid," Devon murmured, shaking his head. "How about I look for the call, you do the same, and may the best birder win?"

"And when I win?" she asked cautiously.

"When I win, we'll agree to disagree, and depart without further argument."

"Very well." She turned toward the cabinet—only to discover she and Devon were still holding hands. He realized at the same moment and released her just as she was pulling away. She rubbed her hand against her waist. Devon shoved his through his hair. Stepping apart, they set to opening cabinet drawers.

"I admit I'm a little daunted, competing with Britain's youngest-ever professor," Devon said as they worked.

Beth glanced at him sidelong. Was he mocking her? Or had that been a note of sincerity in his voice? If he'd whistled a birdsong, she'd have been able to interpret it at once, but her ability with human conversation was mediocre at best, and this one certainly had her floundering. She decided to retreat, as usual, behind niceness.

"I'm daunted myself," she said, "competing with an academic wunderkind."

"That's merely a rumor started by my thesis examination panel because they wanted to get away early for a fishing trip."

Beth stared at him with astonishment. "Really?"

He just grinned in reply, his dark eyes glimmering. Instantly, Beth's aggravation discarded niceness and leaped once more into the breach, swinging its fists wildly and suggesting she close the wall up with a dead professor. Turning away, she rummaged through the birdcalls, not even seeing them.

For a while, Devon searched quietly alongside. But all too soon they were elbowing each other . . . leaning past each other to grab at something that looked like a possibility . . . *humph*ing and *tsk*ing and smacking at hands . . . completely missing the caladrius call lying among several other antique whistles . . . then seeing it finally and both snatching at it with such urgency they knocked it clear off the tray. It flew past them, fell to the floor, and rolled through a gap between two shelving units.

"Now look what you've done!" they said simultaneously.

"It wasn't my fault!" they replied in chorus.

And shoving at each other, they squeezed their way through the gap to crouch in the dark narrow space behind, groping around the floor for the little wooden call. Thighs pressed against each other; shoulders rubbed; etiquette rules exploded left, right, and center. Finally, Beth's fingers stumbled upon the call, and she clutched it in triumph.

Unfortunately, Devon did the same.

"Let go!" she hissed at him.

"You first!" he hissed back.

"How dare—"

"*Shut up.*"

Beth gasped in genuine shock. "I beg your pardon!"

He relinquished the call, but only so as to slap his hand over her mouth. Beth's heart leaped with what was almost certainly alarm and not delighted excitement.

"Shh!" he whispered. "I heard something."

Beth nodded. Devon moved his hand away, and together they shifted apart two boxes on the shelf at eye level so they could peer through to the passageway beyond.

*Tap-tap.*

Beth slapped her own hand over her mouth. A bird was tiptoeing delicately over the dusty floor—a dull brown bird, not much bigger than a magpie, with dainty legs and a small black beak. *Vanellus carnivorus*, her brain automatically recited.

Rabid flesh-eating lapwing.

It was the most vicious, deadly little bird this side of the Mediterranean. With scant effort it could bring down a grown man and the horse beneath him, and the servants attending him, and their horses too. Almost its entire population had been exterminated, leaving only two specimens in the highest-security aviaries.

And one in this basement.

Suddenly, Beth could not breathe. This was not due to her hand over her mouth; rather, she simply could not remember the process of inhaling air. The lapwing's claws tapped gently against the floorboards, providing an eerily calm counterpoint to her crashing heartbeat. She and Devon were sitting ducks, with no easy way of escape. As it passed where they crouched behind the shelf, there came a tiny click of fang against beak, and the warm vanilla scent the bird used to attract prey. Instinct urged Beth to follow that scent, to tuck herself into coziness beneath the lapwing's soft wing. Intelligence managed to restrain her, however, and the lapwing continued farther down the passageway, its lure diminishing as it went. Beth and Devon glanced at each other, exhaling with relief—

The lapwing froze.

It cocked its head.

"Damn!" Devon swore. Grabbing Beth's arm, he hauled her up with him and pushed her toward the gap in the shelving. "Run!"

Beth did not need telling, but this was probably not the time to complain about it. She squeezed through the narrow space, hoisted her skirts, and without daring to look back began to run. The lapwing clacked its fangs and beat its wings excitedly. *Tap-tap-tap* went its claws against the floor, just as they would against her bones.

"Faster!" Devon urged from behind her. Beth refrained from explaining that attempting to outrace certain death while dressed in four pounds of embroidered cotton and lace, a whalebone corset, a linen coat, and several layers of undergarments, not to mention her hat, was no easy task. She kicked aside document boxes that had been stored haphazardly on the floor. Devon pulled old field journals from shelves, flinging them over his shoulder as he ran. The lapwing chattered with delight.

Coming to the chamber door, Beth pushed it open and they rushed through, the lapwing nipping at their heels so closely, they could not shut the door on it. With the deadly scent of warm milk on a stormy night swirling around her, Beth lifted her skirts even higher, so that Devon might have seen the entirety of her calves had he been so inclined, and sprinted down a dim corridor. Ascending a flight of stairs that led to a chamber displaying various taxidermied land birds, they found a museum curator singing to himself about nocturnal city adventures as he dusted a *Struthio disco*, or flat-beaked ostrich.

"There's a rabid lapwing in the building!" Devon shouted at him. "Evacuate everyone!"

Squeaking in alarm, the curator tossed his duster wildly and fled.

*Snap!* The lapwing caught the duster in its fanged beak. Feathers and wood splinters exploded everywhere. Devon knocked down the taxidermied ostrich, to little effect: the lapwing tunneled through it in seconds, emerging in a cloud of sawdust. It shook its head and chattered as if it was having marvelous fun and slaughtering them would be the icing on the cake.

Halfway across the room and moving fast—but probably not fast enough, she feared—Beth grabbed a kiwi from a pedestal and threw it, creating one poignant airborne moment for the flightless bird before the lapwing leaped up to snatch it.

*Snap!*

"This way!" Devon shouted, racing in the same direction the curator had gone. Beth followed, spurred on by the hideous sound of the lapwing gobbling up the taxidermied kiwi. They rounded a corner—

And almost stumbled at the sight of Miss Fotheringham and Miss Fotheringham strolling toward them along a corridor. The tiny, elderly birders were deep in discussion about something that made them giggle like little girls.

"Rabid lapwing!" Devon shouted in warning.

The Fotheringhams looked up with wide eyes, their giggles collapsing into gasps.

*"Run!"* Devon added, for they seemed rooted to the spot. This advice failed to stir the women, however, and Devon and Beth were forced to veer around them or else die on the altar of good manners. Not looking back, they turned another corner just as the screams began. Stumbling to a halt then, they stared at each other, white-faced.

"We can't help them," Devon said. "We'd be killed ourselves."

"Only a fool would try," Beth agreed.

*Thud!*

*"Aagghhh!"*

"Damn." Devon's expression twisted with conflicting emotions. Abruptly, he bent to pull up one trouser leg and draw a knife from the sheath strapped to his calf. Straightening again, he cocked an eyebrow at the sight of Beth holding up her own blade, which she had taken from a skirt pocket. "I thought you were a nice girl," he said.

She looked him in the eye steadily. "That doesn't mean I'm weak."

Devon grinned. "Very well, let's at least try to injure it, giving us all a chance to escape."

Taking a deep breath, they turned.

And saw Misses Fotheringham round the corner, lapwing writhing in a sack fashioned from a hat veil.

"Thanks for leaving us the catch!" one of the sisters called out cheerfully.

"Jolly decent of you," the other added.

Beth and Devon glanced sidelong at each other. "Um," Devon said.

"Three thousand pounds at least for one of these," the first Miss Fotheringham said, holding up the sack. Beth could see through its silk tulle that the bird's beak and feet had been bound with frilly garters. "I wonder where it came from."

"Wherever it did, it's good luck for us," the second Miss Fotheringham said. "A lapwing capture *and* the caladrius call in our possession, all in one afternoon!"

"But *I* have the caladrius call," Beth said without thinking. Beside her, Devon winced.

"Is that so, my dear?" Miss Fotheringham held forth the netted lapwing in the manner of a weapon and smiled meaningfully. The bird's sweet odor flashed through the air.

Sighing, Beth took the call from her pocket and handed it over. With a brusque nod of farewell, the Misses Fotheringham marched along the corridor toward the museum's lobby, heels clicking sanctimoniously against the floor. Beth and Devon stared after them.

"I'm not sure why I bother being polite," Beth said, "considering how rude everyone else is."

Devon gave a brief, dry laugh. "Things are only going to get worse with this new contest. Really, I can't think of a more foolhardy idea than offering Birder of the Year *and* tenure."

"Reckless," Beth agreed.

Nevertheless, the gaze they shared was filled with longing— for a permanent departmental office, that is, and their own aviary, and a lifetime's supply of free tea and biscuits. Then Devon's mouth began to slide into a crooked smile, as if he simply could not keep his wicked charm suppressed for long.

Beth sighed. "I fear you are also very rude."

"And yet, you're still staring."

Her jaw dropped with incredulity—no, outrage!—no, horror! But while she was thus occupied searching for the most appropriate synonym, Devon leaned forward to whisper.

"I suspect you may be rather impolite yourself beneath all those good manners, Miss Pickering."

Beth's mouth snapped shut, and she drew herself up to the dignified height of five feet six inches (although to be honest, three of those inches included her hat). "I am not. Some of us can be fine ladies *and* rational creatures in the same form, sir, regardless of what novelists may suppose. You will not disturb my calm waters. Furthermore . . ."

"Yes?" he prompted when she fell silent.

She frowned. "Stop smoldering at me like that."

Now he was the one who frowned, although it somehow managed to be mischievous, and a smile lurked at the edge of his mouth. "Smoldering?"

Beth gestured awkwardly. "With your eyes like that. We can't have a reasonable discussion while you are smoldering."

His frown swayed out of mischief right into wickedness. "Why, Miss Pickering, I thought I couldn't disturb your calm waters."

Beth bristled so much she feared becoming like the thornbacked owl, an unsurprisingly rare species that tended to explode when touched. Taking a deep breath to settle herself, since there did not seem to be a convenient tea station installed in the museum corridor, she said politely, "Good afternoon, sir. I shall be on my way."

"Of course." He stepped back, gesturing along the corridor. "After you."

With a gracious nod, Beth turned and marched away. Traversing the lobby, ignoring Devon's footsteps behind her, she flung open the museum's exit door. But as she went through to the wide doorstep beyond, a sudden burst of light flashed in her eyes, causing her to stumble back with startlement.

"Madam, look this way?" someone called in a French accent. "And perhaps a smile?"

Another burst of light had Beth raising her arm as a shield. At once, Devon moved in front of her with an unexpected protectiveness that charmed her more than she wanted to admit.

"Sir!" came the voice again, loud, enthusiastic. "The name's Mirou, reporter with *Le Petit Journal*. How does it feel to have saved all these people from a deadly bird?"

Lowering her arm, Beth peered confusedly around Devon's shoulder at the scene before her. Two gentlemen in rather cheap suits, one holding a box camera, the other a notepad and pen, were standing in front of the museum, smiling rapaciously at her and Devon. Beyond them huddled a trio of museum employees, and beyond them, cluttering the street, a small but excited crowd of onlookers.

"How did you know about the bird?" Devon asked suspiciously.

The two men glanced at each other. "We happened to be here purely by coincidence," said one, "investigating, uh . . . the plight of the urban sparrow!" He pointed to a poster on the wall beside the museum door, which in fact advertised an exhibition of the *urbane* sparrow, a bird of an entirely different (and snazzier) feather altogether. "Can you share your feelings about being a hero? And who is this pretty girl with you? Did you save her from certain death as well?"

Devon and Beth stared at him in mute bemusement.

"Show us the bird!" urged the man with the camera. "I'll photograph it for the newspaper."

"We don't have it," Devon told him. "Didn't you notice the women who came out not five minutes ago?"

"Women?" The reporters looked at each other again, confused.

Devon frowned. "Two of them, carrying a bird trussed up inside a hat veil?"

"No, doesn't sound familiar." The reporters shook their heads slowly. Devon seemed astonished by this, but Beth was entirely unsurprised that two elderly ladies had gone unseen. And she certainly had no interest in talking to newspapermen. Doing so went against all her scientific and academic instincts, since there was no surer way of getting oneself misquoted in a public forum.

"If you'll excuse me," she said, "I have a train to catch."

"Allow me to escort you," Devon offered, holding out his arm.

"No, thank you," Beth replied stiffly. "While it's been a pleasure escaping death with you, and I wish you all the best despite your general villainy, I should like to be alone now."

"Madam, I will not leave you exposed to danger."

"The lapwing has been caught," she reminded him.

"I'm talking about the newspaper reporters."

Beth glanced at the men in question. One was eyeing her up and down then writing his observations in the notepad; the second was preparing to take another photograph.

"Very well, if you insist," she said, shifting a little farther behind him, so as to be more hidden from view. "I will accommodate your vanity by walking with you to the next street corner."

"Most kind," he murmured, smiling facetiously. They departed the museum's doorstep, both taut with silence.

They jostled their way through the crowd, the reporters shouting questions as they went.

They strode along the street with every pretense of not knowing each other.

And arriving at the next corner, they parted ways without a word, set on never meeting again.

(Then traveled the same route back to Hôtel Chauvesouris, took the same elevator to the seventh floor, and walked down the same corridor to where their rooms were located side by side—but as both vehemently refused to notice this, the narrative is powerless to offer any comment.)

# CHAPTER FOUR

A wise woman allows nothing to ruffle her feathers;
*she* is the ruffler of feathers.
*Birds Through a Sherry Glass*, H.A. Quirm

ACROSS THE STREET from the Musée des Oiseaux Magiques, in a quaint little coffeehouse, two gentlemen with identical black suits, bowler hats, and brushlike mustaches sipped black coffee as they watched the crowd disperse.

"That couldn't have gone better, Mr. Flogg!" declared one. *"A Triumphal Success!"*

"It was all we hoped for," said the other. "Did you *see* that man, Mr. Fettick?"

Mr. Fettick nodded, his eyes shining with the memory. "Tall, dark, and handsome indeed. We couldn't have asked for a more perfect hero to walk into our little trap. Cheers!"

"Cheers!"

They raised their coffee cups in mutual congratulations.

Just then came the sound of a throat being cleared with the discomfort of someone who is about to eat crow. At the table behind them, a man sitting hunched in a trench coat, hat brim pulled low, glanced around the otherwise empty coffeehouse. "The blackbird has landed," he whispered intensely.

"Did you hear someone speak, Mr. Fettick?" asked Mr. Flogg.

"I'm not sure, Mr. Flogg," replied Mr. Fettick.

*"Hmph."* The man rose from his chair and scuttled to sit at their table. Glancing around nervously once more, he pulled the hat brim even lower.

"Good job, men," he murmured as Messrs. Fettick and Flogg sipped coffee. "I admit, I didn't like your plan at first. Too grandiose."

Mr. Flogg gave him a tight smile. "Monsieur Badeau, if the International Ornithological Society wants to create more interest in ornithology and encourage university enrollments, something truly attention-grabbing is required."

*"'More Bang for Your Birders,'"* Mr. Fettick added, and Mr. Flogg jabbed a finger at him in agreement.

"I know, I see that now," Monsieur Badeau said. "Indeed, when the Fotheringham sisters came out with the bird in their—"

"No," Mr. Flogg interrupted, shaking his head definitively. "Not them."

"But they caught the lapwing."

"I don't care if they caught seven lapwings; for your competition, you need the kind of winner who will attract a broad audience. You need that man."

He pointed out the window, and although the street was now empty, they all knew whom he meant.

"That man was Devon Lockley," Badeau said darkly. "He's a complete rascal. Copious brainpower but all he wants to do is *enjoy* life instead of spending his days in the noble pursuit of writing scientific papers for his peers to argue over. It's disgraceful. And while he may be an Englishman and a professor at Cambridge, he was educated at Yale. *Yale!* The place isn't even two hundred years old! It barely qualifies as a community learning center."

"He's an Englishman?" Mr. Flogg repeated. "What a bonus! With the British Tourism Board helping to fund this competition, we couldn't really set up a *foreigner* to win International Birder of the Year."

Mr. Fettick sighed happily. "A university professor, handsome, athletic, with simply divine legs—"

"Ahem," Mr. Flogg interrupted.

"—in summary, this Devon Lockley is *'An Eagle Among Sparrows.'* Young people will flock to university ornithology courses just to be like him."

Badeau muttered something inaudible that nevertheless perfectly encapsulated the attitude of a man for whom "athletic" means walking from the lecture theater to the tea station three times a day. Then he huffed in surrender. "Fine. But someone's going to have to recover that lapwing. You know what the boss will say if you lose his precious bird. Feathers will fly, and not in a good way!"

"Don't worry," Mr. Flogg murmured with professional reassurance. "There's no need for concern; we know what we're doing. That's why IOS employed us, after all. The plan is set, journalists have been alerted, and our agents will see to it everything goes smoothly. Just relax, monsieur, and wait for the enrollments to, ha ha, roll in."

"But what about the girl?"

Messrs. Fettick and Flogg exchanged a confused glance. "Girl?"

Badeau flicked a finger toward the museum. "Beth Pickering. She was standing there at the door."

"I thought she was just a museum employee," Mr. Flogg said.

"She's an Oxford professor. Moreover, she's a genius when it comes to birds." Badeau paused, frowning. "I wonder why she left with Lockley."

"Perhaps they're lovers," Mr. Flogg mused, staring out the window as if he could still see Beth and Devon on the doorstep.

The monsieur barked a laugh. "An Oxonian and a Cantabrigian? Never! 'Rivals' would be more likely."

Mr. Fettick raised his eyebrows at Mr. Flogg, whose mouth began twitching. "Rivals, you say? The pretty lady and the dashing young man?"

Badeau nodded solemnly. "Pickering is entirely capable of beating Lockley to the bird, regardless of your *plan*. If you want to knock her out of the competition, make sure you get to it quickly—and quietly, so there's no scandal."

"Oh, I think we know exactly how to handle this," Mr. Flogg said. Mr. Fettick chuckled.

"Good." Badeau frowned, glancing around yet again. "This conversation never happened," he said, then slunk back to his table to brood.

"By Jove! That's dastardly!"

Hippolyta stared at Beth over the stacks of luggage in their hotel suite. *"Vanellus carnivorus?"* she exclaimed. "It's a miracle no one was killed. Oberhufter has gone too far this time!"

"Absolutely!" Beth agreed, looking around for a pot of tea to soothe her jangling nerves. She couldn't seem to stop recalling the danger she'd just been through: Devon Lockley's flashing grin, the feeling of his hand over her mouth, and, oh yes, the deadly lapwing that had tried to slaughter them.

"I will be speaking to the authorities upon arriving in England!" Hippolyta declared. "Criminal behavior cannot be tolerated."

"Yes," Beth said. And when Hippolyta glanced at her oddly—"Er, I mean no?"

Hippolyta's eyes narrowed. "You seem discombobulated, Elizabeth. Your hat is askew, to say nothing of your vowels."

Beth checked again for a pot of tea, or a cup of tea, or even a tea bag she could chew on at this point. "Being chased by a carnivorous—"

"It is that Cambridge professor, isn't it? That Devil Lovely."

"Devon Lockley," she tried to say, but Hippolyta was already half a sentence ahead of her and moving fast.

"He is a blighter. I heard he spent the past few years in America and only recently transferred to Cambridge. Apparently the Yankees gave him a scholarship when he was fourteen, on account of his genius."

"Genius," Beth scoffed.

Hippolyta nodded in agreement. "Those upstarts wouldn't recognize true genius if I gave a lecture in San Francisco's Palace Hotel. It's no wonder he's so arrogant. Mark my words, Elizabeth, there's nothing worse than a conceited person! Besides, he may have been born innocent," (she sounded dubious as to this) "but anyone associated with Oberhufter is soon corrupted. The way he stole the caladrius call from you—"

"The Fotheringham ladies did that."

"Cahoots!" Hippolyta shouted. Then recollecting that complete phrasing was usually helpful: "They were in cahoots with each other, I am sure of it. They and Lady Trimble and the whole diabolical cadre of bird snatchers."

Beth did not point out that she and Hippolyta belonged to the same cadre. The first unspoken rule when it came to Hippolyta Quirm was that honesty seldom represented the best policy. (The second rule: it was *tea* in her silver flask, regardless of smell, color, or that half-empty bottle of rum sitting on the shelf. Which also handily illustrated rule one.)

"I'm certain you are right," she murmured with only the smallest twinge of conscience. Devon might be guiltless in this matter, but she did not like the man, nor respect him, nor desire in the slightest to slide her hand through his wayward black hair. He was a bird-stealing fiend, never mind his various charms! They were fiends too, the whole lot of them! And she was a mature, sensible woman, despite the evidence of this paragraph.

She sighed, her heart drooping.

"Buck up, dear!" Hippolyta boomed. "I have—we have a caladrius to catch, and no unscrupulous men shall stop us. Fortune favors not only the brave but the decent and honorable!" She thrust out her hand sidelong, palm up. "Ticket!"

One of the three footmen standing to attention behind her stepped forward with a small card, which he placed tremulously in her hand. Hippolyta passed it to Beth.

"Here is your train ticket. The hotel maid has packed your things, although there is still much to organize before we leave."

Beth inspected the first-class ticket amazedly. "How did you manage to get this so quickly?"

"I stole it from Oberhufter's room."

———

THAT EVENING, HERR Oberhufter himself, along with a rather weary Devon, departed Hôtel Chauvesouris for the Gare du Nord station. A gentleman of Oberhufter's caliber does not need anything so trifling as *tickets* to secure passage on a train. (Especially if he blackmails the railway company president into giving him free travel.)

They proceeded along the seventh-floor corridor toward an elevator, trailed by their butler, valet, and two footmen pushing a luggage trolley. Dinner had been a light, hasty affair, and Oberhufter was munching on an emergency cheese sandwich as he walked. But as the elevator door opened before them with a jaunty *bing*, the sandwich drooped, half its contents falling to the floor.

*"Mein Gott!"* Oberhufter shouted.

"Huh," Devon added more succinctly.

Misses Fotheringham lay moaning on the floor of the elevator chamber, bestrewn with lapwing feathers. The bird itself was nowhere to be seen.

"What happened here?" Herr Oberhufter demanded.

A Miss Fotheringham hauled herself to her knees. "Masked man in a black suit," she said, spitting a feather from her mouth. "Attacked us. Took the lapwing. Sister, are you alive?" She grasped the other Miss Fotheringham's shoulders, shaking her.

Oberhufter waved his sandwich impatiently. "Never mind all that! Focus on what's important, Elvira! Where is the caladrius call?"

"Gone!" Miss Fotheringham cried as she slapped her sister's face. "Wake up, Ethel! Wake up!"

Ethel was in fact awake and yelping at being struck, but this did not daunt Elvira, who continued slapping, shaking, and at one point punching her sister. Oberhufter turned away as the elevator door slammed shut on the scene.

"Who was that masked man?" he demanded of the world in general.

Devon shrugged a reply. In truth, he was rather surprised by this evidence that Oberhufter hadn't been behind the lapwing attack in the museum after all.

The man bit heavily into his sandwich. "I'm shocked!" he declared, although it sounded, through the mouthful of bread, more like he was shoffed. "This is the work of that reprehensible Quirm woman, I guarantee it. Well, well, Hippolyta. I take my hat off to you. If I was wearing a hat, that is. And if you were here. And if you wouldn't just steal the hat to whack me with it."

He chewed thoughtfully for a moment, then looked around with sudden concern. "Where *is* my hat? Someone fetch me a hat! At once! And why for the all the sausages in Germany are you just standing there, Lockley? Summon the elevator!" Taking another bite of sandwich, he muttered about dumb associates (or possibly "yum, opiates!" which might explain quite a bit).

Devon pressed the elevator button. *Bing!* The door slid open to reveal Misses Fotheringham wrestling on the ground, hands around each other's necks. Oberhufter stepped in, moving to one side so Devon could enter next and the servants thereafter, maneuvering the trolley. With such a crowd, Misses Fotheringham were forced to relocate their skirmish to the rear of the chamber.

"Let's get moving!" Oberhufter demanded as the valet

placed a hat upon his head (having first surreptitiously removed the one already there). "The caladrius won't catch itself!"

A footman reached for the control button to close the door—

"Hold that elevator, by Jove!" boomed a deep, galumphing voice. Oberhufter spat out a mouthful of chewed sandwich, which struck the footman's cheek then slid down the front of his uniform. The footman did not so much as blink. He held the door open as Mrs. Quirm swooped in like an exotic bird-of-paradise that had just flown through a haberdashery store, and peremptorily employed her furled umbrella to clear space within the chamber. She was followed by Miss Pickering, more discreetly attired in a simple beige traveling suit, its sleeves barely puffed. With her chestnut brown hair gathered tidily beneath a straw boater and delicate spectacles settled on her nose, she looked so much like a schoolteacher, every man in the elevator stood up straighter.

"Sorry, pardon me, thank you," she murmured. But her attention was focused on a book she held open in one hand, and Devon doubted she even knew whose company she'd joined. Whatever it was she read filled her eyes with enthrallment, and as she turned a page she seemed to hold her breath in anticipation. Watching her, Devon found himself holding his own breath too.

He was being foolish; he knew it. The woman might be pretty, but she was also a rival in the field, an academic foe, an associate of the unscrupulous Hippolyta Quirm, and *so very* pretty the air around her seemed to glow. The spectacles alone made him want to ~~kiss her until they fell off~~ invite her to dinner at a nice seafood restaurant. He could still feel her warm, soft lips against his palm from when he'd hushed her in the museum's basement, and his nerves tingled, begging to touch her again.

"Atrocious!" Oberhufter shouted. Devon jolted, then realized the man was complaining about the ladies' servants, who were angling an overburdened luggage trolley into the elevator. "Typical Quirm behavior! Taking up all the space! I might have known!"

("Aagh, that's my hand someone's standing on!" cried a Miss Fotheringham.)

"You know nothing!" Hippolyta shouted back at Oberhufter. "Your head is emptier than a cuckoo's nest!"

Rolling his eyes, Devon just happened to glance again at Beth Pickering and caught her staring at him with startlement and—was that interest? His pulse leaped. But she immediately jerked up her chin, tightened her expression into haughtiness, and pivoted on a heel to face the elevator door. Devon grinned. With a side step and a little angling, a little shoving at the luggage trolley, he insinuated himself into the space beside her. She was so rigid, a person could use her as a ladder for observing bird nests. She stared at her book with such fierce intent it was obvious she saw not one word on the pages. Devon weighed whether he should nudge her or whisper in her ear.

He had not yet decided when she turned a page in a crisp, emphatic manner that warned him to try neither, on pain of being publicly educated as to his flaws. With any other woman, he might have taken this as a challenge, but there still existed some question as to just how sincere she'd been when she said she wanted calm waters. Veering on the side of gentlemanly caution, a neighborhood he seldom visited, Devon shoved his hands into his coat pockets, where they could not get up to any mischief.

*"Hurry up!"* Hippolyta shouted, banging the tip of her parasol against the elevator floor. "I have yet another award to add to my pile."

The door slid shut with an ominous clank. A footman moved the control lever, and with a tremor, the chamber began its descent. Beth tipped toward Devon, then righted herself mere inches before a delightful collision could occur. Devon's body flashed hot. The woman smelled of lavender and pencil shavings, as if she'd just come from hiding in a bush to sketch birds. She was the perfect height for him to cuddle her close and kiss the top of her head—and the moment Devon thought this, he suddenly longed to make it happen.

"Such codswallop!" Oberhufter shouted. "Your pile will be a mere pebble compared to my collection!"

"Funny you should mention a pebble," Hippolyta retorted, "since we all know that is the size of your—"

"Cheese sandwich, anyone?" a footman interjected loudly.

Devon angled his head toward Beth so that he might see what she was reading. Immediately, she closed the book by clapping her hands together. The resultant *thud* served to reprove him—or, at least, would have, had he any scruples. Instead, he touched one finger to the book and tipped it in her hold so he could see the title.

*Behavioral Ecology*—he read in the two seconds before she tipped the book back. He met her fierce gaze, and the air between them grew so charged, Nikola Tesla could have invented three things just by looking at it. Without blinking, Devon tipped the book again.

*—in Ornithological—*

Beth yanked it with such force away from his reach that she dropped it. A furious little sigh expelled from between her lips, and it was all Devon could do not to grin with triumph at having provoked her.

"Rotten blighter!" Hippolyta shouted.

"Harridan!" Oberhufter retorted.

*Bing!*

The elevator juddered to a halt at the fifth floor and its door opened. Everyone turned their heads to stare at two ladies waiting in the corridor. Both were resplendent in the latest fashion, hats magnificently plumed, feather boas hanging in a bright froth about their necks.

"Good afternoon," one said pleasantly. "Is there room in there for us?"

Hippolyta frowned. "Are those ostrich feathers you're wearing?"

"Rainbow ostrich, from South America," Beth identified from over the rim of her spectacles. "Only five hundred of the species still alive."

"And is that a liar-bird quill in your hat?" Oberhufter demanded, brandishing his sandwich.

The women glanced at each other, then laughed. "Who are you?" one asked. "The fashion police?"

"No," Hippolyta replied ominously. "We're ornithologists."

"Oh dear," murmured the first woman, growing pale, but the other stared them down.

"I purchased this feather from a reputable ornithologist in Paris!" she proclaimed.

"No, you purchased it from a smuggler," Oberhufter said.

"You should probably run while you can," Devon advised with a grin.

Squealing, the women turned and fled.

"Dreadful!" Hippolyta and Oberhufter exclaimed in unison.

Then, exchanging a startled look at this agreement, they immediately scowled again.

"I heard you plagiarized your book!" Oberhufter shouted.

"I heard you plagiarized your personality!" Hippolyta shouted in return.

The door slammed shut, the elevator resuming its descent.

Devon crouched to retrieve Beth's book from the floor, thus narrowly avoiding being struck by Hippolyta's parasol as she thrust it toward Oberhufter.

"You're a thieving beast!" she growled, whacking the hat from the man's head.

"You're predictable!" Oberhufter retorted, grabbing hold of the end of the parasol and attempting to wrangle it from her.

Rising again, Devon managed, purely and innocently by chance, to be standing even closer to Beth. He handed her the book and she took it with a nod of thanks, inspecting it for damage before securing it in her traveling satchel. The spectacles followed, and Devon looked around for some reading material so he could induce her to put them back on again.

"Aaargh!!" Mrs. Quirm roared, prodding Oberhufter with her parasol.

"Aaargh!!" Oberhufter roared, crashing back against the elevator's wall. The chamber shuddered, causing Beth to stumble. Devon automatically put a hand against her waist to steady her.

He expected that she'd move away, but she didn't, and electricity sizzled through him, rousing instincts a man really didn't like experiencing in a crowded space. He wanted to undress her brain, stroke her perspective, make her gasp out the most fascinating theory she hid from all other men. (He also wanted to kiss the hell out of her, but that went without saying.) Only the steely willpower developed over years of bird-watching in icy rain, and teaching undergraduates first thing Monday mornings, kept him from drawing her closer to his side.

"And furthermore—!" Hippolyta declared.

"Pigs will fly," Oberhufter interrupted, "before you win Birder of the Year!"

"I say, do you mean the hog parrot of Borneo?" Elvira Fotheringham piped up from the floor.

"Oh, be quiet, sister," Ethel Fotheringham snarled. They began wrestling once more.

Beth's eyes widened as she realized the sisters' presence. She looked around like she expected the lapwing to leap up and begin an attack; not seeing it, she turned to Devon with a quizzical frown. He just met her gaze silently, his mouth curving up at one edge. *Ask me and I'll tell you. Say my name and I'll give you all you want.*

She did not speak, but neither did she turn away. Devon's smile faded. Their mutual gaze deepened. Had a lapwing indeed been in the elevator, it would have been fricasseed the instant it took flight.

"You will never beat me, Oberhufter!" Hippolyta roared, flailing her parasol with such fury it knocked the hats from two footmen and nearly put out the eye of a third.

"Just wait, woman!" Oberhufter growled, throwing his sandwich wildly. All the servants ducked. *"Mein Gott!* I'll have you over my knee yet, and then you'll know a beating like you've never had before!"

Instant shocked silence filled the chamber. As the elevator thunked to a halt, a footman had the door open so fast one might suspect him of possessing superhuman strength.

Hippolyta stepped to the threshold of the chamber and swung about, skirts whirling, to glare at Oberhufter. The elevator door slid across to collide with her, but she did not move even so much as an inch. Devon was only aware of this at the periphery of his attention, however, for he could not seem to look away from Beth. Nor, apparently, could she break whatever force kept them locked together.

"When I am once again Birder of the Year," Hippolyta intoned, "I shall have your name stricken from the ranks of the Ornithological Society, Oberhufter!"

The door withdrew slightly, then banged into her again.

"When I am Birder of the Year," Oberhufter shouted, "I shall have you banned from ever picking up a birdcage again, Quirm!"

Devon blinked. A ripple went through Beth's expression in response.

"Heinously gormless faradiddling cockalorum!" Hippolyta roared with a tour de force of English eloquence, while the door tried in vain to force her out of its path.

"*Gehirnverweigerer!*" Oberhufter's voice made the servants cower.

"Ahem."

Devon turned his head, as did everyone else, to see a dark-suited man in a bowler hat standing in the hotel lobby, holding a briefcase and folded newspaper, politely blank-faced behind his mustache as he awaited his turn to use the elevator.

Mrs. Quirm harrumphed, and whirling, she stormed off.

"Good afternoon, gentlemen," Beth said politely, and followed.

Devon flinched at the sudden loss. He reached out unthinkingly to stop her, or even just to touch her one more time—

But she was gone.

"*Bäh*," Oberhufter said as the ladies' footmen hastened to exit with their luggage trolley. "The sooner I am Birder of the Year and get to gloat over that woman's tears of defeat, the better." He clapped his hands. "Another sandwich! Now! More cheese this time!"

"*Aaargh!*" cried Elvira Fotheringham as her sister pounded her head against the floor.

Devon sighed. Another lapwing feather drifted past, scenting the air with vanilla, blood, and wicked magic. Watching it, he had a sudden premonition that this was going to be a long summer indeed.

♡

# CHAPTER FIVE

Integrity is the hallmark of the master ornithologist,
trust me on this.

*Birds Through a Sherry Glass*, H.A. Quirm

THE TRAIN ARRIVED at Calais after midnight. Gas lamps lit
the station, but the sea beyond was dark and still, and
dampness made the air feel tired. A ferry waited to carry the
train passengers on to Dover in England, and a veritable scrum
had formed as everyone made the transfer. Beth clutched her
satchel for comfort as she trudged along the dock, the noise
and jostling of the crowd making her feel twitchier than a
white-eyed hurricane sparrow. The day had been far too long,
with far too many people in it (not to mention a deadly lapwing), and she wished she could hang back until everyone else
had boarded the ferry. But it was going to be a matter of first
on, best seated, and no one cared more about seating arrange-
ments than birders. Should Hippolyta find herself farther from
the exit than Mrs. Huang of the Chinese Avian Tracking Society, someone was liable to end up overboard.

Excitement for the competition ran high. Señor Perez had
glued yellow silk feathers to his wheelchair, Mrs. Nnadi's hat
bore a mechanical bird—at least until Miss Eliza Wolfe

"accidentally" knocked it off with her NEXT BIRDER OF THE
YEAR flag—and Monsieur Chevrolet was for some reason out-
fitted in a Scottish kilt that only just covered his excellent
thighs. (Beth noted several people staring at it intently, as if
trying to manifest a sudden breeze.) Hippolyta, however, focused all her energy on Herr Oberhufter, some ten feet ahead.
His luggage trolley was preventing her from overtaking him,
and such was her frustration that she vibrated even more than
an African sacred ibis in mating season.

Suddenly, the trolley met a crack in the dock's surface and
lurched to an abrupt halt. "D—!" said the footman, his curse
reduced to polite punctuation by the clatter of toppling suitcases. The crowd swarmed past him. Oberhufter vanished
from sight.

"Great galloping Jove!" Hippolyta exclaimed. Shoving
aside two ladies wearing large SO I ♥ IOS badges, she pursued
Oberhufter into the night, leaving Beth suspended in stunned
astonishment.

"What a disaster!" cried the footman pushing their luggage
trolley. Beth turned to give him a reassuring smile.

"Don't worry, Samuel, we'll just catch up with her on the
ferry."

"I mean, I can't find Mrs. Quirm's cosmetics purse!" The
poor man was as frantic as a student who hasn't studied for
exams. "I think I must have left it on the train!"

"Oh dear," she said. Hippolyta felt the same way about her
cosmetic purse as Beth did about her satchel: like it was an
extension of herself, containing the necessities of life. And
while it might seem that Beth's field journal, binoculars, and
emergency supply of birdseed were more ornithologically valuable than mere toiletries, Hippolyta had once caught a poisonous

goldfinch using a hairnet and rose-scented lip rouge, so Beth was not about to scoff.

"I can't go back for it," Samuel said. "I need to guard the luggage." He gave Beth a wide-eyed, imploring look.

*No*, said her brain instantly as it contemplated the veritable forest of people, suitcases, birdcages, outdoor furniture, and at least one personal commode that she'd have to navigate in order to reach the train. But "Yes, all right," said her mouth, of course. "I'll fetch it."

Samuel grinned. "Thanks, miss!" He waved to someone—at least, that was how it appeared, confusingly, to Beth, until he pointed at the locomotive, and she understood he was giving her directions. "If you go down the other side of the train, it'll be quicker."

"Hm," Beth replied wearily. A drop of rain splashed against her hand; squinting at the sky, she winced as another fell onto her face. Samuel handed her an umbrella from the luggage trolley.

"Good luck," he said. "I believe in you!"

A little taken aback by this enthusiastic declaration of faith in her purse-fetching ability, Beth murmured thanks, then hurried away. Moving around the head of the locomotive, she balked at how eerily quiet it was on the other side, between the train and the imposing terminal building. Darkness stretched before her, speared here and there by dim lamplight from a few carriage windows whose blinds had not been fully closed. She questioned the wisdom of proceeding, but there was no time to dither. The ferry would be leaving soon.

"Blast and botheration," she muttered as she hurried alongside the train. Rain began to drizzle more steadily, requiring her to open the umbrella. Beneath its black oilcloth, the night seemed even more ominous. Beth paused, thinking that she really ought to turn back.

Suddenly, a low, sinister whistle slid through the darkness. Beth stopped, every hair on her arms rising. She knew that sound. A strix owl was calling out in distress.

*Nonsense*, she told herself. *I'm imagining things.* The strix owl was a vanishingly rare bird located solely in the Scottish Highlands. It would not be crying in the dark of a French ferry terminal.

And yet there went the sound again, coiling around her heart, making her shiver with a disconcerting chill.

She crept forward, listening intently. Perhaps a storm had blown the bird across the Channel. Perhaps it had escaped from an aviary. Whatever the case may be, she was constitutionally incapable of ignoring a bird in trouble.

Just then, the darkness ahead rippled. Beth instinctively edged closer to the train, angling her umbrella like a shield. A man was creeping along the side of the building, a small pipe between his lips. As he passed through a shaft of light, Beth recognized Herr Oberhufter's secretary, Mr. Schreib (or possibly Schreib's identical twin, her brain offered with a pedantry she really did not appreciate right now). He blew on the pipe, and once again the whistle of a strix owl echoed uncannily through the night.

*I knew the bird couldn't be here!* Beth thought with rather smug gratification.

*Er, please note that this is a trap*, her brain countered, her heart pounding in agreement.

Another figure emerged from behind Schreib. "I wish they'd hurry up and get here," he grumbled, huddling within a black trench coat. "I'm freezing."

"Trust me, Cholmbaumgh, they'll come," Schreib said. "And then we'll kill two birds with one stone."

"But what if the footman couldn't convince—"

"Trust me," Schreib reiterated, and blew the whistle again.

"I almost feel sorry for Miss Pickering," Cholmbaumgh said over the eldritch cry. "Nice lady. She's not going to know what hit her."

Beth gasped. The sound might have revealed her presence, but luckily at that moment both men chuckled in a manner she could only describe as unequivocally malevolent, and which a less educated person would call "nasty." She urged herself to flee, but a lifetime of remaining perfectly still while watching birds had overdeveloped the habit, and she was frozen to the spot. Any second now the men would notice her, and all would be lost.

Suddenly, a hand clamped over her mouth. She had no time to panic before an arm came about her waist and she was being pulled against a strong, masculine body (or perhaps one of a lady athlete—Beth did not wish to judge). Her heels bashed against boot-clad legs and her umbrella swooped as she was hauled into the space between two carriages.

Supposing herself about to be murdered, Beth found her life flashing before her eyes. But it had not even finished going through her childhood before she was set again on her feet and turned around. The hand lifted from her mouth, to be replaced immediately with one finger. A dim strand of light from the station's lamps showed that she'd been rescued by Devon Lockley.

He took her umbrella and closed it. The latch clicked slightly, and both Beth and he held their breath.

"Is someone there?" came Schreib's voice. Its sharp tone

seemed to echo with the smack of a fist. The sound of footsteps began to move slowly near.

Devon crouched down, pulling Beth with him, and they crawled under the wrought-iron gangway platform of one carriage. Huddled together, they barely breathed as Schreib approached.

"Hello?" the man called out. Beth watched wide-eyed as he stalked past the gap between the carriages, closely followed by Cholmbaumgh, who paused, glancing in, his expression writhing with shadows and smoky lamplight.

Beth's life resumed flashing before her eyes—

And Cholmbaumgh shrugged, then moved away.

Devon exhaled in relief. Beth attempted to do the same, but the breath shuddered in her throat.

Devon grasped her hand in a firm grip. With his other hand, he stroked her arm. Outrageous! Rakishly scandalous! Actually quite soothing! Beth began to relax, despite being huddled closely with a scoundrel in a small, dark space.

Unchaperoned.

While danger stalked nearby.

For the second time that day.

She should pull away and hasten to the safety of a well-lit public space. But the prospect of being captured seemed more of a concern in that moment than her reputation, not to mention the fact that no one had touched her beyond her hands in years, and she was finding it more pleasant than she cared to admit. Perhaps sensing this, Devon advanced his ministrations, brushing a loose strand of hair away from her cheek.

Tingles went through Beth like a thousand tiny stars. She stared at the man, transfixed. His face was as faint as an albino owl in the darkness, his eyes some other nocturnal metaphor she could not summon from the sparkling haze that had been, merely ten seconds ago, a perfectly good brain. She wanted—

Nothing specific, actually. Just *wanted*, with a depth of feeling she'd experienced only once before, when a rare amphibian crow hopped across the sand in front of her. Obviously, the drama of the moment was to blame, since she had no desire whatsoever for Devon Lockley. He was an adversary in the field, an academic rival, an obnoxious villain with a gorgeous smile that came close to dissolving her kneecaps every time he turned it on her . . .

Beth felt herself drifting helplessly toward him . . .

He moved closer to her . . .

*Toot!*

They jolted apart in shock. For a moment, the world comprised nothing but shuddering heartbeats and rushed breath.

*Toot! Toot!*

"The ferry!" they gasped in unison. Scrambling out from beneath the platform, they emerged on the sea side of the train. Immediately, Beth spied Cholmbaumgh and Schreib—!!

—standing on the rear deck of the ferry, panting heavily from having done a mad dash, as the boat chugged out to sea. Workers were maneuvering the boarding ramp across the dock and wheeling away emptied trolleys.

"Blast and botheration and *bloody hell*!" Beth fumed.

Devon gave her an amused look. "Surprisingly well said, Miss Pickering. I don't suppose you are any good at swimming?"

Beth felt her face grow white. "I'm sorry, but is that a joke? Are you joking? In this moment? Are you mad?"

"No more than any other ornithologist."

"How can you be so calm in the face of this disaster?!"

His face creased in a bemused frown. "Disaster?"

"We are stranded on this dock," Beth explained in the I-am-not-calling-you-an-idiot-but-that's-because-I'm-nice tone she used when explaining to students, yet again, the basic metaphysical attributes of the plica semilunaris in prognosticating thaumaturgic passeriformes. "Although we escaped assault, that is small consolation under the circumstances. The others now have a head start in the competition. I've lost all my luggage apart from this one satchel, I doubt I've enough money on me for a new ferry ticket, and—" Her breath tripped in exhaustion. "It's *raining*."

Turning away from him, she tucked her hands under her armpits in a futile effort to warm them. A few dockworkers peered over curiously, but Beth could not summon even the basic courtesy of nodding to them. She stared out at the ferry, which was now no more than a blurred cluster of lights diminishing into the mist.

*Thunk!*

She jerked at the sudden sound. But it was only Devon opening her umbrella. He lifted it to shield her.

Beth turned to stare at him amazedly. He looked back with equanimity. The air between them, washed faintly gold from lamplight, glinted as raindrops drizzled through it. The sea's whispering was interspersed with the bell-like sounds of halyards clanking against boat masts. Beth did not know whether she ought to take the umbrella in her own hand, or insist Devon share in its shelter, or just dive into the harbor and swim away so as to avoid embarrassment.

"Thank you," she said as a last recourse.

"It's the least I can do," Devon said. "If I hadn't noticed you lurking behind the train, I'd have walked into a trap. I should have known Oberhufter wouldn't have left his binoculars on the train."

"I wasn't lurking," Beth retorted. "I was pausing with a sensible discretion."

Devon's mouth quirked. "One day I'd like to read whatever dictionary it is that you use." He tilted his head to regard her more seriously. "Are you all right?"

"Fine," she said in Automatic British. "You think Oberhufter was behind this?"

"Actually I'm not sure. His footman may have sent me back to the train, but Oberhufter himself is not that sneaky. If he wanted to do away with me, he'd just have had me thrown off the train."

"Why do you work with a man like that?" Beth asked curiously.

Devon shrugged. "My departmental head asked me to spend the summer helping his daughter train her pet falcon. In other words, spend the summer being maneuvered into marriage." He shivered dramatically. "Chasing the deathwhistler with Klaus Oberhufter was a better option. It also meant I could ensure the bird ended up in a sanctuary rather than the weapons laboratory he planned to sell it to. Why do you work with a woman like Quirm?"

"I'm trying to prove a connection between psychic territories and the phylogenetic relationships of thaumaturgic birds," Beth explained. "But I keep getting denied funding, so I need a field partner with resources. Hippolyta fit the bill."

"According to Lady Trimble, she uses you as her personal servant."

Taking umbrage at such an *utterly ridiculous* claim, Beth

grasped the umbrella and stepped back. Devon kept a firm hold on her gaze, however, his eyes dark and amused and seeing far too much. Beth lowered the umbrella defensively. "Hippolyta respects my judgment," she said, "and therefore relies on me."

"She'd throw you off a cliff if it got her a bird."

Beth thought of the several cliffs she'd rappelled down in order to inspect nests while Hippolyta stood at the top, shouting instructions. "I admire her ambition."

"So you don't think she was the one responsible for us being lured into a trap?"

"Oh, it's entirely possible she was."

"But you just said—?" He broke off, frowning in confusion.

"Hippolyta and I may be associates, but there's no space for loyalty or friendship when it comes to ornithology."

"That's true."

A lonely little moment of silence followed. Beth lifted the umbrella again, glancing at Devon. He stood beside her, hands in his coat pockets as he looked out over the sea. He seemed forlorn, and she surprised herself by feeling sympathetic toward him. Perhaps the man wasn't completely bad. He'd just saved her life, after all. And more importantly, he'd kept the deathwhistler from a miserable fate.

"I have a little money," she said. "Enough to buy us tea somewhere in town."

Devon turned back to her, the forlorn mood replaced by an amused frustration. "Miss Pickering, we've just established the ruthlessness of ornithologists. You ought to leave me out here alone, wet and cold."

Beth applied within for a witty response but came up blank. She was not used to playing with conversation—she was barely used to conversation at all. Unless a person was speaking about birds, or pointing to birds, or asking her to please tell them all the fascinating details she knew about birds, she generally avoided engaging. Moreover, inherent shyness, mixed with her attending university from a prodigiously young age, had not been conducive to her developing social skills. Even in Oxford's ornithology department, as a female professor of twenty-four among predominantly old men, she seldom socialized beyond polite nods, observations of the weather, and joining in the occasional excitement about who stole Professor Humberton's sandwich from the faculty lounge. And Hippolyta rarely required more than intermittent noises of agreement.

Besides, how was she supposed to be eloquent when the outrageous fellow didn't even wear a tie, let alone the civilizing influence of a waistcoat? She tried for dignity but hit indignation instead:

"You are being presumptuous. Perhaps I intend some trickery that involves buying you tea."

Devon took a step toward her. "Will you poison it?"

"I might," she said, lifting her chin and absolutely refusing to retreat.

He set a finger beneath the rim of the umbrella, tilting it back. His eyes were full of dangerous promises as he looked down at her unblinkingly. "I might push you into the water," he said.

Hot sparks went through her. "I might get you a croissant along with the tea," she countered.

His mouth twitched. "I might tie you up, gag you, and put you on the next train to Istanbul."

The sparks set fire to an unmentionable part of her body, and it was all she could do not to squirm. "You might," she agreed, "but before you can, I'll telegram my bank for funds to get you a ferry ticket."

The twitch became a slanting smile. "Ah, I see the plan now. Bedazzle me with courtesy, then leave me in your dust. Very cunning, angel, but alas, I have my own money."

*Angel.* Well! Really! Humph! Villain! And other emphatic words that sadly failed to halt the blush speeding toward her face! She'd never been called a nickname before (except in the deep privacy of her own imagination, that is, where she kept a list of suggestions should anyone want one, although no one ever did). She attempted a reply, but her voice seemed to have swooned.

"I'm sure I've enough to buy us cake along with the tea," Devon continued, reaching into his coat pocket and withdrawing not a wallet but a small, narrow object.

"What the fuck?" he said, staring at it in shocked bewilderment.

Beth did not chastise him for this vulgar language, primarily because she was secretly thinking the same thing. "You have the caladrius call," she said in a bland tone that concealed the emotional chaos swirling beneath it.

Devon looked at her with eyes that seemed even darker than usual, due to the pallor of his face. "I have no idea how it got in my pocket."

"Sure you don't," Beth murmured sarcastically. Being nice did not mean being a complete idiot.

"I'm serious," he insisted. "Would I lie to you?"

"Yes. You'd lie and steal my bird and send Mrs. Trimble to spy on me and—"

*Splash.*

Beth's jaw fell as she stared at the midnight waters into

which Devon had just thrown the caladrius call. "Why on earth did you do that?"

"To prove I wasn't lying," he said. "I genuinely don't know why it was in my pocket."

She turned her incredulous stare upon him. "So you just *threw it away.*"

He pushed a hand through his hair, frowning slightly and biting his lower lip as he considered the sea, which now contained one of the most valuable tools for capturing a caladrius and winning Birder of the Year.

"Perhaps not my smartest move." Then he shrugged, and a smile sauntered back onto his lips. "Well, it's done now. Let's get moving."

"Er, fine," Beth said, striving to overcome her discombobulation. "We'll find somewhere to have tea, catch the morning ferry, and be in England before noon."

"Or," he said, "we can hijack a boat and sail across the channel tonight."

Beth gasped. "What a terrible suggestion!"

"I forgot, you are a proper lady. Of course you disapprove of hijacking."

"I disapprove of *sailing.* A steamboat would be faster."

Devon exhaled a laugh that deepened his smile and made him look so gorgeously wicked, she half expected him to transform into a carnivorous lapwing and bite her neck. "I do declare, Miss Elizabeth Pickering," he said, "we may be birds of a feather after all."

She bristled. "Please don't address me that way. For one thing, we aren't so well acquainted."

"We've survived peril twice together already," he pointed out.

"Yes, but Elizabeth isn't my name."

"Mrs. Quirm calls you that."

"However, I am in fact Bethany. I introduced myself as Beth to Hippolyta, and she just assumed it was for Elizabeth."

His stare turned quizzical. "You've never corrected her?"

"Heavens no! That might hurt her feelings."

He seemed momentarily at a loss as to how to respond. But then he smiled again. "Very well, Miss Not-Elizabeth. What do you say to that fishing trawler docked over there?"

"I say it looks filthy and will probably fall apart halfway across the Channel. But that is better than remaining in Calais."

"Hey!" cried out a nearby dockworker in a wounded voice.

*"Je suis désolée!"* Beth apologized, then hurried after Devon toward the fishing trawler as if she was not an intelligent woman who knew better than to go off alone in the middle of the night with a reprehensible, American-educated scoundrel who might just be someone very dangerous to her indeed.

# CHAPTER SIX

*The field ornithologist is a sophisticate, at ease with
the diversity of people she meets in hotel lobbies and
salons around the world.*

*Birds Through a Sherry Glass*, H.A. Quirm

As it turned out, hijacking a trawler was easier said than done.

To begin with, there was the matter of boarding. "I wish I'd sought a special license to wear trousers," Beth mused as she stood at the dock's edge, eyeing the narrow but hazardous distance between herself and the trawler's deck.

Devon felt his heart lift on unexpectedly soft wings toward her. "Take my hand," he offered. "I'll help you."

She stared at him as if he'd tried to pass her a fanged ostrich. Then, dismissing this small but swooningly delightful opportunity for moonlit romance, she closed her umbrella and made a nimble leap. Devon held his breath, but she landed neatly on the trawler's deck with a complete lack of coy, feminine vulnerability and only the mildest dishevelment of her hat.

Devon's heart swooped back and curled up inside him. With a self-mocking smile, he leaped after her.

Then came the difficulty of operating the trawler.

"I see the wheel," Beth said, sheltered once more beneath her umbrella as she surveyed the deck, "and piles of rope, and clearly the chimney holds some purpose. But how does it all go together to create locomotion?"

Devon pushed back his wet hair and sighed. "To be honest, I don't know. But we're scientists; surely we can figure it out."

There was no chance to do so, however, because just then another obstacle arose: the trawler's four occupants rushing from the cabin, clad only in long woolen underwear. They appeared about as happy to be hijacked as might be expected.

*"Merde!"* they shouted. *"Qu'est-ce que vous faites, connards?!"*

At once, Beth and Devon leaped back. "Why are they calling us flycatching loons?" Beth asked, her umbrella trembling.

"That's *fou fatal contopus*," Devon told her. "I'm fairly sure they mean something more earthy." Drawing a gun from a holster beneath his coat, he pointed it at the fishermen.

*"Enlever mon passeur de perruches!"* he commanded.

The men glanced at each other, frowning confusedly. "Take off, my budgie smuggler?" one hazarded.

"Er . . ." Devon did not avert his attention from them as he asked Beth, "How do I say, 'we're birders and we need you to follow that ferry'?"

"Don't ask me," she said. "I will never move them in French, unless it be to laugh at me."

He turned his head then to stare at her. "Really? Shakespeare, at a time like this?"

"Anytime is a good time for Shakespeare," she replied patriotically.

"This is what you learn at Oxford? With such an impractical education, you have no hope of winning Birder of the Year."

"And—and Yale offers an education so practical, it may as

well be a technical institute!" she retorted, clearly unfamiliar with sniping, but giving it her best shot. "I suggest you just go home and await my award acceptance speech."

Devon grinned. His hand longed to reach up and brush away a raindrop glimmering on her cheek. Other parts of his body expressed longings so Shakespearean he almost laughed at the irony. "You are a martinet," he told her amiably.

"And you are scandalous," she countered.

"*Ahem*," contributed a fisherman.

Returning to his senses with a jolt, Devon turned to find all four men leaning back against a large equipment box, arms crossed, watching the scene in fascination. He scowled. Gesturing with his gun toward the misty sea beyond, he ordered them in brusque English to follow the ferry. And apparently the barrel of a Webley Mark I spoke a universal language, because they jumped to obey.

While the fishermen worked, Devon kept his weapon trained on them. Beth, however, paced the lantern-lit deck, chewing her thumbnail with no consideration for the glove encasing it.

"I'm sorry for the inconvenience," she told the captain.

"Please forgive us," she told the first mate.

"You are ever so kind," she told the two crew members, smiling with the kind of warmth that suggests something is about to burst into flames.

"Really, just *dreadfully* sorry," she reiterated to the captain.

And so on, until the fishermen ended up assuring her it was *perfectly fine* she had pirated their boat. Whereupon she relaxed and began instead to ask about their operations, mingling hand gestures and pidgin French, apparently intent on getting her mariner's license at the end of the journey.

The fishermen patiently explained each rope's purpose and the fundamentals of steam engineering, and even let her steer the wheel for a while. Not a mile out to sea, they began bringing her tea, and jam sandwiches, and a coat that she declined on the basis of being quite warm, thank you (although Devon, smelling it from where he stood on the other side of the deck, suspected she preferred freezing to stinking of old fish). In return, she taught them several bird whistles and extracted from each man a promise to never shoot down an albatross should they happen to stray into the Southern Hemisphere while trawling for mackerel.

Devon watched all this with a cynicism that had been polished by years in the ornithology field. The woman truly was fascinating, and he would have gladly kissed her in Calais had the ferry's horn not interrupted. When she laughed with the fishermen, everything inside him sighed with a longing he could not repress. But . . .

But . . .

Er, there *had* been a but within that train of thought, he was sure of it. He just couldn't seem to remember where.

No one offered him sandwiches. Indeed, all he got were menacing looks and more than one muttered promise that he would *"nourrir les poissons"* the moment he let his guard down. Knowing *poissons* did not actually mean *poison* somehow failed to reassure him. Apparently what was good for the goose was not good for the gander after all. He made himself an uncomfortable seat upon a coil of rope, hunched in his coat against the endless drizzle, hungry and tired and thinking thoughts so impolite, Beth probably would have fainted had she known them.

As night labored on through murky darkness, Devon

drifted asleep despite himself. Upon awakening in the faint, blue-toned light before dawn, he looked out with relief at the town of Dover, its black silhouette glinting here and there with lights like slumming stars. The boat was dawdling into harbor. The fishermen stood around the wheel, talking quietly and casting him vicious looks. Surprised that they hadn't turned the boat around while he slept, Devon nodded to them as he crossed the deck to where Beth sat on an equipment box, sheltered by a makeshift canvas roof.

She was rigidly upright, clutching her satchel against her midriff protectively, but her eyes were closed, and Devon indulged in a moment of observing her without fear of being chastised. She must have been freezing in her light skirt and jacket. He wanted to wrap her in his arms—merely on the scientific principle of sharing body heat, of course. He wanted to remove her hat and unbind her glossy hair slowly, pin by pin. It would reach almost to her waist, he guessed with the expertise of a man who had unraveled many a coiffure. It would feel like silk against his skin. He'd brush it back, then tip her chin so as to kiss her soft, lucent throat until she opened those heavenly eyes and saw him . . .

*Saw him.*

His heart, decidedly unimpressed with such a dangerous notion, silenced all further thought. Removing his coat, he draped it over her.

"Wake up, angel," he whispered. Then louder: "Wake up, we're almost here."

"Strix owl," Beth muttered, then wakened with a jolt. She blinked up at him dazedly, her eyes brimming over with shadows.

For a moment, Devon forgot to breathe. The emotion visible in her gaze was so stunning, and made her so beautiful, so haunting, it was as if she'd risen from the sea like a forgotten daughter of Poseidon. But then she rubbed a hand across her brow, and when he saw her again she was guarded once more.

"I must have dozed off," she said.

"We're almost here," he repeated. "Dover."

"Already?"

*"Already?"* he echoed incredulously. "It's taken at least three hours. This boat is a tub."

She sat even straighter. "It's an eighty-six-foot steam drifter with a tonnage of—" She stopped herself. "In any case, the gentlemen were kind to bring us at all."

A laugh broke from him, and he hastily turned it into a cough. Solemn, Beth regarded his damp, crumpled shirt, then the coat enveloping her.

"This is yours," she said. The words snagged a little on her breath. "You gave me your coat."

"You looked cold," he said gruffly. "I—I didn't want you to be cold."

His brain sighed in self-disgust. Beth touched the coat, and Devon found himself shivering like it was his skin she'd laid those finely gloved fingers upon. Her wondering expression might have broken his heart had she not quickly hidden it away.

"You look colder," she said with a brief, shy glance at his damp shirt. "And that is a worrying cough you have." She handed him back the coat. "But thank you for your kindness."

Devon came so close to blushing he could feel its heat in his throat. No one had ever accused him of being kind before. Mesmerized, he reached vaguely for the coat and missed; it dropped to the deck. He barely noticed. In the dreaming twilight, he knew nothing but her.

The first moment he'd seen the woman at that tedious bird-ers' meeting, standing alone at the edge of the room with her gaze fixed on the exit door, he'd thought she looked like an angel visiting earth and finding it horribly boring but, being angelic, not wanting to complain. Pretty face, lovely eyes, em-inently kissable. But now his attraction was becoming compli-cated by a far more treacherous emotion. He *liked* her. She was Sunday morning, a bird in the hand, fresh chalk for a clean blackboard. And damned if he wasn't in—

"Ahem."

Turning, blinking, they both looked at the fisherman standing beside them.

*"Ton manteau, crétin,"* he said, holding out Devon's coat.

Beth smiled at the man in a way that sent jealousy rampag-ing like feral carnivorous ostriches through Devon's blood. "How gracious," she said. Then she flicked a reproachful look at Devon. "Isn't that gracious? He's offering you tea and toast—you know, croutons."

Somehow, Devon did not think so. He took the coat, then hurried away before wishes, or French fishermen, eviscer-ated him.

Finally, as daylight seeped red-gold and glimmering through the harbor, they docked at the Admiralty Pier. Devon gave the trawler's captain a handful of francs and got a scowl in return. He climbed onto the pier, heavy-limbed, cold, and determined to find a place that served coffee. Beth, however, took a ridiculously long time with farewells. Devon watched bemusedly as she shook the hand of each fisherman, murmur-ing a few words, eliciting smiles and much doffing of caps. It appeared she was thanking them, wishing all good things upon their families, and inviting them to call upon her should they ever find themselves at Oxford during the Michaelmas term. And they were *thanking her right back*. Devon rolled his eyes.

At last they handed her up onto the pier, saying things in rapid, impassioned French, which Devon suspected were instructions on how to kill him and steal all his money. Grasping her elbow, he proceeded to ~~tow~~ guide her solicitously toward the train station at the end of the pier.

"Good heavens!" she declared, clutching her hat to keep it on her head. "This is altogether vigorous of you!"

"I'd just like to leave Dover sometime before winter," he said. "And without an entourage of angry Frenchmen," he added, glancing over his shoulder to where the men were standing on the trawler's foredeck, arms crossed, watching him balefully.

"They are merely excited for us," Beth said. "Because they understand so little English, it was no use telling them about Birder of the Year. My own French being weak, all I could think to say was that you were my beloved husband—my *épine dans mon coeur*, giving me a vacation in England—an *angoissant vexation*."

Devon laughed. "I'm pretty sure you told them I'm a thorn in your heart who distresses you with his anger."

"Oh." Her expression blanked. "I must go back at once and explain!"

"No, you must not," he said, increasing his stride. She stumbled to keep up with him.

"But what will they think of us?"

"That we're evil boat thieves. It doesn't matter, we'll never see them again."

"But—"

Suddenly, her boot met a crack in the dock and she

stumbled. Devon caught her before she fell. Glancing back again as he did so, he saw the fishermen bristling. One reached for a harpoon.

"There's no time to waste!" he said, practically dragging her along. "We must hurry if we want to have any hope of catching the caladrius!"

"Yes," she said, her mood suddenly changing, as if she'd come fully awake and remembered what she was about. "You're right. We must run!" Now she was tugging on him.

Devon found himself actually trying to slow her down before she did either of them an injury. "The station is right there. Don't worry, Miss Pickering. It's all going to be fine."


"IT'S A DISASTER!" the ticket clerk cried, waving his cap in agitation. "We don't understand how it happened! The track is absolutely melted! Not just buckled but *melted*, I tell you!" He jammed his cap onto his head, then immediately yanked it off and waved it again, nearly whacking the engineer who stood with him, gazing mournfully at the mess of warped tracks alongside the platform. "There's no point asking about tickets, mister. We're not getting a train in or out of here for days."

"Feuerfinch," Beth said.

The clerk and engineer stared at her as if she were mad, or possibly German. But Devon made a thoughtful sound in his throat. "Interesting theory, Miss Pickering," he said.

Beth opened her mouth to remind him that he was not the only academic genius standing on the dock, thank you very much, but something in his eye suggested that he'd appreciate the excuse to tease her. So instead she leaped down the twelve inches from platform to tracks, eliciting a shocked gasp from the ticket clerk at such unladylike behavior. A small red semiplume lay trapped between pebbles; crouching, she picked it up gently and held it to the morning light. Pinkish-gold traces of magic lingered around the soft bit of fluff, shimmering here and there as a breeze tried to restore the feather to flight.

"Feuerfinch," she said again, envisioning the snazzy little bird, with red wings and an orange breast, hopping over the tracks as it breathed tiny but potent flames onto them. She'd never seen one in the wild, and her heart sighed happily over the feather even while her brain peered at it closely, taking mental notes of the enthralling details.

"I'm impressed," Devon said.

Beth couldn't decide whether he meant impressed by her or the bird, so regretfully set aside the compliment. "Someone has employed a feuerfinch to deliquiate this iron," she said. "The luteofulvous threads of psychokinetic ignition still emanating from this *fringilla accendo* semiplume confirm it."

Looking up, she saw the engineer lean sideways toward Devon. "What's she talking about, mate?"

"A magic bird melted your tracks," Devon translated.

"Cor blimey!"

"The feuerfinch is extremely rare and only found in the Black Forest," Beth said, peering up at the arched roof of the station as if the bird might still be flapping around beneath it. But all she saw was a quiet, wingless morning shimmering with dust. Regarding the tracks once more, she noted fragments of the magical threads that provided a lingering trail of the bird's movement. Tracing it with her gaze, she realized the little creature had attempted flight several times but failed.

"Someone clipped its wings!" she said, rising from her

crouch with the force of dismay. "They mutilated the bird so they could use it as a weapon!"

"The IOS competition is heating up," Devon said, his voice grim. "Literally, in this case." They exchanged a silent gaze weighted with professional fury for whoever had harmed the feuerfinch, then Devon glanced northward, frowning. "We should hurry."

"Yes," Beth agreed, and stepped on a track, raising her arms in advance of climbing back onto the platform. But suddenly Devon was reaching out, taking her hands in his.

"Up you come," he said.

He lifted her so precipitously, Beth stumbled onto the platform, colliding with him. He held her steady . . . she stared at him in a daze . . . and after several moments the clerk and engineer cleared their throats awkwardly. Coming to her senses, Beth moved back. With a sardonic smile, Devon released her hands and turned to the clerk and engineer. Beth took the opportunity to discreetly flex her fingers, which thrummed with the sensation of his touch.

*Villain*, she reminded herself. *Rival.*

*Pretty*, her heart replied with a sigh.

"I'm afraid this was sabotage," Devon explained to the workers. "There's a race for a special bird, a caladrius—"

"Ahh, so that's what those blasted orthonogogists were going on about," the engineer said, nodding with belated comprehension. "I thought a caladrius was some kind of kitchen utensil. Couldn't understand why they were in such a tizzy about it."

"They actually demanded the use of our staff vehicles!" the clerk added. "Didn't even line up in a proper queue!"

"You have vehicles?" Beth said hopefully. "Carriages?"

"Bicycles. Or we did. The ornologists wanted them all. Offered enough money that we could get a new portrait of Her Majesty for the waiting room, so of course I said yes. I brought out the Special Transactions form (3A), the Purchaser Identification form (2F), the form for—"

"You gave them all necessary papers," Devon interrupted.

"Yes! But they ignored that and just took the bicycles!"

"You mean they *stole* them?" Beth gasped.

"No, they paid money," the clerk said. *"But they didn't fill out the proper paperwork!"*

"Oh dear," Devon murmured.

The engineer peered suspiciously at Beth. "You're one of them, aren't you?"

His tone was so sharp, she leaned back. Devon took a small, gliding side step closer to her—an act she'd observed a horned blackbird making in defense of his mate—and she went all steamy inside. Not even admonishing herself that *steamy* was a highly unscientific term could seem to stop it.

"Of course she isn't," Devon said, smiling with such languid charisma that both clerk and engineer blushed. "We're innocent, mild-mannered geologists. Entirely down to earth."

He nudged Beth with his elbow, but she hesitated. While an ornithologist should be able to lie on the spot—for example, *No, sir, I did not see the bright-red sign saying "private land, no trespassing" beside the gate, which was definitely already open*—she had never mastered the ability. Just then, however, she glimpsed a figure lurking by the entrance to the station and recognized it as Oberhufter's secretary, Schreib. Immediately she gave the clerk and engineer a brisk nod.

"We are indeed geologists! Rock-solid characters, honest to a fault."

"But you knew about the magic bird," the clerk pointed out.

"Didn't you as well? I thought it was obvious."

He squirmed and shrugged in the beam of her polite smile.

"We've got a lot on our plates right now," she continued, "so we'd very much appreciate a timely furnishment of intelligence as to any means of locomotion that might be available nearby, for which we will offer commensurate recompense, of course."

The two men gave her a stunned look, then turned to Devon.

"Tell us where in town to find horses," he said. Then, with a sidelong wink at Beth: "Please."

The steaminess began to form a sauna in the pit of her stomach.

"If you're not orgthologists, why are you so desperate to get horses?" the engineer asked suspiciously.

"We have a rock emergency."

"Oh. Well, that makes sense. But look you, there's no point running around Dover. Those maniacs will have been through it like a plague already."

"We have to try," Beth said. "It's a matter of—"

"Life and death?" the clerk interjected with a doubting smirk.

"Worse! Tenure! And surely with a bit of door knocking, some cash on offer, we'll find a kind, good-hearted person willing to help. This is Britain, after all."

# CHAPTER SEVEN

Fortune favors the bold ornithologist—which is to say,
having a fortune will get you all the favors you need.
*Birds Through a Sherry Glass*, H.A. Quirm

RETURNING TO THE station an hour later, they found the clerk leaning against the ticket desk, still smirking as he watched them trudge in. "Let me guess," he said. "The price for horses has increased somewhat since yesterday."

"Seven hundred pounds," Devon said grimly. "And when we explained the situation was urgent, it went up to eight hundred. I've never encountered a more unscrupulous lot of people, and I teach university students."

"We didn't bother trying the whole town," Beth explained. "We came back here to see if our associates left our luggage behind; then we'll start walking."

"I may be able to help you after all," the clerk said. He glanced at something behind them; looking back, they saw only a black-suited, briefcase-toting gentleman of the type ubiquitous in England, standing farther down the platform as he innocently perused the train schedule. "As it happens, I have a horse you could borrow," the clerk explained, drawing their attention again. "She's old but still has a leg on her, and I'm willing to take—"

"Two hundred pounds," Devon offered promptly. And, as the clerk hesitated, he added: "I'll also fill out any necessary forms. *In triplicate*."

"ONLY ONE HORSE." Beth sighed as she watched Devon check the tack on an ancient gray mare. She tried to be glad for him that he'd obtained his own transport, but it was going to be a *very* long walk north to Canterbury, where the nearest train station was located.

On the other hand, she was relieved to be parting from the dastardly fellow. Men had always been vague shapes at the edge of her awareness, rambling on about sports or telling her how to do something she'd mastered in adolescence. The exception was Professor Gladstone, Beth's head of department and former mentor. An octogenarian who smelled of pipe smoke and slightly damp tweed, he had eyes permanently narrowed from too much peering through binoculars and no small finger on his left hand after it was bitten off in the wilds of Colombia by a feral undergraduate suffering from coffee withdrawals. As a young woman, Beth had been awed by the professor, but his repeated suggestions that she try to smile more and show her intelligence less, so as not to intimidate her male peers, destroyed that feeling. And no other man had even approached her interest.

Devon Lockley, on the other hand, had literally dive-bombed it, then set up camp right in the middle of her brain. And worse—after just two days in his company she'd begun using loose language, arguing, even veering dangerously close to banter. Much more of this and she might become *sassy*. Going their separate ways was entirely wise, sensible, proper, and other words found in the index of an etiquette manual. It was only that the prospect of blistered heels from her damp shoes weighed heavily on her mood.

She summoned a bright smile. "I wish you good luck," she told Devon pleasantly. "If you happen to meet Hippolyta, would you please pass on my regards?"

"Tell her yourself," Devon said without glancing back as he arranged the stirrup.

The words struck Beth like a punch to the stomach. Her smile became so bright it might have served as a lighthouse, warning against hidden rocks.

"Well," she said. "Goodbye."

She waited a second, perhaps a second and a half, before concluding he was going to ignore her. Then widening her smile to a degree that hurt, she turned away.

Devon caught her by the wrist, and she looked back at him confusedly. A similar confusion creased his face.

"I *meant*, 'tell her yourself when we catch up to her.'"

Beth's mind went blank, all its protocols lost in surprise. "Oh."

Devon angled his head, regarding her with a mix of amusement and incredulity. "Did you think I'd just abandon you in Dover?"

"Why not?" she asked. "I'd abandon you, were the situation reversed."

"No, you wouldn't. Besides, if I left you here, you'd probably blunder into a group of smugglers and be so busy apologizing for having disturbed them that you'd fail to notice they'd tied you up and shipped you off to scrub floors for some crime lord in Australia."

"I wouldn't mind going to Australia," she said primly. "I've always wanted to see the fanged emu."

Devon rolled his eyes, but he was grinning, and Beth warmed at the sight of it. Before she could chide him (or, God help her, giggle) he set his hands on her waist and lifted her into the saddle. Astonished, disoriented, *steamy*, Beth caught hold of the saddle horn to keep her balance. Devon swung up behind her, and as his body pressed against hers, she went from steamy to flaming hot faster than an active volcano.

"I . . . sorry . . . I can ride astride," she said.

"Sure," Devon answered easily. He waited while she squirmed, shuffled, and tugged at her long skirts, trying to rearrange herself without revealing too much leg.

"Um," he added after a moment, clearing his throat.

"Er," he said shortly thereafter.

Then suddenly he was dismounting, his boots hitting the ground with a decided *thump*. Confused, Beth looked down at him as he pressed his forehead against the horse's flank.

"Is something the matter?" she inquired.

"I'm fine," he said. "Just need a minute." His voice was rather trembly, and Beth thought with some alarm that he might be falling ill.

"Perhaps you ought to sit down," she said.

"No, no. It's only a muscle spasm."

"Oh. In that case, you should massage it."

He laughed.

While she awaited his recovery, Beth gnawed her gloved thumbnail, squinting northward and trying to estimate how long the journey to Canterbury would take and what birds they might see along the way. But her thoughts were interrupted by a shout; looking up, she noticed the French fishermen beside the dock, talking excitedly as they pointed to her.

"Oh! Hello!" she called out, waving.

Cursing, Devon instantly hoisted himself up behind her in the saddle and reached for the reins. "We need to leave," he said. "Now."

"But it's our friends! And this is a perfect opportunity to clarify that you're not an angry husband." She went to wave again, and Devon caught her arm.

"There's no time."

Just then, the fishermen began to sprint toward them, roaring and brandishing a thin, pointed object.

"I beg your pardon," Beth said, "but there is always time for good manners. Besides, I left my umbrella behind, and they clearly want to return it."

"That's not your umbrella," Devon said. "That's a bloody fishing spear. Hold tight." He flicked the reins, urging the horse to gallop. "Gee-up!"

Nothing happened.

He flicked the reins again. *"Gee-up!"*

The horse lifted its head, perused the neighborhood for a moment, then began to stroll forward.

*"Arrête, agresseur de femme!"* the fishermen roared, drawing closer.

Beth twisted, trying to look over Devon's shoulder at them. "They're saying 'Wait, kind lady!'"

"Yeah, somehow I doubt that," Devon muttered. Knocking his legs against the horse's sides, he thus inspired it to shift up from a stroll into an amble.

*"Nous allons te tuer!"* shouted the fishermen.

"They're inviting us to tea," Beth translated.

"Ha! Run, you beast!" Devon squeezed harder and the horse at last began to trot.

*"Aider!"* Beth called to the fishermen. *"Aider!"*

"Don't you mean *adieu*?" Devon asked tartly.

"Of course, yes. *Adieu!*"

But it was too late. The horse had rediscovered its spirit and was gaining speed. "They will think us so rude," Beth complained.

"I can live with that," Devon said. "Focus on imagining yourself finding the caladrius."

Beth attempted to do so, but her imagination seemed more inspired by the circumstance of Devon's arm wrapped about her waist, his body supporting hers, the two of them bouncing together in the saddle as the horse galloped toward town. Indeed, she became so inspired, she would have stepped down for the sake of her dignity, had that not been a sure way to ruin her dignity forever, considering the speed at which they traveled.

"Oh dear," she said.

"Are you all right?" Devon asked at once.

"Just a muscle spasm."

A small moment of silence followed. Then: "Oh dear, indeed," he said. "Just keep holding on. I'll get you there soon."


In the shadows of the Dover train station, Mr. Flogg slid a finger across his mustache, smoothing its dark hairs as he watched Devon and Beth gallop north. "You were right, Mr. Fettick," he said. "Separating them from the other ornithologists was a brilliant ploy. It hasn't even been twenty-four hours and they're already working together closely."

"Yes, '*A Golden Team!*' indeed," Mr. Fettick agreed. "There's a lot of potential in this rivals-to-lovers concept."

"It's publicity magic!" Mr. Schreib enthused from where he stood alongside Mr. Cholmbaumgh, rolling a paper cigarette in a rather awkward attempt to fully embody his role as a thug.

"Much better than just having Lockley as the lone hero. Everyone loves a romance."

"I'm not sure IOS will," Mr. Cholmbaumgh said. "After all, there can only be one Birder of the Year."

"That's true," Schreib said, frowning worriedly. "Someone's going to end up a loser, and then what will happen to the romance tale?"

But Mr. Flogg dismissed this concern with a wave of his hand. "An all-round happy ending isn't necessary."

"Hm," Schreib murmured doubtfully.

"The bird's capture is the important thing. After that, people will move on to the next sensational news. Besides, we haven't figured out the details. For now, much work remains to be done." He pointed at Schreib. "You go alert the local newspaper as to events. Now that the professors have begun their road trip, all manner of *'Delectable Moments'* will occur, and someone needs to report on them. You"—now he pointed at Cholmbaumgh—"go talk to those French fishermen. Give them some reason to visit Canterbury. They add a fun international flavor."

"And what will you be doing?" Cholmbaumgh asked boldly.

Mr. Flogg's mustache flicked. "As the brains of this operation, Fettick and I will be doing the most important work of all."

"Oh?"

"Yes. Consulting with each other over coffee. Now saddle up, everyone, ha ha. We have a romantic adventure to organize, and I will be very cross if it ends up being madcap."

# CHAPTER EIGHT

When in doubt, remember that you have the wisdom
of an ornithologist, the patience of an ornithologist,
and several tools in your ornithologist's kit bag that
can serve as weapons.

*Birds Through a Sherry Glass*, H.A. Quirm

DEVON'S ASSURANCE OF a quick journey to Canterbury contradicted any definition of "soon" that Beth had experienced. After almost two hours' travel, she had become numb from top to most especially bottom; moreover, intimate contact with a male body had gone from titillating to tedious in the extreme. The horse trudged morosely beneath their combined weight. The sun beat down with remorseless vigor on unending billows of farmland. Beth began to fear she might do something drastic, such as remove her hat and announce herself to be *bloody well fed up,* if she did not get hold of a cup of tea before too long.

"We're never going to reach Canterbury," she said. "We'll perish from dehydration before we even glimpse the cathedral's tower."

Devon sighed with equal weariness. "It must surely be just around the cor—"

"*Aaarrrghhhh!*"

A blur of darkness leaped from behind a tree. The horse shied, and Devon pulled the reins to settle it.

"Monsieur Tarrou!" Beth exclaimed, staring down at the president of the Parisian Ornithological Union, who now blocked their path. He wore an elegant three-piece suit, accessorized with a large spotted handkerchief tied around his head, which had sadly failed to prevent sweat from cascading down his face. As Beth and Devon watched in amazement, he held up a wrought-iron birdcage and shook it. The bird inside fluttered unhappily.

"Give me the horse," he demanded, "or I'll set this bird upon you!"

"A sparrow?" Devon said, unimpressed.

The monsieur spat a laugh. "What kind of ornithologist are you?" he asked, his tone prickling with contempt (or possibly just a normal French accent). "Can you not see the little black speck on its tail?"

"Leechsparrow!" Beth said, gasping.

A nasty grin slid across Monsieur Tarrou's face, redirecting rivers of sweat. "Ah yes, the famously clever Professor Pickering. If you don't want that cleverness sucked out through your ear by the leechsparrow's magic, you'll get down from the horse. Now."

They dismounted.

"Good choice," Monsieur Tarrou said. Clambering on the horse, he galloped away, his maniacal laughter mingling with the frantic cheeps of the leechsparrow. Seconds later, two footmen emerged from the shrubbery, laden with suitcases, and sprinted after their master.

"Wait!" Beth called out, to no avail.

"Well, damn," Devon said, setting his hands on his hips as he frowned after the POU president. "That man really is a louse."

Beth was too upset to condemn this language. Indeed, such was her unhappiness, she actually took off her hat and fanned herself with it. "This is altogether dreadful!"

"It will be all right," Devon said distractedly.

"No, it won't. Monsieur Tarrou does not have the address for the clerk's brother in Canterbury. He won't know where to take the horse. What if it ends up in some dreadful situation? Perhaps even a slaughterhouse! And, oh, that poor little bird!"

She was so caught up in worry, she did not notice Devon approaching until he was upon her. Suddenly, without a word, he scooped her up off her feet.

For the first time in her life, Beth squealed. She knew she sounded like an undergraduate but could not help herself. Dropping her hat in surprise, she clutched at Devon, fearing he might let her go. But he cradled her easily in his arms, as if she were featherlight, and began to stride north.

"What are you doing?" she demanded, trying to sound outraged.

"Employing a little chivalry," he said. "A fine lady should not have to trudge along a dirty road."

"We cannot travel miles on only one pair of legs!" Beth protested. She smacked his shoulder, and he gave her his most charming, teasing grin. It was too much. Hatless, hungry, and not having slept properly for two days, Beth felt her resistance crumble. Naughtiness rose within her, accompanied by a swarm of fluttery giggles.

Thankfully, just in the nick of time, she saw over Devon's shoulder a horse-drawn carriage emerge from the hazy southern horizon. It was traveling at speed, sunlight flaring off its polished black surface. Beth's humor abruptly vanished.

"Traffic," she said.

Devon stopped, turning to frown at it. "Hm," he said, setting her on her feet.

Beth brushed wrinkles from her skirt as if she could brush away her improper behavior. Hippolyta would have a fit were she to see her now—and the fact that it would be a fit of laughter did not ease Beth's mind at all.

"Do you think it's ornithologists?" she asked, squinting through the sunlight at the carriage.

"I don't know," Devon said, his face growing somber. He drew his gun. "But in about five minutes it will be."

"Oh, another hijacking." She eyed the gun warily. "You're not actually going to shoot anyone, are you?"

"Of course not," he said. "I'm a scientist, not a criminal. Well, not a murderous criminal, anyway." He glanced at her with a roguish smirk. "Can't practice ornithology without a little trespassing, a little theft, a little seduction of farmers' wives."

Beth decided it wisest to ignore that. "I only ask because Hippolyta is forever shooting people, and it's costing me a fortune having to send fruit baskets to them in the hospital."

Devon laughed. Then he strode to the middle of the road, all long, swirling black coat and dusty leather boots, the kind of man comfortable navigating danger zones like jungles, crocodile-infested swamps, and the hallway outside the student canteen at noon. Pivoting on a heel, he extended his arm, pointing the gun at the approaching carriage.

Beth moved to stand beside him. She reached only as high as his chin but consoled herself with being his superior in all particulars except height (and devilry). Straightening her gloves and trying not to notice their grubby state, she reached up to adjust her hat before recollecting she'd left it on the road. Indeed, it lay not too far away—and yet, she did not run to retrieve it. Something uncharacteristically wild inside her thought, *Let it fly!*

"Let's hope these people are as amiable as the fishermen," she said.

Devon looked at her askance, his expression a mix of disbelief and exasperation. Fortunately, before they could begin a debate on the definition of *amiable*, the carriage arrived. Its driver yelled out, pulling urgently on the reins, and dust flew up from beneath the horses' hooves as they came to an abrupt halt. The carriage shuddered.

Taking an authoritative step forward, Devon aimed his gun directly at the driver. "Stand and deliver!" he commanded in the same tone he used when telling students there would be no extensions allowed for their essays.

"Hello there!" The driver, a young man with ragged hair and a nose resembling that of the northern goshawk, rose from his seat. "This is a private vehicle, gov'nor. I'm standing, but if you want something delivered, you gotta send it by train."

Devon blinked at him for a moment. Then he lifted the hand holding the gun and rubbed its thumb knuckle wearily against his forehead. "This morning has been far too long."

"Hello, young sir!" Beth called out. "Terribly sorry about all this! Just to clarify, we are, unfortunately, hijacking you. I understand it will be distressing, but we'd appreciate any help you can give in making things go smoothly. Thank you so much!"

Both men stared at her. Then Devon set a hand against her back and bent to say quietly, "You evict the passengers. I'll deal with the driver."

She did as he asked at once, since compared with the feeling of his touch, and the intimacy of his voice so close to her ear, hijacking suddenly seemed a whole lot less scandalous.

DEVON WATCHED BETH hurry to the cab, her posture impeccable despite the haste, her hips swaying in a moderate yet alluring fashion . . . Then he abruptly recalled himself and frowned up at the driver.

"Take us to Canterbury and I'll—"

"Kill me quick rather than slow?" the boy supplied.

Devon startled. "What? No! I'll pay you."

"Cor, that's even better! Can you give me a black eye, though? Or a cut on my arm, so's I'll get a fascinating scar? Nothing attracts the ladies like a fascinating scar, you know."

Devon just stared in response.

"Fair enough," the boy said. "But you might want to watch out for your missus."

"Why?" Devon asked.

"The passengers are a bit—"

*"Aaaaahhhhh!"*

BETH LEAPED BACK from the carriage's open door as a hand emerged, pointing a long white finger at her.

*"Be gone, you evil felon!"*

She stared into the carriage. It held two passengers, one a

small-boned gentleman, the other a woman so rigid she might have been mistaken for a statue were it not for the shrieking voice. Beth attempted a polite smile.

"My good lady—"

*"Repent of your wicked crime and leave at once!"* was the response.

Beth blinked, her smile fading. "Er . . ."

"Is something the matter?" came Devon's calm inquiry as he walked across, the young driver crowding behind him. "Why are the passengers still inside?"

*"Brigands! Malefactors! Repent or go to hell!"*

"That's why," Beth said.

*"Fornicators!"*

Devon cast a mild look at Beth. "What have you been telling them?"

She might have bristled, but the woman was attempting to whack her with a purse, and it proved an effective distraction. Hauling her smile back into duty, and summoning several nice points of etiquette as reinforcement, she opened the door wider and unfolded the step.

"Thank you for your advice," she said to the woman. "It's very thoughtful of you. However, I must ask you to exit the carriage. Apologies, but this is a hijacking, and—"

"Silence! We will not be relinquishing this vehicle to the forces of iniquity! *Desist and depart, you vile outlaws!*"

"Not happening," Devon said. "Just get out and we won't break—"

Beth shifted adroitly in front of him. "I'm afraid we must insist. Tenure is at stake!"

"We're going to Canterbury on business," the gentleman piped up, his gray mustache bobbing. "Perhaps instead of hijacking our carriage, you might simply ride with us? There's room, and we packed sandwiches for the journey."

"What kind of sandwiches?" Beth asked.

"Turkey."

"Oh." She tried to step back but was prevented from doing so by Devon's presence immediately behind her. Before she knew what was happening, he lifted her onto the step plate. The consequent eruption of hot tingles in her blood was such that she could right then have been awarded a doctorate in volcanology. Stumbling into the carriage, she landed gracelessly on the bench seat opposite the passengers. Devon turned away to speak to the driver, leaving her at the mercy of bird-eating zealots.

"How do you do?" she asked as she settled herself, arranging her skirt and trying to smooth her hair, which had become disarrayed with the loss of her hat. "May I inquire as to your names?"

"Wilbur Podder, and this is my wife, Muriel," the gentleman answered. "We're journ—"

"Journeying north," the lady interrupted. She speared her husband with a vehement frown. "For God's sake, Podder, don't chat to the depraved criminal."

Beth winced. "I assure you, ma'am, notwithstanding the insistent borrowing of your carriage, we aren't criminals."

"Well . . ." Devon said as he climbed into the carriage. Shutting the door behind him, he dropped into the seat beside Beth. "I am planning to steal a dictionary for Miss Pickering, but other than that, no, we're not criminals. Just ornithologists."

He leaned back, crossing one leg over the other, and Beth felt the carriage jolt into sudden movement—or maybe it was her pulse. Devon gave her a sidelong glance full of amused complicity, as if she was equally a scoundrel and, goodness, weren't they having fun?

*Yes*, answered a traitorous part of her brain. Aghast, Beth immediately looked away and discovered the Podders staring wide-eyed at her and Devon.

"You're ornithologists?" Mr. Podder asked. "Are you going for Birder of the Year?"

"Yes," Beth replied, torn between delight that they'd heard of the competition and dismay that she might now have to endure a sociable discussion about it. "Professor Lockley and I—"

"Professor Lockley?" Mr. Podder's eyes widened even farther as he surveyed Devon. "I didn't realize! Goodness, you're younger than I was expecting."

"Er . . ." Devon gave him a confused and rather wary look. "You were expecting me?"

Mr. Podder flushed. "No! I mean yes! I mean, *in general*, you're younger than I would expect for a professor."

Beth stiffened, clearing her throat, but before she could inform the gentleman of her even more impressive youth, Mrs. Podder leaned forward to pat Devon on the knee in a manner that made her seem amiable indeed.

"Did I say 'go to hell'?" she simpered, smiling beatifically. "A small misunderstanding! A mere slip of the tongue." Reaching into her purse, she withdrew a notepad and pen. "Don't mind me, scribbling is my remedy for travel sickness, ha ha. So, how are you finding the competition thus far?"

As she waited, pen poised, Devon's wary look deepened. But Beth answered politely, "It's fine, thank you for asking." (Of course, being British, she would have given this same answer even were she waist-deep in an utter catastrophe.)

"Glad to be back in England?" Mrs. Podder inquired.

"Certainly."

"Uh-huh, uh-huh." The pen's tip began moving rapidly across the notepad. "Where do you plan to go from here?"

Beth drew breath to respond, but Devon interrupted. "Why do you ask?"

"Oh, just making casual conversation," Mrs. Podder explained, trilling a laugh.

"You know, chitchat to pass the time," Mr. Podder said. "Will you be traveling together?"

"Yes, what exactly is the nature of your relationship, may I ask?" Mrs. Podder added, looking up keenly from her notepad.

Beth felt as if a dozen phoenixes were going up in flames beneath her skin. "Professor Lockley is an esteemed colleague of mine," she managed to answer.

"Esteemed, hey?" Mrs. Podder murmured, scribbling so emphatically, Beth supposed she must be very queasy indeed from the carriage's jostling.

"I say, would you be willing to pose for a photograph?" Mr. Podder asked as he brought forth a Kodak box camera. "It'd be a nice little memento of our hijacking."

Devon's expression turned from wary to outright ornithological. "I don't think—"

*Thud.*

Something heavy hit the carriage roof. In the startled silence that followed, a faint whirring could be heard.

"What is that?" Mrs. Podder asked with alarm.

*"Stand and deliver!"* came a shout from above.

The carriage juddered to a halt, throwing Beth from the seat. Devon caught her just in time.

"I'd say you're about to meet one of our colleagues," he told the Podders.

The whirring increased. Looking out through the window, Beth saw someone descend from the roof to the road with the assistance of a helicopter parasol. Then the carriage door was flung open and a young woman appeared before them. She was attired in tight breeches, tall boots, and a white lace shirt, with auburn curls tumbling loose about her shoulders and a wicked grin upon her face, all of which would have been an attractive vision were it not for the pistol she aimed at the passengers.

"Hello there," she said. "Welcome to your hijacking."

"Scoundrel!" Mrs. Podder shouted in reply. "Deplorable fiend!"

The woman laughed delightedly.

"Actually, this is Miss Rose Marin, a professor from Edinburgh University," Beth said. "She's a renowned expert in seabirds."

"And a crack shot," Miss Marin added. "So no one think of resisting." She gestured with the pistol that they should exit the cab, then demanded they hand over their weapons. Upon receipt of Devon's gun and Mrs. Podder's pen, she leaped into the cab and slammed its door shut.

"See you at the award ceremony when I accept Birder of the Year!" she called out cheerfully before ordering the driver to move on. As the carriage sped away, they glimpsed her through its rear window, lounging comfortably on one bench with her boots propped up on the other as she bit into one of Mr. Podder's sandwiches.

"Damn," Devon and Mrs. Podder said in unison.

"It's not so bad," Beth argued. "At least we have a nice day for walking."

*Boom.*

They all jolted as thunder shook the air.

TRUDGING THROUGH RAIN along the apparently endless road, Beth regretted yet again that Devon had not allowed her to retrieve her umbrella from the fishermen. Indeed, she'd have informed him of his error in decided language, were her teeth not chattering too much for speech. He, too, was silent as he tramped at her side. Mrs. Podder, on the other hand, had a lot to say. She muttered unending curses upon ornithologists everywhere and the universities that bred them, and Beth honestly couldn't help but sympathize. At one point, a carriage rushed past, but such was the deepening murk that trying to wave it down would have invited the risk of being run over. So they walked on until, finally, at the cusp of evening, a sturdy white building came into sight.

It was the Chaucer Inn.

"Thank God!" Mrs. Podder declared with complete disregard for the fact that God was more likely responsible for the storm than the building. She shoved past Devon, barged through the front door, summoned the innkeeper while the others were pausing to sluice rain off their clothes, and thus secured for herself and her husband the last remaining room.

"Are you sure?" Beth asked the innkeeper when she and Devon got their chance to inquire. "Not even one room left? Not even only one bed?"

"No," the innkeeper reported brusquely. "A group of French fishermen arrived about an hour ago and took two rooms."

Beth felt Devon's gaze upon her but dared not return it. "How unfortunate," she murmured.

*"This is all your fault, Wilbur,"* Mrs. Podder could be heard griping as she and her husband followed a maid toward the stairs. "I knew we should have just stayed with writing house-keeping advice." Glaring back at Beth and Devon through her dripping-wet hair, she shouted, "Heed my warning, innkeeper! Don't give that pair a room, whatever you do. They're unholy demonspawn."

"As opposed to holy demonspawn," Devon explained to the wide-eyed innkeeper.

"We're actually scientists," Beth clarified. "We're in the middle of a competition, which is why we—"

The innkeeper gasped. "You're not ornologistics, are you?"

"Something like that," Beth said.

"Very cold, tired ornithologists," Devon added.

"My daughter's awfully excited about this Birder of the Year contest," the innkeeper told them, suddenly bright-faced and smiling. "We read all about it in the paper. She wants to be a ornologist when she grows up."

"I'll talk to her if you like," Beth offered. "I have a brochure on Oxford's ornithology program in my satchel."

The innkeeper stared at her amazedly. "You'd do that? Even though you're soaking wet and I've refused you shelter?"

"Of course," Beth replied. "I'm happy to help." From the corner of her eye, she noticed Devon smiling and shaking his head.

"Hmm," the innkeeper said, frowning a little as he considered the situation. "I assume you two are married?"

Beth gave a nice little laugh, Devon a decidedly more impolite one. "No," they said in unison.

"Pity. This is a decent establishment."

"Please don't worry on our account," Beth told him. "By the

way, would your daughter like a free pass to the London Aviary? And I think I have a . . ." Rummaging in her satchel, she drew out a small golden feather. "Yes. A plume from the magical pileated deathwhistler."

The innkeeper took it, the brochure, and the aviary pass delightedly. "Thank you! My, what a shame you're not married." He fell into a meaningful silence.

Beth glanced sidelong at Devon and found him already glancing at her, one eyebrow raised. She hesitated for the slightest moment—but was so cold, her conscience had frozen over. She gave him a tiny nod.

He promptly turned to the innkeeper. "Oh, did you say *married*? I thought you said *merry*. We're certainly not merry in this weather, are we, my darling wife?"

"Certainly not," Beth agreed. "Darling husband," she added belatedly.

He put his arm around her, pulling her close and tucking her cozily against his side. With her brain still back in the moment after the innkeeper had spoken, and her body urging her to appreciate this *far more interesting moment* as much as possible, Beth found herself unable to move. Devon's grip was strong and unfaltering, his presence enveloping her with such warmth, she felt surprised her clothes did not begin steaming. He kissed her hair, even while her brain was glancing around saying *Wait, what?*, then gave the innkeeper a steady look.

"Right," said the innkeeper, grinning broadly. "Married it is. In that case, I do have one room I can offer. But I must warn you, there's a slight bed problem . . ."

# CHAPTER NINE

Even the drabbest bird can prove magical.
*Birds Through a Sherry Glass*, H.A. Quirm

"S EVEN," DEVON SAID as he stared at the jumble of beds stacked haphazardly atop each other in the small, dark room. "Seven beds."

"And barely enough space to stand in," Beth added, chewing her gloved thumbnail. She might not understand about wiles, but she wouldn't be an animal biologist if she didn't appreciate the perils of being alone for the night with an unscrupulous rake, especially considering he had just embraced her. *Embraced her! And kissed her hair! In public, moreover!* She half expected someone to knock on the door with a summons for them to appear at the marriage registry office.

"At least we're out of the rain," she said, trying to persuade herself she'd made the rational choice. "And that bathroom at the end of the corridor does look inviting." She glanced briefly at Devon, then chewed her glove some more.

"Your bribing the innkeeper certainly paid off," he said as he sorted through the provisions they'd been given. "Candles, towels, bedding, nightshirts, a tray of food, even a bottle of wine. So long as we avoid the Frenchmen, and don't get attacked by mad birds or birders, we should have a comfortable night."

Beth frowned. "I did not bribe the innkeeper."

"Offering to talk to his daughter, gifting her an expensive feather . . ."

"I meant that sincerely. We are not all heartless cynics, Mr. Lockley."

"I'm not heartless," he said. "For example, I'll allow you first use of the bathroom." And he handed her a towel and nightshirt, smiling so adorably he could have illustrated the encyclopedia entry for *fraudster*.

Beth gave him a chiding look in return. "You're only doing that so while I'm gone you can eat all the pie."

"Now who's the cynic?" he retorted.

Beth opened her mouth—and closed it—and opened it again. But speech did not avail itself of either opportunity, so, with a huff instead, she turned on her heel and marched for the bathroom, trying to ignore the sensation of Devon's infernal gaze on her as she went.

When she returned sometime later, clean and warm and dressed in fresh white cotton, it was to discover that Devon had rearranged the stacks of beds, creating more space. He'd managed to fit two mattresses side by side on the floor and dressed them with sheets and blankets. He'd even set the food out like a picnic. Candles glinted around the room, and a red-gold sheen from the fire he'd built in the small hearth swayed and flickered to the sound of dreamy piano music coming from the dining room below. Altogether, the scene couldn't have been more romantic were it set in a honeymoon suite.

"Goodness," Beth murmured, unsure if she meant this as a

general statement or a reminder to herself of how she must behave.

"There's no space for privacy," Devon said. "But no need to fear, we're adults—"

Which sounded to Beth like an excellent reason for fear.

"—and scientists. You'll be quite safe from shenanigans."

"If you suppose I am even *thinking* about shenanigans, you are in cloud cuckoo land," she told him archly.

He gave her one of his smug, provoking looks. "I've been there many times."

"What?"

"What?" he echoed in a defensive tone, then relaxed once more. "I mean Yakushima Island, of course, where the cloud cuckoo lives." Taking a nightshirt and towel, he departed for the bathroom, leaving Beth to ~~tremble nervously~~ *bristle indignantly!* alone.

AN HOUR LATER, they sat facing each other cross-legged on one of the mattresses, both dressed in voluminous white nightshirts, both flushed with the warmth of the fire, and neither willing to admit that they were slightly tipsy.

"You're scared," Devon said, smirking, as he reached for the last piece of ox tongue pie. In the rich, heavy firelight, it looked almost good enough to eat, despite his experience with it thus far, and he needed something, anything, to counteract the sour taste of the wine.

"I most certainly am not!" Beth retorted, sitting a little more erect. "It is sensible of me to avoid corruption when it is placed like a lure before me."

Devon broke off a piece of piecrust and put it in his mouth.

He was at least enough of a gentleman to not speak while eating, but his eyebrows moved with eloquence, and Beth turned even more prickly.

"Very well," she said. "I'll submit, just this once. Go ahead and ask again."

"Knock knock."

She sighed. "Who's there?"

"Hoo."

"Hoo who?"

"Why, Miss Pickering, I did not know you were an owl."

She stared at him, and he took another bite of the dreadful pie so he wouldn't laugh. She was beautiful in the drift of golden light and silvery shadow, with her hair a long damp braid that had left distracting wet patches down the front of her nightshirt, and her bare fingers a great deal more interesting than he'd expected. Their ink stains, scratches, and short, crooked fingernails attracted him as no manicure had ever done. But then, everything about her attracted him. Even her weary exasperation.

"That's your idea of a witty joke?" she asked.

He did laugh then, almost choking on the pie. "No, darling, that's my idea of a joke suitable for your ladylike taste. You'd almost certainly combust in flames of offended dignity if I told you something I considered witty."

"*Tsk*," she said, shaking her head. The wine had failed to loosen her attitude (although she was tilting a little to one side), and Devon suspected that, if he really did tell her a risqué joke, she'd lecture him until he surrendered with a promise to become a better man. And God, how awful would that be? Iniquity was an excellent defense against vulnerability, and he had no intention of relinquishing it, not even for the sake of a beautiful woman.

He reached automatically for his wineglass, drank what was in it, and grimaced as his throat burned. "I can't believe you gave away that deathwhistler feather. Selling it would have bought us a decent bottle of chardonnay, if nothing else."

"Unlikely," she said. "It was just an underwing covert. Besides, the calamus was—" She broke off, shaking her head. "Sorry."

Devon frowned mildly in confusion. "Why?"

"I talk too much about birds," she said with wry amusement. But she would not meet his gaze, and he noticed her fingers twisting in the billows of her nightshirt.

"I'm an ornithology professor," he said. "I don't think it's possible to talk too much about birds. 'The calamus was—' what?"

She looked at him then, her eyes dark at first with suspicion but slowly lightening as he smiled encouragingly, then beginning to shine with outright excitement. "It was marred with significant vertical cracks," she said, her words racing after each other as if they'd been waiting offstage, clutching their scripts and jiggling their knees, desperate for an opportunity to be spoken. "This might indicate the deathwhistler was an unhealthy specimen, or it might have been in the process of pulling the feather out to facilitate molting, or else you caused the damage during your theft of the bird." She gave him a reproachful scowl, and he tried not to grin. "Also, the plumulaceous portion was yellow, which suggests a juvenile bird, although it's hard to be certain, since the deathwhistler retains its first underwing coverts until late in the transition to adulthood. In any case, the feather's value was sentimental only." She sighed. "Coming away with just one small covert I found in the dirt seemed appropriate for that particular venture."

Devon tried not to wince as a strange little pain flicked through him. "I don't apologize for stealing the bird," he told her, "but I *am* sorry you didn't get the chance to observe it more. If it helps, my measure of the wing chord placed the bird's age somewhere in its third year."

Beth gazed at him wide-eyed, seemingly having forgotten the necessity of breathing. "Did you happen to notice the unusual formation of its beak?" he asked, just to keep the delightful expression on her face.

The delight flared even brighter, warming his heart. "Yes! I actually took a note of it . . ." She leaned sideways, reaching for her satchel, and brought out a field journal and spectacles. Opening the book at a steep angle, so as to protect its contents from him, she shared her observation of the deathwhistler's mandibular rostrum. While he listened, Devon regarded her thoughtfully, trying to decide how much of her defensiveness was from mere caution and how much from actual dislike of him. He found neither particularly daunting. More than once, he'd spent hours on a freezing, windswept beach, coaxing some wary shark gull or sword-billed sanderling closer so he could study it. Convincing a woman to talk to him was easy in comparison. And he very much wanted Beth to talk—about birds, or anything, really. He'd luxuriate for as long as he possibly could in the precise, polysyllabic tones of her voice and the interesting things she had to say.

So he started detailing the deathwhistler's measurements, keeping his manner light, and sure enough, Beth gradually lowered the book. She wrote his descriptions alongside a sketch she'd made of the bird, her penmanship delicate and clean, turning his words into something lovely. Her eyes looking up at him over the rim of the spectacles were wing-dreaming skies he wanted to lie back and stare at for hours. And when she bit the end of her pencil while listening to him explain the deathwhistler's toe structure, he had to lay a pillow across his lap to hide the effect it had on him. Conversing with this woman was like the most delicious foreplay, only with technical descriptions of an avian species in lieu of touching.

At last, the hearth fire burned low. "We should probably go to sleep now," Beth said reluctantly, putting the journal away. Devon felt a strange little swoop in his heart, as if he'd been abseiling with a rope that had suddenly slackened. Beth reached up to remove her spectacles, and he had to force himself not to catch her hand, stop her, since he couldn't think of a reason for doing so beyond *you're so damned sexy when you wear them, I want to keep handing you things to read*. Which, he guessed, she'd find impolite.

"I'd like to take the earliest possible train tomorrow," she said, her voice brisk again now they had stopped discussing birds. "I'm certain Hippolyta already has a plan in action."

"And you want to catch up with her."

"I want to *beat* her. We may have been associates for the past couple of years, but that doesn't mean we aren't rivals now in this competition. To be honest, I'm glad I missed the ferry. It means I didn't have to tell her to her face that I was parting ways with her." She lowered her head as she carefully packed the spectacles into her satchel, and Devon could have sworn he heard her muttering in a self-deprecating tone, "I'm not sure I have enough apologies in me for that."

"Maybe, if she was the one who lured us into that trap in Calais, it was her way of not having to tell you that *she* wanted to part ways."

"Maybe. But why would she involve you?" Beth shook her

head. "Really, it could have been anyone who did that. Ornithology is hardly a walk in the park. Er, except when it is an actual walk in the park to observe birds, of course."

He grinned at her. "Very true. As for the train, there's an eight o'clock to London we can catch. The innkeeper has agreed to knock on our door if we're not awake on time."

A tight little pause followed.

"I appreciate your assistance thus far," Beth said slowly, "but we should probably keep in mind that there can be—"

"Only one Birder of the Year," he recited with her. "Yes, I remember." The pie turned over in his stomach. Standing, he gathered plates and empty wineglasses, then stepped across the thin space of bare floor to stack them on the hearth shelf. Vapor arising from the clothes hung to dry on bedframes made his breath feel hot. Lust spiraled like a small, frantic bird in his gut. Scowling, he vehemently wished himself somewhere more comfortable, such as the Indian jungle during monsoon season.

A small noise made him turn, and his blood leaped as he found Beth standing close to him, an empty plate in her hands.

"I hope we won't have a long walk to the train station," she said, even as Devon contemplated which of her cheek or throat or earlobe he would most like to kiss first. "My shoes are quite ruined. It was discourteous of Miss Marin to hijack the carriage rather than simply share."

Devon huffed a laugh. "Discourteous certainly is a nice way to describe having a gun pointed at you," he said, and held out his hand to take the plate from her.

At that same moment, she leaned forward to place it atop the others on the hearth shelf. His fingers brushed against the front of her nightgown. The plate clattered onto the shelf.

"Sorry," Devon said, stepping back.

"Sorry," Beth said, stepping back at the same time.

"It's fine," they both answered at once.

He tried to go around her, just as she tried to move out of his way. He shuffled in the opposite direction—so did she—and they laughed nervously. There simply wasn't enough space in the room, although at this point Devon suspected there wasn't enough space in the entire world for him to comfortably breathe, knowing that Beth Pickering existed.

His defenses cracked, and a gaggle of devilish inclinations rushed through the gap. He caught Beth's hand, setting his other hand on her back. She looked at him in surprise.

"Have you ever seen American bald eagles perform their sky dance?" he asked as he swayed her into a side step. The piano strains of what might have been Vivaldi's "Summer," had the pianist enjoyed any talent, arose from below. Following the rhythm, he led Beth in a step back toward the hearth again. "It's breathtaking."

"A courtship dance," she said warily, although her free hand rose to lie against his upper arm. It was such a light, tentative touch, Devon barely felt it, yet tremors went through his body in response. Why had she done it? To encourage him? Or merely to keep her balance? He looked down at her, seeking answers, but she would not meet his gaze. With another woman, he'd make an educated guess, but this one was all sincerity and sudden knives, and he simply could not be sure.

"The reeling flamingo of Peru somersaults during its court-ship dance," she said. "And uses magic to flip rocks as well. The bigger the rocks, the more likely it is to find a mate."

"I flipped a couple of these mattresses to stack them out of the way," Devon answered with a boyish smile as they side-stepped again, their movement slower this time, their hands growing warm.

Beth sighed. "Are you ever capable of engaging in conversation without bantering?"

He lowered his eyes so she wouldn't see the shadow flickering through them, then looked through his lashes at her. His smile slid languorously into wryness, even as he danced her back toward the embracing heat of the hearth fire.

"I do believe *you* were the one, Miss Pickering, who spoke of courtship."

She sniffed indignantly, but he noticed the way her ears reddened. And the sweep of her eyelashes. And every fine thread of light weaving through her soft, ruddily brown hair. He was caught—the dance forgotten, his very heartbeat seeming to slow to a whispering stop. Somewhere beyond the room, people were traipsing up the inn's stairs, opening and shutting doors, talking to each other. But it felt like the room of seven beds had broken off from the universe and was out drifting among stars and wild dreams.

*My God*, he thought. Just two days in Beth Pickering's company and he'd begun using poetic language, telling inane jokes, and even veering dangerously close to thoughtfulness. Much more of this and he might become *gentle*.

He stepped away from her abruptly. Taken by surprise, Beth rocked a little, and Devon reached out instinctively, catching her around the waist to save her from falling, despite the fact that she was really in no danger of it. She gasped, sending his pulse into a wild flutter at the sound. Despite all his academic genius, he did not know what to do; staring into her deep sky eyes for some kind of answer, he felt like he was the one falling. Beth pressed her hand against his chest, and when she did not use it to push herself away from him, but seemingly to anchor him to her quietness, it was as if he, too, was being saved.

"You truly are an angel, aren't you?" he whispered.

"Not as much as you'd think," she said. And it might have been an offer, or it might have been just him dreaming. Either way, he could not seem to help himself. The narrative gravity drew them together slowly; so slowly, either one of them might have stepped back, packed their clothes, and left the room before the other moved an inch.

But they did not leave. And so the momentum or some unknown magic kept going, until at last their lips met.

BETH HAD BEEN kissed before. Many times! As a woman of the world, she was quite seasoned in the matter. Why, she *could not even count* how many men had kissed her gloved hand when greeting her. Then there had been the *copious* times she'd been kissed on both cheeks by villagers grateful for her capturing a bird that had been threatening their lives (granted, elderly women villagers, but the point remained). Kissing was an altogether banal event. Certainly it did not compare to the sight of a sooty shearwater taking wing for its annual migration south.

And yet, as her lips pressed against Devon's, every sensible thought within her scattered in a rush of pure sensation. Sooty shearwater? What even was a bird?!

Devon shifted his mouth across hers softly, like a wing-stirred breeze. Beth closed her eyes, sinking into the feeling. Her brain melted into a lush, gold-spangled reverie. She yielded to the gentle urging of his lips and parted hers, welcoming him, wishing for him. Devon responded at once, placing his hand against the back of her head as he deepened the kiss. So many lightning flashes sparked in Beth, she could have been plugged into a socket and used to illuminate a small city. Devon's mouth was a velvet lapwing feather, stroking her into magic, luring her gorgeously into danger. She felt somehow both blissful and desperately yearning at the same time. A dozen perfectly decent scruples went up in flames as she shifted restlessly, hands reaching in search of something she didn't know how to classify in the hard length of his body.

Devon stepped away from her suddenly, his breath shaking. He shoved back his hair. Beth stared unseeing into the middle distance.

"Um," she said.

"Er," Devon agreed, not looking at her either.

"Good night, then," they chorused.

Without further word, they crawled onto opposite ends of the mattresses and tucked themselves beneath blankets, feet toward each other. A stunned silence descended upon the room, leavened only by the soft whisper of rain.

*Oh dear*, Beth thought to herself. That had been nothing like a kiss on the hand. Indeed, she'd place it in a whole different genus. Certainly it had been more romance than she'd experienced in her life thus far. She was obliged to declare herself scandalous indeed!

And not entirely upset about it.

Her brain, however, dropped a heavy stack of memories, sending reverberations through her nervous system and making her cringe. There was no need to inspect them; she recited their contents to herself daily: playground taunts because of her book-hugging awkwardness; offended silences when she let her intelligence show; even a full-color chart of the many rejections from her classmates, who were always several years older than her. In short, evidence to prove incontrovertibly that she was not good company.

No doubt Devon had only danced with her because he was rather drunk and she just happened to be there. As for the kiss—it was meaningless, an accident of circumstance. She should not harbor any foolish hopes. After all, the man was forever staring at her, thoroughly dumbstruck; he called her angel, which suggested he could not remember her name; and he was currently hunched so tightly at the other end of the mattresses they could have safely run a flock of geese through the space between them. The conclusion was undeniable: he disliked her utterly.

This was why she avoided society unless heavily armored with niceties that were sure to please. She'd let her guard down tonight, and it had been lovely, so lovely, but at the same time extremely misguided.

Pulling the blanket over her head, she closed her eyes so firmly not a single tear could escape.

And when she woke in the morning to find Devon gone, she was not surprised.

# CHAPTER TEN

Always be aware that, for every bird in the hand, there
may be two in the bush just waiting to attack you.
*Birds Through a Sherry Glass*, H.A. Quirm

BETH WASTED NO time in dressing. She'd been left behind
by everyone now, and while it was no more than she expected, and the ache she felt was purely biological (no doubt
from eating ox tongue pie the night before), it did shake her
back into her good sense.

*I need to act strategically*, she told herself as she pulled on her
fire-dried clothes.

*Intelligence has never been more essential*, she averred as she
pinned up her hair.

*Every minute must be used to my best advantage*, she added
while folding sheets and blankets into a neat pile. From now
on, she had to place her own interests first if she wanted any
chance of winning the competition. And that was what really
mattered. Not tingly feelings. Not foolish romantic wishes.

**Tenure!**

"I shall be ruthless!" she declared aloud. "After taking these
dishes down to the kitchen, and talking to the innkeeper's
daughter as promised, I'll run for the train, and no one had

better get in my way! Especially not that scandalous reprobate, Devon Lockley! If I never see him again, it will be too soon!"

Gathering up her satchel, lifting her chin to the veriest height of dignity, she opened the bedroom door and stepped out.

Just as the bathroom door at the far end of the corridor opened and Devon emerged, fully dressed and wiping his freshly shaven jaw with a towel.

They both came to an abrupt halt, staring at each other. Devon's face went still; Beth's heart swooped like a bald eagle doing a courtship dance.

After what seemed like an eternity, Devon blinked. "I was just coming to wake you," he said.

"I was just going downstairs to order breakfast," Beth answered.

They went on staring, their expressions growing tight as each tried to determine if the other was lying.

"We can walk down together," Devon suggested, tossing the towel back into the bathroom without looking.

"Very well," Beth agreed, restraining herself from rushing to pick up said towel and hang it neatly. Had she needed a reminder of just how wicked this man could be, such careless handling of laundry would have served perfectly! But no such reminder was necessary, not when her lips still zinged with the touch of his kiss, and her brain still zapped with ideas after their late-night conversation, and she felt alarmingly *sassy*.

Besides, the unkempt fall of hair over his forehead offered more than enough proof of wickedness. He might as well just go ahead and approach her with slow, firm paces, look deep in her eyes, and with a sultry hint of a smile, invite her to brush back that hair. *Villain!*

A villain who hadn't left her behind after all.

"Miss Pickering?" he said, and Beth shook herself out of reverie to see him still standing at a polite distance, gesturing toward the stairs. "After you?"

She lifted her chin to the veriest height of dignity—only to recall she'd already done so as several muscles in her neck twinged with the strain. "Of course," she said primly, and turned on her heel before she could see the amusement on Devon's face.

She took two steps, then stopped. The sound of familiar voices rose from beyond the stairwell's corner.

"I hope the housemaid was right and it is them staying here. We really need a straightforward execution today," said one.

"I'm sure it's going to end with a bang," said the other, chuckling.

Beth gasped. *Schreib and Cholmbaumgh!* Somehow they'd tracked her and Devon to the inn.

Instantly, Devon was at her side. But before they could decide in which direction to retreat, Schreib and Cholmbaumgh rounded the corner and halted mid-step, staring up at them in astonishment.

Without thinking, Beth threw the dishes at the men. As they ducked, shouting, she and Devon ran into the room of beds. Devon slammed the door shut behind them, turning the key in the lock. They leaned back against the wooden panel, and seconds later it began to shudder with furious knocking.

"Let us in!" Cholmbaumgh shouted.

"We only want to talk to you!" Schreib added.

"Do you think us complete idiots?" Devon called out.

"Well, you did get your doctorate from Yale," Beth said, "so you can hardly blame them."

He gave her a dark look. She shrugged defensively. "I'm sorry, I can't seem to help it. There must be some contagious aspect to your impishness."

His eyebrows elevated at speed. "Did you just call me *impish*?"

"Cheeky?" she tried again.

The eyebrows plummeted. "Sharp-witted," he said. "Devilish."

*Thud!* The door shuddered again. Beth barely noticed. Looking at Devon, she tried to think of another bantering comment, but her brain was too busy contemplating a career change from science to romantic poetry reading.

*Thud!!*

"The lock won't hold for long," Devon said. "We'll have to go out the window."

Without further conversation, he grasped Beth's wrist, tugging her across the room. They clambered up two stacked bed frames, moving with the ease of professional bird chasers. Devon opened the window, then moved aside.

"After you," he said, gesturing to the morning air beyond.

Beth tilted forward to peer out. They were situated on the inn's second floor, as a consequence of which the ground was worryingly far below and, even more worryingly, was comprised of bare stone. A drainpipe only two feet away from the window provided a convenient escape route, but its agèd state warned of a possible shift of genre from adventure to tragedy.

Beth tilted back again, frowning at Devon. "Really, this

insistence on 'ladies first' is not chivalrous when a risky descent is involved."

"I thought you'd rather not be in a position where I could see up your skirt," he said.

*Thud, bang!* contributed Schreib and Cholmbaumgh, apparently smashing their bodies against the door.

"I believe we can allow some leeway in etiquette," Beth said, glancing out the window again. The ground winked back with a flash of morning light against a lingering rain puddle. "Besides, you already saw my petticoat last night when I hung it up to dry."

*Bang, thud!*

"I'm heavier than you," Devon argued. "Should the drainpipe come away from the wall because of my weight upon it, you'll be closer to the ground, therefore safer."

Beth stared blankly at this dubious argument, Devon stared back, and the pursuers kicked the door so vehemently it cracked.

"Oh, very well," she said, hauling up her skirts and climbing onto the window ledge. "But this is a mark against your character."

"I'm flattered you're keeping notes." Taking hold of her arm, he steadied her as she reached for the drainpipe.

"You needn't grip so firmly," she grumbled.

"Just—careful," he said. And again as she pulled away to grasp the pipe—"Careful!"

"My gloves are going to be ruined," Beth muttered as she began her descent. A great crash announced the men's conquest of the door, and Devon swung himself hastily onto the pipe. Seconds later, Schreib and Cholmbaumgh appeared at the open window.

*"Oi! Stop!"* they shouted, brandishing their fists.

"While that's an entirely reasonable request," Devon called out, "I'm afraid we can't just now."

"Dreadfully sorry!" Beth added.

"Damn!" came the response, and the men disappeared from view.

"Hurry before they get downstairs," Devon said.

Beth frowned. "I'm going as fast as I—"

"Hey!" came a new voice as a window flung open beside her. Startled, Beth clutched the pipe even tighter. A young girl leaned out to gape wide-eyed at her. "Who are you?"

"Professor Pickering," Beth said. "Forgive me for not shaking hands."

"Are you the bird lady my dad told me about last night? The one who gave me a feather?"

Beth smiled. "Yes."

"Is it a real, actual deathwhistler feather?" the girl asked, propping her elbows on the window ledge and staring with fascination.

"Indeed," Beth assured her. "An underwing covert, which is a type of feather that birds use to—"

"Excuse me," came Devon's tightly measured voice from above. "Pedagogical diligence is all very admirable, but this really, *really* isn't a good time for a lesson."

"Right." Beth gave herself a little shake. "Sorry," she said to the girl. "I'll send you a letter all about it when I'm next at liberty to write!"

"Are you doing that contest?" the girl asked as Beth recommenced the descent.

"I am."

She waved vigorously. "Good luck!" Then Devon passed her window, and her eyes grew so wide she might be compared to the yeti owl of Siberia. "Oh gosh. Are you a birder too?"

"Yup," he said with a grin.

"If I go to birding university," she asked as he continued down, "will I meet more handsome men like you?"

Devon laughed. But Beth, reaching the ground, called up, "You should hope not! Handsome men are all too often scoundrels!"

"You think I'm handsome, Miss Pickering?" Devon asked, and only the fact that just then she glimpsed Cholmbaumgh and Schreib through the inn's dining room window saved Beth from making a sassy, bantering reply. A moment later Devon dropped to the ground beside her and, catching her hand in his, pulled her into a run across the courtyard toward a gated fence, beyond which lay the road.

"Really, this constant towing of me is unnecessary," Beth complained.

"I'm not towing you," Devon said. "I'm using you as ballast." And yet his grip loosened, so that she might easily withdraw from it if she wanted. Beth, however, did have to admit he provided a convenient ballast for her too. She tightened her own grip, Devon pushed open the gate, and they dashed out.

And came to a sudden, jolting halt at the sight of the French fishermen standing at the inn's entrance, all peering at a map one of them held open.

"Damn," Devon muttered. He very nearly yanked Beth's arm from its socket as he began towing her even faster up the street.

Determined not to surrender every nicety, Beth called out

in wayward French. "Hello! I see you there!" *("Bonjour! J'ai peur, sauve-moi!")*

Immediately, all four men began shouting and pointing to her. Beth was surprised to hear a tone of anger in their voices. Then Cholmbaumgh and Schreib emerged from the inn, plowing into their ranks, and a skirmish immediately broke out.

"We should go to help our friends," Beth said, glancing back with concern.

Devon laughed darkly in response. "No, thank you. We'll be lucky to outrun any of them as it is."

Just then, a milkman's wagon drove past the group. Devon's eyes lit up, and thus Beth received half a second's warning before he tugged her into the middle of the road.

"Oh no," she said. "Not another hijacking."

"Do you want to escape Schreib and Cholmbaumgh and get to the train on time?" Devon asked as he pulled a gun from beneath his coat. Beth stared at it in surprise.

"I thought you gave that to Miss Marin yesterday."

He cast her a wry look. "What kind of ornithologist would I be if I didn't keep a hidden weapon?" Extending his arm, he pointed the gun at the milkman, who gave a startled shout and reined in his horse.

"We're taking your wagon!" Devon called out.

"Dreadfully sorry!" Beth added with a small wave.

They clambered onto the driver's bench, forcing the milkman to its edge. Snatching the reins, shouting "*Hyah!*" Devon sent the horses into a gallop. The wagon juddered wildly, and bottles rattled against each other in their crates.

"Stop!" the milkman wailed, clinging desperately to the bench. "You'll spill the milk!"

Devon flashed a sidelong grin at Beth. "Shall I tell him not to cry over it? Or shall I butter him up instead?"

She clicked her tongue with exasperation. "It's bad enough you keep hijacking people, do you have to add the crime of cheesy jokes?"

She heard the pun a moment after she said it and winced. The man was corrupting her even at the subconscious level!

Devon laughed. "You are the cream of the crop, Miss Pickering," he said. And it was like he'd kissed her again—the warmth, the tingles, making her blush like a fool.

"Oh God, please stop!" the milkman begged. "Hijack me if you must, but no more bad puns!"

"Sorry!" they said in unison. And Beth lowered her face to hide a smile as the wagon carried them into the sunlit wind.

"So THIS IS goodbye."

She stared at the train ticket in her hand. It had taken almost all her money, but that was fine, she would visit a bank the moment she arrived in London. And then she would buy new clothes, new shoes, perhaps a new field guide while she was at it, something scholarly—

"Miss Pickering," Devon said for the second time, and she drew a deep breath before raising her head to smile at him pleasantly. He smiled back, of course he did, all heedless flair and confidence, entirely untroubled by their parting.

Her heart drooped. She did not like this man, nor respect him, nor feel any ache at the thought she'd never again talk with him about birds, or kiss him in a tiny, secret room while a storm raged outside.

But oh, what a ruthless liar she was to herself.

"The train is still fifteen minutes away," he said. "Perhaps we could wait for it together? Solely for practical reasons, you understand—in case our pursuers turn up?"

"Yes," she said almost before he finished speaking. Then realizing how daft she was, she flushed and turned away. But Devon turned with her, his arm brushing hers in a devastatingly casual manner.

"Hmm," he said. "Where can we sit?"

Beth considered the matter calmly, as if the thought of sitting with him was not akin to the memory of dancing with him by candlelight. The station comprised two platforms, dissected by train tracks and overarched by a cavernous roof. The southbound one was empty, the advertisements pasted to its wall fluttering a little in a warm, dusty breeze. But the northbound one, on which they stood, bustled with passengers heading for London. Beth sighted Monsieur Chevrolet and Miss Eliza Wolfe, the former seated at a wrought-iron table dressed with lace cloths and a tiny vase of flowers, the latter perched daintily on a travel trunk beneath a parasol held aloft by a footman. They were casting disdainfully murderous looks at each other while their servants brought them tea, arranged their luggage, and in Monsieur Chevrolet's case, performed an emergency manicure. Beth tried to determine how she might traverse the platform without being noticed herself.

Devon laid his hand on her back. "Why don't we find somewhere private—?"

*"Aaaahhhhhhh!!!"*

It took Beth a second to realize the scream hadn't come from her, primarily due to its being not excited but terrified. Devon instantly moved to shield her, which was ~~delightfully~~

~~protective~~ blastedly annoying, as she could not see what had happened. More screams arose, and people began to run. Stepping away from Devon, Beth turned, trying to find the source of the panic.

And came within a wingspan of dying as a deadly frostbird swooped down, a sinuous blur of long white feathers and silvery flares, trailing icy sparks that scorched the morning with a promise of carnage.

# CHAPTER ELEVEN

*Ornithologist* is another word for *hero*.
*Birds Through a Sherry Glass*, H.A. Quirm

THE FROSTBIRD'S SCIENTIFIC binomial was *Ardea ignis*, due to its thaumaturgic emanations being cold enough to burn instantly through muscle and bone, although in Greenlandic it was more colloquially known as—

"*Run!*"

Devon's voice broke through Beth's thoughts in the same moment he began pushing her toward the station's waiting room. All around them, mayhem reigned. Larger than its cousin, the Kievan firebird, and far more dangerous, the frostbird darted above the panicked crowd, breathing gusts of high-pressure air. Luggage exploded in great bursts of blue-white ice. People shoved and bashed at each other, desperately trying to reach shelter. Just in front of Beth and Devon, a woman fell to her knees, and they stopped to help her up.

"Please," she cried, clutching at them. "My Louis—I can't find my Louis!"

Beth's pulse skipped. "What does he look like? How old is he?"

"Not even two years old!" the woman sobbed. "Green and gold, with—"

"I'm sorry, what?" Beth interrupted confusedly.

"You mean his clothes?" Devon said.

Now the woman was confused. "I mean my suitcase. My Louis Vuitton suitcase. It's worth a fortune!"

Beth gritted her teeth. Devon's face looked pained. They propelled the woman toward the waiting room, then dashed to crouch behind an overstacked luggage trolley. Their bodies pressed together in the limited space, but Beth had no time for tingling.

"Frostbirds aren't normally aggressive," she said. "It's not attacking out of malice; it's frightened. Which means we'll never get it to land."

"Agreed," Devon said. "And the train arriving might scare it away into the city."

The thought of that disaster darkened their shared glance. Beth opened her satchel, rummaging through its contents, while Devon peered around the trolley, tracking the frostbird as it spiraled toward the apex of the station's roof.

"Fascinating," he said mildly, then turned back to her. At the sight of the object she held up, his expression blanked. "What is that?"

"Just something I invented in my spare time." Unwrapping a web of string from around a narrow metal pipe, she unfolded that pipe at two hinges, gave a brisk flick, and thus transformed it with practiced efficiency into a long-handled net.

"Clever," Devon said. "What's your plan?"

"I need some bait." She scrutinized him in such a way that he leaned back defensively.

At that moment, a voice called out from farther along

the now-abandoned platform. "Miss Pickering? Are you there?"

"Miss Wolfe!" Beth recognized the woman from her refined American accent. "Are you safe?"

"Yes. If you want to try catching the bird, I have a red scarf I'll donate to the effort in exchange for a share of the reward."

"Another person with a faulty dictionary," Devon muttered.

"Thank you!" Beth called. "That will do perfectly for a lure! If we—"

*Screeee*, the frostbird interrupted as it glided the length of the station. The crackle of magical energy echoed eerily through the silence. Tiny icicles formed on Beth's hair. She watched with trepidation and more than a little wonderment as the bird flew out of the roofed area, glowing alabaster when it met the morning sunlight. It's long, ribbonlike tail feathers spread, the rime of ice along them flashing, and for a moment Beth thought it was going to leave. But it soared up to perch on the roof of the signalman's box.

"Now!" Devon urged. "While it's—"

"Excuse me," came a polite masculine voice from directly behind them. Beth and Devon turned their heads to see a young man in an ill-fitting suit crouch down, smiling eagerly. He held a notepad and pencil in his hands. "The two of you are orthogolists, right?"

"What are you doing here?" Devon demanded. "You're in danger. Find shelter!"

The young man just nodded, smile widening. "The name's Spencer, from the *Canterbury Times*. By sheer chance I happened to be on the scene and would love to ask you a few questions."

They stared at him incredulously, but he went on grinning

like ~~a lunatic~~ an entertainment journalist. "Are you competing for Birder of the Year? Have you any special plans to catch the caladrius? What about this bird? I heard someone say it's leafy, but it looks more like snow to me."

"Lethal," Devon corrected him. "As in, it will kill you when I toss you to it, if you don't get into that waiting room and close the door behind you. Right. Now."

The smile shriveled into a pout. "I say, jolly poor sport!"

Devon's expression grew darker, and Mr. Spencer hurried away. Beth and Devon looked at each other, stunned. Then they rose from their crouches.

"I'll get the scarf from Miss Wolfe," Devon said.

"I'll be ready with the net," Beth told him.

He nodded, then jogged away down the platform toward where Miss Wolfe hid behind a bench seat. The thud of his boots matched Beth's heartbeat. She turned to watch the frost-bird in case it reacted to his movement.

Such a magnificent creature! (The bird, that is, not Mr. Lockley.) Beth had never seen one outside of a field guide, for the species lived in the most remote areas of the northern polar zone, avoiding humans. It certainly would never have migrated of its own volition to England in midsummer, but she also couldn't fathom anyone releasing such a rare and perilous creature to help eliminate their rivals for Birder of the Year, even with tenure at stake.

Something in the back of her mind cleared its throat officiously and tapped a memory Beth could not quite see. But there was no time to think about it. Removing her jacket, she draped it over the net, tying the sleeves around the handle to keep it in place. Goosebumps from the bird's magic rose beneath her cotton shirtwaist, uncanny but not unpleasant, and she tingled with more than cold. Really, only one thing was better than engaging with a wild magical bird (belatedly remembering your cup of tea but discovering it still warm).

"Ready, Miss Pickering?"

She glanced up to see Devon striding back along the platform, scarf in hand. Ice shards cracked beneath his bootheels and glinted on the sweep of his long dark coat. He was unsmiling, focused on the frostbird, and he looked so strong, so expert, that Beth's stomach flipped at the thought of such a man having kissed her.

Then again, she was strong and expert too. She might be uncomfortable around people, but when it came to birds she knew exactly what she was doing. Tugging on the jacket's knotted sleeves once more to ensure they would hold firm, she stepped out from behind the luggage trolley. Devon halted, raising the scarf and waving it slowly above his head. The frostbird stirred on its rooftop perch, letting out a haunting, lucent cry.

"Once it takes flight, drop the scarf and run," Beth instructed.

Devon did not even glance in her direction. Beth frowned, wondering if he'd heard her. But it was too late to inquire: the frostbird's lush wings spread, and with another cry it sprang aloft, shedding ice crystals as it aimed straight for Devon.

He tilted his head, watching it. The air began to crackle and splinter into ice, but Devon remained motionless, even while the frostbird sped closer . . . closer . . .

Beth began to run. The bird blew a deadly gust of polar magic toward Devon, who did not even flinch in response. Using a fallen suitcase as a springboard, Beth leaped, lifting her net as high as she could in a double-handed grip. It intercepted the stream of magic less than two feet in front of Devon and instantly turned to solid ice. Beth braced herself.

*Thud!*

The bird flew into the frozen net and dropped, stunned. Ice skittered across the ground.

Immediately, Beth tossed the net aside and crouched beside the frostbird. With gloved fingers, she stroked its long neck, checking for signs of life. A steady pulse reassured her. Further hurried observations suggested the bird was unharmed beyond its stupor, and she breathed a sigh of relief.

Devon squatted beside her. "That really was very clever," he said.

Beth, however, was in no mood for compliments. "Why did you just stand there?" she demanded in her most severe, teacherly voice. "You could have been killed!"

He shrugged. "I trusted you to act in time. I wanted to watch it fly. There was something odd about how it used its tail feathers."

"Oh." Beth found her mood veering in the direction of accepting compliments, after all. Besides, she agreed with him, confound the man. "I noticed that too," she confessed, watching as he gently employed Miss Wolfe's scarf in binding the frostbird's wings to its body. "Almost as if it was going against its natural instincts."

Devon looked up at her thoughtfully, and a whole library of ornithological theory filled the quiet between them. Once again, Beth felt a vague memory of frostbirds drift into her awareness, then out again. But before either she or Devon could speak, the passengers began to emerge from shelter, chattering more excitedly than a flock of garden sparrows in springtime. Devon hastily finished binding the frostbird's wings; Beth stood to act as a guard. But she was almost knocked down by Monsieur Chevrolet charging onto the scene, followed by Miss Wolfe. An iron cage swinging from the latter's hand whacked several times against the monsieur, even though Miss Wolfe had to extend her reach considerably to make this happen.

Suddenly Beth felt enclosed by a warm shadow as Devon rose to stand beside her, his arms crossed, expression tight and cold, as he stared at the other two ornithologists. "Mind you don't step on the lady's feet," he said in a tone that implied a further clause, *"or else I will break your legs."*

"It's fine, Mr. Lockley," Beth said nicely. "Miss Wolfe brought a cage to protect the frostbird. We should thank her."

Devon drew breath to reply with something Beth guessed would be not remotely close to thanks, but at that fortuitous moment a woman in a tweed dress and hat appeared.

"IOS," she announced, holding forth a silver badge in much the same manner as a police inspector arriving at a crime scene. Beth noted the engraving of a phoenix, symbol of the International Ornithological Society, before the woman pocketed the badge once more. "Mrs. Hassan, Kent division. By complete and pure coincidence, I just happened to be present. Which one of you bagged this bird?"

"It was my scarf that allowed its capture," Miss Wolfe said immediately. The crowd of passengers gave her a hearty cheer, and she smiled and waved to them.

"I provided vital supervision, without which disaster might have ensued!" Monsieur Chevrolet offered. Cheers sounded again, intermingled with a few whistles in appreciation of the gentleman's fine mustache.

Mrs. Hassan turned to Beth. "What about you?" Her tone

made it clear that she'd witnessed the whole thing. "Perhaps, in a thrilling display of ornithological skill gained from your university education, you and the handsome young Professor Lockley here partnered to capture the deadly bird and save everyone?"

"*Ooh!*" said the crowd.

Beth looked to Devon in the hope he'd supply a response. But he seemed as taken aback as she felt.

"Handsome?" Monsieur Chevrolet muttered sulkily.

"How did you know who he is?" Miss Wolfe asked, eyes narrowing with suspicion.

"And I wouldn't call him young," Monsieur Chevrolet added. "Besides, he got his degree in *America*."

"Pardon me, I must dash," Beth murmured, and turned to hurry away before anyone could further inflict conversation upon her. But she'd not gone a dozen steps before Devon appeared at her side.

"You were wise to leave," he whispered. "Whoever claims that bird's capture will have to transport it to an aviary, which means being diverted from the competition."

"I wonder if that was the intention all along," Beth said. "Perhaps someone wanted to eliminate competitors. Why else would they deploy a trained frostbird?"

"Shh," Devon hissed. Glancing around warily, he caught her arm and guided her even farther along the platform. Beth considered rebuking him for yet again manhandling her, but refrained out of fear he'd stop doing it.

"I agree with you," he whispered. "I also think the lapwing in Paris was trained; otherwise it's hard to understand how we all survived, including whoever stole it from the Fotheringhams."

Beth stared up at him. "The lapwing was stolen?"

"Yes, the—" He stiffened, abruptly somber. "Damn."

Alarmed, Beth followed his gaze to the station's entrance, where a group of men were strolling onto the platform. "Oh!" she exclaimed. "It's our French friends!"

At Devon's sigh, Beth frowned reprovingly. "They're nice people."

"You say that about everyone."

"Not everyone." She gave him a pointed look, and he grinned in response, biting his lower lip in a way that sent her stomach reeling.

"Why, Miss Pickering, whatever has befallen your good manners?"

"*You* have," she said sternly, although humor danced beneath the words. Turning away lest she start giggling, she waved to the fishermen. *"Bonjour!"*

"If only Hippolyta Quirm could see you now," Devon murmured, tapping his knuckles against her arm amiably. Her stomach, only just recovered, swooped all over again. But the fishermen had noticed them and began to run, shouting with a wrath that took her by surprise.

*"Merde alors! Agresseur de femme!"*

"Goodness me," Beth murmured a second before Devon shoved her protectively behind him. In the next second, the fishermen arrived, shouting mere inches from Devon's face and brandishing their fists. Beth tried to step forward so she might calm the situation, but Devon extended his arm, barricading her.

"Really, this is silly," she said. "Just let me explain . . ."

But there was no point: none of the men listened, nor even seemed to require her existence to justify their dispute. She was on the verge of walking away, to find a quiet spot in which to read while awaiting the train, when a cheerful voice sounded behind her.

"I say! What ho!"

The men's voices stumbled into confused silence. Everyone looked around at the young *Canterbury Times* journalist, Mr. Spencer, who had joined them. He held notepad and pencil in anticipation of an interview.

"My French is a bit rusty," he said to Devon, "but I believe they're accusing you of beating the young lady. Do you have any comment? Perhaps the stress of competing for Birder of the Year drove you to it?" Turning to Beth, he aimed the pencil at her like a weapon. "Ma'am, have you any bruises I might detail for my readers? I'm certain they—"

Devon scowled. "Bruises? This is preposterous!"

"*Prépuce?!!*" the fishermen raged. One lunged for Devon, who hastily stepped back, almost knocking Beth down as he did so. This whipped up a veritable storm of French fury.

"Mr. Lockley has not beaten me!" Beth averred, quite horrified.

The journalist noted this down. "In that case," he said helpfully, "may I suggest you offer some proof that you are friendly with each other? Perhaps a gesture that transcends language, if you know what I mean."

He winked so broadly, it was a wonder he didn't pull a facial muscle.

Devon expelled a sigh of exasperation. Turning to Beth, he gave her a look so intense, her stomach forgot swooping and donned a sparkling leotard to begin performing arabesques instead. "What do you think?" he asked. "Shall we illustrate our goodwill toward each other?"

Beth thought back to their demonstration of marital association for the innkeeper yesterday. A brief hug seemed like a reasonable solution to the current dilemma. "Yes," she agreed.

Devon immediately stepped close and set an arm around her back. Beth girded her loins in anticipation of being embraced.

Instead, he swung her into a dip.

The world swayed, filling with sunlight. Staring up at Devon, she felt her sudden bewilderment melt in the heat of his regard. He raised one eyebrow questioningly, and all at once she realized his intention. For about half a second, she considered saying no. But words to that effect could not be found anywhere inside her (although to be fair, she did not exactly search for them). She gave the slightest nod, and Devon smiled.

Then he bent and kissed her.

The fishermen gasped. The journalist gasped. But Beth did not hear them. Indeed, the entire world might have gasped, clutched its handkerchief, and swooned dramatically among the stars, and she would not have noticed. Devon kissed her with such brash, cheerful vigor that all her senses were bowled over. She tried to remind herself that he was a villain who disliked her utterly, but the *fun* of the moment banished such thoughts. She wanted to laugh. She wanted to climb into the kiss and build a home there, grow a bright garden, and wake every morning to joyful birdsong.

Then it ended, as suddenly as it had begun. Devon lifted her straight again. But the camaraderie in his eyes kept her off-balance, and he tucked her in close against his side to hold her steady.

The fishermen began to laugh. They clapped Devon on the

shoulder and took Beth's hand, squeezing it in a rough, sympathetic manner that had her feeling giddy all over again. *"Pardon"* was babbled in French and English by all parties; the journalist urgently scribbled notes and demanded to know names; and the crowd of passengers began to cheer and whistle. But Mrs. Hassan was tapping her IOS badge against her jaw, staring at them intensely, and Beth felt a chill, like a sharp sliver of frostbird magic, penetrate her heart. A woman's reputation was everything, and she imagined IOS would entirely disapprove of her kissing a man in public. Think of the damage it might do to the public's ideas about ornithology!

Just then, a train arrived, the sound of its horn breaking the scene into pieces. With a final *adieu*, the fishermen departed, the journalist ran to interview Mrs. Hassan, and Beth found herself standing alone with Devon in taut silence. He still had an arm around her, and she slipped away from it. Straightening her satchel, she frowned at a fascinating patch of concrete beside her feet.

"So this is goodbye," she said, just as she had what seemed like hours ago. Back before the world filled with shimmering frost and kissing. Really, the concrete was *so very fascinating*, she could not tear her gaze from it.

"Miss Pickering," Devon said. When she did not look up, he set a finger beneath her chin, lifting it. She tried to avoid meeting his gaze, but one accidental glimpse of it, all shining darkness and sultry eyelashes, arrested her.

"We're catching the same train," he pointed out.

"But we're making different journeys," she said. After all, fun was lovely and kisses were sweet, but tenure was forever. And birds were her only friends. People, on the other hand, showed interest in her only when they wanted something. Beth had no doubt whatsoever that Devon's charm would end just as soon as the caladrius flew into sight, leaving her with a whole lot of regrets to add to her stack of unhappy memories

Retreating from his touch, she offered a polite, collegial nod of farewell. He stared at her silently. The morning sun glowed red-gold around him, flaring in rainbow fragments where the frostbird had shed its icy magic in his hair. But his eyes were almost black with an emotion too intensely human for Beth to identify. Farther down the platform, a group of buskers began to play music that soared above the hum of the crowd. Beth thought wryly that someone ought to capture the scene with a kind of rapid, repeat-action camera, then display it in motion on a large screen; people would surely pay good money to watch and weep over it.

She did not weep, however. She turned away and hastened away to board the train, alone, ruthless, and without looking back.

# CHAPTER TWELVE

The lady ornithologist's reputation is most exposed to
danger when traveling alone; therefore, it behooves
her to always carry a petite revolver, a personal supply
of tea, and a false marriage license should the
necessity for one arise.

*Birds Through a Sherry Glass*, H.A. Quirm

THERE FOLLOWED WHAT seemed so much like a dark moment of the soul that Beth did not even bring out her field guide to read on the train. Seated between a window and an elderly lady occupied with a crossword puzzle, she took only brief intermissions from brooding to use the bathroom and secure tea and sandwiches from the dining car. Her nerves performed a long, angsty monologue about the kiss on the platform, and startled every time someone walked down the carriage aisle, in case they proved to be Devon. She was at last driven to the extreme of *removing her glove* to chew upon her thumbnail, a misdemeanor that inspired grim looks and mutterings from the elderly lady.

"My apologies," she said. "I'm a little frazzled, due to being in a competition."

The lady's eyes widened. "You're not an orthinocist doing the Birder of the Year competition, are you? I read about it in the papers yesterday."

Beth nodded hesitantly.

"Upon my word! How marvelous!" The crossword puzzle was flung aside and the woman grasped Beth's arm in an act that ought to have been declared a felony. "It's in Ipswich! The caladrius! My grandfather told me so last night!"

"Your grandfather?" Beth echoed.

"Yes, at our weekly séance. We get together for a nice chat through the heavenly veil. He said—" She paused to clear her throat, then intoned in a spectral voice: "'The caladrius bird will be in Ipswich, Gladys, and will cure your arthritis.'"

"Uh, thank you," Beth said, blinking rapidly to forestall a bemused frown. "I shall take that under advisement." And with a polite smile, she turned toward the window and resumed her dark moment.

Of course, the caladrius might indeed be in Ipswich, for all she knew. She possessed no idea of where in Britain to begin searching. Sensibly, she ought to return home to Oxford. In the quiet, well-ordered environment of her boardinghouse room, she could regroup and make a plan for tracking down the bird. She could even visit one of her favorite places in the world, the Bodleian Library, to research it in more depth and perhaps come up with some clues as to where it might most likely nest in Britain.

But after the past two days' adventures, the very thought of *quiet* and *well-ordered* sent a great rush of dreariness through her heart. Sitting alone in her small room . . . sitting alone in the library . . . she could not bear even the thought of it. Far better to make London her initial base. Even if she talked with no one, at least she would be surrounded by the city's vivacious energy and noise.

Disembarking at Paddington Station, she stood on the platform for some time, not at all looking for Devon among the other passengers, simply trying to devise a route ahead. Besides, he never appeared. Perhaps he had gotten off the train before she did. Perhaps he'd decided to bypass London altogether. He might be anywhere—she might never see him again in all her life—she did not care.

"Are you quite well, dear?" a woman asked, pausing beside her. "You just gave the most dreadfully mournful sigh."

Flushing, Beth smiled and apologized and hurried out of the station before her emotions could catch up with her again.

Her first call was to the bank, where she withdrew enough money from her savings to fund a substantial engagement in the competition, although it meant that any dream of traveling to New Zealand to study the giant carnivorous moa flew out the window. Then she spent the day traipsing around the city buying maps, nets, a cage that collapsed to fit in a suitcase, clothes, and a new straw boater. It was an endeavor more exhausting than chasing demon ducks along the shores of Greece, and within hours her feet had begun to ache, but she continued onward, as ruthless with herself as any ornithologist ought to be. And to her surprise, everywhere she went she heard people discussing the caladrius.

"My sister was eating chips on the beach in Brighton and the caladrius stole one from her," claimed a woman in the department store where Beth purchased stockings.

"My husband says the bird can't really cure illness, it's just a story being used by the Tories to distract from their mismanagement of public health," declared a woman in the boutique where Beth purchased gloves.

"IOS actually stands for the Invisible Order of Secrets," said a man on the tram she caught across town. "They're conspiring to take over the world using avian magic. Mark my words, before long we'll all be flying in feathered machines instead of taking trams."

Only her exceptional manners prevented Beth from laughing aloud at this. IOS undertaking a secret scheme? Nothing was more ridiculous! (Goodness, that gentleman at the back of the tram, facing away from her, looked like Mr. Cholmbaumgh. She must be tired indeed for her imagination to come up with such a fancy!)

Stopping for afternoon tea in a small café, she idly perused a newspaper that had been left on the table. As she turned to the second page, however, her mouthful of cucumber sandwich became in sudden, real danger of being ejected. For there, in several excited paragraphs, was a report of the lapwing's capture in Paris. Beth was most surprised indeed to learn that Professor Devon Lockley had singlehandedly brought down the bird, thus saving two frail old grannies and a pretty young woman from certain doom.

"I beg your pardon!" she muttered indignantly, and was forced to drink an entire pot of tea before her nerves settled enough to relinquish the idea of writing a strident letter to the editor, and instead to continue on with her shopping.

Finally, come evening, and so thoroughly worn out she kept thinking she saw Cholmbaumgh skulking behind her, she retired to the Minervaeum Club, London's premier private establishment for academics. The grand Georgian building on Cromwell Road in Kensington was owned by a mysterious figure rumored to be the scion of either a smuggler or a royal duke, but who clearly possessed a good heart despite this, for they set annual membership at a mere half sovereign to anyone with a doctorate and a tolerance for interesting conversation. Considering most scholars lived on the cusp of either wretched poverty or explosive fortune (literally explosive, in the case of chemists), this generosity was much appreciated and often reciprocated by grateful donors who wanted their peers to enjoy the same inspiration the club's atmosphere, not to mention the club's wine cellar, had given them.

Beth had always loved the place. The air smelled gently of old books, the beds were soft, and pacing the halls muttering theories to oneself was considered normal behavior. She hadn't visited for some time, since Hippolyta was not a member, and walking into the warm dustiness of the lobby felt like a truer homecoming than returning to her Oxford boardinghouse ever did. Sounds of philosophical debate could be heard from the Platonic Drawing Room, interspersed now and again by the *boom!* of scientific debate from the Paracelsus Lounge. The floor beneath her trembled from someone making a forceful rejoinder about the benefits of nitroglycerin as she crossed to the check-in desk, dreaming of finally being able to eat quality fare, such as bangers and mash with spotted dick for pudding, after enduring French cuisine for far too long.

"Giggleswick," said the gentlewoman clerk as she handed over a room key.

"Excuse me?" Beth asked vaguely, half-lost in visions of custard.

"That's where I reckon you'll find the caladrius," the clerk elaborated. "Giggleswick in North Yorkshire. On account of the limestone. It's got special healing properties, has limestone. The caladrius would be drawn to it."

"I see," Beth murmured. She couldn't remember having mentioned her business but clearly must have. Picking up her suitcase, for she was in a hurry to settle in, then visit the dining room, she turned—

"I can't believe I'm talking to such a famous orothologisist!" the clerk exclaimed.

Well, perhaps she could spare a minute or two. She turned back with a smile—

"I squealed out loud when I read about you kissing that other orothologisist on the train platform!"

Beth's smile vanished, taking her good manners with it. "Excuse me, what?"

"And you look just like your picture!" As Beth watched openmouthed, the clerk rummaged behind the desk, producing a newspaper, which she proceeded to flap excitedly, almost smacking Beth in the face. "It's today's *Evening Standard*. Will you autograph it for me?"

"Picture? My picture is in the newspaper for *kissing a man*?!" Beth went so white, there existed some danger of her being reported as a caladrius sighting. Accepting the paper from the clerk, she stared in horror at the headline on its front page.

## ROMANCE TAKES FLIGHT IN BIRDER COMPETITION

There followed a sensational account of this morning's frostbird capture and her kiss with Devon. They even reported her name, presumably supplied by one of the other birders present at the Canterbury station. The fact that it was misspelled as Peckerine offered some consolation . . . but the even more factual fact that all her colleagues would know it was her took that consolation and bashed it into a miserable, blithering heap of woe.

This was all the fault of that reprehensible, bird-thieving, manhandling villain, Devon Lockley! Granted, she had consented to their kiss, even knowing that a newspaper reporter stood right beside them, but that was beside the point! Indeed, the point was so far away it appeared as no more than a smudge in the distance, whereas her outrage loomed overwhelmingly large.

Requesting that dinner be sent to her room, she went upstairs with a speed inspired by (a) significant aggravation, (b) terror that someone she knew would see her and ask about the newspaper article, and (c) *aaaaagghhhh*. Coming to the Hypatia Bedroom, she locked its door behind her and leaned back against the paneled wood, closing her eyes and trying to calm herself by imagining a beautiful scene:

~~Winning Birder of the Year.~~

Wringing Devon Lockley's neck.

MEANWHILE, DEVON WAS not giving Miss Beth Pickering the slightest thought. He did not ruminate on her soft blue eyes. He did not recollect her scintillating intelligence, which in turn did not spark any degree of warmth whatsoever in his nether region. Furthermore, there failed to be a single moment in which he yearned for their reunion so that he might take her in his arms and kiss her with such a blissful thoroughness she forgot he was a villain. Instead, he spent most of the day shopping for supplies necessary to help him track the Beth . . . er, the *bird*.

Finally, late afternoon, he met with his cousin, Professor Gabriel Tarrant, at a geography conference in Kensington. Gabriel was listening attentively to an ancient lecturer drone on about some limestone block in some village somewhere and showed no pleasure in Devon's sudden appearance. Certainly he refused to leave with him. An appeal to familial loyalty failed; a charming smile failed. Eventually Devon resorted to threats of telling Granny that Gabriel was being rude to him—upon which, his cousin grudgingly relented, accompanying him down the street to the Minervaeum Club. In its warm, book-lined, tobacco-scented Shakespeare Lounge, the two men sat in leather armchairs older than themselves, surrounded by a selection of England's greatest minds (and the people in whom those minds were located), and Devon began a new round of appeals.

"I need your help with this Birder of the Year competition."

"No," Gabriel said.

"If—"

"No."

Devon bit back a decidedly familial word. He and his cousin might have served as a mirror to each other were not Gabriel objectively more handsome, more orderly—and probably more intelligent, although no one could understand his explanations of thaumaturgic geography well enough to determine the matter. But their characters might have been two roads in a yellow wood: they could not have diverged more.

Behind his inscrutable facade, deep inside his almost midnight-colored eyes, Gabriel *might* have hidden a sense of whimsy; if so, however, he never revealed it. Once, when he was a child, a classmate called him Gabe. He'd responded with nothing more than a silent, unblinking look, whereupon the classmate immediately transferred to another school, and no one had risked being chummy with him again. Except Devon, that is. But then, Devon approached risks the way other people approached a warm, cozy bed at night.

Within their family, Gabriel, who was the elder by a year,

got constantly held up as an example of what Devon himself could become (although whether this was meant as encouragement or a warning depended on who said it). But the fact that he was currently and fastidiously using a napkin to wipe the rim of his wineglass, whereas Devon had already finished half his own drink, demonstrated the unlikelihood of that.

"I'd ask someone else to help me," Devon lied, "but you're the only thaumaturgic geographer I know." The fact that Gabriel had also been his best friend until they were separated by Devon's being sent to America did not require stating. Both men knew it, and both men would have been horribly uncomfortable acknowledging it aloud, even between themselves. In that, at least, they were the same. Matters of the heart stayed in the heart, behind several locked doors and barricades.

"I need a list of sites in Britain where magic is especially concentrated," he explained. "Thaumaturgic birds are often attracted to places like that, and the caladrius, being very powerful, is hopefully no exception. It's reported to be a freshwater bird, so I'm particularly interested in lakes and rivers with strong thaumaturgic energy."

"That's confidential information," Gabriel replied sternly.

"Which is why I'm asking confidentially."

Gabriel gave him an all-too-familiar look of mingled confusion and aggravation. "That's not how it works, Devon."

"I know," he answered easily. "And I'm prepared to continue twisting words and their meanings for as long as necessary until I get what I want, so you might as well save us both time and just say yes. For one thing, there are simply too many ways I can blackmail you into agreement. For example, when you broke Aunt Mary's favorite—"

"I recall." Gabriel frowned into his wineglass, where floated what was either a bubble or a speck of dust. Wrinkling his nose, he set the glass aside. "Fine. Yes."

Devon grinned. "Cheers, coz. You're the best. Are you staying here at the club while you attend your conference?"

"Mm."

"Perfect. You get started writing down place-names, and I'll buy you dinner. I haven't seen you for months. We'll have a proper chat."

"Chat," Gabriel echoed dourly. "First you want me to illegally share information; now you want to *chat*. I'm going to need more wine."

It took Beth three drinks before she finally soothed her aggravation about the newspaper article. By the time she poured a fourth, thus emptying the teapot, her mind was ready once more to focus on the competition—mainly because her body was tired of traipsing down to the bathroom at the end of the corridor, thanks to all the tea. Sitting cross-legged on the bed, she consulted her map of Britain, along with several newly purchased field guides, and took copious notes as she brainstormed theories about where the caladrius might be found. It seemed an impossible task, but she wasn't England's youngest professor for nothing.

"I shall be unrelenting until I win!" she declared, brandishing her pen like a sword. "Unrelenting and utterly ruthless!"

*But you're an angel*, Devon whispered in her mind.

*Crack!*

Beth blinked in startlement as the pen hit the far wall. She hadn't even been aware of throwing it. Rushing to check there was no damage to the wall, she picked up the pen, then turned again toward her work . . .

And stopped. Heart twisting oddly, she stared at the spacious room with its elegant furnishings and its bed that was large enough for her to sleep in even with all her papers strewn across the counterpane. Altogether it represented a remarkable improvement upon her situation last night, at the Chaucer Inn, in the tiny, bed-filled room with Devon. No uncomfortable borrowed nightshirt. No sleeping on the floor.

No one to talk to about birds, or dance with, or kiss in the swaying firelight.

Sorrow came upon her with all the suddenness of an owl upon a mouse. The familiar dull ache of being essentially alone, something she'd felt even before her parents died of cholera— something not even Hippolyta's bombastic company had assuaged—now sharpened into a hot, raw pain.

*I miss him*, she realized. *It's only been a few hours, but I miss him so much. He's a villain; he pulled me out of my perfectly calm waters and disturbed me right through my very being . . . and I miss all of it: the hijinks and hassles and chaotic fun . . .*

*I miss the me I was with him.*

Sinking to the floor, she leaned back against the wall and stared wearily at her work set out on the bed. It was just a few steps away and yet she felt drained by the thought of returning to it, as if she'd need to traverse an abyss instead of a rather shabby rug. But return she must. It was all she had: her career, and skies filled with birds.

For the first time in her life, that seemed inadequate.

Then she heard a tiny noise. Another followed, and another, as the occupant of the neighboring room moved around, seemingly right next to where she sat, on the other side of the wall. Closing her eyes, she listened, taking comfort from someone else's presence. And finally, she grew settled again.

The fact was, Devon had behaved in a reprehensibly ungentlemanlike manner, with his constant banter and all his towing of her. She was *fortunate* to be rid of him! So very, very ~~lonely~~ fortunate.

Sighing, she tipped her forehead against her knees. But the universe did not take this cue to send Professor Lockley bursting in with flowers and chocolates, so she hauled herself up and got on with work.

DEVON SAT ON the floor of the Margaret Lucas Cavendish, Duchess of Newcastle-upon-Tyne Bedroom, leaning back against the wall, listening to tiny sounds from the room behind him as if they were ghosts of the breath he kept losing whenever he thought about Beth Pickering. But he did *not* think about her! Absolutely not! He was too busy working on how to win Birder of the Year.

He read through Gabriel's notes over and over again. He drew circles on maps and wrote down every theory that occurred to him. Crawling onto the bed to fall asleep sometime around midnight, he dreamed of Beth (which, please note, does not count as thinking about her) and woke in such a state of mental exhaustion, the world seemed no more than a blank darkness. Then he realized his notebook was lying open across his face.

Lifting it, he peered sleepily at the place-names Gabriel had listed for him. Nine sites, scattered widely across the island, equal in their potential lure for a magical bird. It would take months to explore them all. And even then, he might be on entirely the wrong path. The caladrius could be anywhere.

Except . . .

He sat up, brushing the hair away from his eyes. The bird wasn't anywhere, of course. It was *somewhere*, or else there would be no competition. Realizing that, his perception shifted radically, and he understood at once where he needed to go next.

As for where he longed to be—well, he wasn't thinking about that, was he?

IN HER OWN bedroom, Beth woke face down on the map of England. As her vision slowly came into focus, she saw the circle she'd drawn and the words scrawled next to it:

*Ornithologists are ruthless!*

She ran a finger sleepily across the sentence. Among all the thoughts she'd corralled in the night, that one alone offered her certainty. In fact, she suspected it was the key to everything.

Climbing off the bed, she washed, then hastily donned a dress she'd bought yesterday (soft white, printed with lilacs and trimmed with lace, about as appropriate for a serious-minded scholar as a gossip magazine would have been, but perfect for ~~if she met Devon again~~ traveling in the heat). As she bound up her hair and set a straw boater upon it, she gazed out the window at the brightening sky. Sparrows flecked rooftops, pigeons squatted upon chimneys . . . and somewhere out there in the long expanse of Britain, a caladrius perched.

In a cage, waiting to be won.

Nothing else made sense. A group of leading ornithologists

in all their professional ruthlessness would never organize a competition for Birder of the Year based on mere hope, a rumor, a white-winged dream. Once she'd taken that into account, Beth had become convinced that that they held the bird in their possession and presumably had contrived some plan for arranging its "capture" by their chosen winner. A plan she intended to overturn, outscheming them to win Birder of the Year for herself!

Granted, she didn't understand people, let alone their motivations, which would make outscheming them rather tricky. But she was always open to learning a new subject. And certainly this would be easier than traipsing randomly around the kingdom with binoculars and a big net. She didn't have to find the caladrius; she only had to find someone who would reveal its location.

And she knew exactly where to start.

It was time to go home to Oxford.

# Chapter Thirteen

The garden sparrow is as beautiful as the swan
(although not as delicious when roasted).
        *Birds Through a Sherry Glass*, H.A. Quirm

IN A COFFEEHOUSE overlooking Paddington Station, Messrs.
Flogg and Fettick sipped their third round of black coffee as
they watched passengers enter the terminal.

"I'm not happy, Mr. Flogg," grumbled Mr. Fettick. "When
we sent Schreib and Cholmbaumgh to frighten our professors
into escaping the Chaucer Inn together, it was specifically so
that they'd remain in each other's company. But here we are
now, with *The Lovers Parted!*"

"It's fine, it's fine," Mr. Flogg soothed him. "Every narrative
benefits from some conflict. The professors will reunite, feeling
more keen than ever, mark my words. After all, we're tracking
them to make sure they do."

Mr. Fettick sighed. "What if they don't, though? The newspaper articles have already been published! We might have to
print a retraction."

Both men shuddered.

"No, it's fine," Mr. Flogg reiterated firmly. "A night apart
will make our lovebirds' hearts grow fonder. We can leave that

up to human nature—what *we* have to do is pave their way to success in the competition. But not too quickly, mark you! IOS and the British Tourism Board want to get their money's worth first."

"But not too slowly," Mr. Fettick countered. "The professors need to look clever, so that people will appreciate the value of a university education."

"True." He sighed. "This project certainly is a challenge. Let's imagine we're a pair of bird experts. Where would we go next?"

Mr. Fettick hesitated, only too aware that his own degree in French history left his head in entirely the wrong place for thinking like a scientist. "Well, I'd personally go to question the IOS chairman, Professor Gladstone. But that's because I know he's involved. Don't worry, they'll never think of it."

Mr. Flogg's brow creased in the shadow of his bowler hat. "They're geniuses; of course they'll think of it. Drat! We'd better organize a surprise to meet them at Oxford University should they turn up there. Something to slow them down a bit."

"What kind of surprise?"

Mr. Flogg merely smiled fiendishly and bounced his eyebrows.

"Ah," Mr. Fettick said, perking up. "*That* kind!"

Setting down his coffee cup with a clank, Mr. Flogg stood in a manner that would have been dramatic were he not a pasty-faced fellow with a prissy little mustache. "Quick! To the telegram office!"

FOLLOWING A HASTY meal in the Hildegard of Bingen Breakfast Room, Beth caught a hackney cab to Paddington Station.

Entering the terminal, she immediately looked around for ~~Devon Lockley~~ Cholmbaumgh, still feeling a little on edge after having imagined yesterday that the man was lurking behind her. But all she saw were a few pigeons and one rather fine specimen of *Parus major* (and, less interesting, several dozen people). This failed to ease her nerves, however. As she purchased a ticket and made her way across the platform, she had the oddest sensation that someone was watching her . . .

"Miss Pickering!"

At the familiar voice, her pulse stumbled. Turning, she smiled politely.

"Hippolyta."

"Thank goodness, by Jove!" the woman boomed, ringlets and ruffles flouncing as she rushed forward to take Beth's hand. Footmen followed in her wake, barely visible beneath armloads of luggage. "I've been beside myself!"

"Er," Beth said, looking down at the yellow gloves Hippolyta had given her.

"You know how bad I am at stitching! They're my favorite gloves, and the seams are beginning to fray! But you're so clever, I'm sure you can have them tidied up in a jiffy."

"Um," Beth said, to no effect. Hippolyta hustled her aboard the train in such typical style that she began to wonder if she'd only imagined the past two days.

"Oberhufter is traveling east like a fool," Hippolyta said as they settled into a first-class compartment, "despite all signs pointing clearly to the caladrius being in the Cotswolds."

"Actually, I—" Beth began.

"It shall be my great pleasure to laugh in his face when I win Birder of the Year! Has there ever been a more aggravating person in all the field of ornithology?"

"You—"

"No, indeed!" Sighing loudly, she frowned at the compartment doorway. "I can't believe no one has come to ensure we're settled in and have all we require. Such poor service!" She leaned back as one of her footmen spread a blanket over her lap, then forward as another rearranged the pillow behind her. "Elizabeth, be a sweetheart and go inform the steward that we require tea and biscuits, would you?"

"Yes, of course," Beth said automatically, rising from her seat.

"And tell him to remove that ridiculous mustache of his before he returns. It reminds me in the most disagreeable manner of my late husband."

Beth entered the corridor with some trepidation. It was crammed with people hurrying to organize themselves before the journey began, and the air hung turgid with cigar smoke and perfume. "Sorry . . . sorry . . . pardon me . . . sorry," she murmured as she wove a careful passage. But no one heard her over the clamor, or even saw her, apparently, as elbows, suitcases, and shoe heels impacted with her body. Beth found herself driven to the verge of frowning. Why people—?!

(That was the full extent of the sentence. Extroverts need not trouble themselves asking for an explanation.)

Halfway to the dining car, she paused to lean back against the wall, trying to catch her breath. Never before had she felt so driven to homicidal inclinations. (Although not really. After all, murdering someone on the train led to appalling consequences, such as bloodstains, delayed timetables, and fictionalized accounts in cheap novels.)

"I told you so," came a voice through the open door of the compartment next to her. "*Birders on the Oxford Express.*'"

"I'm impressed. Your instincts are sharper than a lapwing's claw, old chap."

Beth's innate curiosity made her glance through the open door. She saw two men in dark suits and bowler hats, each with a briefcase resting on his lap. They did not look like ornithologists, despite their conversation. They looked like they belonged to the species of gentleman who travels around selling commodes.

"What if she lets herself be influenced by that atrocious woman?"

"Then we bring out a deadly—"

He stopped, and as two mustachioed heads whipped in her direction, Beth hastily looked away. Seconds later, the compartment door slammed shut.

Bother! Just when the conversation had been getting interesting! Beth had no qualms about eavesdropping, since it was how a lot of biological science got done, but she couldn't extrapolate anything from that brief snatch of information. Perhaps if she leaned closer . . .

"Hello, Miss Peckerine," came a rich, amused voice.

Beth almost gasped as she looked up to see Devon walking past. *He's here!* her heart cried out with joyful excitement. *He's here*, her brain echoed in significantly darker tones. He flashed her a hot glance, and Beth felt herself begin to melt. In a panic, she said the first thing that came to mind.

"Villain!"

He stopped in his tracks.

*Oh dear*, she thought, pulse scattering wildly through her body, as he reversed himself for three steps then turned to face her. He wore a black gabardine coat to his knees and a gray shirt, black trousers, oh my goodness rugged black boots, as if he were intending to scout for a nocturnal bird or set a woman's heart aflutter. And still no tie, waistcoat, or even the basic masculine dignity of a hat. Passengers muttered complaints about him blocking the corridor as they sidled past, but Beth did not even notice. All she saw was his ~~gorgeous~~ infuriating eyes looking down at her with dark intensity as he set a hand against the wall beside her head. He held her gaze for several decades, then looked at her mouth, then farther down.

"Pretty dress," he said, and Beth melted to such a degree she had to press her legs together.

"Why are you here?" she demanded.

He lifted his gaze, and as their eyes met again, it felt like coming home. *Which was ridiculous*, Beth told herself. She'd only known the man a short while. He was the *opposite* of home. He was an unmapped horizon, or a bar chart without category names along the x-axis. She'd been right to leave him in Canterbury, and thank God here he was—er, so she could leave him again, that is! She would push him away this very instant and march off down the corridor!

All right, perhaps not *this* instant, but the next one, for sure!

"I'm chasing the caladrius, same as you," he said.

"So you're going to the Cotswolds also?" She rather impressed herself with how seamlessly the lie glided off her tongue.

He smiled. "That's my ruthless girl."

"I don't know what you mean," she answered haughtily.

"No? On a completely different subject, I learned today that a shilling is all it takes to buy information from a railway ticket officer about where a passenger is heading."

Beth gasped. "Cheat!"

"Liar," he countered.

They stared at each other. All that prevented a sudden, shocking bout of tongue kissing and bodice ripping was the crowd of passengers bustling around them. Devon leaned forward, whispering in her ear.

"I'll race you to Oxford University. May the best ornithologist win."

Beth drew breath to answer that she was most definitely not going anywhere near the university, nor the city in general, nor indeed the entirety of Oxfordshire at all, thank you very much, and furthermore do not stand so close to me in this reprehensibly scandalous manner—

But he was already gone.

*Well!* She'd show the scoundrel exactly how ruthless she could be! Tea and biscuits forgotten, she turned sharply on a heel, and begging forgiveness, expressing regret, she forcefully apologized her way back down the corridor (while behind her, had she known it, sat two extremely excited publicists, shaking hands and congratulating each other).

Arriving at Hippolyta's compartment, she found the steward already there, pouring tea from a silver teapot as Hippolyta watched him closely, lest a mustache hair fall into her cup. The woman glanced up as Beth entered.

"Where have you been? It's not safe to just wander about on a train; someone might step all over you."

"Sorry," Beth said. Dropping to the seat, she took a napkin from the table and pressed it against her face. "So dreadfully hot!"

"Have a cup of tea," Hippolyta suggested. "That will help."

The steward handed her an already poured cup. Thanking him, Beth stared into the rising steam. Here at last was a reservoir of peace—and yet, it looked entirely inadequate for her needs. She could do with wine instead. Or maybe vodka.

"You really don't look the thing, Elizabeth," Hippolyta said. "Drink up. It's important to take care of yourself."

"You're right," Beth agreed. But it was an automatic response, for no Englishwoman worth her salt took care of herself if there was an opportunity to sigh instead and gaze wearily into teacups.

Hippolyta gave her a stern little frown. "I hope you will listen to me."

"I have," Beth assured her. "And I think—"

"No, dear, I meant listen to me now as I practice my acceptance speech for Birder of the Year."

"Oh, I see." Her brain trudged forward with its habitual answer, *yes, of course.*

"No," she said.

Hippolyta blinked at her. "I beg your pardon?"

Beth set down the tea and straightened her spine, although she could not quite manage to look Hippolyta directly in the eye. Infuriated with herself for having succumbed so easily to the force of Hippolyta's personality, she gathered that energy, transformed it into courage, and said, "I'm going to find another seat and then continue on with the competition alone."

Hippolyta's mouth fell agape. "By—by—!"

"Sorry," Beth said, getting to her feet. "It's been . . . nice . . . knowing you."

While Hippolyta sputtered and huffed, she reached for her suitcase in the luggage tray above, accidentally knocking the table in the process and making dishes rattle. Tea leaped from her cup onto a napkin, where it proceeded to sizzle, blackening the linen. Beth stared at it for an empty moment, then lifted her expressionless gaze to Hippolyta.

The woman shrugged. "You'd have thanked me when you woke in the hospital. Competing against me would have been too anguishing for you, especially since I'm going to win."

Beth almost laughed. "Goodbye," she said, and turned away.

But then she stopped, her pulse skittering. This woman had been the closest thing to a friend she'd ever known. Memories stirred: walking a sunlit Italian shore, sipping iced tea as they searched for the double-beaked sandpiper . . . hauling herself up a rock face in driving rain while Hippolyta shouted directions from within the shelter of an umbrella on the ground below, only to discover the rainbow auk's nest was a mirage . . .

"By the way," she said, not bothering to look back. "My name's not Elizabeth. It's Beth."

And she left, gently closing the door behind her.


DEVON SLAMMED OPEN the compartment door and flung himself onto the seat with a loud sigh. Gabriel looked at him over the fine silver rim of his reading spectacles. "Are you all right?"

Devon scowled. Had he known his cousin would ask questions in this obnoxious and invasive manner, he'd not have asked for his ongoing help. "I'm fine," he said.

Gabriel regarded him in a vaguely considering but mostly bored way, then went back to perusing his newspaper. Devon exhaled with relief. He did not wish to talk about what had just happened in the corridor with Beth, most definitely and absolut—

"I suspect I've been a villain," he said.

"Again?" came the impassive response.

He shrugged and nodded.

Gabriel turned a page in the *Times*. "I assume it involves the woman you refuse to discuss, the one to whom you were villainous in Canterbury, judging from the report in this newspaper."

Devon glared, to no effect. Gabriel merely turned another page, studiously ignoring him.

"Fine. Maybe the same woman," he relented. "She's my professional rival but I always seem to end up flirting with her."

He propped his feet up on the opposite bench, and Gabriel shifted away from them, frowning.

"For a genius, you are remarkably obtuse. Has it occurred to you to just behave nicely with the woman?"

"Has it occurred to you to visit your wife?" Devon shot back.

Gabriel's expression turned so icily lethal, it could have been employed by Her Majesty's armed forces as a weapon of mass destruction.

"Forget it," Devon said (the universal masculine code for *I'm sorry but am too proud to actually say so*). "I appreciate you coming with me. We should have brought Amelia along too, had an adventure of the cousins, just like old times."

"What an abysmal idea," Gabriel muttered. Even in childhood, it had been his stance that two was a crowd, three a catastrophe. Closing his newspaper, he folded it in a brisk, efficient manner. "I've agreed to use my standing as an Oxford University professor to get you into their ornithology department offices without suspicion, but there will be *no* adventure."

"Come on, have some fun. We both know I saved you from

the terminal boredom of listening to that lecture about the Foreskin Phenomenon—"

"'The Fordwich Phenomenon of Thaumaturgic Erosion Trails, Illustrated by the Transportation over Loam of the Saint Augustine Limestone.'"

"I think I died a little just from hearing that title."

Gabriel didn't bother replying, instead setting his paper on the table at an eighty-nine-degree angle, then nudging it the final degree to perfection. Devon tried not to sigh.

He hadn't expected to see Beth again. But when he'd arrived at Paddington Station, there she'd been, buying a ticket, looking as frazzled as he felt—but also gorgeous, *gorgeous*; how had he ever thought her merely pretty? Rossetti would go down on his knees to beg the honor of painting her. (Were he still alive, that is, resurrection being a step too far for Devon's expensively educated imagination.) What was a mere scientist to do in response to such a woman?

Stalk her, apparently. He grimaced. Iniquity was not feeling as good as it used to.

He stood abruptly. "I'm going for a stroll."

Gabriel stared at him with bemusement. "A stroll? On a train?" Then his eyes narrowed. "You're going to spy on that woman."

"Am not," Devon retorted. Really, who was the idiot who'd suggested bringing his cousin on this trip? Oh yes, the same idiot who was now planning to sneak along the train corridor and spy on a woman because he missed her face, and the way she chewed her thumbnail, and how her eyes lit like a summer sky at the very mention of birds.

With a groan, he leaned against the compartment door. "Tell me not to do it."

"Don't do it," Gabriel said.

"You truly think I shouldn't?"

"You want to know what I truly think? *Truly?*"

"Yes."

"I think that the Fordwich Phenomenon is a perfect example of how—"

*Thud.* The compartment door slammed shut on the rest of that sentence. Devon turned to head along the corridor, promising himself that after one quick glimpse of Beth, he'd go back to being an intelligent adult. No more allowing his heart any influence on—

His pulse erupted.

She was standing at the far end of the corridor, talking to an attendant. Sunlight coming through the train windows flickered like bright phoenix wings against her profile and illuminated her hair with a reddish halo. *Angel* was too feeble a word for her. She was heaven entire, embodied in a woman's body. She was every superlative in every ridiculous emotional dictionary printed in a man's heart. Devon wanted to walk up to her, take her in his arms, and feel the grit of his past turn to gold. But he could not move. Time had stopped, breath had stopped; he stared, entranced, wishing helplessly that she'd turn and smile at him. Then she actually *did* turn—

Panic gripped his body, flinging it through the open door of a compartment.

"Egad!" came a unified cry from two elderly women seated together therein. Hands fluttered; hat feathers threatened to take flight.

"Ahem!" came a loud throat clearing from two men seated opposite. Mustaches bristled; fingers tapped on briefcases.

Apologizing, Devon tried to back away, but the women

took in his appearance with one swoop of their lorgnettes and began verbally assailing him.

"Sit down! Sit down at once, young sir! Rest those legs of yours. No need to be shy; this is a public compartment!"

"*Actually*, as we tried to tell you, it's not," said one of the men, to no avail. The women tugged on Devon until he dropped to the seat between them.

"You look like you've seen a ghost, poor lad," said the woman to the left of him, patting his knee.

He smiled. "A celestial being, in fact. Beautiful, with eyes like the sky."

"Ooh, this is a boy in love," said the woman to the right, patting his other knee. "So why are you sitting with us instead of her?"

*Because you practically kidnapped me*, he wanted to reply, but instead increased the wattage of his smile, blinding them to anything beyond its charm. "She's my rival in a competition."

The women gasped. The men shifted in their seats, glancing at each other with taut silence.

"You're not an othologist are you?" asked the woman to the right.

"Yes, I'm a—"

"Cockermouth!" shouted the woman to the left.

The men jolted, almost dropping their briefcases. But Devon only frowned with mild confusion. "I beg your pardon?"

"The caladrius will be in Cockermouth. The town in Cumbria. Wordsworth was born there, and you know what he wrote about birds."

"Er . . ." Devon didn't read poetry, but in any case he couldn't see how it would influence the caladrius, unless the bird had evolved considerably since last observed.

"Nonsense," scoffed the woman to the right. "It will be in Scotland! Everyone knows it likes the cold." She eyed Devon shrewdly. "You should take your celestial being to Gretna Green, just over the Scottish border. Marry her there and catch the caladrius at the same time!"

Devon choked on his breath.

"What's your name, dear boy?" asked the woman to the left, patting his arm now and murmuring something about Brussels (or possibly "big muscles"; Devon wasn't exactly paying attention).

"Devon Lockley," he told her.

"Ooh, the boy in the paper!" exclaimed the woman to the right. Both ladies lifted their lorgnettes to inspect him more thoroughly, and Devon glanced toward the compartment doorway in much the same way an archaeologist glances at the suddenly closing stone door of a pharaoh's haunted tomb.

"You kissed the girl," said the woman to the left, "so you *have* to marry her!"

"Um . . ."

"And you certainly can't elope to Gretna Green!" argued the woman who'd suggested it in the first place. "You're famous! You need to marry in a cathedral."

"Er . . ."

"The people will demand it!"

"You should have all white flowers, in honor of the caladrius!"

"And release doves at the end of the ceremony!"

"And you'll need to get a proper haircut!"

By this time, the men on the opposite bench were so tense, they appeared on the verge of shattering. Devon himself felt a headache coming on. He promised to use the ladies' suggested marriage proposal, autographed their handkerchiefs, and finally effected an escape.

Beth had disappeared from the corridor, and with a doleful sigh he returned to his own compartment. Looking up from a geography textbook, Gabriel arched one eyebrow.

"What happened to you?"

"Admirers," was all Devon managed to say before collapsing on the seat. He ran a hand across his face, through his hair. "Why people?"

Gabriel shrugged. "I wish I knew," he said, and blessedly went back to reading his book.

Devon stared out the window, thinking about ~~reuniting with Beth~~ catching the caladrius, ~~kissing Beth~~ presenting the caladrius to the IOS committee, and ~~sinking himself into Beth's warm soft depths like a man experiencing a little death and temporarily visiting heaven~~ winning Birder of the Year and the best reward of all, ~~Beth's love~~ tenure.

# CHAPTER FOURTEEN

A bird endeavoring to win a mate is often as
unscrupulous as a certain German ornithologist who
shall go unnamed for legal reasons but who can be
identified by his brash manner and redolent cologne.
*Birds Through a Sherry Glass*, H.A. Quirm

BETH DISEMBARKED THE train at Oxford Station with a great weight upon her. Namely, her suitcase, which she was used to leaving in the care of Hippolyta's footmen. Nevertheless, determined to beat Devon to their mutual destination, she wrapped both arms around it and ventured forth with such speed, several shocked pedestrians muttered to each other, "There goes a feminist!"

They might have been relieved to know, however, that the real reason for this speed was because arriving before Devon would surely lead to *meeting with* Devon, and at this point Beth would have swerved around a dozen caladriuses if they got in the way of her doing that.

Granted, a plain owl of a woman had little chance of winning the heart of a man like Devon Lockley—but she hadn't become a doctor of ornithology, Britain's youngest professor, and Huttingdon Primary School's Most Reliable Student (1873), by surrendering when things got tough! Besides, she didn't aim so high as his *heart*, only his smile, maybe a kiss or two . . . and she wouldn't turn up her nose at being stuck in a hotel bedroom with him again either, should fate absolutely insist upon it.

Stopping at her boardinghouse lodgings on St. Aldate's to drop off the suitcase and despair briefly over the dust that had accumulated while she'd been away, she collected her bicycle, then set off for the Museum of Natural History, wherein Oxford University's ornithology department was located. Twice, students from her classes waved to her, and she felt compelled to pause and check in on their welfare, encourage their summer reading, and inquire about any interesting birds they had seen. Consequently, it was twenty minutes before she finally reached Professor Gladstone's office. Standing outside the door, her determination began wavering as she stared at the nameplate that someone, in an old and hallowed student tradition, had sabotaged to read "Professor BadStoned."

"I'm doing this in the name of science," she reassured herself as she drew the pin from her hat and inserted it in the door's lock. Nevertheless, her breath ran away to hide at the back of her lungs. Gladstone's secretary had informed her that the gentleman departed some time ago for the Peak District, which was indeed his annual tradition, but in the excitement of the competition Beth had forgotten it. At least with him being over one hundred miles away, it should be safe to search his office for clues about the caladrius.

On the other hand, being a teacher, Beth naturally expected the worst. Slipping cautiously into the warm, cluttered room and closing the door behind her, she turned toward Gladstone's desk—

And the breath shook out of her.

Devon sat in Gladstone's chair. With one leg crossed over

the other, his elbow on the armrest and his jaw set between thumb and finger, he looked exactly like a professor willing to spend no more than three minutes listening to your excuse for missing the exam—except for the smug smile that clearly conveyed *ha ha, got here before you.*

Beth's heart soared like an American bald eagle, even while her brain closed its eyes, knowing the fatal plummet that was sure to come.

DEVON HAD TAKEN only one step into Gladstone's office before he wanted to walk right back out and go in search of the strongest whiskey Oxford offered. An imposing clutter of books, maps, papers, and taxidermied birds packed the space so thoroughly, it seemed time could find no access. He smelled ash from a pipe that must have been smoked weeks ago, and noted a portrait of King George III on the wall with a dodo bird mounted beside in it what he suspected was a non-ironic placement. As a student at Yale, he'd visited offices like this often, trying to explain to stern-faced professors how his grades could be so good while his behavior was *so very bad.* In contrast, his own office at Cambridge was little more than a desk, a comfortable chair, and a jar of peppermints to share with anxious students.

But he was also willing to bet that somewhere amid this antiquated mess lay a clue as to the caladrius's whereabouts. And more importantly, he expected Beth would be along soon to uncover it. So he sat behind the professor's desk and waited for her, like an Alaskan cat-catching warbler waiting for its prey. Like an utter scoundrel.

And then she arrived, so sweet and summery in her floral

dress and pale gold boater that the grimy shadows in both the office and his heart seemed to fade away. *Home*, he thought with a silent sigh. Which was ridiculous, considering he'd only known the woman for a short while. And yet somehow, Beth Pickering had become a safe hearth for him.

"What are you doing here?" she demanded with a censorious frown. Devon struggled not to grin delightedly.

"Fieldwork, same as you." Leaning back in the chair, he set his booted feet on the desk in a deliberate provocation. And sure enough, her frown deepened. He loved to see it. He wanted to push her against the crammed bookshelves and kiss all the most interesting places on her body until that frown was twisting with pleasure. But more than that, he wanted to be the kind of man this bookish, brilliant woman might come to like. So he just sat quietly.

"Villain," she said, not fooled in the least.

He shrugged. "Ornithologist. I'm actually surprised we're the only ones here. At the very least, I thought you'd reunited with Mrs. Quirm."

"I left her on the train, heading for the Cotswolds."

He grinned. "Ruthless woman."

"Ruthless enough to shout for a custodian to drag you out of here and have you arrested for trespassing and—and—academic espionage."

It was a lie. She was *flirting* with him. Did this mean she liked him? Not that it mattered, since she would absolutely stop liking him when she learned of his fundamental defect, but nevertheless the question remained, *did she like him*? And what could he do to get her liking him even more? (A subsidiary question, *was he going to recollect sometime soon how to breathe?* was dismissed as being unimportant.)

He continued regarding her in silence, partly because it made him appear masterful, and partly because his body had a most emphatic response of its own to those questions, and he desperately needed time to drag it back into control. Never before had he been more thankful for the challenges of receiving a university education at a young age, alone in a foreign country; it had taught him, if nothing else, how to hide all kinds of feelings behind a calm facade. Finally he stood, rounding the desk.

Beth did not move, although judging from the darkening storm in her eyes, she was feeling rather woozy too. Devon walked toward her, coming so close he felt the anticipation sparking off her as their arms almost, *almost* brushed together . . . and then he veered away.

"I'm not here for academic espionage," he said, crossing to the bookshelves while Beth struggled to inhale behind him. He randomly inspected books, wooden birds, snuffboxes. "Gladstone is chairman of the International Ornithological Society."

"And?"

He cast a wry smile over his shoulder at her. "And you know there's something suspicious going on. Carnivorous lapwing, feuerfinch, frostbird: three trained magical birds, the first appearing in Paris on the same day news of the competition was published. Only people with advance knowledge, and access to such rare birds, could have been involved. IOS is the obvious suspect, and therefore, by association, Gladstone. Tell me that clever brain of yours hasn't reached the same conclusion."

"Why would IOS do such a thing?" Beth asked—but he knew it was in a Socratic way, already having her own answer and wanting to elicit his. *So she fancied playing teacher with him, did she?* He liked that game. Turning back toward her, he prepared to make another seductive approach.

But Beth walked away. Captivated, he watched her move to Gladstone's desk, where she donned her spectacles and began shifting papers, opening drawers. Finally his brain shook itself back into action.

"Perhaps they want to create drama," he said. "And keep ornithologists busy."

She glanced up at him over the rim of the spectacles, approval in her eyes, and Devon's stomach went all twinkly like it used to do whenever he got an answer right in school.

"Why wouldn't ornithologists be busy enough hunting the caladrius?" she asked.

Time to turn her game back onto her. "Why do *you* think, Miss Pickering?"

"I think the caladrius isn't in the wild at all," she said, her tone far lighter than the statement warranted. Devon was rather stunned that she'd just come right out and said it. He couldn't imagine any other competitor doing the same; indeed, had Hippolyta Quirm or Klaus Oberhufter been standing in this room instead of her, they'd probably have whacked Devon over the head with the taxidermied dodo by now and stolen his wallet.

Picking up a notebook, Beth flipped through its pages. Devon waited breathlessly for the next word out of her mouth, as if it would be gold.

"It seems to me that IOS would not run a competition without being confident of there being a good outcome," she said as she paused at one page, then another, assessing their contents. "Even with dozens of ornithologists on the job, finding one small white bird in all of England is like trying to find a needle in a *Philetairus socius*'s nest. This suggests IOS has possession of the caladrius and intends to rig the contest as they see fit. I came here to present my theory to Professor Gladstone in return for some answers. But he's not here. He may have left behind revealing information, however."

"How angelic of you to tell all of this to your rival," Devon remarked.

Setting down the notebook, she shrugged. "Prevarication seems rather pointless, considering we're both operating under the same conclusion. We are, aren't we?"

Their eyes met, and between them shot an understanding so mutual, Devon had to think very fast, very firmly, of cold showers and ice storms.

"We are," he said. Turning away with some effort, he put his hands on his hips as he regarded the cluttered room. "Although we'll be lucky to find any proof of our theory in this mess."

Beth lifted a piece of paper from atop a ramshackle stack and stared at it. "You mean like a letter between Professor Gladstone and the IOS secretary, explaining everything?"

"Seriously, there's a letter?" he said, striding across.

"What?" She looked up at him vaguely, then at the paper again. "Oh. No, this is just his grocery list. But I mean, such a letter would be the ideal proof."

Devon laughed. "My God, I love—"

"Of course!" she exclaimed suddenly, snapping her fingers. Startled, confused, Devon felt himself actually blushing.

But she was not even looking at him, let alone cognizant of what he'd almost said. Casting aside the piece of paper, she began to stride across the office. Devon shifted awkwardly on his feet, not knowing, for the first time in years, what to do. As Beth disappeared through the doorway, he hurried after her like a duckling.

"Where are we going?" he asked as they made their way along the dusty corridor.

"I am going to my office," she said.

He almost tripped over his feet, for entering Beth Pickering's office was even more a titillating prospect than being invited into another woman's bedroom. When she stopped at a door and began rummaging through her satchel for the key, it was all he could do to not lean seductively against the wall, smile, and call her beautiful out of sheer habit.

Opening the door, she astonished and delighted him by not shutting it in his face. He followed her into the room, looking around surreptitiously so as to see everything while still appearing rakishly insouciant. It was all exactly as he'd guessed it would be, from the scrupulously tidy desk to the watercolor paintings of birds set in a precise line on one wall, to the books he was willing to bet were shelved alphabetically—and, in one corner, a rubbish bin overflowing with scrunched papers, which was the officewares equivalent of her battered fingernails.

Beth said nothing, but the awkwardness of her movement as she walked behind the desk revealed just how shy she felt in allowing Devon to see her professional space. He was touched, and also more enamored of her than seemed reasonable for a man who had spent the past decade of his life developing unsentimentality into a fine art. Usually by this point in his relationship with a woman he'd be suggesting interesting ways to mess up that desk of hers. But instead he found himself fighting back the desire to buy some beeswax polish and offer to polish her furniture until it shone. And the fact that this wasn't a metaphor disturbed him considerably.

Shoving his hands in his pockets and a bland expression on his face, he watched Beth remove her hat as if she were at home, brushing back fine strands of hair that drifted over her cheekbones and the soft curve of her mouth. His hands fisted, and when she began opening desk drawers and shuffling through their contents, his capacity for lewd metaphor came rushing back in a great torrent. From sheer self-preservation, he forced himself to look away. On the wall behind her were several framed qualifications, and he could imagine how they must daunt her students. The woman was *accomplished*. He also suspected she put those qualifications up not to daunt but to reassure people that she knew what she was doing, because she was nice (and ignorant of human psychology).

"Aha!" she declared, holding up a three-ringed binder triumphantly.

"Proof?" Devon asked.

Opening the binder, flipping to its third page, she bit her thumbnail as she read. "Circumstantial evidence. Last term Professor Gladstone asked for an inventory of all the birds in both his and the department's aviaries that had been included in his T-2 research program. I thought I remembered having seen the frostbird's name somewhere, and here it is." She tapped the page. "Along with the carnivorous lapwing and feuerfinch, among others."

"Huh," Devon said. "Interesting indeed. But the most important question is . . ."

When he paused, she looked up over the rim of her spectacles at him. "Yes?"

"Why is Gladstone getting you to do an inventory for him? That's work for a secretary, not a professor."

Her expression went utterly blank for a moment. Then she blinked, and blushed, and looked everywhere but at him, muttering something about "diligence" and "happy to help" and quite possibly "better than washing dishes." Devon took pity on her—and on himself, since if he remained on that subject, he'd likely find himself in prison for smacking Gladstone in the face.

"What is T-2 research?" he asked.

"I don't know. Professor Gladstone kept it secret. But considering what we've experienced of those birds, probably it involves training them."

A grim pause followed.

"But I must be wrong," Beth murmured, frowning at the inventory. "It's hard to believe even Professor Gladstone would do that. He's a misogynistic reactionary who teaches outdated science, is callous toward his students, and only leaves the tea bag in for less than two seconds . . . But clipping a bird's wings? Manipulating its instincts and exploiting its magic? That represents a corruption unlikely in such a reputed ornithologist."

Devon's knew his face displayed more skepticism than an entire consortium of scientists, but the second Beth looked up at him, so troubled by this threat to her essential goodwill, he smiled. "Perhaps we should draw up a chart of all the possibilities and formulate a hypothesis from that."

The ring binder swung shut. "What kind of chart?" she asked eagerly.

He took a step forward, intensifying his gaze. "A radar chart."

Beth drew in an audible breath of delight, and thus encouraged, he took another step. With the desk between them and the shadows looming like outspread wings behind her, he glimpsed what she must look like in a lecture theater: mesmerizing, and more beautiful than he could ever describe.

"I should clarify something," she said, her voice trembling slightly. "I intend to win this competition regardless of what charms a conniving villain might try to work on me."

Devon set a hand on the desk and leaned forward. "Is that so?"

"We can make a chart, we can even indulge in some analysis, but there can be—"

"Only one Birder of the Year," they chorused.

Devon repressed a sudden wistfulness. "I have a particularly interesting algorithm I'd love to show you," he said.

Then the clever, clever woman turned his world upside down. Setting her own hand on the desk, she leaned forward until her face was mere inches from his. "I know how to plot variables, Mr. Lockley. I read more than field guides, you know."

He watched courage crackle and flare in her lovely, halcyon blue eyes, behind the spectacles. It sparked fires all through his body. "You smell like lavender," he murmured.

She blinked, thrown off-balance, but did not retreat. "It calms birds."

It was doing the opposite to him. He'd tried being good, being restrained, but she was simply too delectable. "I'm going to kiss you," he warned.

Instantly her face turned red, her expression lighting with the same desire that had propelled Devon through Spain and France, then across England in helpless pursuit of her. He moved the last tiny distance, even as she moved to meet him in the middle. Their breath mingled, their lips parting.

*"Aaaaggghhhh!"*

A scream rang out from the museum's courtyard below. Beth jolted back, her eyes growing wide. Devon bowed his head with a frustrated sigh.

*"Tsk,"* she said, pulling off her spectacles as she frowned toward the office window. "Students."

Devon looked up fiercely through his eyelashes at her, determined not to lose the moment's impetus. "I—"

But what words might have followed, he'd never know for sure. *I want you? I'm in love with you? I'm so impressed you won the Audubon Award for Academic Excellence three years in a row?* The truth was lost as another scream broke out, chilling his blood. It was not a human sound, after all. He straightened; Beth turned to him, her face white. They stared at each other in stunned silence as the air began to shake with percussive magic.

"Whooper swan," they identified in unison.

And then they began to run.

## Chapter Fifteen

Faint heart never won fair lady, nor fabulous bird either.

*Birds Through a Sherry Glass*, H.A. Quirm

Down the stairs and through the Arctic birds display chamber they raced, their boots thudding on the stone floor, Beth's hat tumbling unnoticed from her head. Outraged museum patrons scattered before them with cries of *Egad! How rude!* and *Good heavens, Agnes, did you see the thighs on that man?!* In the courtyard outside, they found several people huddled on the grass, moaning and weeping, while others staggered about aimlessly, clutching their ears. A loud, thumping bass note of avian magic assaulted the air, but no bird was to be seen.

"Which way?" Devon shouted to a nearby woman. She stared at him dazedly, her face streaked with tears of blood.

"North!" called out a dark-suited man, waving his bowler hat.

"The park!" Beth said, seeing it in her mind's eye: sunlit grass, gentle tree-lined paths, occupied by dozens of picnickers and pedestrians at this noon hour.

They ran from the courtyard and along the footpath, barely noticing people cowering behind trees and in doorways as screams echoed from the park ahead. Arriving in moments, they discovered a large black swan circling the field. It was shrieking intermittently and exuding a booming magic that sounded like an orchestra's drum section had jammed itself into a tin box. Several groups of picnickers huddled beneath large umbrellas or blankets, clutching their cushions and hampers, unable to flee without risking attack.

"*Major cygnus malleus,*" Beth identified as she came to a halt beneath an elm tree.

"This one, you can't touch," Devon warned. "Its magic will break your bones."

Beth abstained from rolling her eyes due to the urgency of the moment. Maybe later she would commission a badge showing her qualifications so that men would stop advising her on the basics of her job. "If we can get it to land," she said, "we can use one of those umbrellas to pin it down."

"It's attracted to shiny metal objects," Devon added, looking around as if expecting a mobile jewelry vendor to be in operation nearby.

"Hm. Perhaps if we—"

"FEAR NOT, GOOD PEOPLE! I SHALL SAVE YOU!"

Startled, they turned to see a young man emerge from the trees nearby, waving both hands in general greeting as he jogged onto the field. His shoulder-length hair and cheap, oversized suit fluttered in the breeze. Overhead, the whopper swan screeched.

"Who the hell is that?" Devon said.

Before Beth could supply a response, the man held up a coil of thin braided leather and, with a flick of his wrist, sent it unfurling dramatically. Then he whistled in three short, loud bursts to the bird.

"Oh my God," Beth gasped.

"Jesus," Devon muttered at the same time.

*Eeeeeeee!* the swan added in a distinctly more pagan tone.

"STIFFEN YOUR SINEWS and STAY WHERE YOU ARE!" the young man urged the picnickers, none of whom appeared to require such instruction. "I'LL CATCH THE BIRD!"

He whistled again, and the whopper swan shrieked with aggravation. Soaring high, its wings rapping the air with every beat, it reached a pinnacle and began to turn . . .

"It's going to dive," Beth and Devon said in unison.

*Crack!* went the young man's whip.

*Boom!* responded the swan's magic.

The air shattered into a thousand discordant splinters. Beth and Devon clamped their hands over their ears, to little effect. Thaumaturgic noise slammed through every cell of their bodies, making them stagger in pain. People screamed, leaves exploded through the flashing sunlight, and the young man hollered as he cracked the whip again. The whopper swan tucked in its wings and began to plummet.

Once more the young man whistled, but the sound was lost in pounding shocks of magic. A tragedy in three acts played out rapidly on his face: smugness, confusion, horror. He dropped the whip and cowered, arms wrapping defensively over his head. The swan skimmed inches above him, then soared again. *Thump thump thump* went its wings, considerably more steady than Beth's heartbeat. She shot an ornithological glance at Devon; he gave her a brief, silent nod, then took off running toward the nearest group of picnickers. Without hesitating, Beth dashed for the young man.

"Excuse me, may I?" she asked as she snatched his whip from the ground.

"Aahhh!" he replied from his hunched position, which she took for permission. Quickly tying the leather rope into a lasso, she began to spin it overhead, building momentum.

*Boom!* The swan emitted another thundering bass note as it circled, preparing to dive again. Assessing its likely trajectory, Beth adjusted her stance. From the corner of her eye she noted Devon hurrying toward her, picnic umbrella propped against his shoulder. Excitement rushed through her, intensifying as it synchronized with the swan's magic, pounding hard until she began to feel more than human. Her vision filled with sunlight and sable wings.

She threw the lasso. It fell over the swan's back and instantly she tugged, tightening the noose. The bird tumbled, its magic scattering like the discordant sound of grief.

*Whoosh.*

Devon swung the open picnic umbrella with a strength Beth could only imagine (i.e., him using it to lift her easily and set her against a wall, holding her there while he kissed every qualification out of her brain), and he ladled the swan out of the air. In one swift moment he brought it down safely, immediately tipping the umbrella over it as a shield.

*Screeee!* cried the bird in fear. But all that could be heard of wild, wing-rapped magic was a soft scratching against the canvas. Devon stomped on the umbrella's long handle. It snapped, and the canopy dropped fully. Setting a booted foot upon it for added security, Devon shook the hair off his face and looked sidelong at Beth, bouncing his eyebrows.

"Good job," she said. "Perhaps a Yale doctorate is worth something after all."

"Why, Miss Pickering," Devon replied wryly, "it seems the farther we travel into England, the more impolite you get."

Beth pursed her lips in indignation (and because she could not immediately think of a witty reply). Luckily, just then the young man unfurled himself, rising on his knees. His nose was bleeding as a consequence of the bird's percussive magic, but he appeared otherwise unharmed.

"Blimey!" he shouted. "That was awesome! How did you catch the bird with just one toss of the rope?"

"Expertise," Beth told him.

"That's what comes of being a UNIVERSITY-TRAINED ORNLITHOLOGIST!" he said, his voice ringing through the shivering silence across the field.

"Um," Beth said, bewildered. "Are you all right?"

"I am now!" He leaped to his feet and began to applaud her with such loud enthusiasm, Beth winced. "You SAVED MY LIFE! This day shall be remember'd to the ENDING OF THE WORLD! HURRAH FOR ORNLITHOLOGISTS!"

Beth glanced at Devon, who appeared equally bemused. Behind him, picnickers were beginning to emerge from beneath their umbrellas and behind the shelter of trees. The young man turned to them, his clapping intensifying, and after a moment they obediently began to clap also.

"Who are you?" Devon asked with a suspicious frown.

"Laz Brady, good sir!" He used the back of his hand to wipe the blood dripping from his nose, then held out that same hand in an offer of a handshake. Devon didn't even glance at it, and he snatched it back faster than a seagull snatching a sandwich from a picnic. "I'm a mere wag who DREAMS of becoming a proper ornlithologist one day! I thought perchance it was enough to know a bird's song, and to be able to tell a blackbird from a starlink—"

"Starling," Beth corrected.

"—but clearly if I WANT TO BE A HERO and SAVE LIVES, I need to ENROLL IN A UNIVERSITY SUCH AS OXFORD, CAMBRIDGE, OR THE SORE BONE—"

"Sorbonne," Devon corrected.

"—and get a \*\**DEGREE IN ORNLITHOLOGY!*\*\*"

Beth and Devon looked at each other. "Huh," they said in unison.

"What will you do with the bird now?" Laz Brady asked eagerly.

"Transport it to the departmental aviary," Beth said. Pausing with her hands on her hips, she contemplated the umbrella, beneath which the whopper swan was chittering pathetically. "It might be difficult, however, without a cage or even a black-out bag."

"You mean one of these?" Laz asked, whipping out from beneath his jacket a sack of black canvas.

"Gosh," Beth said. "You just happened to have that on you?"

"Of course! When a man DREAMS of—"

"Never mind," Devon interrupted, snatching the sack. He cast an impatient frown at the young man. "Just stand there. *Quietly.*"

Laz nodded, bouncing on his heels and positively radiating mute excitement.

Together, Beth and Devon worked with swift efficiency to bag the swan, subduing its magic within quiet, heavy darkness. They had just completed this task when a small crowd began to approach them, pale and tremulous.

"You saved us!" exclaimed a woman, blinking eyes that were streaked with red from ruptured blood vessels. "I thought that noise would shatter me!"

"You're heroes!" enthused an elderly man, and everyone nodded in agreement.

"Can I have your autograph?" asked a girl, holding out a handkerchief and pen.

"Um," Beth said trepidatiously. This was the part of bird catching that Hippolyta managed, and quite frankly she'd rather face another dozen whopper swans than talk to these people.

"We were just doing our job," Devon said with the precise degree of humility required to make it clear they *profoundly excelled* in that job.

"Hey, you're the otholigists from the newspaper!" the woman said, pointing at them. "The ones having a romance."

"Ooooh," chorused the crowd.

"Are you betrothed?" asked the elderly man.

"Are you going to catch the caladrius together?" asked another. "It's in Cardiff, you know!"

"Kiss for us!" urged the girl, flapping her handkerchief.

Immediately Laz took up the cry. *"Kiss! Kiss!"*

"Kiss! Kiss!" The crowd began to applaud, whistle, and stamp their feet.

"Goodness me," Beth murmured. Inside her brain, etiquette squared up to a sudden rush of aroused nerves. She felt assured of its victory . . . then Devon grinned at her, and etiquette collapsed beneath a rappelling squad of desires, all bedecked in hot-pink armor.

"Ma'am?" he asked, sounding so American, the desires whipped out star-spangled flags and began fanning her into a high heat.

"Fine," she said, brittle and haughty despite how shaky she actually was. She shook back her hair and tilted her face, lips stiff with anxiety as they awaited his kiss.

But instead, Devon took her hand gently in his, tugging on the glove finger by finger until he could slide it off.

The crowd went wild.

Beth's nervous system did the same. A kiss would have been somehow safe in its familiarity, but this introduced a whole new kind of eroticism. Devon slipped the glove into his trouser pocket, and suddenly Beth apprehended she was in danger—beautiful, luscious, very real danger that she did not particularly want to escape. His thumb stroked her naked fingers, and just like that she was conquered by desire, colonized, and had an embassy of lust erected beneath her heart. She gazed into Devon's eyes, bespelled by the coppery glints amid the darkness. He did not look away from her, even as he bent his head slowly, wickedly, holding her and the crowd in a moment of awed anticipation . . .

Then he kissed her hand.

"Aaaahhh," gasped the crowd in unison with Beth's heart.

It was the lightest of kisses, but it reached deep inside her to stroke some exquisitely sensitive nerve and illuminate her inner darkness like the magical flash of some bird whose name she could not even begin to remember in that moment. She could barely remember her own.

All around them, the crowd cheered, but might as well have been birds chirping in the trees. Devon closed his eyes, and Beth felt his breath sighing over her knuckles as he kissed her again, slower, heavier, as if he was sinking into a dream.

"Uh . . ." the crowd murmured awkwardly.

Beth's stomach fluttered, and her brain released a thought it did not know it was thinking.

*I want him so much.*

She would have pulled away then, citing proper etiquette as

a defense against getting hurt, but Devon seemed to sense it and straightened, his mouth sliding into a complacent smile that Beth suddenly realized was his own form of defense. As their eyes met, the wary, fragile truth leaped between them.

Devon laid her hand to his heart, holding it there with his own. A silent thunder beat against her palm, and Beth swallowed heavily. He'd caught her. He'd pulled her from the aching, empty summer and offered a sanctuary for her in his midnight. Etiquette, wounded and bleeding out, urged her to move back from him. But she could no more do that than she could believe in a conclusion based on uncontrolled experiments.

People forgotten, swan forgotten, they gazed at each other across a private, quiet sky.

The crowd began clearing their throats and shuffling impatiently.

*This was not fun anymore*, Beth thought. *This was falling in love.*

"ROMANCE: ANOTHER REASON TO STUDY ORNLITHOLOGY!" Laz declared, making them jolt. They stumbled back from each other, blinking in disorientation. Over Devon's shoulder, Beth glimpsed two dark-suited figures lurking behind an elm tree.

Her instincts shook. "We have to go," she whispered.

Devon regarded her soberly, taking in her sudden concern. Without a word he returned her glove, then bent to gather up the bagged swan. Turning away from the crowd, he set a hand against her back to guide her toward the park gates. The fact that he did not question her, nor hesitate to do as she advised, made Beth tingle all over again.

Then he gave Laz a frown that equated to a failing grade,

and her tingling became a decided twang. "Do not even think of approaching a thaumaturgic bird again until you've had some training," he ordered.

"Yes, sir!" Laz saluted briskly. "I shall follow your inspiring example of ornlithololgical study at one of the EXCELLENT UNIVERSITIES here in England and abroad!"

"Right."

And they walked away, leaving a dozen blushing, whispering picnickers (and two highly satisfied publicists).

♥

# CHAPTER SIXTEEN

One swallow does not make a summer—unless you
create an aviary for yourself full of bright flowers and
one magical sun-rousing swallow, that is.
*Birds Through a Sherry Glass*, H.A. Quirm

THERE'S ONLY ONE conclusion we can reach now," Beth said,
pulling her glove back on as they walked back to the
museum.

"I agree," Devon answered firmly.

"Someone is trying to help us," she said.

"Someone is trying to kill us," Devon said at the same time.

They stopped in the middle of the footpath, staring at each
other.

"What?" Beth said.

"What?" Devon said.

Beth shook her head and continued toward the museum.
"That's the kind of faulty thinking I expect from a Cambridge
professor," she said with a fine hauteur.

"And yours is the kind I expect from someone who thinks
a demonic strix owl is a cuddly bit of fluff," Devon countered,
shifting the whopper swan more comfortably in his arms as he
kept pace with her.

Beth gasped. "I never said such a thing!"

"But you think it, don't you?"

She lifted her chin and glared at the path ahead, all bristling indignation. "It is possible that I might, but that is irrelevant."

"I swear, when this competition is over, I am going to buy you a new dictionary."

Beth flicked him a disdainful sidelong look, but humor tugged at her mouth. "Villain," she said lightly.

"Angel," he retorted.

They shared a smile of camaraderie that made Beth's nerves flutter even more than the kiss had done. Devon ducked his head, staring down at his feet as if he suddenly needed to remind himself how to walk.

Arriving back at the museum's courtyard and finding it abandoned, they passed through an uncanny silence, the stunned aftermath of the whopper swan's magic. Bags, books, and half-eaten food lay scattered on the grass. Behind the great, honey-colored museum, the sky hung breathless, shocked. Beth couldn't help but shiver.

In the next moment, Devon moved closer to her, his height a bulwark, his warm shadow a promise that she would be safe no matter what flew out of that sky at them. *Such machismo nonsense*, Beth thought with an internal huff.

*Squee!* her heart replied, hugging itself. She could still feel the softness of his kiss against her hand. She wanted more than anything for him to kiss other places on her body. Forehead . . . cheek . . . places she dared not name even to herself.

(*"Tenure!"* her brain shouted, but it could not be heard over the throbbing of those unmentionable places.)

"After we take the swan to safety," Devon said, "shall we go for coffee to discuss what happened?"

"Uughhgnnngggh," Beth answered, and was relieved to hear it come out as a calm, casual "All right." She despised coffee, but that scarcely signified at a time like this.

Her excitement was dashed, however, almost as soon as they entered the cold, white-tiled antechamber of the departmental aviary.

"Professor Gladstone didn't want the bird after all?" the aviary keeper asked when they presented her with the whopper swan in its blackout bag.

"Professor Gladstone?" they echoed in identical tones of suspicion.

"You must be mistaken," Beth said. "Professor Gladstone is in the Peak District."

The aviary keeper shrugged, cradling the swan to her plump bosom as if it were a sad child rather than a deadly magical beast. Behind her, the grimy, glass-paned wall of the aviary seemed to flicker as birds leaped and flew and stalked each other through the trees. Their songs and murderous cries filtered dimly through to the antechamber, and Beth's brain automatically identified them even as it multitasked itself with wondering if Gladstone was still in Oxford, why he had released the whopper swan, and whether she should order cake along with her coffee during the ~~date~~ professional meeting with Devon.

"His signature was on the request form," the keeper said as she rocked the swan gently. "The men said he wanted it for a practicum class." Leaning across her desk, she shuffled with her free hand through a stack of papers until she located the one she wanted. "There," she said, holding it out.

Taking the form, Beth brought out her spectacles and perused it quickly. "This was filled out several weeks ago."

"How can you tell?" the keeper asked, wide-eyed.

"Several letters are crooked, and the signature, while true, is more rigid than usual. Professor Gladstone strained his wrist just before the end of term, and it temporarily affected his penmanship."

The keeper gasped in delighted amazement at such deduction.

"Also, the date written here is June the thirteenth." She returned the form to the stack, five levels down, from whence the keeper had taken it. "Professor Gladstone obviously prepared it in advance of his departure and left it with someone to use whenever they needed," she said as she aligned the stack's edges neatly.

"Who were the men that came for the bird?" Devon asked.

The keeper shrugged. "They never gave their names. Two fine-looking chaps, dressed in expensive suits."

"Schreib and Cholmbaumgh," Devon muttered darkly.

"Maybe," Beth said. "But there were two men standing at the edge of the park, watching us catch the swan, and I could have sworn I saw them on the train from London too."

Devon raised an eyebrow. "Mustaches, bowler hats, carrying briefcases?"

"That's them," Beth and the aviary keeper said in unison.

Devon nodded. "I saw them on the train too. And I'm fairly sure one of them was in the Hôtel Chauvesouris lobby when we were leaving for the ferry."

"I was obviously wrong about someone trying to help us," Beth said.

"I need something stronger than coffee before I answer that," Devon said. "Then again, I think I might skip a drink altogether and just get straight on a train for the Peak District. Obviously the person with the real answers is Gladstone."

Beth's heart sagged, but she reminded it sternly about her desire to win tenure. "That's a good idea," she said. "I might do the same."

"We should go together," Devon suggested, and Beth's heart perked up. "We're still rivals, of course, but it's only sensible that we keep company until we know who is setting birds on us, and why." His posture seemed uncharacteristically tense, but his tone was casual, so casual, he made it sound like they were discussing merely crossing the street.

"Sensible indeed," Beth answered with the same nonchalance, even while her heart lifted so high she thought it might take flight.

Devon smiled. "Besides," he added, leaning close with a glint in his eye, "it will be more fun."

*Thwomp.* Her heart collapsed back in a dreamy, glimmery swoon. She smiled before she even knew what she was doing, and Devon's pupils dilated in response. Realizing she'd done that to him, Beth curved the smile like a western grebe curving its neck to attract a mate. Devon rocked slightly on his heels, and Beth could only conclude from this evidence that she'd stumbled by pure accident onto her feminine wiles. She inhaled with surprise at the same moment Devon quietly sighed. It was like the soft promise of a kiss, reaching between them to—

*"Ahem,"* said the aviary keeper.

Dazed, Beth pulled herself out of the absorbingly sensual moment and turned to give the woman a polite nod—and Devon, turning alongside her, nudged her elbow with his in a friendly manner that forced her to nod a second time while trying desperately to recall the mechanism of speech.

"Good day, Mrs. Daughty," she managed at last. "Thank you for your help."

The keeper did not immediately reply, instead scrutinizing her as if she were a bird just brought in from the wild. "You look different from when I saw you last term, Professor."

"Oh?"

"Almost . . . happy. I haven't seen you look happy in, well, ever."

"Ha ha," Beth said. Turning away, she pulled off her spectacles, despite wishing she could keep them on so that the world—and Devon's suddenly solemn expression—would remain a blur. "I have to go home for my suitcase," she told him. "I'll meet you at the station."

A shadow of worry slipped through his eyes. "You *will* meet me?"

Biting her lip, Beth nodded. Then she swept out of the aviary faster than a cat escaping an Alaskan warbler, before her feminine wiles did something terrifying.


"WELL, THAT COULDN'T have gone better," Mr. Fettick said to Mr. Flogg. They were nibbling on buttered scones at a table in Jabbercoffee, a small, slightly crooked coffeehouse opposite the Lamb and Flag Passage in Oxford, to which they'd retired after witnessing the whopper swan's capture. "Our two professors did exactly as we hoped. *'Birders in Blissful Moment After Saving the Day!'*"

"I myself would have removed some of the prurient behavior from the scene," Mr. Flogg said with a disapproving little sniff.

"But we *want* this to be a romance," Mr. Fettick reminded him.

"Yes, but if they could close a door on the more explicit details—"

"He only kissed her hand, man."

"Twice. And he took off her glove to do so. And, well, there was a good deal of *gazing* . . ."

Both men flushed intensely. Mr. Flogg gulped tea; Mr. Fettick dolloped marmalade onto his scone bottom. Finally, after a long, rather titillated moment of silence, Mr. Flogg cleared his throat briskly.

"In any case, we must congratulate ourselves. The whopper swan provided excellent drama on what was shaping up to be a slow news day."

"That young Lazarus Brady did a marvelous job," Mr. Fettick said. "One couldn't even tell he was acting! We shall have to hire him for more scenes."

They smiled with the particular satisfaction of men who have paid someone below minimum wage for excellent results.

"Furthermore," Mr. Flogg said, "we've managed to slow our professors down. Almost certainly they will be resting together after such a rousing experience—"

"'*Resting*,'" Mr. Fettick sniggered, inducing Mr. Flogg to scowl.

"Furthermore, the caladrius remains safely tucked away, university bookstores everywhere have sold out of ornithology textbooks, and tourism companies report being besieged by inquiries. Everything's perfectly on track!"

*Tinkle tinkle.*

The little copper bell above the coffee-shop door rang. Messrs. Flogg and Fettick glanced up to see Cholmbaumgh enter. He stopped abruptly, staring at himself in the ornate mirror that hung opposite the door. The sight made him jolt, rabbitlike, and no wonder, for his eyes were rimmed with shadow, his jaw unshaven, his jacket severely wrinkled. Noticing the publicists, he trudged over and dropped into the empty chair beside Mr. Flogg.

"I'm exhausted," he said. "First I chased Miss Pickering while she cycled from her lodgings to the university, then I chased her back to her lodgings, then onward from there to the train station. I'm all for allowing women to advance in society, but must they do it on wheels?"

Mr. Fettick frowned. "What are you talking about? According to the most likely narrative, Miss Pickering should at this moment be somewhere in private with Mr. Lockley, enjoying an intimate conversation, the particulars of which we shall politely not consider. This has all been plotted with care, down to the decidedly expensive fact that no hotel in Oxford currently has a vacancy of more than one room."

"I didn't understand half of what you said, mate," Cholmbaumgh admitted, "but unless it was 'Miss Pickering got on a northbound train some twenty minutes ago,' your plot has a hole in it."

"Egad!" the publicists exclaimed. Mr. Flogg whipped off his bowler hat in a frenzy of astonished dismay. Mr. Fettick dropped his scone bottom, sending marmalade splattering across the plate.

"Ornithologists really are ruthless," Mr. Flogg said. "How could she leave him after he was so romantic in the park?"

"I'm starting to think we should have listened more closely to Monsieur Badeau when he warned us about Miss Pickering," Mr. Flogg said gloomily. "I didn't expect the pretty girl to show her own sense of agency."

"Where is Lockley?" Mr. Fettick asked.

"On the train," said a new voice. Everyone turned to see Schreib approach the table. "I followed him there and saw him get on, just now. He bought a ticket for Hathersage in the Peak District."

"That's where Miss Pickering was going," Cholmbaumgh said. "Excellent news! They're together after all."

Mr. Fettick shook his head. "Not excellent news. Professor Gladstone's country house is just outside Hathersage."

"Blast!" Mr. Flogg cried. "Who'd have guessed they would outsmart us in this way?"

No one answered, but in the quiet floated a long list of teachers, thesis committee members, university staff, students, and casual bystanders who could have warned them that Beth and Devon, having obtained their doctorates and professorships at an uncannily young age, were probably going to be pretty clever.

Mr. Fettick sighed extensively. "So much for slowing them down. They weren't supposed to go to Hathersage for ages yet. We need at least another week of them traveling around the countryside, having adventures, and altogether inspiring the population. *'Birders Give Wings to Britain's Imagination!'*"

"We can't damage the train tracks again to stop them," Mr. Flogg mused. "Apparently that was 'over the top' and 'a threat to public safety.'" He rolled his eyes.

"Why don't you just throw another magical bird at them?" Schreib asked.

Mr. Flogg shook his head. "If we're too repetitive, we risk getting stale. Besides, I'm sick of being pecked, frozen, and covered in feathers. I'll never be able to enjoy a scented candle again after dealing with that carnivorous lapwing. I can't believe I'm saying this, but it's possible to have *too much* vanilla aroma."

"Maybe we should just tell them the truth and ask them to collude with us," Mr. Fettick said.

"They're scientists," Mr. Flogg argued. "There's too much risk that they'll be *ethical* about the whole thing."

A doleful silence fell over the group, broken only by the dry little sound of Mr. Flogg scratching his mustache. Then suddenly, he straightened. "Maybe we can't stall them, but I have a new idea!" He directed a cunning smile at Mr. Fettick, whose eyes lit up.

"Ooh, I can see your mind whirring, Otis."

"It's waltzing, Chester. *Waltzing!* Gather round, boys, let me tell you the new plan. 'A Fresh Wind for Famous Lovebirds.' We need . . ." He began ticking off items with his fingers. "Train tickets, details of every hotel in Hathersage, the address of the village telegraph office, something with which to blackmail the local constable, birdseed . . ."

# CHAPTER SEVENTEEN

Courtship dances are not only for the birds.
*Birds Through a Sherry Glass*, H.A. Quirm

Beth was delighted to find that Devon was right about the journey north being "fun." The moment they settled into a private compartment on the train, he closed the curtains, removed his coat, and brought Beth to a state of bliss by taking a long nap, thus allowing her two peaceful hours to read the latest *Ibis* magazine.

Upon his awakening, they visited the dining car and enjoyed wine and scallops, steamed cod, and assorted petit fours, while Beth revealed all the fascinating details of the *Ibis* articles and Devon listened with every sign of enthrallment. Indeed, he barely shifted his gaze from her face as she spoke, a rapt smile on his face, leading Beth to reflect that, despite all appearances, he really was a serious academic at heart.

It did feel a little dangerous to think about his appearances, however, especially since they currently retained the soft, lush-eyed look of sleep, and his lips glinted, wine-dewed, in the lamplight, and the way he stroked one finger slowly against the goblet as he listened to her created such a flutter in her stomach, she began to worry that the scallops were off. What would it feel like to have that finger stroke the source of those flutterings? Would she ever have the courage to suggest an experiment? And if she did, would he be willing?

"Yes," he said, and drank wine, smiling, as Beth's intellect scattered to the winds.

"I—um—I beg your p-pardon?" she stammered.

"Whatever that dreamy expression on your face is about, yes."

"But you don't know what I was thinking."

He set the wineglass down and leaned forward across the table. "I'll always say yes to you, Miss Pickering."

In that sizzling, breathless moment, Beth's brain ran around desperately trying to retrieve its intellect, and her heart just ran around until she felt quite giddy. But she'd survived two thesis defenses, and there remained in her that same strength, allowing her to at least say, "That is good news, since I want the last petit four."

He grinned and sat back in his chair, gesturing to the plate. "As you wish."

But when they changed trains in Suffolk, "fun" took a nosedive sharper than that of a gannet hunting fish. Each purchased a copy of the evening newspaper, and after boarding the westbound train, they settled in to read, hoping to save themselves from the torment of small talk. This they achieved with remarkable success by becoming utterly dumbstruck the moment they saw the front-page headline.

———

### LOVEBIRDS SAVE THE DAY AGAIN!

———

The article spent two paragraphs describing their capture of the whopper swan—and five thereafter analyzing in depth the kiss that had followed. Included were profiles of Professor Beth Pickering, "England's Cleverest Woman," recently returned from tracking dangerous birds through the wilds of Europe, and Professor Devon Lockley, "The Sightly Scholar," for whom hearts on either side of the Atlantic beat fast.

Beth, beginning to hyperventilate, looked around instinctively for tea. But considering they'd not only got her name right this time but also included a horrifyingly accurate illustration of Devon's kissing her hand, she really needed something like chloroform. On the seat opposite, Devon was biting his lip in what appeared suspiciously like an effort not to laugh.

She considered leaving him to sit elsewhere, but the train was jam-packed. She then considered chastising him, but that would require her to discuss the article, and although her inner sense of etiquette was now so thoroughly plucked and seasoned she could have served it for American Thanksgiving, the thought of such an intimate conversation while they were in the forced proximity of only one train compartment terrified her. *Actually kissing him* would be less daunting than talking about it.

She dared to glance at him again, and intuited from the hot intensity of his stare that he was sharing the same thought. Immediately she retreated behind the newspaper and spent the remaining half hour of the journey pretending to read it while her brain indulged in visions of being kissed by the Sightly Scholar until her breath came so fast it could have outpaced the train.

Arriving in the picturesque village of Hathersage just as the sun was beginning to set, they stood on the train station platform with their suitcases at their feet and stared out over the softly rolling hills. Old, red-gold light glossed the land, tempting its outlaw ghosts from the shadows of plump ash trees and brightening farmhouse windows. A fragrance of grass, sun-baked stone, and rail dust freshened their senses after hours of being indoors.

"Magnificent," Beth breathed.

"Truly," Devon agreed.

"It must have a wingspan of six feet at least, for us to see it from this distance."

Devon squinted against the light as he watched the enormous hawk swoop over farmland. "*Buteo colossaeus*," he murmured. "It can kill a cow with one swipe of its claws."

They sighed in happy unison. Beth's hand twitched with a desire to sketch the bird, and Devon's hand stirred as he imagined inspecting one of those long brown feathers—and despite their standing three feet apart, each shivered as if their fingers had brushed against the other's.

"The locals call it Little John," Beth said, clutching at ornithology to keep her steady. "It's the only one of its kind remaining and is too old now to endanger livestock. Professor Gladstone pays the farmers an annual stipend to not shoot it so he can come every summer to work on a longitudinal study of it."

"Where is his house?" Devon asked, entirely casual, but with a sidelong glance at her that conveyed, *I want to do a longitudinal study of your body.*

Beth swallowed dryly. "About half a mile west of the village."

"Half a mile? In these shoes?" Devon frowned down at his thick-soled boots, in which he'd tramped across much of America.

"I lost my hat running for the whopper swan and am going

to get terribly sunburned," Beth said, even as twilight filled her vision with shadows.

They turned their heads and stared at each other.

Ten minutes later, the innkeeper of the George, Hathersage's coaching inn, consulted her reservations ledger while they panted from having practically run there. "Why, yes, we can accommodate you," she said, smiling. "A telegram came in just this afternoon, booking out most of the inn, but luckily there is *one room left!* And with an excellent view of the sky, in case an interesting bird just happens to fly past."

Beth sighed. Devon rolled his eyes. "You know who we are," he said wearily.

*"I do!"* she burst out, causing them to lean back. "You're the othologists I read about in this morning's *Lady of the House.* You were rivals from feuding universities until your eyes met across a crowded museum display of dodo bones!"

"O . . . kay," Devon said.

"If we tell you the truth, will there be more than one room available?" Beth chanced.

The innkeeper laughed more than an Australian kookaburra establishing its territory, thus ending any hope of rational conversation. They followed her upstairs.

"Here we are," she announced, flinging open a door.

Beth and Devon peered across the threshold into a large candlelit chamber, at the center of which stood one bed frothing with white lace, scattered with rose petals. Perfume did not so much waft from the room as emerge at force 7 on the Beaufort scale.

"By *pure coincidence*, our last remaining room is the honeymoon suite," the innkeeper said disingenuously. "There's a complimentary bottle of champagne on the nightstand, and I'll have a special dinner sent up to you. Please feel welcome to autograph anything you wish."

She hurried away, leaving Beth and Devon standing witless in the corridor.

"Why do I feel that she's going to be on the other side of the door this evening, with a glass to the wood, trying to listen?" Devon said dryly.

Beth gasped, her face reddening. He gave her a tired look. "I apologize—"

But Beth's attention had not been on him. "Shh," she hissed, and tugged his arm until they were both huddled behind the open door. "Down there," she whispered, pointing in the direction of the corridor's end. Eyebrows raised, Devon stared at her until she frowned and flicked her finger again. He carefully peered around the edge of the door.

A gentleman bedecked in nothing more than a silk dressing gown was backing out of a room farther along the corridor. "But, my sweet *Leibling*," he protested to whoever was inside. "Be patient. I just want to get us more wine."

"Oberhufter!" Devon murmured grimly.

"By Jove!" came a booming cry. "Never mind the wine, get back into bed, you buffoon! I haven't finished with you yet!"

The blush drained from Beth's face. "Hippolyta!" she tried to exclaim, but her voice had hidden itself beneath a blanket and refused to come out.

"*Mein Gott*, you are insatiable, woman!" Oberhufter declared, untying the sash of his dressing gown as he strode back into the room, slamming the door shut behind him.

Devon was silent, seemingly captured by some imagined

vision, the details of which Beth most definitely did not want to inquire about. She rubbed the heel of her hand across her brow as if she could erase her own imagination.

"Hippolyta told me she was going to the Cotswolds," she said, bewildered.

"Suffice it to say, she lied."

"What are they doing here?"

Devon raised an incredulous eyebrow. "I should think that was fairly obvious, even to a nice woman like yourself." He paused for a heartbeat, then added wickedly, "The same thing we're going to be doing."

The words charged through Beth's sensibilities like an avian metaphor she would have made had her brain not short-circuited. She opened her mouth, then closed it helplessly.

"Visiting Gladstone, I mean," he added.

"Oh. Yes." She nodded vigorously. "We must get there before them."

A moment's very interesting silence followed.

"First thing in the morning?" Devon suggested.

Beth understood what he was really asking. After all, she might be nice, but that did not mean she was stupid. And she knew exactly how to answer.

"Yes," she said.

Suddenly, a raucous laugh from Oberhufter and Hippolyta's room echoed down the corridor. Beth flinched. "But we can't stay here," she said. "Sorry."

"It's fine." And without even one attempt to argue, Devon picked up his suitcase, took her hand, and led her back downstairs. As they slipped past the innkeeper and out into the cool gray evening, Beth found herself wondering if his manhandling continued in all situations . . . and for a wild, corrupted moment she regretted the loss of the magnificent honeymoon bed.

"This way," Devon said, tugging her eastward.

Then, fifteen minutes later: "This way," he said, tugging her to the north.

But it was no use. They found only two other inns, both of which had been fully booked via telegram that very afternoon. Directed at last to a private boardinghouse, they were welcomed on account of their pitiful expressions (and willingness to pay double).

"We're at full occupancy, but I do have one room you can use," the landlady said as she ushered them into a cozy, dark-paneled foyer. "However, I'm afraid there's a small issue with the beds . . ."

"NONE," DEVON SAID in a dull voice, shaking his head as he surveyed what appeared to be a disused office. It contained a solid oak desk, an old filing cabinet, stacks of books, and—"No beds whatsoever."

"But cushions!" Beth said brightly from behind an armful of them. "And a blanket. We can . . . make . . ."

Her voice faded as Devon pinned her with a dark, vehement stare. Her heart (or at least something) began to squirm.

"Three cushions and a blanket is not going to be adequate for our needs tonight," he said. His tone could have melted railway steel faster than a feuerfinch.

Beth clenched herself into stillness, even while she raced frantically through her vocabulary for a clever response. But she found only bird facts and the dusty remnants of a joke she'd told in 1887.

Her eyes were eloquent, however, and Devon obeyed their request, striding toward her. She tossed the pillows aside, he caught her face in his hands, and they were kissing even before the narrative could summon a metaphor in preparation.

Beth's good manners were instantly immolated. She reached for Devon with a kind of homing instinct, clutching his coat lapels, pulling the solidness and wildness of him closer to her heart. He wrapped his arms around her, encompassing all the shy uncertainty, desperate hunger, and textbook facts about courtship that tumbled confusedly within her. As their tongues slipped against each other in the secret dark, Beth wanted more, more, even knowing that a hundred years of this would not be enough, even as her bones seemed to melt into something that felt like pure liquid gold. Had the caladrius appeared in the room at that moment, interrupting them, Beth would have shot it.

Slowly, their kissing gentled, grew lush and silky, easing the storm of passion into true feeling. Tugging at the pins in her hair, Devon had it unbound in seconds, his hands smoothing the satiny ripples. His tenderness, and the palpable longing Beth could feel in his touch, brought her to tears. All the lonely years dissolved. Devon kissed away from her mouth in a glimmering trail down her throat, but before she could miss him he came back, kissing each sliding tear before touching his damp lips to hers again reverently. For the first time in a life of endless academic successes, she discovered what real happiness felt like.

Outside, night sank over the world, leaving only a soft wash of lamplight in the room. It swayed with breezes that slipped through cracks in the window frame and down the ashy chimney. Neither of them noticed. Without pausing between kisses, their fingers tangled while they worked to remove Devon's coat and unbutton his shirt. As the cotton parted, Beth brushed a hand against his exposed chest, smiling when she felt the pulse beneath it tumble into disarray. Her fingers were snowy in comparison to his warm-colored skin. Ancient Greek script was tattooed across his left pectoral major: *the wind is blowing, adore the wind*, she translated, tracing the letters.

"Pythagoras," she whispered, utterly seduced. His breath catching, Devon set a thumb beneath her chin and tilted it up.

"Let me see that beautiful cleverness," he said, his voice husky with desire.

"Now you're the one who needs a new dictionary," she told him, her smile slanting. "Cleverness is incorporeal, therefore cannot be beautiful."

"To hell with semantics," he said, and bent to kiss her again.

*Knock! Knock! Knock! Knock!*

At the sudden loud rapping, Beth jolted. Her forehead smacked into Devon's, and they stumbled back with cries of pain.

*Knock! Knock! Knock! Knock!*

Beth looked around for a giant woodpecker, despite their being endemic to Prince Edward Island, thousands of miles away, but Devon, scowling beneath the heel of the hand pressed against his forehead, strode toward the door.

"Wait!" Beth whispered urgently. "Your shirt."

He stopped as if he'd collided with a wall of pain. For a moment, he did nothing but breathe; then he rebuttoned the shirt, tucking it impatiently into his waistband, before flinging open the door. On the other side, the boardinghouse landlady leaped back with an alarmed squeak.

Beth watched, fascinated, as Devon harnessed his temper

and transformed it in less than a second into calm, endearing charm. "I'm sorry, you startled me," he said, pushing a hand through his hair, smiling at the woman until she blushed. "Can I help you?"

"Um—um—" the landlady said, struggling to manage her flustered nerves. She held a folded newspaper, and Beth sighed even as she saw the heave of Devon's shoulders that suggested he was doing the same.

"I just wanted to let you know," the landlady said, "that I have a proper bedroom free after all . . . 'Mr. and Mrs. Smith.'"

She winked broadly, and Beth realized the pseudonym they'd given when checking in had not withstood their portraits' existence in the evening news. Devon glanced back over his shoulder at her, and his expression was so scandalous, she went from pleasantly warm to steaming hot.

Hurrying over to the door, she offered her own smile to the landlady. "Thank you for such kindness. Is there any chance the new room has two beds, since we are after all merely professional colleagues, entirely innocent of all improper behavior?" She asked this as if she wasn't standing disheveled, her hair unbound and lips swollen from kissing, beside an equally disheveled man—as if her good reputation wasn't almost certainly destroyed, her job no doubt gone, and the entire birding circuit sniggering over newspapers at her thoroughly shocking behavior. *Kissing a man! Sharing a room with him! Going about in public without a hat!* Nice customs might curtsy to great kings (and grovel before Hippolyta Quirm and Herr Oberhufter), but they demanded scrupulous obedience from England's lady professors.

And yet, when the landlady murmured apologies for there being only one bed, all Beth felt was secret erotic delight.

"Before we go downstairs," the woman said, "perhaps you'd be so kind as to provide an autograph?" Holding forth the newspaper in one hand, a pen in the other, she shrugged obsequiously.

"Of course," Beth said, taking the pen.

The landlady turned her head. "They said yes!"

Suddenly, a small crowd of people in nightclothes and dressing gowns swarmed the corridor, all with paper in hand and questions bursting excitedly from their lips. *Do you think the caladrius is in Hathersage? How can I become an opthologist like you? When are you getting married?*

Beth and Devon signed their names, and smiled, and provided the kind of opaque responses professors are skilled at giving when they don't have a clue how to answer. After some ten minutes, every item was autographed, the caladrius declared practically a native of the village, Devon's physique contemplated almost to the degree of tape measures being produced, and the crowd shuffled away, leaving Beth to sag against the doorframe while Devon rubbed his face wearily.

"Come now, let's get you properly settled," the landlady said with a beckoning gesture. As Devon turned away to get the suitcases, she leaned closer to Beth. "Don't worry, dear, discretion is our motto at Chattering Elm Cottage. I won't breathe a word about your being here. By the way, do you have plans for a big church wedding? Or perhaps an intimate ceremony in a garden?"

Beth could practically see the headline in tomorrow's newspaper. She managed not to sigh. "Conjecture on the potential connubial eventualities of our currently emergent relational situation in all its frangibility would be inadvisably precipitate and, to any perspicacious individual, contraindicated by prudence. Wouldn't you agree?"

"Er . . ." The landlady's expression fell slack.

Devon stepped into the dazed silence, carrying both suitcases. "Shall we?" he asked, nodding toward the corridor.

They were led downstairs to a room near the back of the house. It proved to be warm and comfortable, lit by gas lamps and smelling of freshly laundered sheets.

It was also clearly the bedroom of a child.

"My daughter was happy to volunteer her room for the night," the landlady said as they stared at the toys cluttering the edges of the room, the frilly pink curtains, and the bedspread printed with kittens and butterflies. Beth felt herself lose most of her color, at least half her appetite, and every last fragment of her sexual desire.

"Thank you," she said as good manners marched triumphantly back into her brain (wiping their feet first, of course). Visions of Devon pinning her against a wall and expertly denuding her of her virginity skulked away to weep quietly in a dark corner of her subconscious.

"I'll bring you a supper tray, shall I?" the landlady suggested. "It's bangers and mash tonight."

Devon muttered something that sounded suspiciously like *not anymore, it's not*, but the landlady only smiled obliviously and dashed off, newspaper pressed against her heart, leaving the ornithologists drooping more than blackbirds in a rainstorm.

# CHAPTER EIGHTEEN

Ornithology is not all running around with nets.
Sometimes you need to sit quietly and watch a bird's
heart unfurl before its wings do.
*Birds Through a Sherry Glass*, H.A. Quirm

THE NIGHT'S BREEZE intensified, lamenting the clouded moon in a low, aching voice that made the lamplight tremble. Beth and Devon sat cross-legged on the child's bed, eating dinner from plates in their laps. Beth had turned shy, so they managed no more than a halting conversation about the food and weather until Devon could hardly breathe from boredom.

"I suppose your childhood bedroom looked like this," he said, just for something to discuss that did not involve squalls or sausages. But it was apparently the worst comment he could have made, judging from Beth's suddenly blanched expression.

"Not exactly," she murmured. Setting aside her mostly empty plate, she rubbed her hands against her thighs, staring so intently at the wall beyond Devon's shoulder that he might have supposed the caladrius perched there.

A gentleman would have changed the subject. And Devon really wanted to believe he had at least a few gentlemanlike attributes somewhere inside him, even if they looked like a ruined temple half-lost behind rotting vines. But he'd also spent many of his formative years in America, where changing the subject just when things were finally getting interesting would have led to most of the country's history not happening.

"Oh?" he asked, and putting a bite of sausage in his mouth, he just looked at her, waiting for an answer. He'd done the same thing often enough with his students to be confident it would work—and sure enough, after a fraught moment, she surrendered.

"I was sent to boarding school in Surrey when I was five. Youngest student, most clever, et cetera. That meant a dormitory bedroom, of course. Altogether without frills, and not a dab of pink anywhere in sight."

She became occupied with a loose thread on her dress, and Devon could hear in the brittle silence all the things she'd omitted from her tale, the grief and loneliness and struggle. He speared another sausage bite and said as he lifted it to his mouth, "Plenty of birds, though, I imagine."

That made her smile, as he hoped it would. "Oh yes, birds everywhere. Surrey is a treasure trove of them." She sighed happily, her gaze softening as she remembered. Then she blinked, turning that heavenly look on him, and any control Devon felt he had over the conversation completely unraveled, becoming a tangle of emotion deep inside his heart.

"Your eyes are like a sky spun by wild and beautiful wings," he said.

She stared at him with alarmed confusion. "My eyes are spinning?"

He grinned. "No, spun as in weaving, magic weav— I'm trying to be charming here."

And while she blushed endearingly and almost ripped the loose thread right out of her dress, he took their plates and tilted until he could set them on the bedside cabinet. Straightening again, he leaned forward and kissed her.

She stiffened for the smallest moment but did not pull away, and as he coaxed her lips apart, everything in her eased, soft, warm, and trembling on the same verge of sexual desperation where he was trying to balance as well. They couldn't attend to it in a child's bed, however; not even he was that depraved. So he ended the kiss gently and pressed his mouth instead against her forehead, making her sigh.

"I'll sleep on the floor," he whispered, moving away—

And she caught him, her ink-stained fingers clutching his arms with an ornithologist's strength. "It's a cold night," she said. "Logic dictates we share the bed. If we remain clothed, it will be quite safe."

He raised an eyebrow at that. "Darling, someone should have included at least a little of the humanities in your education."

"I trust you," she insisted, proving that he'd corrupted her indeed, considering she was able to say something so villainous. His wretched, malnourished heart dropped to its knees and began weeping. He flinched, trying not to leap off the bed and run screaming into the night.

"It's cold," she repeated, her voice hushed. And Devon heard it then—what she really meant. What she hid behind her nice manners and apologies. The same thing he hid behind his cynicism: deep loneliness and longing for affinity.

People called him a genius, but he didn't see it that way. He certainly didn't feel superior to anyone. It was only that his brain seemed to operate on a different, far less comfortable frequency than others'. Talk to them about a bird in flight and they'd describe wings, but he'd learned not to say anything about lift-induced vortices and ballistic trajectories, or the exhilaration of his soul as he watched fire-breathing eagles or plain seagulls take to the sky. Even other ornithologists ran out of interest after a while. So he moved through the world in a constant state of dissatisfaction, looking for some kind of connection by making people laugh, and rescuing them from dangerous birds, and having a lot of sex. It never worked, though, because he was only giving a small part of himself, and no one asked for more. Except his professors, of course—they could not get enough of his passion for learning. But they also spent years trying to extinguish his playfulness, so it was really just the same coin, different side. And while his cousins, Gabriel and Amelia, could follow the sharp angles of his thoughts, he'd scarcely seen them since being sent to America at fourteen. Besides, neither of them cared about birds, the heart of his heart.

Beth was the first person he'd met who truly spoke his language. Her presence made the world finally slide into place for him. She was beautiful, unconsciously sexy, and he was drawn to that, of course, but it was only a minor part of how he felt. His attraction to her was so intensely intellectual it affected his very brain function, until it seemed like he walked for her, breathed for her, got hard just hearing her say the words *mandibular rostrum*.

With a sigh, he gathered her into his arms. "Let's be warm together, then," he said, and laid them down together on the bed. Some wriggling ensued, some kicking of feet, as they pushed the bedding back, then hauled it up again to cover them. It was provoking, to say the least, but the laughter was what really got to him, the comradeship as they wrangled blankets and squirmed on pillows and tried to arrange their clothes. Intellectualism gave way to sweet goofiness, and by the time they settled together, Devon reckoned he'd never been so aroused. But Beth was lavender-scented softness in his arms, and he wanted that more than sexual release. He wanted her, his clever angel, his rival, his friend.

Besides, no man could comfortably make love to a woman with that row of china-faced, ringleted dolls smiling menacingly down at him from the shelf beside the bed.

At last, quiet, and nestled together in more cozy warmth than was actually pleasant, they looked at each other in the amber lamplight. The world seemed to melt away. Devon could not have said exactly what he saw in Beth's eyes that kept him absorbed, only that it felt like everything.

He'd never fallen so fast for a woman before. Or perhaps it was more accurate to say that she uplifted him, drawing him out of cynicism into a happiness he was enjoying wholeheartedly; a happiness that had taken him so off-guard, his usual defenses were useless against it. Then again, maybe he didn't want to employ them anymore. Beth was welcome in.

He stroked her hair until she drifted asleep, then still went on gazing as the slow, feather-quiet sway of her breathing caressed him with peace.

"I love you," he whispered, closing his eyes, sinking into dreams.

And behind her own closed eyes, Beth lay awake, holding her heart tight, trying not to break into a thousand bright pieces.

THERE ARE MANY awkward experiences a woman might experience. Being caught without menstrual protection. Not realizing until after getting home that there has been a bit of lettuce stuck in one's teeth since lunch. But surely the worst must be waking in the arms of one's professional rival, with whom one almost surrendered every scruple the night before. It might seem like a cozily romantic moment, but only to someone who's already brushed their hair and applied deodorant.

Beth regarded Devon's quiescent face, mere inches from her own, with considerable anxiety. Was he asleep? Would he remain so if she moved? Had there ever been a more beautiful man in the existence of the world?

Realizing there was no safe way to answer these questions, she did the only thing possible: twisting her lower half toward the edge of the bed, she slithered backward. Devon's arm, hooked over her, slipped until just his hand lay on her arm. She paused, holding her breath, but he did not wake. So she slithered some more—his hand dropped to the mattress—his eyelashes stirred—Beth froze, but as he gave no other sign of waking, she exhaled with relief . . .

And fell off the bed.

Holding her breath, she peered up over the edge of the bed to check that Devon kept sleeping. (Really, it was *unfair* that any man should be so beautiful.) Reassured, she rolled onto her hands and knees and crawled across the room as fast as possible for someone in a long dress and petticoats, to say nothing of her corset. Reaching her suitcase at last, she clutched it in both arms, stood up, and tiptoed toward the door, all the while glancing nervously at Devon's motionless form. Alas, thus glancing, she forgot to look where she was going and collided with a dollhouse. Tiny window shutters clattered. Even tinier furniture tumbled noisily. Holding her breath again, Beth waited, but Devon did not stir. The sable locks draped over his forehead remained in place, the curve of his lips lay in the dream of a smile, and her heart yearned toward him even as she continued on out the door.

DEVON WAITED UNTIL the door closed behind Beth, then turned onto his back. Pushing a hand through his hair, he stared at the ceiling with an expression that would have been entirely bleak except the butterflies painted there made that impossible.

He'd known she would leave him. Everyone did, and of course a woman as intelligent and sensitive as Beth Pickering would be no different. He could only admire that she'd escaped his corrupting influence so quickly, despite how much it hurt.

Which was a lot.

He loved her. It was astonishing; he'd had longer relationships with a block of cheese, but there it was—he interrogated the idea from several angles, set it against various laws of human behavior, and sought a second opinion from skepticism, before concluding that he just loved her, completely, hopelessly, with all the scrappy mess of his heart. No doubt his father would frown disapprovingly, since emotions were an impediment to career success; and his aunt Mary would need an application of smelling salts, since she'd always wanted him to marry a nice American girl and stay in the United States, where news of his exploits would not reach her gardening club; and Gabriel would—

Oops, Gabriel.

Devon groaned. He'd completely forgotten about his cousin,

who was probably sitting at home in Oxford, thinking about the conference he'd missed and cursing Devon's very existence. Devon owed him a humble apology, transport costs, and most likely a signed declaration that Gabriel Tarrant was the Superior Cousin. But it would have to wait. He had important work ahead.

Questioning Gladstone about the caladrius's location.

Securing the bird for himself.

Being awarded Birder of the Year.

And doing whatever was necessary, including relinquishing those other goals, to win over Beth Pickering.

Which meant catching up to her now. Climbing out of bed, Devon dressed in fresh clothes, washed cursorily, and in less than ten minutes was powering toward the boardinghouse's front door.

And there she was.

Standing opposite the dining room entrance, she was eyeing it with trepidation as she chewed a thumbnail. She hadn't left him.

*She hadn't left him.* She was just getting breakfast.

Or, at least, trying to summon the fortitude needed for getting breakfast, considering what sounded like a minor crowd inhabited the room. He smiled. If it had been a flock of birds, she'd be inside already, and he'd have run off without seeing her. Thank goodness for her introversion.

He tilted his head to the side, contemplating her. Gone was the pretty dress; she'd dressed instead in a simple beige skirt and white shirtwaist, presenting the quintessential image of an English lady professor, calm, sensible, restrained—except for her hair, bereft of its pins, which he'd scattered to the office floor last night. It flowed down her back, utterly indiscreet.

His hands tingled with the memory of having been in that hair, the softness drifting against his bare fingers. His trousers began to feel tight at the thought that she was going to breakfast in an unbound state because of him. (His brain flashed images of the caladrius at him, alongside the Birder of the Year trophy, but he did not notice.)

*She hadn't left him. Hadn't crept out with her clothes in her arms before he could ask for anything more than sex, hadn't walked away without looking back while he stood on a transatlantic steamship's deck trying not to cry, just a scared boy no matter how clever he might be.*

Shaking his head, he hastily summoned a rascally expression and ambled toward her.

"Good morning, Miss Pickering."

She did not jolt or gasp, as he thought she might. "Mr. Lockley," she said, bestowing upon him the briefest glance.

Ah, so she was going to be like that. His smile deepened. Someone ought to teach her that standoffish behavior was a siren call to scoundrels. Hands in his pockets, he glided to her side and nudged his elbow against hers.

"Sleep well?"

"Adequately," she replied. But then her good heart had her adding in a softer tone, "And you?"

He loved her, loved her. "Blissfully, thank you."

"I'm glad. However, before we continue, I must clarify something. Last night was a temporary aberration induced by the peculiar stresses of the competition, and the experience will not be replicated. I trust you agree?"

"I do," he said easily. Then he bent to whisper close to her ear. "After all, I never kiss a woman the same way twice."

She did gasp then, looking up at him with an outrage that

wavered when she discovered how near their faces were to each other, then melted completely as she gazed into his eyes. Devon knew he could have kissed her right then and won her surrender. But instead, he offered his arm. She laid her hand on it as if mesmerized, and he escorted her gentlemanlike into the dining room.

BETH WENT WITH Devon in something of a daze. Only fifteen minutes prior, she had reached the firm decision that, although she was desperately attracted to the man, there must exist some doubt as to the sincerity of his interest in her, considering she was a plain little owl and he a worldly rake. Furthermore, her own behavior had gone as far from sensible as it was possible to get without losing one's head entirely (to say nothing of one's virginity). So while she might reasonably continue a professional association with Devon, intelligence led her back to the same conclusion she'd made at the train station in Canterbury: she must forget romance and focus on winning **tenure**.

So how she had gone from Absolutely Setting a Boundary with Mr. Lockley Like the Independent, Educated Woman She Was! to almost immediately thereafter tingling with delight as he guided her across the corridor was a baffling mystery. Even more baffling was the fact that she found little desire within herself for solving this mystery—and, conversely, a whole lot of desire for Devon.

As they stepped into the dining room, all conversation around its long table abruptly ceased as ten heads looked up from newspapers or coffee cups to stare at them. Then, being British, looked politely away again, although with enough throat clearing and newspaper rustling to make it clear the politeness lidded a writhing mass of profanity. Beth and Devon did not say anything; it would have been pointless. The damage to their reputations was clearly now beyond repair (or at least, Beth's reputation, Devon's actually being improved) thanks to the front-page headlines of three different publications.

---

### BIRDER SWEETHEARTS IN TRAIN TRYST

---

### ORNITHOLOGISTS ORDER LOVE FROM MENU

---

### PROFESSORS IN FINE FEATHER

---

Beth's stomach roiled, and she was fairly sure it wasn't just the smell of fried bacon causing it.

"Come along," Devon whispered and, in the gentlest example yet of manhandling, guided her across to the sideboard. Taking a plate, he lifted the tongs set on a dish of grilled tomatoes, then turned to her.

"Some of these?" he asked. Beth looked at him confusedly for a moment before comprehending that he was serving her, not himself. At once, her vocabulary disappeared in a glittering burst of amazement. No one had ever served her unless employed to do so. And from the rather nervous look in Devon's eyes, he'd never done it before either.

*I love you.* The memory of his whispered declaration at the verge of sleep took her glittering amazement and turned it into moonlit snow: romantic but also chilling. For while she might have stayed awake for hours last night imagining he really meant those words and fantasizing about where it could lead, looking at him now, with his eyes like a raven's wing and his beautiful face, and what had been her point again? Oh yes. In morning's light it became clear what he'd *actually* said was "eye of newt," inspired by the windstorm outside to quote *Macbeth*. That made much more sense.

He raised an eyebrow, waiting for her response. She directed him to the foods she wanted, then he pulled out a chair at the table for her and ensured she was comfortably placed. By the time he brought her a cup of tea, Beth's logic had given way to a helpless dream of their wedding day. Eventually he sat beside her with his own plate of food, and she gave him a bashful nod of thanks. He winked in reply. Turning to reach for the salt canister—

She stopped, hand in midair.

The entire company was staring at them, and judging from the range of expressions, also imagining their wedding day.

Snatching back her hand, Beth fixed an unblinking stare on her plate. How was she supposed to eat now?

"Excuse me, sir." Devon's voice wandered casually into the enthralled silence. "May I ask how you developed such an excellent mustache? I've never had luck in growing one. Perhaps you can advise me?"

Beth glanced up through her eyelashes to see the gentleman opposite her blush and stroke his whiskers. He launched into a detailed explanation of their care, and although Devon did not move, Beth could practically feel him nudging her in his friendly way. An ephemeral smile slipped across her mouth, then hid itself away again. Picking up her fork, she began to eat, and Devon guarded her peace by asking the hirsute gentleman about barbers, pomade, and the perils of crumbs, until she'd finished.

After breakfast, they left their suitcases with the landlady and set off for Professor Gladstone's house. Summer was rousing slowly for the day, white-skied and quiet. The long, dusty road coursed through hedgerows and frothy trees, beyond which lay a view of plump hills and groves. Beth's stomach returned to roiling now that she was alone with Devon, no other person in sight to judge her behavior. Good sense, upon being summoned, whispered pathetically that it was unwell and could not attend. She was forced to the meager resort of hugging her satchel for comfort—not a particularly effective thing to do considering the binoculars and hard-edged field journal inside.

But it was important she reset the boundary between her and Devon that she'd been so determined upon this morning, or else the villain might turn her calm waters into an absolute typhoon, and she didn't want that, did she?

*Actually I wouldn't mind*, answered her heart unhelpfully. Ignoring it, Beth glanced sidelong at Devon. "I must clarify something," she told him.

"Again?" Devon flashed a grin. He was kicking at pebbles while he walked, an endearingly boyish behavior that had Beth veering into the middle of the road to escape the charm radiating with devastating power from him.

"Yes, I must—"

*"Hyyyaah!!"*

Suddenly, a great chaos of noise filled the world. Beth felt a moment's confusion before Devon was leaping to wrap his arms around her. As he threw them both into a hedge, Beth's confusion exploded into shock. She stared through a veil of hair at a curricle speeding away along the road, its pair of horses kicking up great clouds of dust.

"Are you all right?" Devon demanded, cradling her against him, his hand brushing the hair away from her face as he searched for injury.

"You saved me," she sighed dreamily—then, hearing herself, forced Proper Etiquette kicking and screaming back into her brain. "I'm much obliged for your timely assistance."

Devon chuckled. The sound vibrated through Beth's heart, causing havoc with its already tumultuous pulse. She attempted to push herself up, but Devon held her closer, so that she was now at risk of suffocation, crushed nerves, and fatally broken scruples.

"Are you sure you're not hurt?" he insisted. There remained no hair against her face and yet he kept brushing. His eyes had turned the color of old fire. Beth went still, like she did when observing a distressed bird.

"I'm quite sure," she said softly. "You should let me up before a newspaper reporter comes past."

He nodded but did not move, except for his hand, which was now sliding down her throat. After the past week, Beth had a good idea where it might end: deep inside her feminine wiles. She tugged herself free, getting clumsily to her feet and brushing off road dust, leaves, and hot tingling sensations.

"As I was saying," she continued a little shakily, "I must clarify something."

Devon gave a huff of laughter. He rose, looking like a pagan god emerging from the undergrowth. At the sight, Beth's good manners rushed forward—not to protect her but to offer themselves as sacrifices on whatever altar Devon might suggest. Appalled at herself, she began striding down the road.

For three steps before stumbling on a pebble.

Immediately, Devon was at her side, holding her upright. "You *are* hurt."

The genuine anxiety in his expression melted away the last of Beth's resistance to him. The man might be a villain, but he was a decent, good-hearted villain, and she could honestly no longer think otherwise. He listened to her, always made her feel welcome, and now here he was caring that she might be hurt. Not letting herself love that would be allowing all her bullies, the people who'd told her she was not worth care, to rule her heart. And it would be allowing them to devalue Devon too, which she couldn't tolerate.

"I'm fine," she told him with a smile. He did not seem convinced, however, and Beth suspected he was on the verge of carrying her all the way to Gladstone's house. Gentle reassurances were not going to suffice. So she pulled away and began striding once more along the road, swinging her hips just a little in the way she'd seen Hippolyta employ when desirous men were on the scene.

"To clarify," she said in her archest tone, "we are rivals, traveling together only as far as Professor Gladstone's house, after which we will go our separate ways."

"Of course," he answered as he followed, his voice easing just like she'd hoped. She cast him a provoking look.

"Perhaps we may shake hands again at the Birder of the Year ceremony, when you congratulate me on winning."

That made him smile, and Beth was relieved to see color return to his face. "You really are an angel," he said. "I'll mention you in my winner's speech."

Edging to the side of the road, Beth skimmed her fingers along a hedgerow, letting the tickle of leaves and twigs send sparks through the heavy smolder Devon's touch had caused in her. "What would you say about me, exactly?"

"Why, that you are a tremendously accomplished woman," he answered. "Clever and capable and beau—"

Alas, just at this most interesting part, a hand reached out from a gap between bushes and yanked Beth off the road. Staggering, she drew breath to scream, but another hand clamped over her mouth, and she was dragged into darkness.

♡

# Chapter Nineteen

If it looks like a blackbird and sings like a blackbird, it
might nevertheless grow sudden fangs and try to eat
your face off.

*Birds Through a Sherry Glass*, H.A. Quirm

*An hour earlier*

GLADSTONE'S SUMMER RESIDENCE, with its comfortable aspect, private aviary, and several accompanying acres for the natural study of birds, reflected his academic character—and the fact that he'd inherited a large income, since no science teacher could afford such an estate.

This morning he was outdoors, endeavoring to capture a leechsparrow. Which is to say, he sat on a mahogany sofa in the meadow behind the house, gesturing with his rosewood pipe to several graduate students who traipsed through the grass, bedecked with protective goggles and earmuffs, wielding heavy-duty nets, as they did the actual work of capturing a leechsparrow. The gentleman himself sipped tea between puffing on the pipe and nudging down his tiny spectacles to frown at the students. His goatee had been brushed and teased into a magnificent state, his bowler hat was unacquainted with bird guano, and the fine polish of his shoes reflected considerable doubt that he'd entered the field under his own steam.

"To the left!" he shouted. "No, fools! My left, not yours! For pity's sake!" He clicked his tongue with contempt, and all throughout England, university students shivered uncannily. "Young people these days," he grumbled.

"Absolutely," averred Mr. Flogg from the far end of the sofa, since despite the inexact nature of Gladstone's complaint, his professional instinct was to always agree with the person paying him, regardless.

"Indeed," murmured Mr. Fettick in a chair opposite.

Gladstone flicked a disdainful look at both men. "You two are no better. IOS hired you to organize a competition that would attract people to study ornithology. We expected to see accounts of diligent, noble-minded scientists using research libraries and crouching in rain-soaked hides. But what do I read instead in the newspapers? *Romance*."

"Romantic comedy," Mr. Flogg muttered unhelpfully.

Mr. Fettick began to open his briefcase. "We brought our latest analysis to show—"

"Listen to me," Gladstone interrupted, knocking his pipe stem against the arm of the sofa in lieu of any available blackboard upon which he could tap a wooden pointer. "I know what I'm talking about. People aren't interested in romance. They want sober, informative reports that use complex words and make them feel stupid, thereby inspiring them to seek higher education."

A moment of silence followed this speech as Messrs. Fettick and Flogg tried to decide if it was satire. In the field beyond, one student was excitedly pointing to a particular spot in the long grass while the others gestured at each other to stay very still.

"Besides," Gladstone continued, "Pickering and Lockley

are from different universities. You can't have a romance between an Oxonian and a Cantabrigian; it's unnatural."

"They're rivals who become lovers," Mr. Fettick explained.

"Also, both universities are represented on the IOS committee," Mr. Flogg pointed out. "We thought they'd be
pleased."

"They are not," Gladstone said. And as he sent a look over
the rim of his spectacles, Messrs. Fettick and Flogg were
prompted to understand that, for all intents and purposes, the
committee was sitting before them, embodied in a gentleman
for whom the cutting edge of scientific progress had come and
gone some forty years ago.

"Arrrgh!" came a sudden scream from the students as a
leechsparrow flew up from the long grass several feet from
where they were focused, its wings flapping violently.

Gladstone took a sip of tea—and yet, when he spoke again,
his tone was somehow even drier. "Now seems an opportune
time to make a few changes to the plan."

"Changes," Messrs. Fettick and Flogg chorused warily.

"Nothing major. Mere tweaks. For example, no more of
this *romance* nonsense. And return to having just one winner—
let's make it Pickering, eh? Throw a sop to the bluestockings.
Show we're all about 'equal opportunity.'" He used his fingers
to make quote marks in the air, and not even a massive dooms-
day weapon over his shoulder would have illustrated more
clearly that he was the antagonist.

"Ah. Have an Oxford professor win," Mr. Flogg said with
the cynical insight of a man whose own degree was in political
history.

Gladstone shrugged and puffed his pipe.

In the field, the students began running in panic, arms flailing, as the leechsparrow dive-bombed them.

"Miss Pickering might not agree with this plan," Mr. Fettick said. "She seems from all accounts to be quite a nice lady, concerned with doing the right thing."

Gladstone blew a smoke ring contemptuously. "Nice? The woman keeps pushing at the boundaries of ornithological science and outright refuses to grade students on a curve. I don't call that nice."

"There is also the small issue of her being just down the road in Hathersage with Devon Lockley," Mr. Flogg added. "We fear they guessed that you have the caladrius bird in your possession and will be arriving here soon, ruining our carefully planned timing and potentially costing a fortune in tourism revenue if the competition is cut short."

"Caladrius," Gladstone said.

Mr. Flogg frowned delicately. "Pardon?"

"Caladrius. Not 'caladrius bird.' There's hardly a caladrius frog for me to confuse it with, is there?"

"So true, of course, indeed," Mr. Flogg murmured, flushing. Mr. Fettick said nothing, but flicked the latch of his briefcase handle, making a spiky little *tsk* sound with it.

"I am not worried about Pickering and Lockley," Gladstone went on. "If they arrive, I shall give them both a thorough reeducation. And if they won't cooperate, we'll just have to resort to Plan B."

"Plan B?" Mr. Flogg inquired nervously.

"Hippolyta Quirm."

*"Oh God, nooooo!!"*

For a moment, both Messrs. Fettick and Flogg were sure they'd been the ones to shout. But it was only a student cower-

ing in the grass as the leechsparrow perched on his head, pecking wildly at his earmuffs. Two other students were bashing
him with their nets in a hysterical effort to capture the bird.

"Go back to London, gentlemen," Gladstone said, "and organize the award ceremony. I'll see to it that Pickering behaves. If she doesn't, she'll lose her job. And I'll provide
Lockley with a sabbatical—behind the bolted door of my cellar. There will be no more shenanigans. No more making rela-
tions public. Just good old-fashioned ornithology."

"But—but—you're proposing to kidnap Mr. Lockley and
blackmail Miss Pickering," Mr. Fettick gasped.

Gladstone puffed out another smoke ring. "As I say, good
old-fashioned ornithology." He snapped his fingers, and three
footmen stepped forward from where they had been waiting
discreetly at the edge of the scene. "Show the gentlemen out,"
he drawled in a bored tone.

As Messrs. Flogg and Fettick trudged despondently away,
blood-curdling screams arose from the students.

"Wait!" Gladstone shouted, raising his hand. The footmen
paused, and Messrs. Flogg and Fettick looked back hopefully.
But Gladstone was squinting across the meadow at his frantic
students. "Once you're done," he told the footmen, "bring me
another pot of tea. I need liquid fortification; I have some failing grades to hand out."


BACK ON THE road, an hour after Messrs. Flogg and Fettick
were thus dismissed, Devon stared with mute shock at the gap
in hedgery through which Beth had disappeared. Three seconds later, his intellect snapped into service once more, and he
leaped after her.

Plowing into a tangle of grasses beneath a heavy oak tree, he scanned the shadows ahead but saw no sign of Beth. Confused, he turned—and there she was, caught in the clutches of a dark-suited man against the back side of the hedge. The fiend pressed one black-gloved hand over her mouth, and in his other held a narrow, pointed object to her throat.

"Don't come any closer!" he warned, "or I'll use this!"

"It's a pen," Devon said.

"And I won't hesitate to scribble on her!" the man growled. "She'll not get the ink out of her skin for weeks!"

Beth's eyes grew wide with alarm. But Devon calmly surveyed the man, thinking of all the ways he'd kill him for threatening Beth. The expensive suit and bowler hat, in addition to a briefcase set neatly on the ground nearby, reminded him of someone he'd recently seen. All at once, he realized: "You were on the train to Oxford."

"Mmmm-mmm," Beth said urgently from behind the gloved hand. Devon gave her a reassuring smile.

"Don't worry, love, I'm going to—"

Alas, the exact manner in which he would have heroically rescued her cannot be related, for he was interrupted by Beth ramming her elbow back into her captor's gut. As the man bent, crying out in pain, she slammed her fist up beneath his jaw. He staggered, she hooked her leg around his, some physics was applied, and in the next moment the man was thudding to his back on the weedy ground. His bowler hat tumbled off and rolled away.

"Eek!" the man squealed, cringing in terror. "Don't hurt me!"

Devon stared openmouthed as Beth tilted her chin. "I apologize for the violence," she said. "However, if people insist on equating my ladylike manner with powerlessness, they are to blame for the consequences. I wouldn't be an ornithologist—not to mention a woman who went through years of schooling with mostly male classmates—if I wasn't able to defend myself."

She stared coolly down at the man, but almost at once her expression wavered. "Are you all right? I didn't hurt you too much, did I? And, oh dear, I fear your hat may be scuffed . . ."

She hurried to rescue it, and Devon instantly moved forward, imparting a mild kick to the man's leg.

"Up you get."

The man scrambled to his feet, pale-faced and sweating. He performed a hasty bow, his sleek black hair flopping over his brow. "Please excuse my unorthodox behavior. I was worried you'd try to run away."

"You've been following us since London," Beth said as she brushed dirt off his hat and handed it back to him. "May we inquire as to your identity?"

"What she means," Devon added, "is, *who the bloody hell are you?*"

"I certainly do not mean that," Beth said indignantly. "There is no cause to be rude."

Devon gave her an incredulous look. "You're joking, right? He just attacked and threatened you."

"For which he has apologized."

"And you threw him to the ground."

"For which I apologized."

"Ha! You know, it's possible to be too polite."

"And sad to be quite so cynical."

They stepped toward each other.

"I'm not cynical, I'm realistic," Devon argued.

"Perhaps you need to imagine a little," Beth said.

He blinked slowly, giving her a look absolutely overflowing with imagination, and she trembled as if he'd reached out and caressed her.

*"Ahem,"* said the man. Remembering his existence, they tore their attention from each other and back to him.

"Who are you?" Devon demanded.

The man's eyes shifted nervously. "I'm with the Protection and Rescue of Enchanting Species, um, Service. We're trying to rescue the caladrius, and you're our only hope."

"I've never heard of that group," Devon said suspiciously.

"We're a secret organization," the man explained. "My colleague and I have just come from Professor Gladstone's house—"

"Your colleague?" Devon looked around, reaching for his concealed gun before realizing he must have left it in his suitcase.

"Yes, he's watching the road to be sure no one comes upon us."

"Such as whom?" Beth asked, looking around now herself as if she expected half a dozen rival ornithologists (and their servants) to appear from behind the greenery. "I extrapolate the chances of—"

*"Please.* Listen." Such was the man's anxiety, he scrunched the brim of his hat in his fists. "There isn't much time! Be prepared, what you are about to hear will shake you to the core. *The Birder of the Year competition is rigged!"*

He paused dramatically, but neither Devon nor Beth evidenced any shaking. "You seem awfully calm about that," he remarked, miffed.

"We already guessed it," Beth said.

"I see. Well, Professor Gladstone, as the chairman of the International Ornithological Society, has possession of the caladrius. And—and he has made a deal with a wicked doc—no, *an evil pharmaceutical organization* that plans to experiment on the bird. The competition is a sham; they intend to simply make their secret agent their winner."

"Why did they even bother holding a competition?" Beth asked. "Why not just hand over the bird?"

The man blinked at her. "Because . . . to cover their tracks."

"How exactly?" Devon asked.

The man's blinking accelerated. "Who can say? It's a secret, evil plot."

"Where did IOS find the caladrius to begin with?" Beth asked.

"Er . . . Transylvania, I think?"

"Who discovered it?" Devon asked.

"And why have other magical birds been attacking people?" Beth asked.

"And how do you know about this secret plan?" Devon asked.

The blinking reached force 6 on the Beaufort scale, threatening to do the man an ocular injury. "Look, the point is, someone needs to rescue the caladrius and take it to London."

Beth's eyes narrowed. "Why London?"

"And how did a conservative thinker like Gladstone get involved in something like this?" Devon asked.

"And why are *we* your only hope?" Beth asked.

The man began fanning himself desperately with his hat. "I-I-I will answer all your questions when there's time. But we need to hurry now! The caladrius must be rescued from Gladstone's house before anyone else discovers it there and tries to steal it for themselves."

Beth and Devon exchanged a sober glance. "Oberhufter," Devon said.

"Hippolyta," Beth said at the same time.

They turned back to the man. "We'll do it."

He exhaled with relief, his shoulders sagging as if half the air in him had been released. "Gladstone has the caladrius secured inside a cage in his library. You need to—"

"If you were just at the house and saw the bird, why didn't you rescue it yourself?" Devon asked.

The man smacked his hat over his face. When he lowered it again, he was smiling brightly. "Do I look like a hero to you? Really, we have no more time for questions. You need to sneak into Gladstone's house, obtain the caladrius, then flee before any of the servants catch you. Make sure you don't separate! This is vital! You must stay together. Er, safety in numbers and all that. Take the bird to London and meet us at . . . let's see, a random place just off the top of my head . . . Kensington Gardens, behind the Albert Memorial on Albert Memorial Road, opposite the Royal Albert Hall. There's a new public aviary just finished being built there: the Albert Aviary. Queen Victoria had it erected in memory of the prince. He loved birds, you know."

"Loved to shoot them," Devon said caustically.

"Why can't we just bring the caladrius to you here, today?" Beth asked. "Since we're in—"

"I said *no time for questions*!" The man flapped his hat at them urgently. But Beth and Devon paused. Morning light fell through the oak foliage over them in soft, bright pieces, like the broken dream of tenure.

"If we bring you the caladrius, will you keep it safe?" Beth asked.

"Yes. It will be protected from all harm, or my name isn't Feh—er . . ."

"Isn't what?" Devon prompted, suspicion darkening his eyes.

"Feth-erlong-ham-*skew*!" The syllables tumbled from the man's throat with increasing desperation. "Mr. Fetherlong-hamsque, PRESS agent. Now hurry, in case Herr Oberhufter and Mrs. Quirm turn up at Gladstone's house before you!"

That propelled them into action. Beth nodded a polite goodbye, and Devon held back branches so she could move easily through the gap in the hedge. As she reentered the road, she noticed Devon casting one more mistrustful look at the PRESS agent. Then he followed her, and they took off running toward the Eyrie.

"Uuughhh." Mr. Fettick groaned, collapsing back against the trunk of the oak tree. Taking the handkerchief from his jacket's breast pocket, he applied it to his face and throat. It came away sodden.

"That was brilliant!" Mr. Flogg whispered excitedly, appearing from around the other side of the tree. His eyes shone with admiration. "*You* are brilliant! I've never seen anyone think so fast on their feet. Your brain must have been in a flat spin!"

"I feel like I need a doctor," Mr. Fettick said, wringing out his handkerchief. "They were so blastedly clever! I didn't expect them to question me quite so much."

"Professors," Mr. Flogg murmured in a tone recognizable to anyone who has had an essay returned to them covered in red ink.

"At least we have control of the story again. And frankly, I think it's going to be even more of a triumph than the original competition idea. Heroic professors rescuing a bird from the clutches of a tyrant! Sacrificing their own dreams to keep it safe! Dangerous henchmen! Romance! A desperate race across the country! Children everywhere will want to be ornithologists after this."

"And Gladstone will learn not to mess with publicists," Mr. Flogg said with dark satisfaction.

Both men chuckled and rubbed their palms together in what anyone would call dastardly behavior—at least until the publicists talked them into a new perspective.

SLOWING AS THEY spied the Eyrie ahead, Beth and Devon glanced back at the road behind them, hazy with sunlit dust. No one followed, and yet they felt a creepy sensation of being watched.

"Do you believe what that man said?" Beth asked.

"Ha! No," Devon answered. "It sounded like complete nonsense. But I do think Gladstone has the caladrius. And if he's training thaumaturgic birds, to exploit their powers . . . even beyond winning Birder of the Year, I want to get the caladrius away from him. Removing dangerous birds from the wild so they can be protected in aviaries and do no harm to people, that's one thing; using the magic of those birds for your own gain, another thing altogether."

"I agree. As for us remaining together . . ."

"You heard the man: it's *vital*."

Beth nodded. "That part is absolutely believable."

"Totally," Devon agreed. Taking her hand, he hurried along a path at the edge of Gladstone's property, and she smiled secretly to herself, letting him lead her.

# Chapter Twenty

The wise ornithologist keeps her friends close and her
enemies tied up somewhere they cannot trouble her.
*Birds Through a Sherry Glass*, H.A. Quirm

A N ORNITHOLOGY PROFESSOR is a master at skulking. Not
only can they creep up on the most jittery little bird without its realizing, but they are also skilled at slipping past farmers, police officers, and students wanting to ask for an extension
on coursework. Consequently, entering Gladstone's house unseen presented no difficulty to Beth and Devon.

Avoiding his various household staff proved simple also as
they made their way along the narrow service corridors.

Ducking into a broom closet to save themselves from the
butler's notice was a snap.

On the other hand, not utilizing that broom closet for the
purposes of grabbing each other, kissing each other, and
generally behaving in a wanton manner that would have jeop-
ardized their mission proved considerably less easy. The darkness and intimacy of the setting seemed to override all
Beth's prudence, which had been growing fragile even in broad
daylight, and Devon hadn't possessed much to begin with.
They managed to refrain, however, due to being consummate

professionals—and, more to the point, being interrupted in their reaching for each other by footsteps sounding just outside the closet door.

A feminine voice rang out. "Mrs. Grant, I've finished with the chamber pots. I'll sweep the entrance hall now."

The door handle began to move. Beth's breath snagged; Devon hastily grasped the handle. They looked at each other with a mix of alarm, trepidation, and simmering lust.

"It's stuck," muttered the woman on the other side. "Darn!"

She began to tug on the handle. Devon tugged back.

"Mrs. Grant!" the woman called out. "I think there's someone hiding in the closet!"

"Nonsense!" came a distant voice. "What a silly idea! It'll be the ghost."

"That makes sense," the woman said with relief. "All right, I'll dust the library instead."

"No, the professor left a bird in there and doesn't want it disturbed. Come help me with these pans."

The handle gave a final rattle, then footsteps could be heard moving away. Beth released a long breath. Devon cracked the door open cautiously, peering out.

"She's gone," he whispered.

"Thank goodness," Beth said.

There followed a moment of riveting silence as they contemplated closing the door again and having another go at wanton behavior. Their overstimulated glands campaigned strongly for this (thus revealing to them the existence of adrenaline a few years before its official discovery, had they but known it); their professionalism, however, sent a belated reminder that the caladrius was within reach and urgently needed their help.

"To the library?" Beth whispered.

"Yes," Devon said. He opened the door—

Then closed it and spun back to her, reaching out to cup her face with a barely restrained desperation. He bent until his lips hovered inches above hers, and Beth went so still she did not even breathe.

"Just be aware," he whispered, "that as soon as I can, I'm going to kiss you until your corset falls off."

"Understood," she said shakily.

A smile flicked across his mouth. A thread of desire knotted around Beth's heart. Her attraction to this man was so deep, it was practically geological. But there was a bird to rescue, a wicked plot to foil, and hopefully still the possibility of tenure to be awarded. So she stepped back just as Devon pulled himself away, and they both sighed.

Reopening the door, Devon double-checked that the corridor was still empty, then they crept out with what was objectively silence, despite the thundering of their hearts. Having visited the house more than once as Gladstone's student, assisting with his annual study of Little John, Beth directed their way. She managed to do so without grabbing Devon's wrist or otherwise womanhandling him, but there was no opportunity to point this out to him in a gently educational manner. And she actually would have rather liked to hold on to him, for she was nervous. Should Gladstone catch her, not only would she bid farewell to her hope of becoming Birder of the Year, but she'd probably end up demoted to the role of remedial tutor for first-year students, teaching the difference between a sanderling and sandpiper, and cleaning blackboard dusters at the end of each day.

Ascending a flight of stairs, they came to a hall lined with marble busts of famed scientists. Along the ceiling, taxidermied birds hung in a gruesomely motionless parody of flight toward the library at the far end. Beth paused at one diverging corridor, peering into its dusty shadows, but this part of the house seemed entirely unoccupied. The quiet only worsened her nerves, however, for if there was one thing an experienced birder knew, it was that danger didn't advertise its presence while lurking in wait to pounce on you. But they reached the end of the hall unchallenged and paused outside the library's half-open door. A sound of disconsolate peeping came from within.

"Well, that's certainly a bird," Devon said. "How much do you want to bet it's the caladrius?"

"Gambling is an illogical pursuit; I never do it," Beth replied. "But extrapolating probabilities from the available evidence, I'd say that is indeed our *Caladria albo sacrorum*."

They shared an excited glance. Never mind the competition; they were about to meet an exceedingly rare bird that hadn't been seen in the wild for decades. Beth's pulse began to speed up, and it was all she could do not to run at the same pace.

Her instincts, however, were trying to stop her altogether. She'd always disliked Gladstone's library, a vast collection of mostly unread books filled with outdated information and archaic science. She would like it even less if Gladstone occupied it at that moment. But instinct must bow before courage. Opening the door wider, she peered inside. Seeing no one, she slipped in, and Devon followed, closing the door behind him.

Whereas Gladstone's university office had been a chaotic jumble, this chamber was so clean as to appear entirely unvisited. Its leather sofas gleamed. The air lay torpid, scented with furniture wax and slowly decaying books. Summer's warmth seemed to have drained away through the old lead-lighted windows.

"There," Beth said, pointing to a round display table at the far end of the chamber. Twigs were protruding from cracks in its surface; they sprouted leaves here and there and glistened with thick golden rivulets of sap. Amid them stood a canvas-hooded item about one foot tall and dome-topped.

*Peep peep* came a sound from beneath the hood.

The lonely little cry pierced Beth's heart. Rushing across, she bent to lift the hem of the canvas a few inches and peer cautiously inside. Sure enough, a cage stood beneath, beautifully wrought with iron bars and scrolled designs. Glimpsing a small white body huddled trembling on a perch, she lowered the hem and stepped back so as not to distress the bird even more.

"It's our caladrius," she said in an awed whisper. "The poor little thing doesn't seem in good condition." Laying a hand atop the cage, she peeped in an approximation of the bird's own voice. Beside her, moving with a professional gentleness, Devon crouched to look beneath the cover, then after a brief moment straightened again, pushing back his hair.

"Judging from the bird's size, soft plumage, and the color of its beak, it's a juvenile," he said. "I'd suggest the altered state of this table is due to unstable thaumaturgic energy, but that seems unusual in a bird past fledging. I know you didn't want to believe that Gladstone would indulge in exploitative research, but this really does look like a bird who has been provoked into overusing its magic. And it's clearly having a negative impact on its health."

His voice was grim, his expression devoid of its usual ease, and Beth knew suddenly, unequivocally, that she loved him. Not even necessarily in a romantic vein; she loved him for who he was, and how he cared about birds, and the fact that he'd assessed the caladrius so confidently with just a quick look.

(There was also the matter of his strong forearms and gorgeous, skilled mouth, but she didn't want to spoil the high-minded moment by mentioning them.)

"You're right," she said. "We need to get the bird out of here." She took the cage by its handle, whispering reassurances to the caladrius as she lifted it carefully. She and Devon turned—

And stopped, staring at the footman who stood in the library doorway with feet apart and arms crossed, looking eerily like a university porter hunting down recalcitrant students.

"Who are you?" he demanded.

"We're Professor Gladstone's associates," Devon lied without hesitation. "He asked us to bring the bird to him."

The footman's eyes narrowed with suspicion. "I've never seen you before. How do I know you're telling the truth?"

"My good man," Beth replied in the tone of voice she reserved for emergencies, such as when a local suggested razing a forest to get rid of a sweet little bloodsucker owl, or a hotel concierge offered her a room overlooking the market square. "If you are deficient in elementary memory retrieval, that is not our responsibility. As representatives of the finest pedagogical facilities (pertaining to ornithology) in Her Majesty's realm, and more specifically, practitioners of academic specialities affiliated with those of Professor Gladstone, we reserve the unassailable right to—"

"Fine, fine," the footman interrupted, holding up his hands

in defense against this linguistic assault. "I believe you. Only a professor would talk like that."

"Quite right," Beth said. They took a step forward, then stopped again, frowning with nervous impatience, as the footman made no move to retreat.

"I still think I should double-check with Professor Gladstone," he grumbled.

Devon nodded. "That's reasonable. You're obviously very intelligent, and I respect that. You run off and double-check, and we'll wait right here for you."

"I shall!"

The footman turned smartly on a heel and marched away, and Devon rolled his eyes at Beth. She bit her lip, repressing a laugh.

"Thank you!" she called out to the footman as he left the room.

*Angel*, Devon mouthed to her. Now she was the one to roll her eyes, but less from amusement than from a confusing mix of shyness, mild exasperation, and being utterly, hopelessly charmed by the rogue. There was no time to sort through the feelings, however. As soon as they saw the footman turn the corner into another hallway, they ran from the library—

And stopped again, hearing voices from around that same corner.

*"What do you mean, 'associates'?"*

Beth's entire body turned colder than a frostbird's breath. "Gladstone!" she whispered.

Instantly, Devon manhandled her back into the library and closed the door behind them. He dragged a chair across to wedge beneath the door handle, and Beth turned the key that was protruding from the lock. Moments later, a *thud* reverberated through the door as someone bashed on it.

"I know you're in there, Pickering," came Professor Gladstone's stentorian voice, sounding bored.

"Open the door!" shouted the footman, thumping it again.

"There's no escape!" Beth gasped, looking around the room as if another exit might suddenly materialize among the books.

"We'll go out the window," Devon said, striding toward the far wall. Hurrying after him, Beth conveyed a lecture as to the danger of this plan, along with charts and comprehensive recommended reading list, via the silent arch of her eyebrows. Devon merely grinned at her.

"Trust me," he said. He unlatched the window, swung it open, and looked down. "Hm, no drainpipe. Well, that's inconvenient. I don't suppose you have a helicopter parasol on you?"

"Oh yes, I keep it under my hat," Beth answered, provoked to sarcasm.

*Thud! Thud!* The efforts on the other side of the door had escalated to kicking, with considerable success: the barricading chair fell, and the key began to rattle in its lock.

Devon regarded Beth mildly. "You aren't wearing a hat."

"Mr. Lockley," she chided, "this isn't the time for bantering. Please confine yourself to helpful suggestions."

He glanced out the window again. "We could climb down using the window ledges, but only if we left the bird behind. And I'm *not* doing that."

Beth had never heard anything more sexy in her life. *I really do adore him*, her heart sighed. *I could kiss him all over this very moment.* (Which was not a particularly helpful suggestion either, but she couldn't blame herself.)

They looked at each other in taut silence, then Devon's eyes lightened, a smile gliding across his mouth.

"Oh dear," Beth said. "You're going to hijack something."

He laughed. "No. We simply have to make a run for it. We'll head back down the way we came, and out the back door. You take the bird and keep going, no matter what happens."

Beth's expression grew wary. "And what about you?"

He cupped his hand against the back of her head and drew her closer, setting a kiss upon her forehead. "I'll be right with you," he said—at least, that is what Beth thought she heard dimly through her nerves' delighted singing.

*THUD!*

With one enormous crash, the door broke open and the footman veritably tumbled into the room, followed at a more sedate pace by Gladstone. Beth did not spare a moment to assess the degree of anger on the professor's face. She was running even before he'd fully entered the room.

"Out of the way!" Devon yelled as he led the charge, using all the authority vested in him by an organization whose goal was to keep a bunch of high-spirited young adults from wreaking havoc impart a valuable education upon its students. Startled by this sudden offensive, the footman instinctively leaped aside, and they barreled past him, past Gladstone—catching a whiff of pipe smoke, a broken gasp of outrage—before speeding down the corridor. They were almost to the stairs before the footman reorganized his wits and gave chase.

Hauling up her long skirt with one hand, Beth began a cautious descent of the stairs, the caladrius beating its wings frenetically within the cage and peeping at her to go more slowly while Devon, one step behind, practically vibrated with the desire for her to hurry up.

"*Stop!*" shouted the footman in their wake, proving once again his unfortunate lack of intellect. More unfortunate, however, at least for Beth and Devon, was that he made up for it with physical prowess: he'd run so fast, he would probably reach them in another few steps.

Glancing over his shoulder, Devon muttered a curse. "Keep going," he told Beth. "I'll catch up."

Beth paused. "What—"

"Go!"

A lifetime of obedience forced her onward, around a bend, down another flight of steps. From above came a terrifying series of noises . . . *thud! crash! "aarrgh!" thud! smack! "nooo!"* . . . but she did not stop until she reached the ground. Racing past the closet in which she and Devon had previously hidden, she took a sharp corner into a musty, unlit corridor. At its end she arrived at an entryway cluttered with raincoats, galoshes, and rusted old cages. Opening its external door, she looked out to the lawn at the side of the house. Not far away was a hedge, some three feet high, and beyond that, a line of elm trees gleaming in the vivid morning sunlight.

Devon arrived, running straight for the door. His shirt was ripped at the collar and his hair disheveled, but he appeared otherwise unharmed. "Quickly!" he urged.

They sprinted across the lawn toward the hedge. Devon hurdled it without pause, but Beth struggled, hampered as she was by her skirts and the fact that the hedge was more than half her height. Taking the birdcage and setting it down, Devon helped her over—which is to say, half dragged her over, with a display of uncouth and decidedly unromantic handling that Beth was nevertheless grateful for under the circumstances. As soon as she was on her feet again, he picked up the cage and they dashed into the shadows among the trees.

"We have to get back to the village and catch that eleven o'clock train," Devon said.

Checking the fob watch pinned to her satchel, Beth frowned. "It's ten thirty now. We'll never make it."

Just then, with impeccable timing, voices sounded on the far side of the trees. Devon stopped so abruptly, Beth collided with him. He reached out automatically with his free hand to steady her, but his attention strained toward whoever was speaking.

"Damn it, you *Arschgeige*!"

"Desist from pushing me, by Jove!"

Beth and Devon shared a knowing glance. Moving forward cautiously, they noticed a narrow lane on the other side of the trees. Parked there was the curricle that had almost plowed into Beth earlier. Herr Oberhufter and Hippolyta Quirm stood a short distance from it, arguing.

"I'm not pushing you!" Oberhufter hollered. "I'm patting you!"

"Reprehensible liar!" Hippolyta retorted, smacking his arm.

"Ow!"

"Violent, pompous clodhopper!" She smacked him again.

Devon caught Beth's gaze then tilted his head toward the curricle. She nodded. They crept between the trees, wincing with every crack of twigs beneath their feet, barely daring to breathe—although they probably could have sung a shanty in two-part harmony and they wouldn't have been heard above the shouts of the field ornithologists.

"Idiot, I told you Gladstone didn't have the caladrius! Your idea to follow Pickering and Lockley was a complete waste of time!"

"We only searched half the house! If you hadn't worn an *orange* dress, we wouldn't have had to flee when that chambermaid spotted us!"

"It's not as orange as your face!"

This insult was not particularly fair, since Oberhufter's face had in fact turned bright red. He grabbed hold of Hippolyta by the ruffles of the aforementioned orange dress and, pulling her hard against him, kissed any further vitriol from her mouth. Immediately, Beth and Devon dashed from the tree shadows. Climbing into the curricle as quietly as possible, they set the birdcage on Beth's lap, she placed her satchel in front of it for protection, and Devon grabbed the horses' reins.

*"Oi! Stop!"*

Glancing back, they saw Gladstone's footman making hot pursuit through the trees. The command alerted Oberhufter and Hippolyta also, and they stared with shocked confusion as the curricle began to drive toward them.

"Lockley!" Herr Oberhufter shouted. *"Was zur Hölle?!"*

But there was no time for conversation. Devon urged the horses into a gallop. Beth, clinging to the bench seat with one hand and the birdcage with the other, heard only incoherent screams from Oberhufter and Hippolyta as they were compelled to leap into a hedge or else be run over. Had she ever diversified her education to include cultural studies, she would have appreciated the karma of the moment. Unfortunately, her only instinct was a British one.

"Sorry!" she called out.

Alas, judging from Hippolyta's roar, she was not forgiven.

They sped along the sloping lane, sending birds flying up

from the hedgerows in alarm and an elderly pedestrian into paroxysms of outrage at the side of the road. The footman gave chase for a while but was soon left in their dust, literally. As Beth tried to keep the birdcage safe despite the wild shuddering of the curricle, she heard nothing from beneath its cover and began to worry that the bird had expired from fright.

Within a few minutes, the lane descended at a steep angle toward the main road, and Devon slowed the horses. They trotted into the village.

"How long have we got until the train leaves?" Devon asked.

Beth reached for her fob watch—and blinked in surprise. The glass surface was freckled all over with tiny white crystals, as if some magical force had tried restoring its original state. But the only performer of magic in the vicinity was the caladrius, and according to all the information Beth had reviewed, its power was healing illness, not actual regeneration.

"Um," she said, holding up the watch.

Devon shot a quick glance at it. "Um," he agreed.

The bird in its hooded cage had no comment.

"We'll just have to hope we're not too late," Devon said.

Looking back over her shoulder at the diverging roads behind them, Beth noticed dust clouds in the distance and realized the race was on. Fear gripped her stomach tight. Forget hope; it was going to take a whole lot of luck to get out of this situation, and as a scientist, she knew that was the most precarious thing of all.

## Chapter Twenty-One

The adventuring woman should not just expect the
unexpected, but *be* the unexpected.
                    *Birds Through a Sherry Glass*, H.A. Quirm

Arriving at the train station, Devon leaped from the
curricle almost before the horses had come to a halt. He
assisted Beth in making a more careful descent with the birdcage, then together they ran up the ramp to the platform. A
clock above the ticket booth assured him they still had five
minutes before the train arrived, but Devon knew he'd not feel
safe until they were on board and heading for London.

Only when Beth stumbled behind him did he realize he'd
kept hold of her hand and was practically dragging her along
with him. "Sorry," he said, letting her go—but immediately set
a hand against her back as he guided her toward the ticket
booth.

"I can walk under my own power, you know," she said with
wry humor.

"You're keeping me steady," he answered, flashing a grin to
hide the fact that he meant it seriously, and far more soulfully
than a licentious rake ought. Somehow over the past few days,
Beth Pickering had become the center of his personal gravity.

Whenever he left her side for long, it felt like his heart was spinning out into darkness. He had to appreciate the irony: after all, he was only in this situation now because he'd been so aghast at his head of department's matchmaking endeavors, and so determined to remain single.

Then again, perhaps Beth's wry comment was her nice, polite way of asserting her personal boundary. And Devon, respecting her, certainly did not want to overstep. So he withdrew his hand—

And she caught it, clutching it warmly with her own. "I'm glad I've been a good influence on you," she said—and the only reason he didn't stop right then and kiss her in demonstration of just how *bad* she inspired him to be was because they had a priceless bird to save, a nefarious cabal of ornithologists to escape, and tickets to buy before all the first-class seats were taken.

The ticket clerk watched their approach excitedly, and by the time they arrived he seemed almost breathless. "It's you!" he exclaimed, his pert little goatee ruffling like a duck's tail.

"It is?" Devon said cautiously.

"The famous ornithologist lovebirds!"

Beth was so astonished that he'd used the correct word, she did a double take. Then she quickly laughed. "Oh good heavens, no. We only look like them. We're literature teachers."

"You're holding a birdcage," the clerk pointed out.

"It's a raven. For a class on Edgar Allan Poe."

"Two first-class tickets for London, please," Devon ordered, releasing Beth's hand as he reached for the wallet in his coat's inner pocket.

"Of course," the clerk said. He slipped a card across the desk—not a ticket, but a color postcard with the Little John hawk depicted on it. "I don't suppose I could trouble you for an an autograph . . . ?"

"Certainly," Beth replied with a smile.

"But we're just literature teachers," Devon interjected. "Not famous at all." He reached beneath the glass screen, seized the tickets, then strode away without another word, leaving Beth to thank the gobsmacked clerk before hurriedly following. As she caught up with him, her hand brushed against his, like a shy question. He reached out to take it, and at once her fingers tightened around his. It was as if they tightened around his heart too.

"You've become quite the liar," he teased, smiling at her.

"Your corruption of me is complete," she said with a valiant attempt at banter.

"Not quite yet," he answered, his banter so on point it might even be described as penetrating. Beth blinked, and flushed, and altogether made Devon adore her a hundred times over.

"Excuse me," the ticket clerk said behind them, dragging a luggage trolley. They leaped apart, for fear of being interrogated about their relationship status and ending up in a newspaper once again, but the clerk did not even notice; he was looking about confusedly. "Where's your luggage?"

"We have none," Devon told him.

It was as if he'd announced that suitcases and steamer trunks had been canceled and that there would be no refunds, not even a handbag. The clerk reared back with shock. "Are you sure?"

"Quite."

"I see." Clearly they were making wholesale edits to a script he had in his mind. He gave himself a little shake. "This is a flag stop; we have to wave down the train so it knows to stop here and pick up passengers. I'll tell Martin up the signal tower to bring out the white flag and—*hey! Stop!*"

At first Devon assumed the young man was merely being emphatic in his explanation of what a white flag signified. But then he glanced up at the signal tower.

"Hey! Stop!" he shouted.

"No, thank you," called down a Miss Fotheringham from the high platform where she stood beside the signalman (or at least the gagged and bound form of the signalman), waving a green flag aloft.

"But we need the train to stop!" the clerk yelled up to her. "Wave the white flag! The white!"

Miss Fotheringham cupped a hand to her ear. "I can't hear you!"

*TOOT!*

Devon and Beth turned to see a train approaching.

And drive past them.

And continue on toward the horizon.

Seconds later, they found themselves looking at empty tracks and a high trail of smoke speckled with disturbed birds. Miss Fotheringham threw down the green flag, cackling.

"I told you we were right to follow Miss Pickering, Elvira!" she called out.

"There's a first time for everything, Ethel!" came a reedy shout from behind the seating shelter farther down the platform. Devon looked around to see a second Miss Fotheringham emerge, pulling a knife from her puffed sleeve.

"Hand over that bird," she demanded, moving toward them.

"This?" Beth held up the cage. "It's empty."

Whether Miss Fotheringham believed her did not matter, for just then *another* shout rang out.

"Stop right there!"

Looking around, they saw Gladstone's footman running up the station's ramp, red-faced with fury.

"For goodness' sake," Beth said. "All this excitement cannot be good for the caladrius."

"*Caladrius?!*" The ticket clerk squeaked, excitement radiating from his every pore. "You have the actual caladrius in that cage?!"

Alas, they could not answer him, on account of being halfway across the platform, making at speed for a secondary exit.

"Stop!" Gladstone's footman insisted, gasping as he reached the top of the ramp.

"Stop!" Elvira Fotheringham demanded, brandishing her knife.

"Terribly sorry!" Beth called out. "Please give Professor Gladstone our regrets!"

"I'll give *you* regrets!" Gaining his second wind, the footman sprinted toward them.

*Crash!*

The ticket clerk had shoved his luggage trolley across the platform and the footman ran into it, causing the trolley to topple and him to go down with it. Pumping a fist, the clerk whooped triumphantly. "For the caladrius!" he shouted.

As the footman groaned and the Fotheringhams reunited in preparation to give chase, Devon and Beth raced down a short ramp into the adjacent lane, where the curricle awaited. Someone, presumably Gladstone's footman, had broken its wheels. The footman's own horse stood nearby, grazing on wild grass at the side of the avenue, and Devon was debating whether he should steal it when a garishly colored bird flew overhead. It circled them, then aimed back toward the village, squawking, *train station! train station!*

"*Psittacus inquisitor,*" Beth identified grimly. Spy parrot.

Devon cursed. His mind began to sink with the weight of every possible decision he might make, and for a terrifying moment he simply could not move at all. Then Beth caught his hand and began tugging him.

"Just run," she said, and he gratefully obeyed.

They reached a crossroads and saw a hansom cab in the distance, speeding through the village. "This way!" Beth ordered, and they turned south, following the road down beneath an arched stone bridge into a vista of sheep-strewn farmlands. Beth's hand grew sweaty in Devon's, and he could hear the strained labor of her breath. Only a frightening silence emitted from the birdcage. Devon wondered if they should leave the road to hide among bushes, but a glance back showed a horseman in pursuit, and he knew it was too late.

"Stop!" the man shouted. "Wait!"

"Devon." Beth slowed her pace, making him stumble a little. "Stop."

"We don't need to be polite to our enemies!" he reminded her.

"No, really, stop! It's the ticket clerk from the station."

Devon glanced back with confused surprise. Indeed, the clerk was galloping toward them—or, more correctly, what appeared to be the footman's horse was galloping toward them with the clerk hunched on its back, his goatee flapping like a tiny blond flag of surrender. Devon felt inclined to keep running, but Beth pulled free of his grip and waved to the clerk. Devon lifted his gaze heavenward, seeking patience, but then turned and stood beside the angel he'd already been sent. Perhaps she was right and they were not about to be captured and forced to deliver the caladrius back into Gladstone's dubious care.

"Look at it this way," Beth said. "We can always hijack the horse."

Devon bit his lip so he didn't laugh. Feet apart and arms crossed, he scowled as the clerk drew up before them.

"I've come to help!" the young man explained breathlessly, slithering down from the saddle and performing an old-fashioned bow to Beth. From the corner of his eye Devon could see her practically melting at the gesture, and his scowl grew more severe.

"You're Professor Pickering, aren't you?" the clerk said, pressing a hand against his heart as if he addressed the Queen herself. "I *knew* you were! I'm a big fan. The way you caught that whopper swan in Oxford with such grace and expertise was an *inspiration* to me as a professional luggage handler. And you must be Mr. Lockley." He flicked a glance at Devon, then returned to swooning over Beth. "I know we have no time for autographs, or even for me to snip a lock of your hair—? Right, no time. But it is my *honor* to assist you. Also the man said you might turn up at the station and that if I helped, I'd get my name in the papers too. He said an evil professor was torturing the caladrius! So I've brought this horse for your escape."

"Thank you," Beth said so sincerely, the clerk hunched up his shoulders with bashful delight. Devon's scowl went from severe to the equivalent of a winter storm in Antarctica. Shifting closer to Beth, he laid a hand on her back—not at all in a proprietary fashion, you understand, simply to have somewhere to put it.

"What man?" he asked.

"He said he was a PRESS agent," the clerk told Beth as if Devon was merely her mouthpiece. "Black suit, mustache, briefcase. He said the caladrius was counting on me. *Me*."

"Gosh," Beth responded obligingly.

"Horse theft is a significant crime," Devon pointed out.

"Not when you're doing it to save a bird!"

At that, Devon's scowl eased slightly. "What's your name?"

"*Bastard!*"

They all jolted at the sudden shout. Gladstone's footman was pelting down the road toward them, followed by the Fotheringham sisters skimming above the road with the aid of helicopter parasols that were sparking and beginning to smoke. Farther back came a hansom cab carrying Herr Oberhufter. Hippolyta Quirm stood in its rear driver's seat, looking like the warrior queen Boudicca, albeit with more orange lace. She whipped the horses into a speed that made Herr Oberhufter's hat bob atop his head. Last of all, following at a respectful distance, were three carriages full of assorted servants and luggage.

"Go!" the clerk urged, flapping his hand. Immediately Beth handed the birdcage to Devon and mounted the horse with an efficiency that rejected another romantic moment. Devon passed her up the cage, then hoisted himself into the saddle, wrapping one arm around her waist as he grasped the reins in his other. There was only enough time for her to call out thanks to the clerk before they galloped off down the road, followed by roars from their pursuers.

"*Halt!*" Oberhufter demanded.

"*Get out of my way, fools!*" Hippolyta shouted at the Fotheringham sisters.

*"Never!"* they hollered in reply.

*Crash!*

Devon glanced back to see the hansom cab tilted sideways against a bush on the verge, the Fotheringham sisters tumbled in Oberhufter's lap, and his hat rolling away down the road.

"Oh no!" Beth gasped. "Is everyone all right?"

Hippolyta's furious *"damn you, Oberhufter!"* provided an answer. Beth slumped back with relief against Devon, and he held her tight, racing toward the hope of some safe, private place where he could embrace her properly, in peace.

Fifteen minutes later, the horse began limping, but almost immediately thereafter they came upon the Sir William coaching inn, in what could have been considered a miracle were they not scientists and, furthermore, this not England, land of hope, glory, and some hundred thousand public houses. They rode into the stable yard and dismounted.

"We'll have to leave the horse here and continue on foot," Devon said.

"Where are we even going?" Beth asked.

He squinted at the sun-bleached horizon. "Sheffield? And catch a train to Dover from there?"

"Good idea." She peeked beneath the cage cover. "Feathers fluffed up, breathing unsteady," she said as she assessed the caladrius's condition. "But beak closed and eyes clear. The seed debris on the cage floor is sprouting, which suggests thaumaturgic activity."

Lowering the cover, she bit her thumbnail, then grimaced at the taste of the dusty glove. Devon tried not to smile in sheer adoration, or for that matter to remove the glove and kiss her thumb, her hand, all the way along her arm to—

"I'm concerned," she said, and he shook his head to restore

focus. "Obviously Gladstone has been provoking the bird to use its power, but a caladrius that's been drawing illness into itself must cleanse it by flying high into the sunlight. How long can a juvenile survive without doing so?"

"I don't know," Devon admitted. "So much of the available information about the bird is mythology."

Beth sighed, her expression sobering. "Why did I not think about its possible fate before I entered the competition?"

"I didn't either," Devon admitted. "I trusted IOS's professional integrity."

"So did I. Obviously I should have been more cynical."

He took her hand before she could attack the thumb again. "Don't think like that. They should have been more trustworthy. Anyway, we're here now, and it's our decisions from this point on that matter. I suggest we take the bird to a sanctuary."

"Which one?"

"L'Abri à Bergerac," he said. "It's where I sent the death-whistler, and I know it to be reputable. They'll protect the caladrius even if the entire IOS executive committee comes knocking on their door."

"That sounds good. So back to France, then. But first, might we purchase some food from the inn? An apple, some nuts, some crusts of bread?"

"I think I can afford to buy us better than that," Devon assured her wryly.

"I meant for the caladrius. Its seed and water supplies are adequate, but it ought to have a varied diet."

Devon tried not to roll his eyes with fond amusement. "And you, Miss Pickering? Are you hungry?"

She blinked with surprise at the question. Then shyness darkened her gaze like a summer storm, and Devon would have bet that no one had asked her such a thing in a very long time. "I'll buy you some lunch," he said, just to watch the storm deepen and her eyelashes lower sweetly, just to make her feel nice. "Will you wait here with the horse?"

She nodded, and he squeezed her hand gently before releasing it and turning toward the inn. But he'd taken only a few steps before he simply *had* to look back, compelled by the gravity between them.

Beth was stroking the horse's neck, murmuring praise and promises of hay. The late morning sunlight blossomed around her, turning her long, loose hair into a wealth of bright treasure. Devon stared transfixed, every other thought forgotten.

And that was how he missed the parrot skimming past the inn before circling to fly north again, singing *here, here*.

BETH WATCHED FROM the corner of her eye as Devon went through the inn's side door. The way he'd held her hand, not to mention the thrilling interest he'd shown in her digestion status, created a fluttering sensation all over her skin, as though she wore nothing but a feather boa. She wished she could forget about the International Ornithological Society for a while and convince him that they should take a room in the inn—a room with only one bed and a sturdy lock on its door.

She gasped at the thought, then gasped again because the first one had not been shock at her impropriety but delight at the imaginings it inspired.

And yet, how could she indulge in such imaginings about a man for whom she held so little data? She'd disliked Devon Lockley . . . been aggravated by him . . . felt attracted to him . . . kissed him . . . fallen in love with him, and it had felt like everything. But what was his favorite bird? Had he ever encountered a ghost owl? Who were his family? Would he mind terribly if she ripped off his shirt and kissed every inch of his naked torso?

*"Hello!"*

The greeting jabbed her awareness; turning, she found a young stable hand beside her.

"Oh," she said, blushing as if he might have somehow discerned her thoughts.

He tugged his forelock. Drops of sweat flicked off it to create tiny, murky puddles on his dirt-streaked face. "Can I help you, mi— Hey, wait! You're that lady from the newspaper!" His gaze flicked from her to the birdcage, then back again at speed, barely giving her enough time to roll her eyes wearily. "The orthilochist lady what's doing the Birder of the Year competition! Cor blimey!"

"Um," Beth said.

"Where's your American lover? Oh no, you ain't back to being rivals?"

"Uh . . ."

"Is that cage for when you catch the caladrius?"

"Er."

"Wait until Jenny hears about this! She loves birds! The flying kind, that is. Well, and t'other kind." He winked in such a risqué manner that Beth took a step back. "Just wait here a mo' and I'll go tell her! Bleedin' hell, an *actual famous* orthilochist!"

"Um," Beth reiterated, to no avail. The stable hand dashed off, leaving her reeling from their conversation.

"Good grief," she muttered. "Why do people have to people?"

*"Vulgar cretin!"* Hippolyta shouted.

Beth almost laughed. Trust Hippolyta to phrase it in a

more blatant way, she thought, turning to raise her eyebrow at the woman—then suffered a belated jolt of alarm as she realized, *Hippolyta!* Ducking behind the horse, she looked around urgently but could not see her former associate anywhere.

"Must you shout, madam?!" arose another voice with no concern for the irony of its own volume. Beth comprehended that Hippolyta and Oberhufter, and God knows who else, were approaching close upon the inn.

She had mere seconds to act before they either passed its frontage and saw her in the stable yard—or stopped and, entering the building, discovered Devon therein. She looked around, trying to assess all possible escape routes, but before she could decide upon one, the inn's side door flung open and Devon emerged at a run. Relief propelled Beth toward him, and he grasped her arm of course, towing her inside the stables. One second later, a hansom cab arrived in the yard, driven by Gladstone's footman and with Hippolyta and Herr Oberhufter crammed into its seat, the Fotheringham sisters each balancing precariously on a step at either side. Behind it came the servants' carriages.

Ducking behind the stable's open door, Beth and Devon peered through a gap between the hinges as the ornithologists climbed down from the cab, squabbling the entire time.

"We won't be able to hide for long," Beth whispered. "The horse proves that we're here."

*Peep*, the caladrius agreed.

Just then, the stable hand entered through the stable's far door. Devon whistled quietly through his teeth and the boy came to an abrupt halt, noticing them in their hiding place. As he drew breath to speak, Beth placed a finger to her lips, urging silence. She pointed in the direction of the yard and mouthed the words *avaricious opponents*. The boy frowned with unsurprising bewilderment.

"I know you're here, Elizabeth!" Hippolyta shouted. "Just hand over the bird and no one will get hurt! Except that Cambridge lout. And, well, you too, a little bit. I'm sure you understand; this is ornithology, after all!"

Comprehension dawned on the stable hand's face. He hurried over, joining them in the shadows behind the door and forcing them to cram themselves farther into the corner.

"You got the caladrius in that cage, yeah?" he whispered. When Beth and Devon nodded, his excitement shone so brightly, he almost looked clean. "Keep your pecker up! I'll bamboozle the rotters while you saw your timber."

Now Beth was the one to frown in bewilderment. But there was no time to request a translation.

"We need to get to Sheffield, to catch a train south," Devon said.

"That's easy. You just go some three hours up the east road. Cut down through the gardens behind here, that'll get you in a jiffy to the village, then Bob's your uncle."

"I don't have a jiffy," Beth said. "Or an uncle."

Devon smiled at her. "He means . . . never mind. Let's go."

"The name's Jack Scrottley, by the way," the boy said, "in case you happen to talk to any newspaper reporters."

He held out his grubby hand and Beth automatically shook it, silently thanking her gloves' manufacturer and reminding herself not to chew her thumbnail anytime soon. Then he hurried away, and as they heard him greet the ornithologists, Beth and Devon ran along the stable's alleyway and out the back door, a booming echo of Hippolyta's voice chasing them like a Siberian saber-toothed canary.

## CHAPTER TWENTY-TWO

Out in the middle of nowhere is often where you find
your answers.

*Birds Through a Sherry Glass*, H.A. Quirm

WHEN HE SAID 'go up the east road,' I did not think he
meant *literally* up," Beth said, pausing to wipe her brow
with the back of her wrist. Since leaving the village of Grindleford, their route had made a moderate but relentless incline
through woodlands, and the day's heat had intensified to such
a degree that they half expected to see a flock of firebirds in the
trees overhead, singing flames across the sky. Their steady pace
slowed, and "three hours to Sheffield" had transformed into
"all damn afternoon to go one-fifth of the way."

To be fair, they'd spent much of that time sitting beneath
an oak tree. Their pursuers not appearing, perhaps having
taken a different route, it had seemed only logical to rest from
the hectic morning and to eat a nourishing luncheon purchased from a baker in the village, whose spectacles were so
scratched he'd barely been able to see them, let alone identify
them as famous ornithologists. This logic had then extended to
gazing around at the lovely, tranquil countryside (reconnais-
sance), noting various birds within it (professional develop-

ment), and drifting slowly, sweetly closer to each other (team building). Their eyes had begun to haze, their lips parted . . . since, after all, kissing would be the *most* logical thing to do, because, er, um, because it would reinvigorate them for the walk ahead . . .

And suddenly the caladrius had embarked upon a bright, trilling song, calling to its peers in the wild. They'd moved apart with surprised laughter.

"We must get back on the road," Beth had said, forcing good sense back into her brain.

Devon had sighed and nodded. "Yes, we ought not loiter like this. At any moment a reporter from the *Morning Herald* might pop up to ask us when we're getting married."

"Ha ha," Beth had said.

"Ha ha," Devon had agreed.

They'd gathered up the leftovers of the food and resumed walking.

Soon after, however, a yaffingale had flown across the road, and they'd felt a professional obligation to stop and admire it, and argue cheerfully about it being a harbinger of rain, and for Beth to make rudimentary notes in her field journal before Devon stole the book to draw a tiny dancing carnivorous lap-wing in the corner of one page. Beth had watched him with a lump in her throat. When he'd returned the book, she'd hugged it while Devon had shoved his hands into his pockets and scuffed a bootheel against the dusty road. They'd smiled rather bashfully at each other, there in the middle of the road, and kissing would have almost certainly ensued had not the yaffingale circled back and deposited a large wad of guano only inches away from them, rather spoiling the mood.

Then a carriage had appeared on the road behind them,

coming out of Grindleford, requiring an urgent dash into the protection of tree shadows . . . and the holding of hands when they emerged again . . . the swinging of those hands . . . light conversation and smiles . . . lingering looks . . .

All of which made for much enjoyment but very little actual progress toward Sheffield.

Finally, they noticed the sun's lowering and agreed they'd have to give up their trek for the day and find an inn before darkness fell. (Granted, sunset wasn't due for another four hours, allowing plenty of time to travel the remaining eight miles to Sheffield—but an ability to do basic math disappears surprisingly quickly when one's brain is being so flooded by the oxytocin hormone that one can barely walk at all.)

Beth sighed. "I wish the train had stopped in Hathersage," she lied. In fact, she'd never felt more blissful than she had this afternoon, strolling the woodland road with Devon. It was even superior to the time she'd been about to join a faculty Christmas party when the fire alarm had gone off, forcing everyone to leave the building.

"At least the caladrius is happier," Devon said, holding up the birdcage to watch its little white inhabitant hop from perch to water bottle to perch again, peeping excitedly at all the sights of the woodlands around it. After leaving the village they had removed the cage cover and pressed a chunk of pear between two bars, and the caladrius had perked up considerably. Its pretty white wings and its delight with the world made Beth smile every time she looked at it.

"Come on," Devon told her, lowering the cage again, his own smile rather sappy. "We should keep going."

Beth sighed. "Can't we just wait here until someone imports one of those newfangled motorcars into England and happens to drive past so we can hijack them?"

Devon laughed. Hooking a finger around two of hers, he lifted her hand and turned it so she found herself spinning beneath their raised arms like in a dance. Then he began walking backward, cajoling her, gently tugging her, until she was laughing and walking, with all her heart willing to go anywhere in the world he might lead.

A FEW MINUTES later they came to the edge of the woods and discovered before them moorlands spreading to a far horizon, bare, brown, and swept with cool wind. Not a single building was in sight. Devon stopped, his heart swooping.

But Beth slipped away from him and drifted forward, becoming illuminated by the clear light from a vast, pallid sky. Tipping her face up to the wind, she closed her eyes, and long strands of hair swept across their lids, brushed her smile, and draped over the arms she stretched out as if she'd take flight.

Devon could not move, not even to glance away from her. The weight of attraction he felt for this woman had become almost unbearable. He'd dawdled all afternoon, taking any excuse to stop along the way, reveling in her company. He found her so endlessly beautiful, decent, fun, and interesting, and he liked her equally as much as he felt in love with her. He wasn't ready to say goodbye yet. In fact, he wished he never had to at all. But his whole life had been a series of farewells: from his mother when she died, from his family when he was sent to Yale, from casual lovers and temporary friends . . . He could not trust in wishes.

"It doesn't look hopeful," he said.

Beth turned to smile at him. "Oh, you never know your—"

She stopped abruptly as the clatter of traffic sounded in the distance. There was just enough time for Devon to utter a curse (and Beth to give him a chastising frown) before a hansom cab appeared around a bend some hundred yards back, dust clouds rising from beneath its wheels and shouts from within its body.

*"Tyrannical woman!"*

*"Idiot! I told you going west was a stupid idea!"*

*"Will you both stop shouting?!"*

*"Don't shove me!"*

Devon reached for Beth to pull her off the road, but she was already running. They sprinted down a mild slope to crouch behind the nearest clump of dusty, dried-up gorse, and seconds later the cab emerged from the woodland. It drew to a halt where they had been standing, almost causing a collision between the several vehicles behind it.

"I swear I saw people on the road here!" the driver called from his high seat.

*Peep!* the caladrius sang, and Devon hastily swept one half of his coat around its cage. Hippolyta rose to stand on the cab's footrest with her hands on her hips, ringlets stirring in the wind as she examined the view.

A yellow gorse flower blossomed in front of Devon, glimmering slightly with avian magic.

"I see no one!" Hippolyta declared.

"The driver's telling the truth," a Miss Fotheringham said from her perch on the cab's left step. "It was two people, a man and a woman."

"Yes, and the woman wasn't wearing a hat," the other Miss Fotheringham said disapprovingly from the cab's right step.

"And the man had a magnificent golden mustache," the first added.

Suddenly a score of flowers burst forth at the uppermost tips of the gorse bush. Beth gasped. Devon drew the birdcage closer and wrapped the other half of his coat around it. *Peep* came from beneath the cotton drapery.

"That's strange," Hippolyta boomed, peering in their direction. Devon suppressed a curse; beside him, Beth tensed in preparation for running.

"Those weren't there a minute ago, by Jove!" Flinging out her arm dramatically, Hippolyta pointed a pink-gloved finger toward the bush behind which they hid.

"What is it?" Herr Obherhufter and the Fotheringham sisters all asked at once.

"Two albino hawks in that tree over there!"

*"Verdammt!"* Oberhufter shouted. "We have no time for hawks and shadows! Lockley will be in Sheffield by now! Drive on!"

With a loud, aggrieved sigh, Hippolyta sat down and the driver urged the horse into a trot once more. Within moments, the cab and its attendant vehicles had disappeared beyond the eastern horizon.

Devon and Beth let out simultaneous breaths of relief. Unwrapping the birdcage, Devon gave the caladrius a mock frown. "Rascal," he chided.

"How did it make these flowers bloom?" Beth asked, gently touching a yellow petal. "Rejuvenation is never mentioned as one of its powers."

"Perhaps it has naturally evolved since last observed," Devon suggested. "Or perhaps Gladstone's attempts to manipulate it have triggered a change to its thaumaturgic energy profile."

Beth frowned. "If it can regenerate things in this way on a consistent basis, and not just as an expression of stress, then *everyone* will want a piece of it."

"Well, we have it now," Devon said, "and we will ensure its safety." He rose and held out his hand; Beth took it, and he helped her up. They gazed out at the scruffy landscape.

"Not a building anywhere in sight," Beth said with a weary sigh.

"I could have sworn there was an inn nearby," Devon murmured. "Mind you, it's been a while since I was last here."

"Oh?" Beth asked, sounding as if she wanted to hear more. He gave her a slightly uncertain look but, seeing her smile, realized the interest was genuine. The woman appeared hell-bent on melting every rough, jaded shard within him and replacing it with a warm haze of delight. He answered her; of course he did—he would give her anything at this point.

"These moors contain a wellspring of thaumaturgic energy. When I was twelve, my cousin Gabriel convinced his parents to camp here at the start of summer so that he could study the effects of magic on the land. He always wanted to be a geographer, don't ask me why, no one really understands him. I may be clever, but Gabriel is something else altogether. Anyway, in those days, wherever he went, I followed—we're around the same age, and we used to be more like brothers than cousins— so they invited me along. He spent the whole time walking hither and yon with a compass and a notebook, muttering to himself, while his sister Amelia and I chased flying pebbles and tried to locate hidden singing rivers. But my favorite part was witnessing a certain nocturnal bird that nests here."

Instantly, Beth's eyes lit up. "Do you mean *Setophaga lapis*, the warbler that turns itself to stone by moonlight?"

He shrugged his mouth. "Maybe."

"Or was it *Lagopus lagopus aoidos*, the grouse that sings epic poetry to the stars?"

"Perhaps."

"My legs hurt," she said at once.

"Oh?"

She nodded. "Yes. And my shoes are full of road dust. I can barely walk."

"Poor darling," he said. "Perhaps we should just camp out for the night."

Her expression could have taken flight into a dream of moonlit wings, but she bit her lip with the most unbelievable pretense of disconcertment Devon had ever seen. Thankfully, she didn't bite her thumbnail—that glove was so filthy now it would have made her ill.

"If you think that's wise," she murmured. Then without even looking, she flung out an arm in the same manner Hippolyta had, pointing to a scattering of trees a hundred yards northeast of where they stood. "That seems like a good spot."

"Can you walk that far?" Devon asked, just to tease her. But she was already striding away, plowing through bracken and wildflowers, weariness forgotten at the thought of an interesting bird.

Devon smiled at her back. In all honesty, he had no idea if stone warblers or poetic grouse lived on this moor. But he remembered vividly what did, and he loved the idea of surprising Beth with it.

After all, he thought as he followed her into the wild, it was *only logical* that they spend a little time away from observers, outside the chase, to experience some private magic for themselves.

THE PROBLEM WITH wanting to see wild avian magic is that it doesn't just appear on command. (There's also the problem of it often proving deadly, but that's beside the point.) Beth and Devon had set up camp beside a few oak trees, building a fire circle and making a bed from ferns, grass, and sphagnum moss. (Only one bed, because ~~the night would be cold~~ . . . ~~the greenery was limited~~ . . . some good reason that they eventually gave up trying to invent.) They had eaten a small supper comprised of leftover pork pie, cheese, and pears they'd bought in the village, as well as nuts from an emergency supply Beth carried in her satchel. They'd even tried discussing their plan for getting the caladrius to the sanctuary in Bergerac, where the little bird would be safe from schemers, at least until it was old enough to be released into the wild. But the specter of farewelling each other afterward drew them into a melancholic silence. Night had begun to rise gracefully from the old, dry land. And still they waited.

"I'm sorry about tenure," Devon said. "And Birder of the Year. But I admire the way you said no to Gladstone."

Beth gave a quiet, droll laugh. A week ago, she'd never have refused Professor Gladstone anything. Who knew that racing across the country, being attacked by deadly magical birds and kissed by a handsome rogue, would be so transformative to one's character?

"It's really fine," she said, and meant it. "Of course, you yourself could still win Birder of the Year. You'd just have to take the caladrius and . . ." *Leave me*, she almost said, but her throat closed, set up a barricade, and threatened to shoot her if she dared approach it with such painful words.

"I'm taking the bird to sanctuary," Devon answered quite simply. "With you."

The barricade in her throat began to preclude breathing. She hastily changed the subject. "I hope the others reached Sheffield without any problem."

Devon cast her a wry smile. "You're such a sweetheart. Personally, I hope they ended up in a ditch."

"I don't. The farther they are away from us, the better. Let them arrive safe in Sheffield—then have someone steal their vehicles and luggage."

He laughed. "I can't believe you said that."

"I've told you, niceties don't mean I'm nice."

He leaned forward, his eyes narrowing as he regarded her. "Do you mean to say all those polite manners and kindnesses of yours actually hide a cynical heart?"

"I'm not cynical," she answered, busying herself with straightening the cover of the birdcage, beneath which the caladrius slept, its beak tucked snugly into its soft back feathers. "I'm realistic. If you're nice to people, they won't . . ."

"Hurt you," he said into her stiff silence. She shrugged.

Devon brushed at a wildflower beside him in the grass, making its tiny petals scatter like fragments of dreams in the thickening dark. "So," he said after a moment. "Who, exactly, hurt you?"

It sounded like a casual inquiry, but beneath the words

Beth heard a coldness that evoked weapons, the gathering of addresses, and a plan for vengeance. Her stomach fluttered as if it were trying to fan her suddenly heated pulse.

"It's not important," she tried to say, but he interrupted her, his voice still so casual, so dangerous.

"Yes it is."

Goodness, how was she supposed to talk again after that? She rubbed at a knotted thread in the cage cover, and her finger seemed to gleam slightly—from the firelight, she guessed, rubbing it against her skirt, feeling it tingle from the friction.

And then words began slipping from her throat, as if of their own volition. "You're kind, but I must confess, 'hurt' is an exaggeration. I've never been beaten, or had my glasses broken—at least, not more than twice. I'm just not liked. I'm a weird know-it-all."

Seeing Devon frown, she bit her bare thumb knuckle anxiously. "That's a verbatim citing of what my peers would shout across the playground or write on the blackboard before class. I promise I'm not so unscientific as to falsify quotes!"

His frown darkened. "I don't doubt you," he said, and Beth's brain spun confusedly as she realized he was angry *for* her, not with her.

"It really isn't important," she insisted. "And please understand, I'm not complaining. They didn't *have* to like me, or answer when I spoke to them, or give me a seat at their table. It wasn't their fault I have no instinct for the principles of social behavior among *Homo sapiens sapiens*. Birds are easy; people are utterly bewildering. At least etiquette rules provide a framework for how to act. They stop me from saying things like '*Homo sapiens sapiens*' and mentioning over afternoon tea the fornication habits of sandpipers. They enabled me to become fr—associates with Hippolyta, and got us across the English Channel in a boat full of fishermen who had knives tucked in their boots. That is why I'm nicely behaved even though I'm not nice inside."

The words stopped there, leaving a stunned silence. Even the moor had gone quiet. *Oh God, had she really just exposed her humiliations like that?* Appalled, Beth lifted her chin, smacked her hands on her thighs, and said briskly, "Let's go look for birds."

She began to rise, but Devon reached out, catching her arm, forestalling her. He let go at once, but Beth forgot that she had ever wanted to move.

"You have moss in your hair," he said. "May I?"

She nodded mutely, and he leaned forward, his fingers gentle as they plucked bits of greenery from the tumbled strands. As he worked, not looking at her, he said lightly, "*I* like you. I like you a great deal. Frankly, anyone who doesn't is a fucking idiot. And anyone who says cruel things, or uses silence as a weapon, is a bully who knows how to be violent without lifting a finger. Don't blame yourself, sweetheart. It's not your fault or your shame."

And while her brain was trying to cope with that, her heart hyperventilating, and her memory preparing a full-on flood of tears, he added: "I promise I will never, ever want to hurt you."

The words made such a warm glow within her, she saw it like stars in her eyes against the night landscape. But she had no idea how to respond. *Thank you, Mr. Lockley*, seemed too polite. *Let me take off your clothes and demonstrate my gratitude*, probably not polite enough. Finally, worried that too long a silence would offend him, she said, "Gosh," and he smiled as he smoothed a stray lock of her hair.

"I know you won't hurt me," she continued. "You never have. You've been . . ." She paused, her breath catching as his fingers brushed against her cheek. "You've been aggravating, nettlesome—"

"Um," he said.

"—and respectful, thoughtful, kind. I haven't *had* to be nice with you. Perhaps that's why I lov—"

She stopped, lacking the courage to finish that word. But Devon wasn't a genius for nothing. He reached out again, cupping her face with his hands, looking almost distraught with emotion.

"No one's ever said such things to me before," he whispered, searching her gaze for a lie. "No one's called me thoughtful or lov—" Now he stopped, swallowing hard.

"Loved you," she dared for the both of them.

Something seemed to break in him, collapsing his expression. He closed his eyes, and Beth pressed her hand against the hard beat of his heart, wishing she could soothe it. "I'm not just being nice," he told her, his voice as velvety dark as the sky. "I meant what I said. You can trust me."

"I do trust you. You're a good man."

She leaned closer, wanting to kiss the humor back into him. But something flashed in the night behind his shoulder, closer than a star, brighter than a fragment of moonlight. Beth stared as the speck of light began to dance.

"What is that?" she breathed.

Opening his eyes, Devon looked only at her. He smiled. "That, darling, is my favorite bird."

# Chapter Twenty-Three

What I learned from birds in love: turn your heart into a dance.

*Birds Through a Sherry Glass*, H.A. Quirm

They went together into the deepening night. But after only a few yards Devon stopped, whistling an ethereal song Beth did not recognize. Then he turned back to her, smiling.

And behind him, a score of tiny stars blossomed in the dark.

Beth stared in wonder. *Linaria ignis fatuus.* The will-o'-the-wisp linnet, a vanishingly rare thaumaturgic species she'd only ever dreamed about. They danced around each other in silence, the disk of cartilage on their foreheads glimmering with beautiful, eerie magic. Devon stood beneath the near-invisible flutter of their night-colored wings, like a sorcerer who had roused them from the secret heart of England. His face seemed part of the magic: a moon to the avian stars. He looked at her with an expression Beth had never seen from another person before.

She remembered the first moment she laid eyes on him, a mere month ago, at the most boring birders' meeting ever held. She'd glanced up from a dusty raisin scone and there he was, trying not to yawn as Professor Singh rambled on at him about mousetwitter claws. Something had stirred beneath her heart. She'd assumed it to be the one mouthful of scone she'd been foolish enough to eat, but now she understood it was the magic of *this* moment, reaching back through time to claim her.

Devon offered his hand, and she took it, stepping toward him like she was stepping into a spell. "Watch," he whispered. And turning her gently, he wrapped his arms around her, keeping her snug as she observed the dreamy swooping dance of the birds all around them.

At first Beth stood rigid, unused to such treatment, but gradually she relaxed, leaning back against the strength of Devon's body, inhaling its warm, musky scent. He tilted his head to rest it against hers, and she felt the drift of a sigh across her cheek.

They stood quietly, absorbed in beautiful magic. One half of Beth's brain, the half that stored her education and considered tweed the height of fashion, wanted to fetch her field journal and begin making observational notes about the linnets. Luckily, the wiser half knew a romantic moment when it encountered one and refused to budge.

Devon began to stroke her arm, heating her through the cotton sleeve of her shirtwaist. The cozy atmosphere molted its feathery softness, revealing something far more provocative beneath. As Beth stirred restively, Devon slid a hand across her breastbone, then down the shirtwaist's row of pearl buttons. Her skin beneath began to tingle. The places he did not touch began to ache with yearning.

"You're not wearing a corset," he said, surprised.

"I left it off today. It's hard enough to breathe around Professor Gladstone without being tight-laced as well."

"That's very . . ."

"Practical?" she suggested.

"Tantalizing. Knowing there's nothing more than fine cloth between me and your naked skin."

There was only one adequate response to that: "Oh. Gosh."

She felt his smile against her cheek. He tucked his fingers beneath the waistband of her skirt, then paused. "Yes?" he asked.

It would have sounded like the enchanted song of *Lothario podiceps*, had her brain not become so swathed in white lace wedding veils that it barely heard him. Her heart, however, was more perceptive.

"Have you ever seen a ghost owl?" she asked.

There followed a moment of silence. "I beg your pardon?" he said uncertainly.

"Do you have a large family?"

"Um."

"What is your stance on the general enmity between museum ornithologists and field naturalists?"

"I say the more information about birds, the better. My family is a fairly normal size, my mother dead, my father retired back to Devonshire, from where he continues to attempt running the Cambridge physics department and my career, and I have no siblings—but I do have cousins who are aggravating enough to compensate, as well as the usual assortment of grandparents, uncles, and aunts. And yes, I've encountered a ghost owl, just once, in the hinterland of Peru. Fabulous bird, gave me hideous nightmares for a week."

"Interesting. Very well, my answer your question is yes."

"Ask me anything, anytime you want," he said, one finger stroking her belly and electrifying her so much they could have boiled water on her and made tea. "I'm happy to slake your curiosity."

Beth reddened, for his words seemed as risqué as his behavior. He continued to slide his fingers farther down—then stopped, his progress thwarted by the unrelenting nature of her waistband. Silently cursing women's fashions, Beth reached behind to unfasten a hook, loosening the band.

"Thank you kindly," Devon said, and proceeded on course.

As he reached between her legs, Beth inhaled air that tingled with linnet magic, imbuing her senses with an exquisite sensitivity. "Oh my holy hens," she gasped.

Laughing softly, Devon began exploring her gently through the layers of her fine linen chemise and drawers, tickling and caressing as her ability to remain upright became increasingly imperiled. He soon settled on one location, circling it, flicking softly, as Beth felt her lingerie grow damp. She gasped, unable to bear the sensation; she bucked against his hand, desperate for more. The bird lights spiraled around each other, and her feelings did the same, magic and pleasure weaving and blurring and suddenly cresting in a flare of ecstasy that made her cry out.

Devon held her secure, his voice a deep whisper in her ear, telling her about the wingspan of will-o'-the-wisp linnets, and their preferred habitat, and other defining features of the species, inspiring an extended series of aftershocks that rendered her breathless and giddy. Just when she was feeling almost steady again, everything swooped, and she wondered briefly, wildly, how she had become airborne. Opening her eyes, she realized that Devon had scooped her up and was carrying her back toward their campsite beneath the trees.

"What are you doing?" she asked dazedly.

"I'm taking you to bed, Miss Pickering."

"But I'm not tired yet."

"I don't intend for you to sleep," he said, and the wicked promise in his smile opened her inner manual of etiquette to a page that had previously been glued shut. "That is," he added, "if you consent."

"Consent?" she echoed with the instinctive caution of a teacher who had learned over the years that words could be deceiving (for example: *my grandmother's funeral is on the day of the test* and *I read every book on the syllabus before writing this essay*). Although she was fairly sure she'd agree to anything he wanted, prudence seemed, well, prudent at a moment like this.

"I require specific information before I answer that," she said.

He sat her down on the bed of greenery, kneeling beside her. "I humbly request to make love to you," he said, cupping a hand around the side of her neck and using his thumb to gently tilt up her jaw so he could kiss her. The brush of his lips against hers was so ephemeral it could have been a gust of smoke from the campfire, making all her nerves clamor for more. "I ask that you allow me to strip you naked and lay you down so that I may lavish attention on every part of your body." He kissed the secret, tender place just beneath her ear in demonstration, and while she was shivering at that, he kissed her earlobe, her cheek, her lips again, whispering all the while about what he wanted to do with her. Growing silent at last as the kisses deepened, he began unbuttoning her shirtwaist. Beth pushed the coat from his shoulders, and after he shrugged it off she set to work on his shirt.

There followed a busy moment of unfastening and unbuckling and tugging at clothes until, before Beth knew it, she was bare of all but her stockings and half boots. The latter she levered off with such force, they flung across the campsite, barely missing the fire.

Devon chuckled. "Please give my regrets to your good manners."

"Never mind them," Beth answered impatiently, pulling him close to kiss him again. Her skin was flaming with anticipation. Her pulse raced with a beat that sounded like *hurry, hurry*. "Tell me what I can do for you."

"Just be here with me," he said, smiling with what almost looked like shyness. "And enjoy yourself, I hope."

She answered that with heavy, luxuriant kisses that delved into passion but still felt insufficient. She wished she could get closer to him, even while their naked bodies pressed and slid together with a silky friction and their tongues met in the secret dark.

"So, do you consent?" Devon asked, his lips barely leaving hers to ask it.

"Yes," she said—and found herself lying back on the grass bed faster than the flight of a peregrine falcon. Reclining over her, Devon abandoned her mouth, instead kissing his way down her throat, over her breasts, all the while reaching fingers once more between her legs. Beth arched, gasping—

Pain shot across her back. "Ow!"

She sat up at the same moment Devon lifted his head in response to her pained cry, and his brow collided with her chin. "Ow!" he said, tumbling over. And then again, "Ow, dammit!"

"Are you all right?" Beth asked anxiously, clutching her jaw.

"There was a rock," he explained as he wrangled himself up.

She tried to turn him so she could investigate his back, but he gathered her in his arms, hugging her close. "Are *you* all right?"

"A twig scratched me," she grumbled with mock petulance.

He laughed. "Sex in the outdoors is a romantic idea but suffers from the reality of being in the outdoors."

But then, as he looked at her, his smile began to dim, and unhappiness slipped across his countenance. Beth felt a familiar chill settle into her heart. She drew hair over her shoulders to cover herself.

"There's—there's something I have to tell you about myself," he said. "I should have done so earlier, but I'm a coward. I knew telling you could change everything . . ."

As he bit his lip anxiously, a hundred dire possibilities rushed through Beth's mind. The man was a bird smuggler. He had a wife hidden in an attic somewhere. He believed in grading students on a curve regardless of their actual achievements.

"When I was sixteen, I was bitten by a basilisk owl," he said. "I escaped petrification, but I—I cannot have children. I don't mind, I never wanted them, but . . ."

Beth exhaled with a relief so strong, she felt light-headed. "I'm sorry that happened to you, but can't see how this changes things between us."

He lowered his eyes. "More than one of my lovers left when they learned it, not wanting a future with someone who couldn't offer them children. And fair enough, of course, but . . ." He fell into a heavy silence that seemed to expect no reply.

"I don't want children," Beth said plainly. "Being a parent would disrupt my teaching schedule. How fortunate that we don't need to worry about contraception!"

Devon looked up at her warily, and she gave him a warm, encouraging smile. "Now I think there *is* something I can do for you," she said. And reaching out in a spirit of intellectual inquiry, she took hold of his *Magna erectus phallus* and gently caressed it as he had caressed her before. Devon made a strangled sound in his throat.

"Professor Pickering!" he gasped. "I just told you my darkest secret and you just smiled and—and—" The word broke apart as she tightened her grip. "Oh my God," he moaned unscientifically, his eyes rolling back.

"The evidence suggests you are either in a state of pleasure or pain," Beth said. "Should I stop? I don't want to hurt you."

He answered with a kiss that quickly restored them both to mindless passion. "Come here," he begged, gathering her close. "Please."

Beth gladly allowed him to pull her onto his lap. But unsure of the etiquette—how and where exactly did one sit when one's seat was so *elaborate*?—she rose on her knees, draping her arms over his shoulders. Their gazes meshed, heavy with desire.

"Beth," Devon whispered. *"Beth."* He said her name again and again, kissing her throat or jaw or mouth each time, as if he were tasting something sweet. "You're like a night full of bird stars and magical dreaming. I am so in love with you."

"Thank you," she replied automatically. Then the words reached through her old, defensive blockade of manners to fill her with happiness. A few grim memories crawled out, trying to scratch and bite her, but she shoved them away. "I love you too."

"In that case," Devon said, "we can reach only one logical conclusion." Taking hold of her hips, he lowered her to complete and delightful corruption.

The heat that had evolved between them throughout their travels blazed now into a wildfire (fortunately metaphorical in nature, considering the tinder-dry conditions of the moorland at midsummer) as they moved together slowly, at first a little awkwardly while Beth grew accustomed to the mechanics involved. She tried to make mental notes for later inclusion in her field journal but quickly lost track of them. Leaves chafed her bare knees, but she did not care. Devon's eyes watered—"smoke from the fire," he insisted, and went on kissing her as if irritation of his corneas was not a serious threat. Their bodies grew slick with sweat, and their backs ached. Finally, grasping blindly for his coat, Devon spread it over the ferns, and they lay down, facing each other in a tangle of breath and limbs. Whispering of skies and thermals and *oh my God, right there, don't stop, I love you*, they ventured a more intense rhythm until the night went utterly dark, and silence enfolded the moorland except for their mutual sighs as they reached fulfillment.

DEVON WOKE AT dawn, yanked from a dream by the obnoxious *chut! chut!* of a red grouse nearby. Aggravation clenched his body, but the moment he saw Beth lying asleep beside him, a shy wonder eased it away. He could scarcely credit that he'd gotten to spend the night with her. And moreover, she was still here in the morning. Granted, there was nowhere for her to go, out here on the moors, but Devon didn't want to consider that. He watched her face grow luminous in the unfurling light, like a sacred pearl drawn out of the dark ocean, like a dream he could not believe was real . . .

He winced, appalled by this degeneration of his rational

brain into cloying sentimentality. He tried to focus instead on how cold he felt, lying naked on the ground, the campfire having burned out—but it was no use. Beth quite simply bewitched him, beyond linguistic sobriety, beyond quantifiable data analysis. She was beauty. She was peace.

She was looking at him.

Devon's pulse leaped up and began running frantically around his circulatory system, sweeping up, shoving things behind curtains, even while he gave her a languid smile. "Hi," he said.

Her eyes grew wide, and she frenetically brushed her hair so that it covered her face and breasts. "Hello," she answered through the shroud. "How lovely to see you. Would you mind terribly going away?"

Devon blinked, taken aback. "Um—??"

"No, don't look at me." She flattened the palm of her hand against his face. "I need to tidy—and wash—and oh God, my teeth." He heard a puffed exhalation, then she groaned. "Don't breathe, don't look, just . . . give me a minute."

"Okay," he said against her hand, trying hard not to laugh.

"Close your eyes."

"Sweetheart, I don't care—"

"Close. Your. Eyes."

He closed them obediently and the hand moved away. The warmth against his body vanished as Beth clambered up. Amused, he lay back, stretching and yawning as he listened to the urgent rustles of a woman getting dressed. The habit of wickedness in him hoped she would come back into his reach so he could pull her down and muss her again in delicious ways, but an unexpected domestic part of his heart smiled contentedly to think she was making herself nice for him, and he drew his coat over himself to conceal, and hopefully subdue, how much it aroused him.

"You may open your eyes now," Beth said at last, sounding so dignified he felt certain her chin was tipped up and her arms crossed tightly. Opening one eye cautiously, he squinted up at her, and smiled to see his suspicions were confirmed.

"There's enough water in the flask for you to wash also," she told him briskly. "But no hope for tea, I'm afraid."

Devon sat up, rubbing his face. "And no hope for wake-up sex?" he asked in an entirely scientific manner—after all, you don't get a result unless you pose a question.

"Gracious heavens!" she exclaimed. "Is that quite the done thing?"

He shrugged. "In some parts of the world, yes."

"Perhaps tomorrow morning, then," she allowed, and all his metaphorical test tubes began bubbling over. "While I'm keen to replicate our experiments of last night, it's more of a priority to get the caladrius safely to Dover."

"You're right," Devon agreed, despite his baser nature. Casting aside the coat, he began to stand, and Beth hastily turned her back. "You've already seen it all," he pointed out as he got to his feet and looked around for his clothes.

"Hhmughhmm," she answered, and he just *knew* she was blushing. For that matter, he was close to doing so himself. He'd had more than enough sex over the years to feel blasé about it the next morning, but it turned out that love made a remarkable difference to the experience. Never before had he lain quietly afterward while a woman stroked his eyebrows, and kissed the corners of his mouth, and generally made him feel so cherished that he'd had to roll her gently over and slide back inside her just so he could breathe.

And it was just as good now—all right, *mostly* as good—listening to her talk about travel routes and buying yet another suitcase and what she wouldn't give for a cup of tea, while she tidied the campsite. Her voice was like music to him, but he heard not one single word of it, too busy imagining when he might be able to get her into a bed.

Once they were dressed and ready to depart, they checked the caladrius, smiling as it shook its feathers and groomed its claws with a youthful, rather clumsy diligence. The morning light seemed to enliven it, but seed husks on the cage floor were threatening to become an enchanted garden, and thin, shining strands of magic wove up the cage bars, so they lowered the cover again for safety's sake. Beth took the cage by its handle and was moving toward the road when Devon caught her wrist, stopping her.

She turned back to him with a politely inquiring expression, so lovely that the sun cast golden strands to adorn . . .

*No*, he told himself sternly. No more sentimentality! (And if his heart could beat in a steady rhythm, that would be rather helpful too.)

"Good morning," he said again, wanting to reconnect with the feeling of intimacy they'd shared last night, the togetherness, before they faced the rest of the world. Really, just wanting *her*, with an intensity he felt might never diminish.

Beth seemed bemused for a moment, then understanding lit her eyes. She smiled—a smile just for him, one he could wrap up, tuck inside his heart, and keep forever. "Good morning, Devon," she said. And putting down the birdcage, she hugged him.

*Oh gosh*, he thought dazedly. So this was what true comfort felt like. He'd never expected to know it in his life, certainly not after his mother died and his father decided the best way to deal with a wayward, brilliant child was send him alone to a far distant country—and yet here was Beth Pickering saying his name, holding him against her heart, and he realized that, regardless of what happened hereafter, he wasn't ever going to recover from this beautiful moment.

FINALLY, THEY SET off for Sheffield. Devon ached all over from having spent the night on the ground, and he noticed Beth stretch and twist her back so many times that he reached over to rub it for her as they walked. And yet they plowed on, encouraged by occasional peeps from the caladrius.

Only seven minutes later, they stopped in front of a stone building.

"Fox House Inn," Devon said, reading the sign hanging above its door.

They stared at it blankly, undecided as to whether to laugh or cry.

"Hello! Good morning!" the innkeeper greeted them as they entered. "Up with the lark, you are!" He looked intently at their faces, then at the cage Beth held, and his eyes lit with excitement. "It's a true honor to welcome you into my humble inn! You're wanting a room? We have plenty available!"

He beamed a rather manic smile that suggested "plenty of rooms available" might be good news for them but was bloody terrible for his bank account, and would they *please* not pretend to be married?

"Excellent facilities, a bird's-eye view of the moors, and our beds are the best you'll find this side of Hadrian's Wall! Soft, warm, like sleeping on a cloud."

Luckily for him, the bird in their cage was not a carnivorous lapwing. Beth contrived a polite smile, and Devon managed not to curse, despite his various aches and pains offering up a few eloquent suggestions.

"Just breakfast, thank you," he said. "And coffee. Strong coffee. Coffee so strong it could lift this entire building and throw it, say, half a mile back down the road."

"And tea, please," Beth added. "Thoroughly steeped. I don't so much need a reservoir of peace as a deep, deep well of strength. We have a long walk ahead of us to Sheffield."

"Sheffield? My lad's taking a wagon there this very morning!" The innkeeper pointed to a young man who was loitering in a doorway behind the registration desk.

"I am?" Apparently this was news to the boy.

"Yes," his father said firmly. "And you're going to give these nice ornith—um, nice *people* a lift, free of charge. We here at Fox House always do our best for travelers! And we have excellent rates too! Just in case anyone—say, a newspaper reporter— happens to ask."

Devon and Beth exchanged a speaking glance. But they allowed the innkeeper to lead them into the dining room and seat them side by side at his best table, and order them a full English breakfast, his gift, no thanks necessary, hospitality was the name of the game here at Fox House in Longshaw, right before the turnoff to Hathersage.

As he bustled away, they set the birdcage on the floor beneath the round table, concealed by the long drape of its cloth, then Beth straightened the cutlery and Devon picked up the newspaper folded neatly on the tabletop. The front-page head-

line almost made him summon the innkeeper and ask for some
rum in the coffee.

———

**THE ROBIN HOOD OF ORNITHOLOGY!**
**Professor Lockley Rescues Caladrius from Tyrant!**
**Pretty Miss Pickering Joins Him in Race to Safety!**

———

"*Robin* Hood? Really?" Devon said, grimacing at the pun
(which, to be fair, only a bird lover would have noticed).

"*Pretty Miss Pickering?*" Beth said, more justifiably.

"And how did they even know?"

"The stable hand at the inn yesterday might have told them,"
Beth said. "Or one of Professor Gladstone's servants. Or even
that Mr. Feh—uh, something."

"The PRESS agent?" Devon said doubtfully, and Beth
shrugged.

"No one can be trusted."

"My cynical angel," he said fondly, reaching out to brush a
knuckle across her cheek. Her tiredness dissolved into a smile,
and the atmosphere between them turned sugary with adoration.

"It *is* them!"

They looked up, startled, at the spirited exclamation from
diners across the room. Two women in matching blue dresses
were pointing spoons at them; at another table, a pair of octogenarian gentlemen whispered and giggled.

Devon and Beth barely had time to sigh wearily before they
found themselves surrounded by diners requesting autographs,
a glimpse of the caladrius, advice on how to become an

orthonogonist, and the date of their wedding. Breakfast arrived in the middle of this, but enjoying it proved impossible. Inn staff joined the diners, and between their enthusiastic clamor and the chairs beginning to sprout green buds in an untimely show of avian magic, neither of them noticed a man entering the room. Only when he slipped through the crowd to seat himself at their table did they realize.

"Herr Oberhufter!" Beth gasped.

"*Guten Morgen*, Miss Pickering," Oberhufter replied, tipping his hat. "Lockley. I've come for the caladrius."

"Oh sure," Devon said sarcastically. "We'll just hand the bird over to you; it's no problem whatsoever."

"You will hand it over," Oberhufter agreed. "As for there being no problem . . ."

He raised a pistol, aiming it at Beth's face. "I guess that part's up to you."

# CHAPTER TWENTY-FOUR

*While you're watching the starling in the field,*
*remember that a hawk may be watching it too.*
*Birds Through a Sherry Glass*, H.A. Quirm

THE CROWD OF onlookers whispered avidly as the three ornithologists stared at each other with a professional degree
of enmity.

"Point that gun away from Miss Pickering," Devon said,
chillingly calm, "or you will regret it."

"Fair enough." Smiling, Herr Oberhufter angled the gun
toward Devon instead.

*Crash.*

Everyone jolted as Beth stood so abruptly, her chair
slammed back against the floor. Face flushed, expression grim,
she slammed her fist on the table. Cups and plates rattled violently. The milk jug spilled. Across the table, Oberhufter stared
openmouthed with astonishment.

"I beg your pardon," Beth said coolly. "But I have just about
had enough. Put your gun down and get some bloody manners, or I swear I will *expel* you."

The gun dropped with a *thunk* to the table. Immediately,

Devon snatched it, flipped it in his hand, and aimed it right back at Oberhufter.

"Apologize to the lady for annoying her," he said.

At his commanding tone, the crowd fairly swooned; one elderly gentleman had to be fanned with a chambermaid's apron.

"Sorry, *Fräulein*," Oberhufter muttered, his voice so faint it sounded less German and more like a confederation of sovereign states dreaming of a kaiser.

"Thank you," Beth said primly. With a polite little nod, she retrieved her chair, sat down, and reached for the cup of tea in front of her, despite it being entirely inadequate for peace at this moment. Drinking from the teapot, however, would have been déclassé. Her hand hurt, her pulse could have outraced a *Geococcyx luna tunica* (the fastest roadrunner in the West), and her own manners had begun to discuss among themselves putting her into a sanitorium.

Under the table, Devon set a hand on her thigh. A week ago, it would have sent her jumping up out of her chair again, but now she felt instantly calmed by his touch. Forgetting the tea, she set her own hand over his, gently nudging his fingers so she could slide hers between them. From the corner of her eye she noticed him draw in a rather tremulous breath.

"*Heiliger Strohsack*," Oberhufter muttered, retrieving a handkerchief from of his breast pocket and using it to wipe his forehead. "Women certainly are liberated these days."

"How did you know where to find us?" Beth asked, making it clear that if he did not answer to her satisfaction, she'd immediately seek out a blackboard and drag her fingernails down it.

"My butler insisted he saw you on the road last night. I

thought it would do no harm to come back and check. Besides . . ." Reaching out somewhat shakily to the rack at the center of the table, he snagged a piece of toast and bit down on it. "Have you heard how loudly Quirm snores? I say, pass the jam, would you?"

Beth reached automatically for the jam dish but then snatched her hand back. "We won't be giving you anything today, Herr Oberhufter!"

"*Ooh,*" said the crowd. They whipped their wide-eyed attention to Oberhufter, but he only shrugged.

"Fair enough." Leaning over, he grabbed it for himself. "I like you, *Fräulein*," he said, straightening, and jabbed the piece of toast toward her. "You're interesting. But Birder of the Year is even more interesting, and the fact that I was willing to shoot you to get the award is why I deserve to win it."

"Whether you deserve it or not makes no difference," Devon said. "The Birder of the Year competition is a sham."

The crowd gasped at this, but Oberhufter guffawed, crumbs spitting from his mouth. "You think I'm stupid enough to believe that?"

Devon leaned back, slipping the gun into his coat pocket. "Actually, I think you're stupid in a broad range of ways. And this conversation has become boring." He nodded—whereupon the innkeeper stepped up behind Oberhufter and tossed a tablecloth over the man's head.

"*Mein Gott!*"

"Let's go," Devon said to Beth as Oberhufter floundered wildly beneath the cloth. They rose, still holding hands, and a breathless "*aww*" went through the room.

"Is that the caladrius?" someone asked Beth as she lifted the birdcage out from beneath the table.

"Oh, no," she answered easily. "This is a handbag. It's the latest fashion."

"Aah," said the crowd. Beth squeezed Devon's hand before he could laugh.

"I apologize for the disturbance," she told the innkeeper. "Thank you for your assistance."

"It's a pleasure . . . *ugh, stay still* . . . to help," he replied, wrestling with the enshrouded Oberhufter. "We here at Fox House are always . . . *ow! don't bite me!* . . . willing to support a noble cause. You're getting the full-quality experience when you stay in our—"

"Right," Devon said, nudging Beth, who was listening politely, albeit a little impatiently, to this speech. "We ought to run."

"This way, Professors!" called the innkeeper's son, waving from the dining room door.

"Wait!" Oberhufter shouted from beneath the tablecloth. "Let's discuss this, *ja*? If we joined forces, we could be undefeatable."

Devon laughed.

"But listen! Quirm is planning to set a booby trap for you at the Sheffield train station!"

"Why would you tell us that?" Beth asked warily. "You're her . . . special friend."

"To say nothing of the fact that you were pointing a gun at us two minutes ago," Devon added.

"That's just sex and death," Oberhufter scoffed. "This is ornithology. None of us want Quirm winning Birder of the Year. Come on, Lockley, let's get back together. We had fun, *ja*? Remember when we stole the pileated deathwhistler from . . . er . . ."

Beth and Devon exchanged a grin, then headed for the door.

"Good luck!" the innkeeper called after them. The crowd whooped, brandishing spoons, coffee cups, and at least one rasher of bacon.

"I can't believe I did that," Beth gasped as they hurried toward the stable yard, carefully avoiding Oberhufter's servants, who waited near the inn's front door. She broke into laughter—then promptly began hyperventilating.

Devon jiggled her hand in his. "You were really quite impressive. Makes me want to attend one of your lectures, just to watch you teach."

She laughed again, although it was as trembly as her heart felt. "I guess that's not the last we'll see of Herr Oberhufter."

"Don't worry," Devon assured her. "We'll catch a train in Sheffield, reach the Dover docks this afternoon, and be eating boeuf bourguignon in a French hotel for dinner. It's going to be plain sailing from here."


"I THINK I just saw Hippolyta," Beth warned Devon as they walked through the Sheffield train station toward its first-class booking hall. Although *walked* was perhaps an exaggeration; after spending two hours in the back of a juddering wagon, every muscle in her body hurt, and *upright creeping* would have served as a more accurate description of her progress. Beside her, Devon did not seem much better.

"Where?" he asked, and she surreptitiously flicked a finger toward a space farther along the platform. But then a small crowd of passengers milling near the train parted, revealing that what she'd actually seen was a brightly canopied stall selling lollies.

"Sorry, my eyes must be tired."

"All of me is tired," Devon said.

"Maybe we should buy some of those lollies, to give us more pep."

"I'd rather have coffee," Devon said. "Or," he added with a roguish smile, "kisses."

"Gosh," Beth breathed, fanning herself with a hand.

"Sadly, the train leaves soon," he said. "So instead of"—he bent to whisper close to her ear—"lifting your skirt, pulling down your drawers, and kissing you *there* until you can't stand . . ." He straightened, brushing back his hair casually, "We should get our tickets."

And while Beth was fanning herself with both hands now in an urgent effort to stave off internal combustion, he opened the door to the booking hall—

And stumbled back, shouting in alarm, as the booby trap Herr Oberhufter had predicted hit him in the face, literally.

Beth glimpsed a flash of yellow and white, a furious blur of wings, and identified *Sula dactylatra sicarius*, the masked assassin booby, with a speed that proved just how clever indeed she was when it came to birds. Unfortunately, that cleverness did not extend itself to avoiding said bird; it swooped at her, slamming a webbed foot against her shoulder before flying out of reach again. Hot magic spiked through her nerves, and Beth staggered in pain, almost dropping the caladrius's cage. An inch higher and that blow would have knocked her unconscious.

"*Everyone run!*" Devon shouted as he turned, arms crooked defensively over his head, to track the bird's movement.

"Hey, you're those orthologigs!" someone shouted.

"Has she got the caladrius in that cage?" someone else shouted.

Nobody ran. In fact, they clustered nearer, voices rising with enthusiasm, as the booby emitted a high-pitched whistle and dove again. Beth ducked, holding the birdcage protectively against her legs, and Devon hunched over her. She enjoyed only the briefest delight in his gallant behavior before he grunted with pain as the booby struck his shoulder blade. Magic speared right through him to crackle against Beth's skin. The bird soared up and they straightened, looking around for some means of capturing it.

"Use your special net, Professor Pickering!" someone in the crowd suggested.

"I've got an umbrella you can have!" another called out.

Devon began removing his coat. "I'll try to catch it," he told Beth. "Worst-case scenario, I have Oberhufter's gun. Stand back, keep the caladrius safe."

She nodded, smiling encouragement. The vitality of the past few days flashed between them, the laughter and the passion, making that brief moment feel like an eternity of perfection. Then Devon smiled quickly, brightly, in reply before turning away. Taking the coat in his hands, he gave it a brisk flap.

The crowd cheered. *"Catch that bird!"* began a general chant, accompanied by rhythmic clapping. *"Catch that bird!"*

Wincing at the noise, Beth backed up, all the while trying to unhook the latch of her satchel one-handedly so she could hunt for something that might subdue the booby. But someone tugged on her arm.

*PEEP!* the caladrius complained as its cage jerked.

Glancing around, Beth discovered Hippolyta standing close behind her, a great deal more colorful than the lolly stand, and significantly less sweet. "Hello, Elizabeth dear," she said, smiling viciously as she clamped one hand around Beth's wrist.

"Let go!" Beth demanded (proving that even the most intelligent woman can be hopelessly naive at times). Hippolyta only chuckled and gripped more tightly.

*Eeeeeee!*

The booby's piercing whistle sounded as it attacked again. Devon flung his coat over it with perfect timing and the bird tumbled, crashing into him in a chaos of wings and cloth. As he staggered, the crowd cheered again with a rather bloodthirsty enjoyment of the show.

"Time to go," Hippolyta snarled in Beth's ear, and began tugging her through the crowd. "Gladstone's waiting for you."

Beth gasped. "How could you do this?!"

"An ornithologist has to play the long game. You'll understand one day."

"Never!" Beth declared. "Help! Help!"

But her voice was lost in the hullabaloo of the crowd as Devon wrestled the booby safely to the ground. Glancing back, Beth saw his face dripping blood, his jaw clenched as he worked to firmly but carefully wrangle the bird inside his coat. He was hurt! In a rush of panic, she began kicking Hippolyta, but the woman's skirts were so layered, it was like kicking a cloud. Suddenly, one of Gladstone's servants appeared before them.

"This way," he said, gesturing toward the train.

"No!" Beth shouted. It didn't matter. The servant snatched the birdcage from her and both he and Hippolyta hauled her across to the open door of a first-class compartment. Professor Gladstone sat within, smoke billowing serenely from his pipe. Beth increased her struggle, but the servant just shoved her through the doorway. She landed hard on her hands and knees on the compartment floor, hair falling around her face. Shaking it back, she glared up at Gladstone.

*"Tsk tsk,"* he said, tipping his spectacles so as to frown over their rim at her. "D-minus for attitude, Pickering. A Birder of the Year and tenured professor deports herself more elegantly than that."

He snapped his fingers, and the servant hauled Beth up, placing her on the seat opposite Gladstone. The caladrius's cage was set beside her, and she immediately laid a protective hand on it.

"Make way," Hippolyta ordered majestically, lifting her skirts so as to enter the compartment. But the servant pushed her back, and she did not even have time to take Jove's name in vain before the door was slammed shut. The servant yanked the window's curtain closed and positioned himself before the door, feet apart, arms crossed. One look at his bulging triceps, to say nothing of the pistol strapped to his thigh, and Beth knew she had no hope of escaping. Outside, Hippolyta bashed on the door, hollering furiously, but then apparently decided on a new tactic. Silence fell. The world shrank to one small train compartment filled with the smells of pipe smoke and bird guano.

"Kabelo, run and tell the engineer that his clock is slow," Gladstone ordered. "We want to be gone before Lockley realizes what's happened and tries to play hero."

"I'm the one you should worry about," Beth said with a fierceness she actually felt.

But Gladstone only laughed. "You talk as if I don't know you, Pickering. You wouldn't say boo to a goose."

"I beg your pardon, but that's not true. There was a goose in Liberia that I—"

*Peep!* cried the caladrius at that moment, wings fluttering madly. At once, Beth forgot everything but her concern for it. Lifting the cage, she peered beneath its cover. The bird was clinging to the vertical bars, scraping its beak against them. Its tail fanned out, twitching; its feathers were fluffed up; and wet splotches of guano littered the cage floor. Even as Beth watched, leaf buds began to appear along the wooden perch.

Setting the cage down, Beth gave Gladstone a somber look. "The bird is distressed."

He shrugged. "It will be fine."

"Its magic has become unstable, thanks to whatever you've been doing to it. I fear that if it doesn't fly soon, to release the thaumaturgic energy, it will become ill or die. We must set it free in a safe place."

*"Set it free?"* Gladstone sputtered, his bushy goatee twitching. "Why would I be so stupid? I will be using my finely honed behavioral training techniques to get it into good performing shape, then touring it around England to demonstrate its healing abilities."

Beth gasped with shock. "But it's only a juvenile!"

"Best time for training. I've had good success with other thaumaturgic birds thus far, and I anticipate plenty of funding to come my way because of it. But the caladrius will be the star in my crown."

"It's not like this is a bird bred for domestication, learning tricks to enliven its existence. You're depriving a wild bird of its natural self-expression, manipulating its magic for your personal gain, and making it sick in the process. I can't believe you would do such a thing."

"You've spent too long among field naturalists, my girl, if you don't believe facts when they're laid before you. I just *told* you I was doing it. And you can hardly condemn me. The funding alone will make me moderately well-off, to say nothing of all the free meals I'll be given on tour!"

Beth shook her head, dismayed. "So this was IOS's scheme from the start."

"IOS." Gladstone hissed a laugh. "They wouldn't know their beak from their tail. I must say, though, the excitement over the caladrius that this competition has whipped up will be helpful indeed in attracting investors."

He blew a smoke ring from his pipe. Behind him, patches of green mold were beginning to appear on the seat back.

"I won't let you succeed!" Beth vowed.

"You have no choice," Gladstone answered calmly. "You may be clever, but you're just a girl."

"I'm a doctor of—"

Gladstone snatched the pipe from his mouth. "You're a *girl*. You could never best a man like me. And you might as well give up on Lockley coming to your rescue. He thinks you betrayed him to take Birder of the Year for yourself. He thinks you left him. You know he does."

Swallowing back a heated reply, Beth forced herself to focus on the spreading mold. Tiny yellow flowers blossomed here and there amid it. *Peep peep*, the caladrius cried as it emitted a surfeit of erratic magic. From the corner of her eye, she noticed the burly servant turning pale. Gladstone just blew another smoke ring.

She glared at him, wishing she had enough courage to

shout that he couldn't have been more wrong! Devon trusted her. They'd walked together in the sunshine, swinging their hands. They'd kissed (et cetera) in the bird-lit night. And his eyes had lit like burnished copper when she told him that she loved him, revealing a depth of emotion surely no man could counterfeit. He would trust her just as she trusted him. Undoubtedly he was even now searching the crowd on the station platform, desperate to find her. And when he failed to do so, he'd realize that she'd been kidnapped.

*Wouldn't he?*

Or would his skeptical heart assume the worst?

As the nasty little fear crept forward, sharp-clawed and sneering, a bitter taste filled Beth's mouth. She realized she was chewing her gloved thumbnail. Grimacing, she removed it from between her teeth and instead laid her hand on the birdcage, as if doing so might somehow reassure her and the caladrius both. Her palm tingled beneath the glove. Her throat tightened.

No, Devon *would* trust her. She refused to believe otherwise. After all, what good was love if it failed at the first uncertainty?

Shoving the fear away, she lifted her chin and stared with supercilious disgust at Gladstone (specifically, his shoulder, since her newfound courage was still a little wobbly).

*Toot!*

The train began to move. And just like that, Beth learned the most important lesson of all: it didn't matter if someone loved you, trusted you, was sure to come and rescue you, when the locomotive power of steam engines was involved.

There now existed a real and present danger of her winning Birder of the Year, and only she could save herself from it.

*Thud! Thud!* Someone outside bashed on the compartment door, no doubt furious that the departure time had been advanced without warning. *"Stop!"* they shouted, confirming her hypothesis. Gladstone chuckled, puffing on his pipe with triumphant equanimity, even as the vine reached out to twine around his bowler hat.

Closing her eyes, Beth repressed tears as the train carried her south toward London and tenure.

♡

# CHAPTER TWENTY-FIVE

*When the going gets tough, find a shortcut.*
*Birds Through a Sherry Glass*, H.A. Quirm

*Three days later*

WHAT A DARK moment!" Mr. Flogg groaned, staring into the depths of his coffee. Across the table from him, Mr. Fettick sighed in solemn agreement.

"I don't see why," Schreib said, taking the last cream puff on the three-tiered communal plate. "Miss Pickering will win Birder of the Year, which is at least half of what you wanted, and IOS is happy."

"But the British Tourism Board is not," Mr. Flogg said. "It was supposed to take longer than this for the caladrius to be 'captured,' so people throughout Europe would be inspired to come across, join in the excitement. And newspaper editors are not happy, since the grand romance they'd been touting has just fizzled away. Not even a dramatic breakup, not even a tragic but interesting death. Furthermore, our plan for a proper finale—our *expensive*, already-paid-for plan—has been ruined. We'll be lucky if anyone employs us after this debacle."

"I'm going to miss sitting in coffeehouses, arranging great adventures," Mr. Fettick said.

"I'm going to miss having an income," Mr. Flogg added.

This time, they both sighed in mournful unison.

Schreib cast a bemused glance at Cholmbaumgh, who shrugged. "But it's not over yet, is it?" the latter ventured. "They haven't handed out the award."

"And Mr. Lockley hasn't rushed to Miss Pickering's rescue," Schreib pointed out.

Mr. Fettick raised his gaze to Mr. Flogg, eyes glinting with hope. "That's true. 'Hope Remains.' What say you, Otis? Do you think we can go for one more spin?"

Mr. Flogg smiled, reaching across the table to grasp Mr. Fettick's hand. "Chester, let's dance."

BETH WOKE TO the sound of sparrows. They were scratching at the windowsill, and for a moment Beth thought she was home again in Oxford, with the city awakening reluctantly to another week of lectures, and her landlady downstairs burning the breakfast eggs. But the pillow beneath her head was soft, wrapped in silk, and she did not smell the familiar greasy smoke.

Her mind lurched through time (pausing here and there as it spotted an interesting bird), then crashed into the present. She sat bolt upright, looking around blearily at the hotel room in which Gladstone had locked her three days ago while word went out that the caladrius had been captured by *"The Extraordinary Professor Pickering from Oxford!"* . . . because *"Girls Can Do Anything (with a Quality University Education)!"* . . . and that Birder of the Year would be awarded in the same hotel's conference room.

Strong light suggested that the morning was well advanced—unsurprising, since she'd sat awake most of the night worrying about the caladrius, Devon, the newspaper headlines, the Dover railway clerk's horse, and even Hippolyta. She'd paced the room, tried for the sixteenth time to pick the door's lock, considered screaming for help again although it had achieved nothing thus far, and torn her fingernails in what she knew was a futile effort to open the bolted window. She'd even waved to passersby on the road below, not caring that such behavior was the height of vulgarity. But no one had seen her to be scandalized, let alone to rush in and perform a rescue. Finally, near dawn, she'd slipped into a troubled sleep.

She missed Devon with a physical sense that took her by surprise, since they had not been together for long. The air at her side seemed achingly empty of his presence. Her hand reached for him over and over again, as if wanting the balance he offered. And the sound of his voice echoed in her mind, warm and smiling, threaded through with the slightest American tone beneath his English vowels. *Beth*, he whispered to her, and she stopped, closing her eyes, listening to it, feeling his strong arms enfolding her.

How had this man quickly become so integral to her experience of being in the world that she felt incomplete now without him?

When the nights began to burn with silence and boredom, she imagined herself back on the moor again, tangled naked with him, loving deep and slow while magical bird stars floated and spun through the darkness beyond the sheltering tree. She remembered walking hand in hand with him on the long, climbing road, and discussing ornithological science over lunch as the train took them north, and working in easy professional harmony to catch the whopper swan in Oxford. So many wonderful memories, so much happiness—more than she'd known in all her life. When she let herself sink into them, she understood why she'd so rapidly fallen in love with Devon. He was extraordinarily lovable.

Why he loved her was more of a mystery, but she clung to the fragile belief of it. Far too often for good sense, she opened her field journal to the page on which he'd drawn her a dancing carnivorous lapwing, and hugged it to her heart as if she were some passionate art student.

She knew that Devon would come for her—perhaps not swinging in through the hotel window heroically, since (a) he did not know where she was and (b) it would cause an atrocious mess of broken glass; but certainly he would save her from winning Birder of the Year.

Not that she didn't intend to save herself, but a girl does like to have someone waiting in the wings, *wanting* to rescue her.

Apart from these dreamy figments of her lover (*her lover! squee!* echoed a gaggle of delighted thoughts, hugging each other and kissing framed memories of Devon), the only people she saw were the servants who brought her food, a suitcase of clothes and toiletries, and last night, a note.

*We will come for you at ten o'clock.*

(Or possibly *Weevils on one's oven eat nice luck*, considering Gladstone's penmanship had reached the degree of impenetrability attained only by medical doctors and senior professors on whose written word other people's futures depend.)

Rising now, Beth ate what remained on the latest food tray, washed, then rummaged through the suitcase with the bittersweet attitude of someone who has already lost two and holds little hope for this one as well. Gladstone himself must have specified the purchases, for brown tweed, gray tweed, and thick woolen stockings dominated the collection, smelling slightly of dust although they were new, and threatening death from heat suffocation before she even got on the stage to accept Birder of the Year. Beth selected a white shirtwaist, then a plain brown skirt on the basis that it included pockets. A woman felt she could do anything if she had pockets. There were no hairpins supplied, perhaps because Gladstone knew she'd use them to unlock the door, so she tore the lace trim off a garter to tie back her hair in a single braid. It was a young girl's style, but when she consulted a mirror, she saw a strong, determined, resilient professor gazing back at her.

Of course she did. She'd always been that, beneath her good behavior. The only difference now was, she felt far less willing to compromise.

Well, that and she knew how to use her mouth to make a man groan with pleasure.

So, improvements all around.

She had just finished buttoning her half boots when the door opened. It was time for the award ceremony. Grabbing her satchel and setting on her head a straw boater that had been among the clothes, Beth marched from the room. In the corridor beyond, Gladstone stood with a small group of servants, his face blurred by the faint mist of pipe smoke. He gave her a scathing once-over.

"Adequate," he said.

Beth tipped up her chin. "If you imagine that I care about your opinion—"

"*Imagine?*" he scoffed. "We are not primary school teachers, Pickering! And my opinion is not at work here, only my authority as your head of department." He flapped a hand. "You don't need that bag."

"It contains the notes for my acceptance speech," Beth lied.

Her satchel had accompanied her to the heights of the Swiss Alps and the depths of the Bodleian Library, and she wasn't about to relinquish it even if Gladstone did frown at her. Indeed, as she noted the covered birdcage being held by a servant, and smelled the thick, acrid scent of avian distress exuding from it, she considered taking the satchel and whacking it several times around Gladstone's head. Only the fact that it contained exorbitantly expensive binoculars made her hesitate.

And perhaps Gladstone saw the uncharacteristic rebellion on her face and ran a hasty mental cost-benefit analysis of further debate, for he huffed in surrender. "Fine. Let's go."

They took an elevator to the ground floor in taut silence. Beth's brain consulted urgently with her nerves regarding escape, but all the cunning ideas she'd developed during her imprisonment took one look at the aforementioned servants and slunk away. She had no intention of accepting the Birder of the Year award, and she'd developed quite the knack for saying no to people over the past week . . . but those servants' muscles really were quite pronounced, and Gladstone's frown plucked at nerves that had become particularly sensitized when he was her thesis adviser. She needed time to build a new plan.

Unfortunately, the journey across the hotel's gilded lobby seemed to take only about five seconds. Arriving at the open doors of the conference room, Beth peered inside. Her stomach flipped at the sight of several hundred people seated therein, including Mr. and Mrs. Podder from Canterbury, looking around wide-eyed, and Monsieur Chevrolet, smoothing his elegant mustache. Onstage, the golden phoenix statuette that was bestowed upon recipients of the Birder of the Year award gleamed atop a pedestal, guarded by the heads of Oxford University and the Sorbonne, who scrutinized each other over their spectacles and down their noses as they waited.

Beth's stomach flipped again. Was Devon in the audience? Was he smiling with sardonic humor and wondering if she'd name him in her acceptance speech?

"Give her the bird," Gladstone ordered brusquely, flicking his fingers at a servant. The man stepped forward, holding out the cage without a word. As she took it from him, Beth lifted the cover and peeked beneath.

The caladrius hunched on its perch, seemingly no more than a puff of trembling white feathers. Beth could hear the rapid staccato of its breath and noted the splatters of wet guano. The cage itself was beautiful, ornately fashioned from gold, but contained no food or water receptacle. She felt the chill of what she'd have called a premonition had she been any less educated. A life without comfort lay before the little bird. Feted for its talent and forced to perform in an endless series of drawing rooms and lecture halls, it would never get the consideration and freedom it needed to thrive. Beth very nearly burst into tears at the thought.

The caladrius did not even peep.

Taking a slow, deep breath, she lowered the cover and turned again to Gladstone. "The bird is unwell. It needs to fly, to release the buildup of its magic."

Gladstone waved a hand impatiently. "Of course, of course. I'll let it tootle around my aviary for a while after I've presented it to the most important people: the Queen . . . the Russian emperor . . . the editor of the *Daily Telegraph*."

Beth stared at him with all the iciness of a frostbird. She noticed belatedly that he was not wearing spectacles, and his hair and goatee had transformed from gray to the blond of his younger days. She could see in his smirk that it was no accident: he'd drawn from the caladrius's untempered magic to heal various injuries time had done to his appearance. Repulsion threatened to not only flip her stomach but spill its contents all over the floor.

"No need for that expression, girl," Gladstone snarled. "Just smile and do your duty by Oxford. And if you don't . . ." He ran the end of his pipe across his throat.

Beth's eyes grew wide with shock. "You'll kill me?"

"What?" Gladstone blinked at her confusedly. "No. Good grief! I'll have your Royal Society Medal of High Achievement taken from you, your professorship renounced, and all sources of funding closed to you forever." He paused, his face hardening once more. "Do you understand?"

Beth's heart cringed. She looked again into the conference room, heavy-eyed and with a dozen apologies crammed unspoken in her throat. Oxford's chancellor was staring out at her now, his face taut with impatience. The audience murmured restlessly. Everyone was waiting for her.

"Well?" Gladstone demanded. "Do. You. Understand?"

"Yes," she said.

Then, tightening her grip around the birdcage's handle, she turned on her heel and fled.


RACING ACROSS THE hotel lobby, Beth knew she would not reach even halfway to its exit before Gladstone's servants caught her. Niceness would not save her this time; bird facts were useless. She needed a dose of barefaced, swaggering bravado. What would Devon do in such a situation?

Better yet, what would *Hippolyta* do?

"Help!" she shouted. "By Jove, help me!!"

Bystanders turned to gape at her with the horror of offended etiquette, for one simply does *not* run through a hotel lobby if one is a decent person (although the occasional handsome spy in a tuxedo, or lovestruck person desperate to stop a wedding, may be forgiven for doing so).

But Beth didn't have the luxury of good manners. "I'm an ornithologist," she called out, "and they're trying to hurt the caladrius!"

A shocked gasp arose from the crowd. Close observers might have noticed the remarkable lack of feathers upon ladies' hats and concluded that newspaper coverage of Birder of the Year had gone deep into the public psyche. Luckily, Beth was professionally trained in close observation.

"Please help me save the bird!" she cried.

At once, elegant ladies and somber gentlemen leaped forth to block the pursuit of Gladstone's servants. A scuffle broke out. A furled parasol was employed, and a walking stick or two. One woman vigorously swung what appeared to be a handbag in the shape of a birdcage. Within seconds the servants had been brought to the floor.

Beth glanced back in amazement, then turned once more toward the exit doors . . .

"Excuse me!" said a young woman, darting in front of her. Beth skidded to a halt mere inches from collision. "I'm from the *Ladies' Home Journal*. I'd like to interview you about—"

"Sorry, no time," Beth said. Smacking the woman's notepad so it skittered across the floor, she resumed her dash.

*"Elizabeth, my dear!"* Hippolyta herself appeared in a perfumed blur of flounces and lacy ruffles, as if summoned by

Beth's imitation of her. The woman was like a flock of seagulls at a beach picnic, Beth decided grimly—never driven off for long. Without even so much as a pardon, she skirted around her and kept going. Running faster now, she felt a breeze, promising freedom (and a lung infection from London's air pollution), as the exit doors flung open . . .

And every beat of her heart came to a crashing halt.

DEVON STRODE INTO the hotel lobby, his long dark coat billowing in dramatic hero style—and stopped abruptly, redness suffusing his cheeks as he stared at Beth. He'd been expecting to disrupt the award ceremony by leaping upon the stage to rescue the fair maiden just in the nick of time, but here she was, fair indeed (although not, scientifically speaking, a maiden any longer), and scowling at him furiously.

"You're in the way," she said, gesturing that he should move aside. Then she added, of course she did: "Sorry. Nice to see you. Please get out of my path."

God, he loved her. Loved her so much he kept bringing *God* into it, and indeed was even at this moment contemplating a grand church wedding if such was required to have Beth Pickering in his life forever. When she'd vanished into the crowd at Sheffield's train station, panic had almost overcome him in a way not even the deadly masked booby had been able to do. Glimpsing Hippolyta and one of Gladstone's servants pushing her onto the train, he'd made a mad dash—but had been too late. Thumping on the side of the train had achieved nothing, and there'd not even been a carriage balcony for him to jump onto like a romantic daredevil. Although he'd known

Gladstone would not hurt Beth, watching that train speed away had felt like part of his heart was being dragged away with it.

Traveling to London in agonizingly slow pursuit, he'd taken a room at the Minervaeum Club and spent two days trying to uncover where Gladstone was keeping Beth and the caladrius. Late on the second day, Gabriel had arrived, taken one disapproving look at the shambles of clothes, sheets, and dinnerware strewn about the room, another at Devon's haggard, unshaven face, and sighed with exasperation.

"Why are you making a disaster out of this?"

"Because it is one!" Devon had replied in a rather hysterical tone he'd not have used had he known he'd be recalling the scene later.

"No," Gabriel had said with stern impatience, "a disaster is when lightning strikes a Neolithic gravesite in Kent, disrupting the thaumaturgic wellspring thereunder and electrifying every metal object in the vicinity. Which is what happened this morning, and I'm heading there now to join the professional response. So let me make this quick. You know you'll see your woman and your bird at the award ceremony. You have time to make a plan. Pull yourself together, all right?"

"All right," Devon had muttered, feeling justly chastised.

So he'd made a plan, and tidied the room, and waited impatiently to rescue Beth.

Except she did not seem to want it.

"I spend half my life chasing deadly birds and the other half applying for funding grants," she told him, chin raised at her favorite haughty angle. "I can rescue myself."

"I know," Devon said.

"Nice doesn't mean incapable."

"I know."

"There was this one time in Greece when a lycan-thropic owl—"

"Get them!" came a shout from behind her. Gladstone's servants had almost wrestled their way out of the crowd. Hippolyta was creeping up with a net she'd had concealed in her hat, as if Beth were some kind of bird. And the young woman from the *Ladies' Home Journal* was excitedly writing on a notepad as she watched the scene. Devon immediately drew his gun, aiming at them all.

"We're leaving," he announced. "And I *will* shoot anyone who tries to stop us."

The entire crowd froze.

"Please don't follow," Beth urged Hippolyta in a tone of sincere concern. "I concluded matters between us days ago, while on the train to Oxford. Having to keep defying you is—well, redundant, and quite honestly confusing."

Hippolyta opened her mouth to reply but was apparently all out of Jove. In her gobsmacked silence, only the rattle of her long, ornate earrings expressed just how furious she was. Devon backed himself and Beth to the edge of the lobby, where large double doors stood open to a tearoom.

"Why are we going this way, instead of out the front door?" Beth whispered from the corner of her mouth.

"I have a plan," Devon whispered back. "Trust me."

"Always," she said—and the only reason he didn't grab her face and kiss her right then was because ~~a crowd of rivals was waiting to leap~~ that was exactly the kind of manhandling behavior he really ought to stop.

Turning, they ran into the tearoom.

And the crowd, with a roar, took up pursuit.

# CHAPTER TWENTY-SIX

Avian magic is beautiful. That's what makes it so dangerous.

*Birds Through a Sherry Glass*, H.A. Quirm

BETH MANAGED THROUGH strength of will alone not to waste breath apologizing to diners and waiters as she and Devon raced between the white-clothed tables at a speed that disallowed autograph requests. Hot on their heels came Hippolyta, Gladstone's servants, the *Ladies' Home Journal* reporter, assorted ornithologists, and various hotel staff. Glancing back at them, Beth felt her straw boater topple, but there was no time to stop for it, or even to count exactly how many hats she had lost in the past week. Devon pushed aside a half-open door and they turned left along a service corridor, then right, Devon seemingly aware of exactly where to go. Passing a laundry room, he shouted, *"Now!"* and a hotel worker pushed a large trolley, piled high with bedding, into the corridor behind them.

*Crash!* The pursuers ran right into it.

*"Aarrghhh!"* Bodies fell in a writhing tangle.

"Goodness me," Beth murmured.

They raced on, coming eventually to a wide door that

opened on the hotel's delivery yard. Devon shut and barred it behind them, then indicated a narrow alley.

"We'll cut through there and head for the South Kensington train station as fast as we can."

"All right," Beth agreed.

They crossed the yard, Devon glancing at Beth sidelong. "You don't seem surprised that I'm here."

"I knew you'd come—"

"For Birder of the Year?" he said, finishing her sentence. His voice sounded like it had its hands in its pockets and its gaze focused on the middle distance: not at all upset about her response, entirely nonchalant.

*"For me,"* she corrected him.

He stopped abruptly, halfway along the narrow alley, caught by her words. Smiling, he cupped a hand to one side of her face more gently than he would hold the most precious and rare bird.

"I will always come for you, Beth. You are my sunlight."

She would have swooned, were it not for the present circumstances. Leaning into the warmth and comfort of his hand, she smiled at him in return. "You are my wild wind."

They gazed at each other with a longing that felt like it could defy time—or that had simply forgotten half a dozen rival ornithologists were after them. The grim alley began to glow with soft, golden spangles, as though their hearts were emanating love as a radiant magic . . .

*Oh*, Beth thought, blinking away from Devon to stare up at the light. *Damn.*


As Beth shifted her gaze, Devon went on helplessly gazing at her, transfixed. He'd thought she was pretty from the first moment he saw her, and she'd become truly gorgeous in his eyes the more he learned about her; but now he could think of no adjective sufficient for this woman. She was beyond description. She was something for which he needed a language of heartbeats and deep, satisfied sighs.

She reached out to touch one long, serene coil of light, and as it slid across her hand she seemed to light with another kind of magic. A very specific, beautiful Beth magic, Devon thought, one that unfurled from her soul in response to ornithology. "Such a comprehensive and elaborately luminescent manifestation of thaumaturgic energy is extraordinary for a juvenile bird," she said.

And even if he hadn't already decided on it, Devon would have known in that moment he needed to marry her, just so he could listen to her talk like that for the rest of his life. But then he realized she was frowning, and he frowned too, abruptly remembering the circumstances in which they found themselves.

"This cannot be good," she said. Holding up the birdcage, she lifted its cover warily.

"Shit," Devon said, magic turning to ash in his throat.

*Pip*, the caladrius responded. It hunched lopsidedly on its perch, feathers dull and gray, tail bobbing, as it squinted wearily at its glimmering enchantment.

"It needs to fly," Beth said, lowering the cover again, "but we can't just release it here, in a London alley." Her tone was brisk, her manner entirely professional despite the anguish on her face. "We need water. And fruit. Mashed banana, applesauce."

"We need to *run*," Devon corrected her.

She nodded, and without further discussion they ran along

the alley, trailing golden magic. Turning down one street, then another, they headed south—

"Hey!"

In the center of road ahead stood a man, waving his arms furiously. In one hand he held a pistol, and before Devon even processed the sight, a shot rang out.

Devon immediately leaped in front of Beth, causing her to collide with him. The caladrius cheeped in fright, wings fluttering against its cage bars. Pedestrians screamed and ran. But the man was focused entirely on Beth and Devon. With the gun pointed skyward, and a thin cigarette hanging limp from between his lips, he shouted rather dubiously, "I'm not going to hurt you!"

"Schreib!" Devon said like a curse.

"Quick!" Beth tugged on his arm. "This way!"

They veered onto a leafy avenue and raced past the Imperial Institute construction site, breath burning in their lungs. Schreib followed, demanding that they stop. Coming to Exhibition Road, they turned south again toward the train station.

"Hey!" came another roar.

"Damn!" Devon swore as Cholmbaumgh rushed for them, waving a cricket bat. Forced to retreat, they ran north, weaving through a crowd of pedestrians and inciting outraged comments and much clicking of tongues as they went. Schreib and Cholmbaumgh trailed them relentlessly.

"What are we going to do?" Beth asked with increasing panic. "The caladrius won't survive this for long."

"We'll have to take it to the Albert Aviary," Devon said.

"The place that agent of PRESS suggested?"

Devon pointed to the lush trees of Kensington Gardens, visible at the end of the road. "It's just up ahead."

He took her hand and they increased their pace even more, the birdcage swinging wildly in Beth's grip. Glancing back at Schreib and Cholmbaumgh, she felt a sudden, uncomfortable sympathy for all the birds she had chased. The men were jogging steadily, appearing almost unhurried, as if they were not trying to catch their prey but herd them. It was a common birding tactic, and she looked away rather queasily—just in time to see Hippolyta and Oberhufter appear as if from nowhere, a few yards ahead.

*"Halt!"* Oberhufter roared.

"Halt!" Hippolyta added in English.

Devon swerved to the far side of the road, Beth struggling to remain steady on her feet. Oberhufter and Hippolyta began to follow, but suddenly Cholmbaumgh flung himself at the field ornithologists, causing all three to collide with furious screams.

"Go!" Cholmbaumgh shouted to Beth and Devon, waving one arm desperately from within the tangle of limbs and lacy flounces. "Run!"

Beth and Devon shared a confused glance but did not hesitate. They raced on to the end of Exhibition Road, where several people were milling around the Coalbrookdale Gates, excitedly watching their approach. From somewhere farther inside the park arose the hearty sounds of what sounded like a full brass band.

"Perhaps this is not a good idea after all," Beth said.

*PEEP!* the caladrius argued.

"We don't have a choice," Devon said, pointing behind them, where not only Schreib but also a crowd of ornithologists were in pursuit, wielding nets, binoculars, and birdcages . . . and was that a helicopter parasol rising above the Royal Albert Hall? . . .

No, it was *four* helicopter parasols, one with Monsieur Tarrou from the Parisian Ornithological Union, the remaining three bearing servants laden with his baggage.

They crossed the road, and the bystanders, cheering and whistling, shifted aside to allow them easy passage through the great iron gates. But as they entered the carriageway, Beth and Devon staggered to a halt, staring openmouthed at what lay before them.

"Oh gosh," Beth gasped.

"Bloody hell," Devon agreed.

♡

# CHAPTER TWENTY-SEVEN

All any of us want, bird and birder, is the freedom to
find our own skies, our own magic.
*Birds Through a Sherry Glass*, H.A. Quirm

HUNDREDS OF PEOPLE lined both sides of South Carriage
Drive. They were waving bird-shaped flags and bird-
painted balloons, and they chanted in exuberant unison, "Caladrius! Caladrius! Go! Go! Go!" Banners had been strung
between trees, proclaiming such things as GET HIGH*er education* WITH ORNITHOLOGY! and BIRDS ARE BRILLIANT! A pair of
clowns in plumed hats danced along the rows of people, handing out boiled lollies and university enrollment forms.

Upon noticing Beth and Devon, the crowd went wild.
(Which is to say, they cheered and clapped in a slightly louder
fashion, considering this was Victorian Britain, where "going
wild" would seem like "disinterest" to tourists from more ~~emo-
tionally healthy~~ excitable countries.)

"Um," Devon said.

"Gosh," Beth said.

*"Caladrius! Caladrius! Go! Go! Go!"* the crowd replied.

And to the left of them, a small child said in the kind of
sweet, lisping voice that somehow managed to be heard clearly

above any amount of general uproar, "Mummy, the bird people are holding hands. Does this mean they got married?"

*"Aahhhh!"* gasped the crowd in delight.

"Uh," Beth and Devon said in unison, glancing at each other. Then looking back, they saw Schreib paused at the gates, struggling to catch his breath. He winked at them, flicking his pistol in a *go on, hurry up* gesture.

"Uh," they said again, utterly bemused. But in the absence of any other option, they continued along the path. The crowd cheered and tossed paper confetti at them. Beth was appalled, bewildered, and overwhelmed, but Devon's grip on her hand kept her steady. The strength of his presence, encompassed by boots and long coat, set with hardened muscles, offered sanctuary for her jittery nerves. Even so, she wanted to stop and find a quiet place beneath a tree where she could bring out her journal, write a risk-benefit analysis of placing the caladrius in the Albert Aviary, and maybe have a cup of tea. But there was no time. She would just have to trust the wind, adore the wind.

As they progressed, the two rows of people merged behind them, and before long they found themselves leading the crowd past the Albert Memorial, upon whose steps a brass band stood, playing Rossini's "William Tell Overture" with a verve that obliterated whatever shreds remained of Beth's composure. Some thirty yards beyond, surrounded by a colorful garden, stood the Albert Aviary. Its great glass dome bore a delicate, finely scrolled copper exoskeleton that created a diamond-paned effect; roses framed the arched, gold-painted doorway; and as sunlight flashed here and there, producing fragments of rainbows, the structure seemed altogether like a fairy-tale castle against the faultless blue summer sky.

But Devon stopped before they reached it, and Beth edged close to his side, tightening her grip on the birdcage's handle—for standing near the entrance of the aviary were two men in dark suits and bowler hats, their identical mustaches twitching with what might have been delight, or possibly itchiness considering the noon heat.

*"Lovebirds Meet Their Destiny!"* exclaimed one in rousing tones.

*"Higher Education Wins the Day!"* declared the other.

As the crowd behind them fell silent with breathless anticipation, Beth and Devon turned to each other, dazed.

"Do you understand what's happening?" Beth asked in a whisper.

"I think we've been played," Devon whispered in reply. "Those are the men who've trailed us since Paris."

"The agents of PRESS?"

"Oh!" Devon's countenance lit with sudden understanding. "Press agents. I can't believe I didn't get that before."

The dark-suited men were watching them as warily as if they were explosive thornbacked owls. Nearby in a tidy line stood the IOS executive committee, obviously as disconcerted by the crowd as Beth herself felt. And behind them, Laz Brady and another young man in Oxford blue held up a banner reading REACH FOR THE SKIES WITH AN ORNITHOLOGY DEGREE.

Comprehension struck Beth so forcefully, she gasped. "This has all been a recruitment drive!"

"I think you're right," Devon agreed.

"But that's insane!"

He shrugged. "Ornithology." Reaching out with his free hand, he gently tucked a loose strand of hair behind her ear.

*"Awww,"* the crowd cooed adoringly.

At that moment, the dark-suited men approached, briefcases in hand like weapons. "Good day, Professors," one said with a polite nod. "I am Mr. Flogg, and this is my associate, Mr. Fettick. Congratulations!"

"Um," Beth said. "Thank you?"

"You have been *"A Beacon of Inspiration"* to thousands of bird lovers across Britain and abroad," Mr. Flogg continued. "Because of your acts of courage and derring-do, not to mention your romantic exploits, inquiries and enrollments to the ornithology departments of all universities have more than tripled this week! At least *twelve* new applicants! The International Ornithological Society is ecstatic and would like to offer you both an excellent employment package, including tenure, at any institution you desire."

**Tenure!** rejoiced one part of Beth's brain. The rest, however, was a tumult of cynicism, overwhelming stimulation, and the desire to run away to some distant moorland where the soft melody of a whispering warbler provided the only sound for miles. Over Mr. Flogg's shoulder, the IOS committee members regarded her with solemn approval, and she smiled politely in automatic response. Then, noting that Gladstone was not among them, she breathed a little more freely.

"That's—" she began.

"But wait!" Mr. Flogg interjected dramatically, causing her to jolt and the caladrius to emit a startled peep. "There's more! The Royal College of Science would like to honor you both with their Medal of Distinction, which comes with a grand cash prize of ten pounds."

"Good heavens," Devon said sardonically, grinning at Beth. He bounced his eyebrows. "We're rich. Ten pounds each!"

"Er, no, that's ten pounds between the two of you," Mr. Flogg explained, scrubbing his mustache in embarrassment.

"Wasn't there supposed to be a *five thousand pound* reward that went along with Birder of the Year?" Devon asked.

The committee members shuffled uncomfortably, looking like Devon had just threatened to steal all their blackboard chalk. "Ah, yes, well, you see . . ." Mr. Flogg extemporized. "There are *two* of you, and as everyone knows—"

"There can only be one Birder of the Year," Beth, Devon, and the committee members joined him in saying.

"Yes, precisely. Because the award cannot be given to two people, it will instead be presented to the International Ornithological Society executive committee itself."

"Which is significantly more than two people," Devon pointed out, but no one heard him over the committee members enthusiastically congratulating each other for this win.

"What about the caladrius?" Beth asked.

"Ah! Wonderful news on that front too," Mr. Flogg continued. "The committee is excited to offer the caladrius an all-expenses-paid tour of the British Isles! Including a very special audience with Her Majesty the Queen's aviary keeper!"

Beth went cold right through. "But that's what Gladstone was going to do," she said. "It's why we took the bird."

"Yes, but *we* are doing it in the name of science, not profit," explained the committee secretary, Monsieur Badeau.

"Entirely different," said the representative of Universiteit van Amsterdam.

"Gladstone has been invited to resign," announced Oxford University's chancellor, in a tone that left no doubt *"invited"* was a professional synonym for *"forced to."* He looked Beth up and down comprehensively, then nodded in approval, and she intuited that there were great things in her future: not only tenure and a corner office, but a higher quality of gloves to wear when she washed the dishes in the faculty lounge. She took half a step back, clutching the birdcage so tightly her fingers hurt.

"Excuse us a moment," Devon said to the committee, then turned away, drawing Beth with him. She felt his mood clench with the same instinct to flee that she had. But there was nowhere to go. With Messrs. Flogg and Fettick and the IOS committee behind them, and what appeared to be half of London before them, they were thoroughly trapped.

"This is dreadful!" Beth whispered. "We can't release the caladrius inside the aviary now; it's just like placing it inside a larger cage. But we can't run either. The poor bird is doomed! Utterly doomed!"

Devon took a deep breath, holding her gaze steadily with his, then exhaled. When next he breathed in, Beth did the same, then they exhaled in unison. It was highly effective, although only if their goal had been to feel rather dizzy. Certainly, calm found nowhere to perch within Beth.

"You have a plan?" she asked Devon hopefully.

"No," he said. "I'm at a complete bloody loss."

*Peep!*

The caladrius's sudden sharp cry drew their attention to the cage. A gold thread of magic was emerging from beneath it, coiling slowly as it rose through the space between them.

"*Ooh.*" A soft ripple of wonder went through the crowd.

The magic began to extend in sparkling ribbons, shooting off tiny pink stars. Floating toward Devon, it encircled him, then wove around Beth, binding them in enchantment.

"*Ahhh!*" The rippling wonder grew louder. Messrs. Flogg

and Fettick stared, mouths agape. The IOS committee began taking notepads and pencils from pockets in their university robes to record the phenomenon.

*Peeeep!*

At the caladrius's shrill cry, Beth's pulse leaped. She hastily lifted the cage cover, revealing the little white bird standing tall on its perch, wings outstretched.

"The caladrius!" several people at the front of the crowd shouted.

"Where? Where?" shouted others.

"Move! I can't see it!"

"Quick, Hilda, get out your sketch pad!"

"It looks nothing like its picture in the newspaper."

*Peep peep!* An intense light burst forth from the little white bird. Everyone winced, and when they looked again the cage was melting away, gold drops falling to the earth, leaving only the handle in Beth's grasp.

"Oh no," she said—

And the caladrius flew up, singing, singing.


As THE SMALL wings flapped valiantly, carrying the bird into ~~clean fresh~~ not-too-horribly-polluted sunshine, Beth's spirit lifted along with it. Fear seemed to dissolve like old thaumaturgic energy being shed in flight. Panic faded into a quiet sigh. The bird flew swiftly upward, trailing magic in long, beautiful feathers of light: all the infirmities it had absorbed since being captured and brought to England by IOS agents, all the pains it had transformed into hope. Throughout Kensington Gardens, plants whispered and stirred. The music of the brass band dwindled into one exquisite melody from a clarinet.

Love filled the air.

It was magic, but more. It was pure healing, right down to the core of life, where only truth existed. Among the crowd below, a plethora of broken words, strained silences, and simple everyday distresses melted away into peaceful resolution. People began turning to embrace each other, weeping tears of joy; making protestations of love, apologies, promises; signing university enrollment forms. Beth noticed the PRESS agents kissing each other with such passion, their bowler hats fell off. Even the IOS committee were in paroxysms of emotion: shaking one another by the hand, even going so far as to pat a shoulder or two. And within the crowd—

*Smack.*

"This is all your fault, Oberhufter!" boomed Hippolyta's voice. "That bird should have been mine!"

Laughing, Beth turned back to Devon.

He was gone.

Looking around confusedly, she was bewildered to discover him on one knee before her. "Oh," she said. The confusion tipped and spun until her thoughts became a blur. All she knew then was the rush of her pulse and the safe, heavy darkness of Devon's eyes gazing up at her.

"Well, this is embarrassing," he said as he took one of her hands in both of his and held it gently, loosely, so that she could slip away from him at any second, should she want. "Nothing like being forced down on one knee in front of crowd by the magic of a tiny bird."

"Sorry," Beth whispered.

He smiled. "No need for an apology, my angel. I don't need magic to know I love you. And I always intended to do this, just perhaps a little more privately. With, you know, flowers and champagne, and a prettier view. Then again, I'm grateful the caladrius is giving me the courage it might have otherwise taken a while to gather."

"*You* need courage?" she asked, amazed.

His smile wavered. "More than you know."

Indeed, his hands were trembling around hers. Beth wanted to take them, hold them against her heart, so he might know how it beat for him. She could not move, however, mesmerized as she was by the enchantment he was weaving, had been weaving this past week, with his good cheer (and his even better kisses).

"You're allowed to say no," he assured her. "You're allowed to turn away and leave, never mind all the people watching right now."

Beth glanced around, swallowing heavily as she realized the entire crowd had already forgotten about the caladrius in the face of the far more interesting spectacle Devon was making of himself. She glimpsed Rose Marin, the hijacking professor from Edinburgh, grinning brightly; and Hippolyta, wide-eyed; and the magnificent mustache of Monsieur Chevrolet . . . and was that the Chaucer Inn landlord and his daughter, waving to her from beside a hydrangea bush?

"But should you wish to stay," Devon continued—then paused to brush the hair away from his eyes with uncharacteristic nervousness. Several onlookers shuffled impatiently; *"get on with it, man"* could be heard within the ranks of the IOS committee. "If you do stay, um, then I'd like to propose that we marriage. Er, get married. We could travel—um, wherever you want. Psychic territories of the giant moa. Eyries of American eagles. We could have fun, rescue a lot of birds, make a lot of—um. Yes. Well. There you have it. Never mind. Goodbye."

He began to rise, but Beth hastily set a hand on his shoulder, holding him in place. Devon looked up at her with a vulnerability, and yet a love, that made her think of the first moment a bird took flight from a tree branch into the peril and promise of the sky. She smiled back at him, entirely certain, and just a little smoldering.

"It requires very little analysis," she said, "for me to conclude that your proposal has copious merits, and that acceptance would be the most profitable response on my part; therefore, please do take remittance of it."

His expression emptied. "What?"

Urgently seeking a translation from within the wreckage of her overwhelmed brain, she received one instead from her heart.

"Yes."

"Yes?" Devon echoed, his own intellect apparently having disappeared somewhere up among the clouds with the caladrius.

Beth grinned. "Yes, please. I love you, Devon. I will most definitely marry you."

Instantly, he was on his feet, grasping her head and manhandling her into a fierce kiss. Beth wrapped her arms around him, clutching his coat, not letting him go.

The crowd screamed with excitement. Banners flew out of raised hands to flap free, like vast wings, in the glimmering air. And a voice shouted out from the general melee.

"By Jove! Good catch, Elizabeth!"

Laughter broke their kiss. Still hugging, they smiled at

each other before lifting their gazes skyward with the irrepressible instinct of ornithologists, seeking wings.

Far above, the caladrius circled the scene, peeping cheerfully, then flew away into mystery.

And a cool breeze began to drift in, promising fresher days to come.

♡

# Acknowledgments

Writing this book was like chasing a wild, magical bird. My warm thanks to Beth and Devon for always knowing what route we should take—and to all the birds who sang outside my window while I worked, providing beautiful inspiration!

This is a historical fantasy, as may be obvious from the magical birds, not to mention the female professor. While every effort was made to accurately depict the various details of life in 1890, I took considerable artistic licence with the big picture; for example, making ornithology a separate department at English universities (in my defense, the widespread existence of deadly magical birds does perhaps justify it!). Thanks to all the real ornithologists over the years whose work brings us nearer to understanding, as poet William Blake called it, "an immense world of delight, clos'd by [our] senses five."

I'm grateful as ever to all the people who were part of this book's journey. Kristine Swartz, I appreciate so much your wisdom and the way you can always find the heart of my stories. Taylor Haggerty, thank you for your kindness, calm guidance, and for never failing to make me smile. Jasmine Brown and Mary Baker, I really value all that you do. Thanks also to Heather Baror-Shapiro and Alice Lawson; Rebecca Hilsdon, Jorgie Bain, and everyone at Michael Joseph Books; and my foreign-language publishers.

My heartfelt gratitude to Stephanie Felty, Anika Bates, Christine Legon, Stacy Edwards, Katy Riegel, Eileen Chetti, and everyone at Penguin Random House. Immense thanks to Katie Anderson for the glorious cover!

Hugs to all my readers; it's such a delight to write for you.

And love, as always and forever, to Amaya, Julie, Simon, Anya, and Myla.

I also want to send thanks to all those who have been in touch about the neurodivergent representation in my books. I don't use diagnostic terms within the context of the stories, because it wouldn't be historically accurate. That neurodivergent people have nevertheless seen something of their own experience in several of my characters means a great deal to me as an autistic writer.

Since I finished writing *The Ornithologist's Field Guide to Love*, I've continued telling myself tales of Beth and Devon's ongoing adventures, such as fighting smugglers and visiting the great moa. So, as a kind of miniature epilogue, I invite you to see them as I so often do: lying hand in hand on the sunlit ground of an American prairie, watching eagles dance.

*Keep reading for an excerpt from*

*India Holton's next book in*

*the Love's Academic series . . .*

THE GEOGRAPHER'S MAP TO ROMANCE

> Speak softly and carry a big telescope.
> *Blazing Trails*, W.H. Jackson.

*Oxford, 1890*

A GEOGRAPHER BEHAVES WITH quiet dignity at all times. Elodie Tarrant had been informed of this maxim repeatedly by professors over the years, and she took great pains to impress it upon her own students. England's surveyors and mapmakers must be known for their decorum so they are not known for their trespassing and shot at. Consequently, Elodie had chosen to cycle to the Oxford train station that morning, rather than run along the streets—walking in a dignified manner being out of the question, considering how late she was.

And this would have been entirely commendable, except for the small but not untrivial matter of her bicycle being a steam-powered velocipede.

Anyone not immediately witness to the spectacle of a helmet-clad woman perched upon a rickety wheeled contraption, with steam clouds billowing around her and a long, un-buttoned tweed coat billowing behind, was alerted to it by the loud rattling, tooting, and random belches of the machine. At least her skirt did not billow—but this was because she had it knotted up around her knees, thus revealing her stocking-clad legs, and so rather failed to argue in favor of dignity.

"Faster!" she urged the vehicle as though this might make some difference to its speed. "It will be a disaster if I miss that train!"

She spoke literally. News had arrived yesterday that, following a large storm, magic was afoot in Wales, igniting trees and sending sheep airborne. The Home Office had called upon Professor Tarrant to manage the crisis. Being one of England's foremost specialists in exigent thaumaturgic geographic dynamics (otherwise known as "magical mayhem" to people who valued their vocal chords), Elodie received many such requests, and usually delegated them to graduate students. But with the Michaelmas term still a week away, Elodie rather fancied a few days of strolling through the autumnal countryside.

Besides, there existed a small chance that this job would require her advanced expertise. The site—Dôlylleaud, a minor village ten miles east of the Welsh coastline—was marked as a level 5 node on the Geographic Paranormal Survey (GPS) map, which recorded all known sources of earth magic along with the fey lines that connected them in a complex web around the world. Level 5 indicated a source powerful enough to send thaumaturgic energy down the line to Oxford and its various libraries, just waiting to explode, then on to London, where an incursion of wild magic would have cataclysmic results.

Immediately, Elodie had packed a suitcase, postponed her milk delivery, and organized to catch the earliest morning train to Wales. It was the perfect rapid response.

At least, up until the part where she forgot to set her alarm clock.

Arriving at Oxford station with less than ten minutes to

spare, she parked the velocipede and was untying the suitcase from its luggage tray when a young man approached, mustache trembling on his thin, dark face as he hugged a clipboard of papers against his chest.

"Professor Tarrant?" he peeped.

"Ah, there you are, Motthers." Elodie turned to him with a brisk nod. He took in her entirely rational ensemble of coat, white shirtwaist, and gray skirt, and then her altogether irrational stockings exposed to general view (one black French lace, the other green, embroidered with flowers), and he winced so deeply his neck disappeared. "Is everything prepared?" she asked.

"Yes, ma'am. I have the Emergency Response kit, two tickets for the train, and a plentiful supply of sandwiches."

Elodie waited . . .

"Ham with cheese," he clarified.

She grinned. "Well done." Removing the helmet, she shook out her long, pale blond hair. It tumbled down in reckless waves—magical hair, literally, having been mousy brown until, at age thirteen, she swam in a moonlit lake she had *absolutely no idea* was enchanted. "Sorry I'm late," she said, sweeping the wayward strands from her face. "I overslept, then I started wondering during breakfast about how Persephone went for nine days in the Underworld before eating the pomegranate seeds, and I quite lost track of time. Do you know?"

"Know what, Professor?" Motthers asked warily.

"How she survived all that time without even drinking water, of course."

"Um."

"Never mind. I'll ask someone from the classics department when I get back." She hung the helmet on the velocipede's handlebars and began to gather up her hair, looking around as if clips might appear midair for her convenience. Then she noticed Motther's dazed stare. "What?"

"T-ticket, ma'am," he said, holding it out in a trembling hand. Elodie took it from him, her hair tumbling down again.

"Much obliged."

But Motther was not done trembling. "There's, um, a small problem."

"Oh?" Elodie asked, not really listening, as she inspected the ticket. It provisioned her with a second-class seat from Oxford to Aberystwyth, after which she and Motthers would take a hired carriage to Dôlylleaud. This was altogether a journey of several long, dull hours, but Elodie didn't mind, feeling that tedium was best described as an opportunity for imagination.

"Just a very small problem," Motthers persisted. "Which is to say, quite large actually, and—and—*problematic*."

"Uh-huh." Elodie experienced so many problems in her profession that they had to be literal disasters before she started worrying. Motthers, however, was only a master's student, and had not yet been caught in a raging flood, let alone outrun fiery boulders that chased him uphill. He needed several more catastrophes under his belt before he developed perspective. As a result, his voice tried to hide behind his tonsils when next he spoke.

"You recall how the telegram yesterday requested aid from Professor Tarrant?"

"Sure," Elodie said, barely listening. Suitcase in hand, she began striding across the train platform, the heels of her sturdy half boots knocking against the ground as if to announce to other travelers that a professional heroine had arrived—

although apparently this was not clear enough for Professor Palgrave, who was forced to leap aside, muttering about "sinful blindness."

"Um," Motthers said, scurrying to keep pace despite his legs being several inches longer than Elodie's (which prompted him to wonder if he should mention the knotted-up skirt, but his courage failed). "It's just, well, it seems a copy was made of the telegram, and someone who shall go unnamed Ralph Sterling delivered it to a second office."

"Oh?" Elodie stopped near the edge of the platform and shielded her eyes with her free hand from the morning sun as she peered south along the tracks for a glimpse of a train.

"To be fair, we're not *exactly* sure who the message was meant for in the first place, you or . . . the other Professor Tarrant."

Elodie continued gazing out beneath her hand at the horizon, mainly because she had frozen. Then, very slowly, she turned to look at the small crowd on the platform.

And there he was.

"*You,*" she muttered with such ferocity, it must be cause for amazement that the gentleman did not spontaneously combust.

He did not even so much as flicker, however. Indeed, he might have been a statue erected in honor of Elodie's worst memory. All the familiar details were present: tidy black hair, almost-black eyes, olive skin, suit so immaculate he could have worn it to meet the pope, were he not an atheist. Absent was any human warmth. Behind him, a graduate student fussed with their Emergency Response kit, but he ignored them, ignored the entire world, staring into the middle distance with an expression so stern it made a rock seem like quivering jelly.

Yet Elodie knew that he'd seen her, without a doubt. He saw everything.

Gabriel.

Professor Tyrant to his students (and several members of the faculty when they thought no one could hear them).

Her husband.

Elodie's face blazed. She thrust the suitcase at Motthers without looking, turned on a heel, and began striding back toward the velocipede.

"P-professor!" Motthers cried out, but Elodie ignored him. She had to get away . . . even while her mind ran headlong into the pit of memory.

SHE'D MARRIED GABRIEL on a Monday afternoon in September, almost exactly one year ago. It had been an accident.

If only she'd not gone to the Minervaeum, London's private club for academics, after attending the annual Thaumaturgic Cartography symposium. If only she'd not felt so queasy from the odors of pipe smoke, steamed pudding, and nitroglycerine swirling through the club's Paracelsus Lounge that she'd decided to open a window. And if only doing so had not brought her close enough to where Gabriel sat with Professor Dubrovic that she'd overheard their conversation.

"Oh dear," Professor Dubrovic was saying. "*Four* Balliol students living upstairs from your flat?" He shook his head sympathetically.

"They are constantly quoting poetry," Gabriel answered, managing to grouch in such refined tones, one naturally assumed he was in the right, because he sounded like he must be. "And they debate Shakespeare's authorship at the top of their lungs. Or perhaps it's just that they want breakfast at all hours—in any case, if I hear another cry for Bacon, I will go quite mad. I need to find new accommodation before I'm driven to *educate* them."

"The place across from me in Holywell Street is vacant," Dubrovic said.

"I know, and it would be ideal. I inquired, but the landlady only wants a married couple."

Dubrovic shrugged. "So get married."

There followed a pause in the conversation, due to a chemistry professor across the room having detonated her pudding. While the other patrons variously cheered or complained, Dubrovic smirked over the rim of his whiskey glass at Gabriel. "No need to look so perturbed, old chap. *Amor est mortuus.* I'm just talking about a marriage of convenience."

Gabriel frowned. "Oh? And where would I find a wife at such short notice?"

*I'd marry you,* Elodie thought with a wistful sigh. She'd adored him since the day they had met in Advanced Principles of Thaumaturgical Cartography, two eighteen-year-olds embarking upon a master's degree far sooner than their peers. He'd gotten there via a first-class bachelor's degree, she by exceptional entry, having spent most of her life in the fields of Europe and Canada with famous geographer parents. They could not have been more different. Regardless, Gabriel Tarrant had from the very start represented her ideal of manhood. He possessed compelling gravitas, exceptional intelligence (and perfectly aligned facial contours).

But he also scrupulously ignored her existence. Elodie could not blame him, however. She wasn't beautiful, she lacked proper refinement, and then there was that time she accidentally dented his expensive, thaumaturgically-charged copper sieve when using it to swat a fly in the classroom . . .

Suddenly, a ringing silence made her look up from the window's latch—whereupon she discovered that Gabriel had, at that moment, become very aware indeed of her existence and was staring at her in a way that made her feel like a map location with a pin stuck in it.

For one frantic second, Elodie mentally cataloged every wrinkle and ink stain on her dress. Then she dragged together whatever dignity she could find within herself and stared right back at him.

"What?" she said defensively.

"You'd marry me?" he asked, echoing the thought she'd apparently spoken aloud.

*Oh, damn.*

"THE OTHER PROFESSORS don't respect me," she explained two days later, back in Oxford, as they walked to a church, the landlady having accepted Gabriel's application. Elodie's hair was unraveling from the intricate arrangement she'd spent hours concocting, her white dress was really far too matrimonial for the occasion, and somewhere along the way she'd lost her quiet dignity, perhaps in the same place as the handkerchief she'd bought for the traditional "something blue." Every few yards she glanced at her husband-to-be, still not quite believing the situation she found herself in. He just stared ahead, giving the impression he was walking alone. Nevertheless, Elodie couldn't stop talking.

"They think an unwed female professor is a terrible idea. That's why I'm agreeing to marry you." (Well, and the fact that she was an idiot, unable to keep her thoughts in her own head.)

"Uh-huh," Gabriel answered, glowering at a nearby oak that was shedding its old leaves onto the footpath.

Actually, now that she mentioned it, Elodie felt quite heated on the subject. "Women have been allowed tertiary education for a hundred years now, thanks to Queen Charlotte's sponsoring it, and yet Oxford's geography staff thinks a woman with a doctorate is some kind of bizarrity. Never mind that there's a female ornithology professor even younger than I am; never mind that I know what I'm doing. I have more field experience than most of them put together, but do they care?"

"How strange," Gabriel said as he watched a squirrel scamper up the tree with a paperback novel in its mouth.

"Yes, exactly! Strange is just how I would describe it. Strange, and yet so very common. Misogynistic. The departmental secretary told me outright that I'd plague other professors with my 'tempting availability.'"

"Hm."

"My mother said that was probably just his way of asking me on a date."

Gabriel almost tripped on the edge of a cobblestone. "What?" he said, looking at her finally, his forehead creased with a frown.

"I know! Can you believe it?"

"Did *you* believe it?" he asked in return.

She huffed a laugh. "No. The only dates Coffingham knows about are the ones he buys at the greengrocers in an effort to be cosmopolitan."

Gabriel glared at the church farther along the street as they continued toward it. He clearly did not want conversation, but if Elodie had ever found an off switch within herself, she'd lost it again long ago.

"When I'm married to you, they'll have to respect me." (For no other reason than the fear that, if they didn't, "Professor Tyrant" might come and *look* at them.)

"So," Gabriel said, "if we do this, I get decent housing, and you gain the respect of your peers? And you think that's a good deal?"

Elodie recognized that he was offering her a chance to withdraw, and she considered it—which is to say, immediately, completely refused it. Her proposal may have been accidental, but the opportunity to marry Gabriel Tarrant was, as her more modish students would say, a no-brainer.

In other words, she failed to apply her brain to it.

"Yes," she answered.

Twenty minutes later, she was standing in a chapel, trying hopelessly to repair her coiffure while Gabriel persuaded the vicar to marry them.

Ten minutes after that, they were pronounced man and wife. Gabriel lowered his head to kiss her.

"Er, we don't do that bit in the Church of England," the vicar interjected, but he could have broken into a flamboyant aria and Elodie wouldn't have noticed. Gabriel mustn't have noticed either, for he went ahead and pressed his lips gently against hers. Although he touched her nowhere else, Elodie felt embraced by his entire being. Her knees began to weaken, and her heart turned to sighs . . .

And he stepped back, not looking at her. As Elodie swayed dizzily, he turned to the vicar and said, "That's an unusual inlay on the altar. Is it Italian marble?"

Afterward, they walked across to Holywell Street, Elodie feeling uncharacteristically shy. They were *married*. It seemed like a magic spell held in place by the gold ring on her finger, which Gabriel had unexpectedly produced. Neither of them spoke, but that was fine, for the memory of their kiss was singing in the space between them. On the doorstep of ninety-nine, Gabriel introduced her to the landlady as his wife. That Elodie managed not to giggle would have made her parents ~~astonished~~ proud.

But the landlady barred the threshold to them. "I've already rented it," she said.

"We had an agreement," Gabriel replied in a tone that would have terrified the woman, were she educated. As it was, she merely shrugged.

"Sorry. Dr. Costas made me a better offer."

"Dr. Andro Costas?" Gabriel asked.

"You know him?"

"Tall. Blond. A *bachelor*."

The woman winked at Elodie. "Yes, well, he's going to supplement the rent with free massages for my nervous condition. He has a special vibratory device." And she shut the door in their faces.

They stood in a silence so comprehensive it could have built a whole new house. Elodie's heart clenched with pain for Gabriel's disappointment, and she almost reached out to pat his shoulder. But, losing courage, she verbalized her sympathy instead.

"You should have secured the keys straightaway."

*No, stop!* her brain shouted in frantic confusion. *That's not what I meant to say!* She began blushing even before Gabriel turned to stare at her thunderously.

And that had been that for their marriage.

———

"Professor!" Motthers squeaked, trying to juggle suitcase, clipboard, backpack, and wits as he hurried after her across the platform. "The train!"

"I won't be catching it," Elodie said, walking faster. In the past year since that wedding day, doubt over her respectability had spread beyond the geography department to most of Oxford and even as far as Shropshire, where her parents declared themselves bemused (but, alas, not entirely surprised) that she would marry a colleague on a sudden whim then abandon both him and her reputation to continue living alone. And Gabriel's search for accommodation had been completely derailed, since an estranged husband was considered even less reliable a tenant than a bachelor was. All in all, the marriage had turned out to be very inconvenient indeed. But having no grounds for an annulment without making matters substantially worse, they were stuck with it.

Each blamed the other—or, at least, Elodie blamed herself, but since Gabriel made no effort to persuade her otherwise, she turned quite happily to blaming him. In short order, they moved from being *acquaintances* to *enemies* without any interesting stop at *lovers* along the way. No conversation passed between them other than a few curt greetings when absolutely required, and one particularly fiery verbal skirmish over whether to stock chocolate jumbles or plain digestive biscuits in the faculty tea cupboard.

Furthermore, Elodie learned to be a veritable escape artist, disappearing through doorways, behind hedges, and down stairwells whenever she saw Gabriel; once she even jumped out a first-floor window—the consequences of which to her ankle were luckily healed now, thus enabling her to move at speed across the train platform. Certainly, a master's student with a flimsy mustache could not stop her.

"But the magic!" Motthers cried.

"Professor Tarrant—the other one—will attend to that. You can join his team."

"But soil contamination from aeolian transportation of explosively thaumaturgized Neoproterozoic-Cambrian rock particles!"

Elodie's heart sank. *Damn*. Motthers was right. Dôlylleaud was sure to be in a bad way. She imagined the starved faces of children deprived of vital sustenance from . . . (she paused to search her memory for the area's main produce) . . . er, pears.

"Fine," she muttered, coming to a halt.

"Pardon?" Motthers asked daringly.

Elodie turned, casting him a brief glare before taking the suitcase back. "Fine. I'll go."

Motthers grinned so widely, his mustache appeared in danger of sliding off. "Hurrah!" Then he grimaced. "Um, er, you might want to . . ."

As he flicked a finger at her lower half, Elodie glanced down and realized that her hem was still knotted. She hurriedly untied it, then began to trudge once more toward the tracks with the air of a French soldier approaching Waterloo. To the south, a cloud of steam signaled the train's approach. With luck, she'd have only a minute to talk with Gabriel before it arrived.

Approaching him was the hardest thing she'd done in a long while, and this was coming from a woman with a doctorate that had required extensive knowledge of trigonometry. She hated the cold-hearted, unforgiving man. Absolutely, completely loved—wait, no, *loathed* him. Arriving at his side, she murmured a greeting.

But Gabriel just went on staring at some unknown vision, his face so beautiful in repose it made Elodie's throat ache. *Ache like I've just swallowed poison,* she amended furiously. Setting down her suitcase, she cleared her throat, and when that failed to elicit a response, tried to decide which exact swear word she would shout . . .

"Do you feel that sound?" Gabriel asked suddenly, not shifting his gaze.

It seemed *good morning* or even *I say, aren't you my wife?* were surplus to his conversational requirements. Elodie found herself thrown from aggravation into utter confusion.

"Um?" she said.

*Um.* A master's degree, a doctorate, a professorship, and all she could say was *"um"*? Her intelligence rolled its eyes in embarrassment.

But Gabriel hadn't noticed, of course. Pulling herself together, Elodie tried again. "You mean do I *hear* a sound?"

"No."

Aggravation stomped back into her brain, shoving confusion aside. "I don't feel anything," she said frostily.

And then she did. A tiny sound scraped along her ear canals, whining like a student who has forgotten it's exam day. "What is that?" she wondered aloud, shaking her head.

"Thaumaturgic resonance," Gabriel said. *Magic.*

They exchanged a glance that was pure geography, all steep hills, underground rivers, and a hot, dangerous flash of lightning. Elodie immediately looked away. She scanned for signs of danger, but the sky with its grand old rooftops and dreaming spires remained clear, sunbright. Nothing seemed amiss.

And yet . . .

A fresh, sweet aroma, almost like sun-ripened fruit, mingled with the familiar damp smell of the River Thames. A haze of green shadowed the far western horizon. Instinct stepped forward to warn her that something magical had gone catawampus.

(No reason why scientific expertise couldn't come with a sprightly lexicon, Elodie always contended.)

She did not need the GPS map in front of her to know that the fey line to Dôlylleaud ran straight in that direction. Nor did she need a thaumometer to tell her that something was coming along it. Fast.

Increasingly troubled, she glanced again at Gabriel, and found him staring at her.

"Arousing," he murmured.

A blush swept across Elodie's face like a matador's cloak, which was a particularly fitting description considering how her pulse rampaged. "I beg your pardon?" she asked with geographic dignity.

"The resonance. It's arousing my nerves in the most disconcerting manner."

"Ah, I see. Yes, me too. The hairs on my arms are standing up." She slid a hand beneath one sleeve to calm them. "And—"

*BOOM!*

PHOTO COURTESY OF THE AUTHOR

**India Holton** lives in New Zealand, where she has enjoyed the typical Kiwi lifestyle of wandering around forests, living barefoot on islands, and messing about in boats. Now she lives in a cottage near the sea, writing books about unconventional women and charming rogues, and drinking far too much tea.

Ready to find
your next great read?

Let us help.

**Visit prh.com/nextread**